Graham grew up in Darlington and has lived in Nottingham, Leeds, and London. He has worked as a factory operative, hospital porter, schoolteacher, special educational needs strategist and trade union caseworker. He served as a Labour councillor for eight years in Brent and has written extensively on politics in various socialist journals. Graham has four adult children and three grandsons. He lives with his partner Joanna in Cricklewood.

For Joanna, Alex, Will, Feargus and Sylvie

Graham Durham

A PEAL OF SOCIALISM

AUSTIN MACAULEY PUBLISHERS™
LONDON * CAMBRIDGE * NEW YORK * SHARJAH

Copyright © Graham Durham 2024

The right of Graham Durham to be identified as author of this work has been asserted by the author in accordance with sections 77 and 78 of the Copyright, Designs and Patents Act 1988.

All rights reserved. No part of this publication may be reproduced, stored in a retrieval system, or transmitted in any form or by any means, electronic, mechanical, photocopying, recording, or otherwise, without the prior permission of the publishers.

Any person who commits any unauthorised act in relation to this publication may be liable to criminal prosecution and civil claims for damages.

This is a work of fiction. Names, characters, businesses, places, events, locales, and incidents are either the products of the author's imagination or used in a fictitious manner. Any resemblance to actual persons, living or dead, or actual events is purely coincidental.

A CIP catalogue record for this title is available from the British Library.

ISBN 9781035856596 (Paperback)
ISBN 9781035856602 (Hardback)
ISBN 9781035856619 (ePub e-book)

www.austinmacauley.com

First Published 2024
Austin Macauley Publishers Ltd®
1 Canada Square
Canary Wharf
London
E14 5AA

Thanks to the archivists of Hull Library Service, Tower Hamlets Archive, the Peoples History Archive Manchester, Darlington Library, the British Library and many local and labour historians. Walter Besser and David Rosenberg provided valuable help with details.

Anna Dolezal, Matt O'Dwyer and Steve Forrest read the manuscript and provided invaluable feedback. Above all Joanna Wilmot read and commented helpfully on many drafts, much love and thanks.

Table of Contents

Chapter 1: Arrivings (1936) — 11

Chapter 2: The Cause of Ireland (1937) — 28

Chapter 3: Search Party — 38

Chapter 4: A Pot to Piss In (1938) — 53

Chapter 5: Uncle Pat's Funeral — 67

Chapter 6: Bombs and Raids (1939) — 92

Chapter 7: The Obvious Irishman — 100

Chapter 8: A Not So Popular Front — 109

Chapter 9: Don't Breathe a Word — 113

Chapter 10: 'We Will Have to Fight Another War in 25 Years' — 136

Chapter 11: The Wench of Bliss (1940) — 145

Chapter 12: An American in London — 155

Chapter 13: Mr Rude — 165

Chapter 14: Brighton Outing — 169

Chapter 15: Old Russia — 179

Chapter 16: Coalminers (1941) — 185

Chapter 17: Aurora — 194

Chapter 18: Clear Out Hitler's Agents (1942) — 208

Chapter 19: White Lines Were Painted (1943) — 218

Chapter 20: Joe Louis — 239

Chapter 21: Fare Thee Well (1944) — 243

Chapter 22: Neath (1945) — 252

Chapter 1
Arrivings (1936)

All were agreed he was the most dependable horse they had ever owned. He gave off a gentle air of competence, never breaking stride and rarely running the cart over a damaged part of the path. The horse, which never had a name, seemed to regard it as his mission to avoid any discomfort to his human cargo. Brigid felt a sadness that she would not see him again nor ever, perhaps, ride the road to Whiddy harbour with the Atlantic breeze blowing her black hair back across her face. The horse needed no blinkers and seemed to prefer to see the landscape ahead, carrying his head high as if proud that even when the wild O'Shaughnessy dog had barked and jumped the week before he had simply held his course.

Brigid envied her brother Conan, his relationship with the horse. It was neither on words or signals but on a quiet respect that each would ensure duties were performed. Indeed, Conan was loved and respected by all. His face, round like a griddle pan, never indicated alarm or even interest, whatever the information that was passed to him. Brigid knew that she would miss him the most for his quiet devotion to her always gave her additional strength.

At Whiddy jetty, Brigid remembered greeting Frank McCormack there a few months before and his insistence, later over supper, that Athlone had the oldest pub in Europe. After Conan and Frank had resolved their plans together and Frank had left, Brigid asked Conan if all the Westmeath men boasted and lied. Conan had replied that he could not say for he believed all men were prone to boasting but that when it came to lying and duplicity no one could beat the English. That summer day Conan told Brigid nothing of his business with Frank.

Now though he helped her dismount took her in his arms and kissed both cheeks, whispering almost inaudibly that he knew she would be ready if Ireland came calling. Looking up to his face she saw no sign that anything but a fond farewell had been spoken and, holding the horse in one arm and his waist in another, she said that all that she loved was in west Cork.

The ferry chugged away and Brigid thought of her mother Mary back on the farm and how she had complained for weeks about Brigid's departure 'for that old pagan country.' Brigid had known better than to point out, as she once had as a girl, that she had named her daughter after a Celtic goddess. That childhood memory of Father Dennis being summoned and talking at her for over two hours about St Brigid had led to her hating her name for years. She realised that her friend Maureen was the only person she had told of Imbolc and that their innocent secret celebrations in the woods, once knee deep in snow, had never been discovered. On leaving the farm, Brigid had promised her mother to find a Catholic church on her first free Sunday in London and that she would pray for Whiddy and Ireland.

The short ride across to Bantry always brought memories of the French fleet, summoned by Tone, one of which lay deep below. It was she believed one of the greatest chances for freedom Ireland ever had but now, perhaps, with talk of the possibility of war another chance may come. The train to Skibbereen and on to Cork was ready but Brigid knew she had fifteen minutes to spare so she strolled to the edge of the lake. Spotting a redshank busily feeding on the other side she tried to capture that image and take it with her to England.

Looking across to Church Street, she recalled her earliest memory of her uncle's house and looking out the window at the funeral procession. She may have been four or five but she recalled the hats of the men walking past, rows of flat caps, and a few trilbies and even, she was sure, a bowler hat. Her uncle Martin was the gentlest of men, and she recalled her shock when he returned declaring 'those bloody murderers, in cold blood.'

Brigid had called on her older sister, Annie the day before and heard again the story of how Annie and her friends at school had managed to chew and spit out messages from and to the IRA before the Black and Tans had reached them. Annie was now a mother of four and so she always added, 'It took a lot for me to do that, Brigid, for spitting is a dirty habit,' and they had linked arms and laughed again at the danger and the absurdity. The day before that she had visited her younger sister Agnes, whose new baby was sickening and had not been churched at the altar of God. Agnes had come a little way down the stairs and it was the saddest parting, for Brigid had taught her to read and had plaited her hair each morning. Everyone knew that Agnes had married a waster and drinker but

Brigid knew Conan would always make sure there was enough to eat and neither Agnes nor her children would be harmed, for even a drunk knew better than to cross Conan.

The train slowly pulled out sending steam across the harbour and a wave of excitement seemed to pass through Brigid's body. She had no husband and did not want one for she knew big events and exciting ideas lay across the water.

*****

Billy was dreaming too. As he slowly awakened, he remembered the magic bridge his father had taken him to, where you could stand with one foot in Yorkshire and one in County Durham. Billy could not remember exactly where, for he had been a small boy, but his dad half-tipped him over the bridge so you could see the speedy Tees below, so clear you could sometimes spot a trout swimming. He was told the tale often of his grandad who had been caught there and although he had been fined five shillings for poaching the magistrate, who was a Methodist circuit preacher, had later paid the fine, knowing the family had no money. Suddenly, his dozing was rudely interrupted by a loud bang on the door.

'It's a Blackshirt come to shoot you,' shouted John through the door. Billy jumped up and splashed cold water from the basin under his arms.

'I'm going to complain to that Mr Mosley personally,' Billy retorted.

They went down the stairs, passing Mrs C at the bottom who grumbled that the noise would wake her new lodger who was working nights. Outside John said she never gave her full name for everyone knew she was Italian and probably a fascist too. Billy wondered again where John had suddenly acquired this interest in political affairs; when he had first met him two years ago, he was sure John could not even name the Prime Minister.

They walked up Temple Road and passed the old Stoll studios. On his very first day in Cricklewood three years before Billy had seen Kitty McShane smoking a cigarette on the street corner. He had written home to tell his mam for he knew she loved the Old Mother Riley films. A letter had arrived back within a week, containing the usual knitted socks but also the hope that Billy would have "nothing to do with that sort." Billy had been bemused by this but thought perhaps Mrs Farrier across the road had heard some gossip on her trips to the cinema.

Turning right along Edgware Road, Billy and John were in a hurry, they ran past the telephone exchange and had just reached their barrow when, coming down Cricklewood Lane on his cart they heard Cyril.

'Hurry up boys; I've some lovely juicy oranges today specially for you, all the way from Palestine.'

Pushing their barrow alongside the cart as they turned left and stopped alongside The Crown, Billy asked, 'How can you be so bloody cheerful, this early in the morning?'

'It's the coffee, keeps me lively, young Billy, mother puts it on the paraffin at three and by four I'm buzzing.'

Billy and John unloaded the oranges, which shone like oil paintings against the pastels of old turnips and assorted vegetables left from the day before.

'That all you got today, Cyril?' asked John.

'Those Jaffas will keep you in pennies till you start a proper job on Monday. I'll settle with you now if that's alright for I've no reason to head to this wilderness again now both you and the old fella on Finchley Road are jacking it in. Can't blame you like, there's no money in fruit and veg anymore.'

John found an old apple and fed it to the horse. 'Hey steady on, Black Beauty will head back Monday if she remembers that.'

With that Cyril shook the reins and shouted, 'Kilburn here we come, good luck lads.'

By lunchtime the oranges were sold and Billy suggested they celebrate with a pint in the pub. John agreed but said he could only stay for one, as he was going to treat himself to a new shirt. Billy knew what that meant; he must have finally persuaded Grace to let him take her out.

'Where you taking her?' laughed Billy. John replied it was none of his business and gave John a playful punch in the arm in return.

'Hey, save that for the fascists,' John replied.

Billy pressed John for details and John explained he had met Tom Stone in the street yesterday and promised to help him make sure Mosley could not march through the East End.

'But isn't Tom the foreman at the factory?' asked Billy. 'We've to report to him on Monday.'

'He's also in the Communist Party Billy and it seems they follow orders, they had been told to go to a rally on Spain on Sunday but now they've been told to go to the East End.'

Billy asked John what he knew about Mosley.

'Not much, but he hates Jews and loves Mussolini and Tom says if he gets to power all socialists will be arrested like Hitler does.'

*****

Brigid was looking forward to seeing Maureen, the only person she knew personally in London, although Conan had given her two addresses and a telephone number only to be used if she desperately needed help or money. Maureen had been at the same school in Bantry and at first Brigid had been shy of Maureen, who was an extrovert at the age of five and was always in trouble with Miss O'Connell. However, by the age of seven they were inseparable and Brigid remembered the time her mother came from a school meeting and declared proudly, 'Miss O'Connell says our Brigid is an example to the other girls, especially Maureen O'Leary.'

When Maureen was fourteen her family had moved away to Cork and they had lost touch, but now on Wednesday Maureen had actually rung the house and asked to speak to her. Maureen was like that; it would not have occurred to her that she could get Brigid into trouble or even sacked. Luckily Brigid had been asked to answer the telephone that morning as the family had gone for an appointment at the hospital and so no harm had been done.

As Brigid had Sundays free, she decided it would do no harm to miss church on her first free day in England and she was excited both to see Maureen after six years but also to explore the city a little for she had barely left the house since arriving at Paddington station close to midnight a week ago. Maureen was not working in a house but in a factory across London in Whitechapel. Brigid found she did not like the Metropolitan Line much especially when it went underground and there was no chance to look out of the windows.

When she arrived, she was surprised to be an hour early for when she had answered Mrs Clark's question as to what she was doing with her first free day. Mrs Clark had made Whitechapel seem a distant place where it was "important to hold onto your purse at all times." Rather than make herself conspicuous by waiting at the station entrance so long, Brigid decided to walk briskly down the street for twenty-five minutes and then straight back retracing her steps so that by then Maureen would be due to arrive. Crossing the road to the London hospital she set off in the direction of Aldgate and then turned left into Leman Street.

Here she could not believe her eyes, several men were running at full speed towards her with policemen chasing them and hitting them with truncheons whenever they could get near enough. Brigid had to squeeze against the wall to let the men pass and she edged down the street until she heard a noise from her left.

'Man down, Miss, can you help us?'

Brigid could not see anyone and glanced up at the street name, Alie Street, so she would know where to return to. She slowly walked down the street and noticed a fine building and looking up saw the lettering Deutsche Lutherische and the date 1762. Suddenly a man appeared with pink blotches on his gabardine.

'He's here, in a bad way with skull cracked open, can you help? Copper hit him hard.'

Now Brigid saw two shoes face down on the step and when she turned into the alleyway, she found the owner with his head dripping blood which had soaked the back of his white shirt red. She bent down to examine the man and saw the wound was on top of the head. Brigid removed her gloves and carefully stored them in her handbag, which she placed in the alcove of the church. Taking the handkerchief which was tucked in her blouse at the wrist, she gently moved the damp strands of hair and the wound was visible, about six inches long but not, as far as she could tell, very deep. She placed her handkerchief along the wound and whilst it turned red quickly it did seem to halt the blood dripping further. She turned to the man who had called her.

'What's his name?'

'I'm sorry Miss, I don't know. We were all being chased by coppers and they caught us and hit him from behind. I pretended to be hit and fell over and they just charged on. My name's Samuel.'

Suddenly the injured man raised a little, resting on his elbows, 'My name's Tom Stone,' he said. 'Thanks for helping.'

Samuel glanced up and down the street and noted that the pursuit by the police and the violence seemed to have moved on.

'If we can get him to the corner here, my cousin will take him into his café.'

Brigid said they needed extra bandaging for the wound before Tom could be moved. Samuel asked them to wait and, in a moment, returned with his white shirt removed and his gabardine tightly pulled up to the collar. Brigid carefully rolled the shirt and placed it gently on top of the handkerchief asking Tom if he could hold it there. Then they gently helped Tom to his feet and, with the occasional buckling of the knees which Samuel buttressed, they slowly reached the corner. Across the street a crowd had gathered, some tending two other men who had fallen, and four men who seemed to know Samuel ran across and picked Tom up by the legs and arms.

'Over to Mendel's,' said Samuel to them. 'In case the police come back.'

Inside the café a couple of injured men were talking to each other in a language Brigid did not recognise. One of the men had his arm in a sling and was wincing with pain; he looked at Brigid and uttered a phrase.

'He says women too, my God,' Samuel explained. 'We like to speak Yiddish still.'

Brigid wanted to explain that she had not been involved in the chase by the police but instead she said, 'I don't know this area, but there is a hospital not far away, can we take Tom and the others there?' At this Tom suddenly sat up in his chair, dropping the shirt and exposing the bloodied handkerchief, 'We mustn't go to the hospital, they're arresting everyone.'

A tall man wearing a skullcap came in from behind the counter. He spoke to Samuel at length, and by his hand gestures was seemingly concerned that the police might smash his shop. When Tom offered to leave, Samuel explained that Mendel wanted them to stay but he was going to close the shop shutters so that no one else would draw attention to them. Samuel said Mendel joked he had never had a goy in the shop and now he has two and one is a Communist. He worries that he hopes the Rabbi doesn't hear about it.

'Why is that a joke?' asked Brigid, thinking of some fearsome priests she had met.

'Because his Rabbi was last seen behind the barricade in Cable Street with a large stick in his hand.'

They all laughed and Samuel added that soon a doctor would be arriving to see if Tom needed stitches, meanwhile tea would be served. Brigid explained that she was not on the demonstration, indeed, she was not sure what the demonstration was about until she heard the word fascist.

'We have a few of them in Ireland too and some went to fight for Franco. But now I have to go, I hope you all make a full recovery and the fascists are driven away.'

Tom asked her name and she gave it but she was anxious not to miss Maureen and so explained she could not stay a moment longer. Samuel insisted on accompanying her to the station despite Brigid's protest. They walked quickly and agreed Brigid should walk a few steps ahead just in case the police recognised Samuel. As they reached the station, Maureen was there and she ran across and embraced Brigid.

'Brigid O'Brien I would have known you anywhere.' Brigid turned to introduce Samuel but he was walking away and she called and waved but he did not turn round.

'And I would have known you anywhere Maureen O'Laoghaire, with those famous high cheekbones.'

Brigid started to tell Maureen about the event of that afternoon but Maureen just said, 'Just like back home, always finding something to fight about.' Brigid was astonished at Maureen's appearance, she knew what a platinum blonde was but she knew no one who had become one.

'You look gorgeous, Maureen, I'd say Jean Harlow eat your heart out.'

Maureen was pleased. 'I thought you wouldn't recognise me Brigid, mind it cost me half a week's wages at the hairdressers, but it gets the boys looking though.'

'Anyone special?'

'Well, there's two, Frank and Henry, but I can't make my mind up so I'm dating them both. No telling now, Brigid.'

Brigid recalled that Maureen was never one to do things by halves. She remembered the only time Maureen persuaded her to skip school; they did not go shopping in Bantry like other girls, but hitched up towards Sheep's Head. It got dark at Durrus and they slept in a barn, until Conan collected them next day. Brigid remembered him saying, 'That is a mighty fine barn, the most useful in west Cork' and only realising what he meant years later.'

It was still a warm day for October so Maureen suggested they take their sandwiches to Weavers Field and they strolled along, Maureen describing her factory job and how she only survived the boredom by chatting to the girls either side of the noisy machines. It appeared they were spinning silk for gentlemen's shirts.

'Someone said one batch was for Stanley Baldwin,' Maureen boasted.

'I hope you put a nasty knot in those,' Brigid laughed.

'We'd all get sacked,' Maureen said. 'And the wages are not bad.'

In turn Brigid described the comfort she had landed amongst at the large house alongside Warwick Park station. She was supposed to look after the children, Bartholomew and Athena, but after supervising their dressing and giving them breakfast they went off to school in St John's Wood and she had little to do until they came home.

'I think Mrs Clark is lonely, she likes me to make tea and take it with her most weekdays. Mr Clark is away in Europe a lot selling military equipment and every week the children get a postcard from Vienna or Berlin or some such. I have to hang them around the kitchen like Christmas cards once the children have read them aloud.'

Maureen agreed the work sounded easy but said she could never work in service, always at someone's beck and call. Brigid agreed saying that it was the only way her family would be happy about her leaving, knowing she had somewhere to stay, but that she would be finding a different job after a while. Maureen made no offer to help, so they sat there a while munching their sandwiches and watching the children from the terraced houses opposite playing hopscotch.

*****

Billy and John were early at the factory gates and once inside the office were asked to sit down and wait for Mr Stone and Mr Willans. The large clock in the entrance hall showed 7.21 am and time seemed to pass slowly until at 8am precisely a tall man in a pinstripe suit entered and stood in front of them.

'Mr Wood and Mr Stainsby, welcome to your first day here, the best supplier of precision engineering to the world. Mr Stone does not appear to have graced us with his company as yet, so I have asked Mr Eastwood here to take you to your work stations. My name is Mr Willans, General Manager of this Cricklewood works which employs some 1,000 men and women. I hope you will work hard and carefully here.'

Only when Willans had turned and marched out did Billy take notice of the tall man with his trouser braces resting on a blue work shirt. He was putting his pipe in his shirt pocket and Billy sensed he was not happy at doing so.

'Right lads, Tom's not in, let's hope he got some sense knocked into him yesterday. Come on.'

Billy was about to reply when he felt a tug at his sleeve and saw John with his fingers to his lips. They followed Eastwood through the factory at speed.

'This is the drill room,' said Eastwood. 'Where some of the finest engineers make parts for planes, cars and all sorts.'

'And tanks,' a voice interceded. 'You forgot tanks.' From underneath a ramp, an even smaller man climbed out.

'Yes, thank you, Tiny,' said Eastwood. 'John Wood, meet your new team leader, Tiny Bennett, the finest engineer in north London. Tiny can fix anything, usually by climbing under it.'

Billy was led away to the left, past a group of women on an assembly line, busy putting screws into speedometers moving rapidly along the assembly line. Back at the entrance, Eastwood told Billy he was going to train him up as a progress chaser making sure all jobs are proceeding on time.

'But first you need to be familiar with the whole of the works and all its departments. I want you to visit each section in turn this week, making sure every tool is in its right place, never on the floor, and sweeping every drop of liquid and detritus up. Understand?'

Billy confirmed that he did, put on the brown work coat offered and selected one stiff and one soft brush from the side room.

Later at one o'clock, the hooter sounded and Billy found John and they stepped into Mora Road for a smoke.

'We've no bloody sandwiches, John; I'll be starving by six.'

From his jacket John produced a beef sandwich and precisely tore it in half. He explained that Tiny had given it to him, saying that it had too much mustard on for his taste. Billy said the workers seemed like a good bunch who did not like the managers much. John agreed and added that there were some good-looking lasses in his section.

'In every section,' Billy replied. 'Seems like half the workers are joining the army and going on holiday to India. Eastwood says soon the women will have all the skills and he does not think that is a good thing.'

After a short silence, Billy started softly chanting, 'The rats, the rats, we've gotta get rid of the rats.'

John joined in; he had really enjoyed the clash the day before. 'We really made those fascists run,' he said.

'Yeah, we did, had one by the scruff but had to let go or a copper would have brained me. Wonder where your new mate Tom got to?'

John said they had been split up when the police charged. He had seemed a good bloke and John hoped he was not badly injured.

*****

Early in the afternoons, Mrs Clark encouraged Brigid to take a short stroll in the neighbourhood. Usually, Mrs Clark would invite her into the drawing room on her return and ask her who and what she had seen. Once Brigid asked if Mrs Clark would like to accompany her but this seemed to cause offence and Mrs Clark said any such gallivanting would not go down well if anyone in the Ministry of Defence heard of it. After a couple of weeks, Brigid began to pity Mrs Clark, apart from the occasional shopping trip and a half-hour with the children after tea each day she really seemed to have nothing to do with her life.

Usually, Brigid liked to walk along the canal, feeding the ducks with breakfast leftovers, admiring the boats and sometimes having a brief conversation with any of the boat dwellers who were visible. One of these said he was an Irishman from Belfast who teased Brigid about living in such a grand house.

'It's getting far too grand round here; someone called it Venice in Paddington the other day. There'll be no scrap to collect if the rich get to buy up everywhere.'

Later Brigid told Mrs Clark about the comment on the neighbourhood and Mrs Clark murmured, 'Venice, how romantic, at school we learnt that Nietzsche said if he had to find another word for music, it would be Venice.'

Brigid had not told Mrs Clark about the incident in Whitechapel but she did say that she thought Paddington Basin was a much nicer area than Whitechapel.

'Too many Jews in the East End, my husband always says,' replied Mrs Clark. Brigid said nothing but this helped her decide she would try to find an alternative job as quickly as possible. She remembered that she had promised her mother she would go to church regularly and resolved to do so on Sunday. She mentioned this to Mrs Clark who said she thoroughly approved although of course they were part of the established Anglican Church. Brigid consulted her boat keeper acquaintance and was surprised to find he too was a Catholic.

'Although I only ever go on Christmas Day, just to keep in touch you see.' He recommended St Agnes in Cricklewood. 'Quite new, not as posh as some churches round here.'

On Sunday Brigid walked to the Edgware Road and caught the number sixteen bus towards Cricklewood Bus Garage. Mrs Clark had lent her a maroon hat with a feather which matched her dark green coat and she felt she looked quite elegant, especially as her brogues had polished up nicely. The bus proceeded and the conductor announced the next stop. 'County Kilburn, the 33rd county.'

She asked him where the stop for The Crown Hotel was and he replied, 'This is Shoot-Up Hill, darling, and at the top I'll tell you where to get off.'

'Cricklewood, The Crown,' he soon shouted and Brigid got off and waited for the bus to depart.

Across the road she saw a handsome building with the words Crown Hotel and Cannon Brewery Co. attached to the front in large gold letters. She crossed the road and turned left, as her boat keeper had instructed, then right and set off up Cricklewood Lane. St Agnes church was on the left, it was a very impressive brick building she thought and the October sun seemed to shine off its roof. A whole family of mother, father and five children were entering the church and only when they all had their hymn books issued could she enter the door. An old man with his silver hair carefully brushed back was issuing the books.

'Good day Miss, I'm guessing you're a County Kerry girl.'

To his evident disappointment, Brigid indicated she was not but simply took her books, not wishing the whole church to know her business. She blessed herself and took a seat two rows from the back. The service had not started and she looked around and admired the way the use of bricks continued inside the church making it seem light and yet somehow entirely suited to its urban surroundings. Looking around she was surprised at how full the church was, she had always enjoyed mental arithmetic and quickly multiplied the average pew occupation by the number of pews, calculating there were around two hundred in attendance.

She could have recognised the nature of the congregation from back home, except there was a much bigger attendance and, in general, a slightly better quality of clothing than in Bantry although there were plenty of worn jackets and coats here too. The priest entered and the service soon took on a familiar rhythm with regular responses required, she smiled to herself as she recalled Conan as a boy getting into trouble for claiming the responses were to stop old Mr Collins and his wife from falling asleep and blowing the windows out with their snoring.

At the end as she turned to go, a man covering his head with his hat behind her caught her eye. He stooped down to lift up a small child and his hat was dislodged again. Brigid filed out ahead of him and waited until he emerged still carrying the girl who could not be more than three years old. She was sure and stepped forward to ask, 'Excuse me, but did you injure your head last Sunday in Whitechapel?' The man stopped and put the child down; he looked alarmed and looked carefully at Brigid and then anxiously around.

'I'm sorry,' Brigid said, 'I've made a mistake,' and she turned round to leave.

'No that's right,' Tom Stone replied catching her up and guiding her back to his wife and older child. 'Mary, this is the kind woman who helped me last Sunday. I am so sorry I have forgotten your name.'

Brigid replied that she was not surprised given the blow he had received and was soon introduced to Mary and the children Patrick and Emily. Mary thanked Brigid and insisted that she come home for Sunday lunch with them.

When Brigid protested that it was unnecessary and she had only done what any passer-by would have, Tom simply said, 'It'll be grand to have some company and, in any case, I'm afraid your fine handkerchief is ruined so we owe you a dinner.'

When Emily, who was "two and three quarters tomorrow", realised a new visitor was coming for lunch she wriggled to be put down and putting her hand through Brigid's she promised to show her all her dollies. Patrick, who was two years older, was not to be outdone and held Brigid's other hand and skipped down the road. The Stone family lived about half a mile away in the bottom of a Victorian house in Chichele Road.

'It's a bit cramped now we have two young ones running about,' Tom said, opening the door. 'But the garden is great for the kids playing, sometimes half the street seems to be out there too.'

Brigid insisted on helping with the cooking although, just like back home, the cabbage, potatoes and leeks were already in their pots and it seemed Mary had left the beef roasting whilst they were at church.

'We don't always all go to church,' Mary said, 'But Tom has had to rest and we wanted to give thanks he is getting better. Don't worry though, my cousin lives upstairs and will have been down to check the roast is not burning.'

Once Brigid had inspected the dolls and Patrick's train set, Mary asked the children to play outside and she sat down with Brigid and poured out cups of tea.

Tom was reluctant to lie down but Mary insisted he rest before lunch saying they could not afford Tom to miss another week's wages.

Mary thanked Brigid again saying that a man called Samuel had brought Tom home late last Monday as his wound been stitched up by a Jewish doctor but he was still groggy and had spent two days in bed and this was his first time outside since.

'He is stubborn and won't go to see the doctor, even now he is suffering bad headaches. He's always thought doctors a waste of money and this time he had an excuse in case he was reported to the police.'

Brigid explained that she had only been passing by whilst visiting a friend as she had only arrived from Ireland two weeks ago. She liked Mary who told her how she had left Wicklow at eighteen herself, and had met Tom at a dance in Nottingham only three weeks later.

'New Year's Eve 1919 was very strange with very few men there, but Tom made a beeline for me and that was that, though we've only been married ten years next month.'

Brigid confided in Mary that she did not like being in service and wanted a job in a factory like her friend Maureen. They continued chatting easily and it turned out Tom was a Scottish Catholic from Glasgow who had moved south to work in the steel in a place called Corby, got sacked for agitating and found work at Raleigh in Nottingham.

'They make bicycles of course but Tom was trained as a car engineer there for those three wheelers. I was a bit homesick for Ireland so we moved here and the Party got Tom a job making clocks, as you know there's no work back home. Patrick and Emily go to the Gaelic Club in Kilburn on a Tuesday and she's quite a dancer for her age.'

Mary went to rouse Tom and so Brigid called the children in and helped them wash their hands. The adults served themselves straight from the drained cooking pots and Tom carefully carved the meat, with Mary cutting the children's portions into small pieces.

'Bless us Lord, and these thy gifts,' said Tom leaving Patrick to add, 'Through Christ, Our Lord, Amen'. Mary looked at her son fondly, gently saying, 'Which we are about to receive from thy bounty.'

Tom popped the meat in his mouth and added, 'And Lord thank you for beating the Blackshirts.'

Mary looked aghast but simply said, 'Daddy is naughty eating with his mouth full.' After the meal, the children went for a quiet time in the bedroom and Mary told Tom that Brigid was looking for a job in a factory.

'No problem at all, Brigid, I'll interview you meself, but don't let anyone know you know me.' Brigid asked what Party she would have to join and Tom looked bemused.

After Mary explained, Tom said, 'Oh no, no need to join the Communist Party but I'd expect you to join a union, that's why our wages are better than service wages.'

'James Connolly was a union man,' Brigid replied. 'So that's good enough for me.'

*****

Tom returned to work that Monday. He had acquired a flat cap to hide his wound and simply told Willans that he was sorry to miss work but fighting fascism in the streets of London was the same task as fighting fascism in Germany or Italy, adding with extra emphasis "or Spain". Willans, he knew, was a rearmament man although he had not approved of the collections Tom organised for Spanish Republicans.

Tom spent the morning checking on the men and women recruited the week before, both checking they were making progress and that they had joined the union. He found John welding and tapped him on the shoulder so that when John removed his mask he could point to his head and simultaneously put his fingers to his lips. When Tiny spotted Tom, he said, 'He's looking like a good worker, Tom, and a quick learner.' Later Tom found Billy sweeping up the metal cut offs from the speedometer workshops and asked him if he and John could spare an hour after work.

It was already getting dark when they met but Tom said it was late closing at the library and they could speak quietly there. They strolled past a handsome water tower and Tom explained what had happened in Whitechapel and how Brigid was coming for an interview on Friday. Round the corner they entered a tiny library and Tom showed them how to register.

John did not dare explain he never read books after Tom said, 'The good people of Willesden voted funds for this oasis of peace and thoughtfully placed it next to a park so that we can all enjoy reading and exercise. I often climb up to the old house at the top of Dolls Hill to sort out a knotty problem.'

Tom explained that the victory over the fascists showed the unity needed to defeat Hitler. He explained he was in the Communist Party and that he thought they might like to learn more. He produced two copies of the Daily Worker and explained that he had to help put the children to bed as Mary was helping at the church later but just to ask him anything they wished about the Party. John walked back with him, but Billy said he would stay awhile as it was light and warmer than his digs.

Billy was fascinated by the reports in the Daily Worker, news he had never heard before. Twenty-seven thousand sets of clothes for Spanish children were being made in Moscow, the Skorokhold shoe factory had exceeded its target by 500%, there was a strike at a Dundee jute spinning works and someone called Madame Despard was planning a visit to Russia at the age of 92. Billy found one familiar item though, New Brighton 2 Darlington 0, leaving the Quakers third bottom of League Division III (North).

The next day Billy asked Tom if he could look through some more old copies of the Daily Worker and he could see Tom was delighted.

'Mary will be pleased to get some more room under the bed.'

Billy joked that he hoped the football scores for Darlington would improve and Tom replied that perhaps Billy would like to support the champions who had beaten Queens Park on Saturday. Laughing at Billy's confusion, Tom explained, 'Celtic, Billy, Celtic, pride of Scotland.'

That evening Billy walked home with Tom and collected a large number of back copies of the Daily Worker, by midnight he had read everyone. Later that week Tom asked him if he had any questions and Billy replied that he had many but one leader article had confused him. It was lunchtime, so Tom suggested they sit on the pallets at the back of the factory and get some fresh air. Billy produced from his wallet a cutting from the paper dated 24 August and he read extracts out:

'History can record few more revolting characters than this Zinoviev gang of assassins now making their final pleas in the trial…they were plotting a campaign of murder and extermination. They are a festering cankering sore and we echo the workers verdict: Shoot the Reptiles.'

Billy waited for a response from Tom but nothing came. Billy waited and then said, 'But I thought Zinoviev was a great Bolshevik, one of Lenin's closest allies.'

Tom snorted and then he spat out, 'Billy, these traitors conspired with Trotsky against the Soviet Union. They are fascists and every one of them deserves to be shot as the workers' demand.' Billy could see Tom was not going to discuss the matter so he simply thanked Tom for the papers and walked away.

Chapter 2
The Cause of Ireland (1937)

It was the hat that Brigid hated the most. Everyone had always admired her hair and, she sometimes admitted to herself, it was a pleasure to comb first thing so that not a single knot remained and she loved to swing it from side to side in front of the mirror each morning. She remembered with a laugh how Uncle Jon had teased her as a child, 'Black hair and black eyes, you'll give your man a real surprise.' No matter how she wore it though her hat never looked right, today she was wearing a beret Grace had lent her but her hair was too thick and kept forcing itself down her back. She knew she would have to go back to the shapeless cover-all most of the women wore. 'Stupid pride,' she admonished herself and tucked the beret in her overall pocket.

Brigid liked to start the day waiting for the girls on the bus from Colindale to arrive for even though it was seven in the morning the liveliest girls were on that bus. Sure enough, this morning when they came walking down from the garage, they had already linked arms and were singing at the top of their voices. Amy was nearest and she linked with Brigid who joined in, 'You're calmer than the seals in the Arctic Ocean; at least they flap their fins to express emotion.'

The song stopped as they saw Mr Willans stood outside the gate, 'Morning ladies, I hope that exuberance leads to record production today.'

Amy could never resist a response. 'Perhaps if Fred Astaire was our manager, it would,' she replied, causing all the girls to laugh. Willans sensed that girl was trouble but said nothing deciding to have a quiet word with Tom Stone about her.

Brigid liked working with a large group and found she was good at the work and soon was helping the slower of the girls catch up. Tom Stone had arranged the job for her and, he claimed, overcome objections from other managers who did not want the Irish amongst the workforce. As the number of women taken on had increased in the six months since she started, Brigid noticed more and more

Irish women had joined and she enjoyed introducing herself and sharing tales of home. One girl, Mairaid was from Clonakilty and they were regular companions at the weekend.

Brigid was being paid two pounds three shillings a week and so she had the money for an occasional cinema trip or even a trip to the centre of London where they would visit the markets. Mairaid liked the Sunday market at Brick Lane whilst Brigid loved the chaos and cheek of Covent Garden fruit market. Brigid and Mairaid would occasionally meet up with Maureen on any weekend when she was not out with Frank, who she had decided was to become her betrothed.

One such Sunday, Mairaid and Brigid had fallen out when they had been teasing each other with tales of the relative superiority of Clonakilty and Bantry Brigid claimed that no song had ever featured Clonakilty and Mairaid responded that the great republican hero, Michael Collins, came from there. They were in a coffee house in Whitehall and Mairaid was astonished when Brigid stood up and left. Later Brigid said she had been suffering from a migraine and needed fresh air but, although they still greeted each other at work, somehow Brigid never arranged to go out together again.

Brigid had a workstation alongside Grace, who chatted amiably enough but mainly about where she and John were going at the weekend. John would find any excuse to have to pass by the speedometer workshop where they worked to chat to Grace and one day he turned to Brigid and asked her if she would like to come for a drink in Kilburn on Saturday to celebrate Billy's twenty first birthday. Brigid was missing her weekend excursions and so she said yes. She had spoken briefly to Billy and he seemed a friendly somewhat withdrawn sort although his job allowed him to tour the whole works so he was very well known. Mairaid had once gossiped about how several of the girls liked him but they were put off by his limp.

Brigid had forgotten to look the next time he passed by and anyway, she reminded herself, she was definitely not looking for a man, crippled or not. Brigid had found new digs above a smart card shop on the Broadway, which she shared with a Scottish girl who worked late on Saturdays refitting the shop windows at a big department store on Oxford Street, and so she invited Grace round so they could get made up together. Brigid had a new maroon scarf but could not afford a new hat. Mrs Clark had taken hers back as soon as she heard Brigid was leaving, calling her ungrateful and selfish whilst shedding a tear although as Brigid reasoned at the time, it was not her job to keep her employer connected to the world. Grace arrived early and they experimented with lipstick and swapped scarves so that Brigid had an emerald accompaniment to the bright red lipstick Grace had insisted she wore.

They met Billy and John outside The Crown; it was a warm spring evening and they stood chatting for a while. Brigid said it was a special day for Ireland and perhaps they could go to Kilburn for a change where they would be music in some of the bars. This was agreed and they caught the bus, Grace and John naturally finding the only empty seats at the back leaving Brigid to sit at the front next to Billy. There was a silence until Billy said he thought they had celebrated St Patrick's Day recently because Mairaid had brought in some delicious potato cakes. Brigid smiled and wished Billy a happy birthday asking him when his birthday had been.

'It's today actually,' replied Billy. 'Though I don't want any special fuss in the pub.' Brigid assured him she would not mention it to a soul but she would be buying him a drink first for it was a double celebration as the 24 the April was the anniversary of the Rising. Billy was pleased that Brigid was pleased but he was not sure exactly which rising she meant but did not want to show his ignorance.

He did not have to for Brigid said, 'As I'm buying you the first drink, can I ask you a personal question, Billy?' Billy nodded and somehow did not mind being questioned how he got his limp which he had refused to tell any of the girls at the factory. He swore Brigid to secrecy and then replied, 'It's nothing heroic, I'm afraid. I was sent to work down here at Smithfield market, humping dead animals around. I was only just fourteen and about half the size I am today. On my second day a horse reversed suddenly with a loaded wagon and crushed my leg against a pipe. Somehow it didn't seem to hurt much but I had a broken foot and somehow it just didn't heal properly. My chances of being the first to climb Everest gone in a flash.'

Brigid smiled but said, 'It must have been hard being alone in London and still a boy really.' Billy had not noticed the bus had reached the end of Kilburn High Road and he was very annoyed when John called out, 'Come on, you lovebirds, it's our stop.'

They went into the Old Bell which was bedecked with the orange, green and white of Ireland with flags hanging from every wall. A band was playing in the corner and Brigid began singing along.

'You may take the shamrock from your hat now…'

Which seemed to stir the others at the bar, some clearly having partaken more than a glass or two, until the whole pub reached a crescendo.

'But until that day, please God, I'll stick to wearing of the green.'

Billy liked the music but he regretted that there was no break in the songs so he could carry on his conversation with Brigid. John suggested they try a quieter pub for as he pointed out, Kilburn has more pubs than Leeds town centre. Grace though said she was enjoying the music and could they stay for one more song and just then a woman wearing a velvet coat leant over and asked Brigid if she would sing a song. Brigid was just about to decline when John said he was sure she would and along the bar came a murmur of approval. The woman asked where Brigid was from and then signalled to the band for a bodhran roll of introduction.

'To celebrate this day of James Connolly and the heroes of 1916, Brigid from Bantry Bay will honour us with a song.'

There was a cheer and, amidst the drinks being carried and the laughter, the pub went almost quiet for a second. Brigid had no option and began for, although she had been singing rebel songs in the farmhouse since she was a small girl, there was only one she was sure she knew all the words to. The band waited with just a gentle fiddle line as an introduction and Brigid began, first asking the crowd to join her in the chorus first:

'So take it down from the mast, Irish traitors

It's the flag we Republicans claim,

It can never belong to Free Staters

For you've brought on it nothing but shame.'

A few men in the corner were singing loudly as Brigid continued, 'Then leave it to those who are willing…'

Suddenly two men charged across the bar the nearest one seizing John by the throat and swinging a punch at his head. The other knocked several glasses from the bar shouting, 'No bastard who murdered Collins is drinking here tonight.'

In turn the men in the corner, who happily all appeared to be the size of oak tree trunks stepped forward grabbing the two assailants and forcing them outside. Grace was helping John to his feet and Billy stood alongside Brigid who looked as though she was ready to fight the next intruder. He whispered to Grace, 'Let's get them both out of here,' and grabbing John's arm with one hand and Brigid's with another he pulled them out of the door, narrowly avoiding the arm swinging fight just outside the door. They crossed the road and John lent against a shop window, a trickle of blood coming from his nostril. Billy looked across and saw policemen arriving, drawing truncheons to confront the fighting men.

'Let's move away or we'll get arrested,' shouted Billy, leading the way. They walked as quickly as they could towards Maida Vale, they were all shocked and Billy looked across at Brigid to see she was still coiled as if wanting to go back and rescue her new comrades from the police van. No one spoke and Billy held back a joke about how he would never forget his twenty-first birthday. As they reached the turning with Carlton Vale a police car pulled up and the driver ordered them to stand still.

The back window was wound down and from the far side a voice said, 'That's her, bring her in.' Two policemen had already got out and now grabbed Brigid, forcing her into the car.

Billy shouted at the first one, 'I'm coming with her,' and the voice from the car said, 'Push off or I'll have you arrested for treason.'

The inside of the car was full of stale smoke which made Brigid cough. The man who had identified her turned and showed his face from under a trilby type hat, without a word he offered her a handkerchief. Brigid refused but then needed to wipe her nose with her sleeve. They sat in silence as the car drove at speed with the driver sounding his horn at any cart or pedestrian threatening his progress. Brigid was looking for any familiar landmark but did not recognise anything on the route. Suddenly the car stopped sharply and Brigid could just see out front an overturned cart of furniture with brown kitchen stools and small tables spread across the road.

'Carry on,' said the man and, as the driver picked his way through the furniture, Brigid noticed a pub sign for The Spotted Dog outside. Moments later they drove into the back yard of a police station and Brigid was hurried inside by the driver and the third policeman. They took her to a small room with only one tiny barred window and the two policemen were replaced by a sergeant and another constable.

'My name's Sergeant Merrigan and I need to get your details down so that the detectives can ask you a few questions. First what's your name and where do you live?'

Brigid said nothing, she needed time to think but realised antagonising the police would only mean more time in the station.

'Could I have a drink of water, please?' she asked.

Merrigan stroked his moustache at the left side with his thumb, 'Give me your name and address and I'll make sure you get one.'

Brigid asked why she was here; she had done nothing wrong. Merrigan was an old hand though and replied he did not know he was only the duty sergeant and he did not want to have to put her in a cell as the station was a bit crowded and the only available cell had not been cleaned recently. Brigid decided that if she pretended to be an innocent girl out for a night to celebrate a birthday, they might let her go but she knew she could not give them any true information for that might lead them to Conor and anyway she could not incriminate Billy, Grace and John in whatever the police were accusing her of.

Brigid had, of course, told the odd half-truth when she was a girl. Once she had been caught out for missing school to go to play at Maureen's house, after her story that she was helping look after Maureen's sick mother was spoilt by her brother arriving to say he'd just bought two lambs from Mrs O'Laoghaire in the market. For that she had missed her supper and spent an hour locked in the old barn. It was to be two hours but the old priest, Father Cosgrave, was visiting and declared that the Lamb of God had saved Brigid from sin. Brigid was required to recite the whole song by heart at Sunday school that week. It came back to her now and she thought a little devotion might help her cause so clasping her hands in prayer she whispered:

'Only by grace is thy worthiness restored,

Behold the Lamb, behold the Lamb

Behold the Lamb of God'

Kerrigan was unimpressed and about to interrupt when Brigid went on.

'My name is Mary, Mary Furlong and I come from Dublin but I've just arrived in London and I was promised a bed to sleep on by a girl I met on the train from Holyhead.'

Kerrigan wrote this down slowly and asked for the name of the girl. Brigid was starting to enjoy this and thought she could risk a name from home, Eileen she replied adding that the girl had never told her full name. She thought of Eileen Flanagan, whilst Kerrigan was writing, the poor girl who had drowned in the harbour during a storm. Merrigan had decided he needed one more piece of information.

'Who were the two men you were in the Old Bell with?'

She suspected Merrigan knew the answer but by now her story was flowing and she was astonished how easily the lies flowed. Merrigan wrote down what she said and left the room telling the officer not to get her any water and not to speak to her.

Brigid looked round but there was nothing to fix her gaze on, only some regulations pinned in the corner which were too far away to read. She rested her head on her hands and closed her eyes, she thought about why the police were interested in her. Did they know she was Conan's sister? If so, what could they have on him and how did they think she would help? Did they want someone to inform on republicans in London? She suspected the latter and knew the next session would be tougher, probably trying to scare her but when the door opened, she was surprised to see the man from the car enter with a tray with a large metal teapot, cups and saucers and a half full bottle of milk. He sat down, signalled for the police constable to leave and carefully poured the tea, passing a cup and the milk bottle to her.

'I'm sorry,' he said, 'The sergeant couldn't find the milk jug.' He began without introducing himself.

'How do you know that song about traitors?'

'We used to sing songs at my granny's every Saturday,' she replied.

'Why did you sing it in the pub?'

'The whole pub was watching me, I felt under pressure.'

'But why that song?'

'It's the only one I know all the words to.'

'Didn't you know it would cause trouble?'

'No everyone liked it back home.'

Soon he got bored, he hurled the tray and pot over, sending hot tea splashing across the floor. He walked round the table and pushed his face into Brigid's.

'Stop this bollocks now, you're not called Mary, you're not from Dublin and when I find out who you are, I'm going to charge you with treason you murdering Irish bitch.'

Brigid said nothing. She thought crying might be a good idea but she could not manage a tear, instead she did her best to look frightened. He left her in silence for several minutes and she raised her hands to her face although she made a careful mental note of his features his large forehead and protruding Norman nose, his stained teeth and the bald patch just emerging on the crown of his head. She pretended to quiver a little letting out a sob as he pulled up a chair and sat next to her.

'I'm sorry,' he murmured, 'I lost my little brother in an ambush in County Kerry, shot in the back as he rode his motorcycle. Sweetest kid, sometimes I just get angry about it. I just want to help you and I will, if you help me stop these murderers. You don't like to see young men murdered, do you?'

Brigid felt she was in a scene from a film. She certainly knew the next part of the script, saying how sorry she was that he had lost a brother so young and she hated all violence, she really did not think she knew anything useful as she knew of no murders but she would try to help. He seemed to lose interest in who she was, though she could tell he did not believe her story. Instead, he wanted to know who she had heard of in the IRA, any names she had heard mentioned in the pub, how many people called Sean did she know.

This latter question almost prompted her to make a long list just for the fun of it but she named two and made-up little stories about them. Three times he mentioned Sean Russell, had she heard that name? Did she know anyone who had met him in America? would she report back to him if anyone mentioned his name? She promised she would and he asked some more questions, lots of names he mentioned but she really did not know any of them except, of course, Russell who was well known and had stayed near the farm on Whiddy and had turned up for breakfast and teased her about her good looks when she was fourteen or fifteen.

The policeman seemed angry again and said he could tell she was lying so he was going to come back tomorrow until she helped him. If she was not prepared to help, she would have to stay in a cell that night and for as many nights as it took. Brigid knew to cry out now and ask him to let her go, promising that she would report on anyone who mentioned Sean Russell or any of the others. He made no reply and left. The constable came back in and the room darkened, she realised she did not know the time but when she asked the man did not reply.

Brigid resumed her resting position, she was tired but she could not sleep, angry with herself for being so stupid as to sing that song, angry that she had drawn attention to herself, angry at John for making her sing and then angry again at her own weakness. Merriman came in eventually and told her there were no cells and she could go, but they would be watching her from now on.

It was a short walk from Willesden Green police station to her room. It was the early hours and there were only a couple of drunks on the High Road and walking up Walm Lane she saw no one, except two beggars sleeping outside the underground station. It was now Sunday and she needed to find John, Billy and Grace first thing and then contact Conan before the story spread. She slept well but a gentle knocking on the door woke her and her landlady Cynthia told her there was a young man waiting downstairs to see her. Brigid was pleased that Cynthia was not much interested in her business, or indeed anyone's, and showed no sign that she thought a nine o'clock call on a Sunday morning to be in any way unusual. Brigid took her time she assumed it was a contact from Conan and she needed to get her story straight.

Downstairs Billy was worried he had been too forward in coming round and indeed in asking Tom Stone for her address. Whilst Tom had given him the address last night, he could not resist asking if Brigid would mind, for he regarded Billy as his protégé and a potential recruit and he did not want Billy to get hurt. Tom had noticed that Brigid, young as she was, kept herself to herself and did not seem the type to want to get romantically involved with anyone.

However, when Brigid eventually came down, looking remarkably well and changed into a white blouse and dark skirt, she seemed pleased to see Billy. She explained that she had been released quickly and she would really like to forget the whole episode and swore Billy to not telling a soul either at the factory or anywhere else. Billy agreed but it seemed Brigid was not fully convinced, for she added, 'That includes Tom Stone.'

She walked back to Billy's digs explaining that she supported the struggle for Irish freedom from England and the 1916 Rising was the attempt to force Britain out of Ireland and establish an Irish Republic. There were some, Billy learnt from her, who gave up the fight for Irish independence and agreed to split Ireland up. Some of these in the Dublin government, Brigid said, were now arresting genuine republicans and were even collaborating with the British to crush the IRA.

Brigid said it seemed that Special Branch were keeping an eye out for IRA sympathisers but she had not been able to give them any information as she knew nothing about what the IRA was doing. Billy kept quiet and tried to make sure he did not forget what Brigid said, he realised he had a lot to learn about Irish history. When they got to Billy's digs, John was just coming out and still had some cotton wool lodged in a nostril.

'I'm sorry you got punched, John,' said Brigid. 'I'm sure you'll never ask me to sing again.' John was on his way to collect Grace so they left Billy and when they got to Grace's digs Brigid simply said she had no information so the police let her go and she would be grateful if they would not tell anyone because Mr Willans would probably sack her. They agreed and John added, 'Best not tell Tom either so as not to put him in a difficult position.'

Chapter 3
Search Party

The firm hand on his shoulder caused Billy to start. Often one of the girls would tap him as he passed on his rounds in search of a missing part but not usually this early in the morning and this was a firm grip and when he turned round, he was astonished to see Mr Willans facing him. Willans had only spoken to Billy once since his first day and that was when he summoned Billy, John and two other new workers for a brief lecture on not getting involved with "British Bolsheviks" who he said pretended to be friends but wanted to overthrow the King. Now though Willans beckoned Billy to follow him and they walked right through the factory to the office.

'Your father's on the phone, be quick, it's most irregular,' Willans said pointing to a handset on one of the desks.

It took Billy a few second to react to Willan's words, for he had never known his father use a telephone. As he picked the receiver up, he assumed the Public Assistance were trying to cut the payments again but his father quickly said, 'Billy it's our David, he's gone missing.'

Billy knew it was a Tuesday morning and the Easter holiday had been weeks ago, so surely David was at school. Before he could ask, Humphrey said, 'I'm at the school; Mrs Perkins came round in her car and said they'd lost David.'

'Where is he now, dad?'

'They don't know, the police are out looking for him.'

Billy wanted to ask a lot of questions but he could hear his dad was upset and clearly unsure what to do. Instead, he just said that he was on his way and would ring as soon as he could.

Billy's thoughts jumbled. When he had last been in Darlington last September, David had just started at the open-air school; he was no longer strong enough to walk too far so caught a special bus at the end of the road.

Billy thanked Mr Willans and walked back into the works where he met Tom Stone. He explained what had happened and Tom told him to travel home to see if he could help.

'I'll square it with Willans no problem, he takes a day off if his daughter has the hiccups.' Tom produced a ten-shilling note and explained it was from the rally the night before and Billy could pay back what he spent on a weekly basis.

'You'd better go and get a train, Billy, let's hope your little brother is safe.'

By ten o'clock, Billy had made the train north and sat in third class, still panting from running up steps, as the steam rushed past the windows and the train picked up speed. He had never been on a train home before; usually he hitched up Ermine Street as Humphrey liked to call it. As he recovered his breathing, he wondered what had happened two hundred miles away and if he would be in time to help. Dave was ten years younger and had always struggled with his breathing since he was small. He was the sweetest boy and he had cried for the first time anyone could recall when he realised Billy had to leave home. Before then Billy and Dave had shared the back bedroom and Billy remembered Dave struggling to breathe and coughing in his sleep, awaking to find his mam and brother anxiously watching him.

Whenever he was well enough, he liked to chase Billy across the beds but recently this effort was too much. After the diagnosis of consumption, whenever Billy came home, he had to sleep downstairs but he could hear from the front room that the coughing had got worse. Billy had been home last year when his mam was persuaded that the new school would have the nurses and the correct exercise programme to help Dave attend classes. Dave did not want to leave Dodmire School and Billy wondered why the nurse could not call there but Humphrey had raised it in the Labour Party ward and Councillor Rodgers had explained that it cost too much to have nurses visiting different schools.

Humphrey later told Billy that it was no use arguing because the council was very proud of the new school which was, apparently, based on the latest Swedish research and involved fresh air and exercise for all children.

The journey seemed to last forever and it was only after they left York that Billy felt useful again, standing by the door and leaping from the train at Bank Top and running over the bridge and down Neasham Road. When he opened the door, his mam was dabbing her eyes with a hanky and in Humphrey's chair a policewoman sat holding a cup and saucer.

'What's happening mam,' Billy asked holding her to his chest.

The policewoman explained that Dave had disappeared from school just after nine o'clock and still had not been found although police had been searching the area.

'I want to go there now,' said Billy prompting his mam to detach herself and remark that she knew that was what her Billy would want.

'We'll find him mam,' said Billy. 'I promise.' The policewoman said she could arrange a lift if someone could sit with his mother.

'Well,' said Billy. 'There's Mrs Burton over the road, she keeps chickens and possibly someone from Toc H would come, there's two in the next street.'

'I've already approached Mrs Burton,' replied the policewoman in an accent that didn't seem local. 'And apparently she is on a Salvation Army trip to Tow Law and won't be back until later this afternoon.'

Billy thought it odd to choose Tow Law as a trip destination and remembered going there in the Sunday school quiz team to be soundly thrashed by their young Bible Study team. He asked if the policewoman could stay a while and she replied she had been ordered not to leave Mrs Stainsby alone.

Billy stepped out in the street and saw Colin Dennis getting into his pop van down at number forty-six. He walked down waving and Colin recognised him shouting, 'Ha, knew ya couldn't stand London for long. Unfriendly buggers down there.'

Billy explained his predicament and Colin remarked that he was well ahead on his rounds today and that, given it was an emergency, he would give Billy a lift over to Haughton and hope his manager was not about. As an extra precaution Billy crouched in the back seat for the company did not allow their trucks to be used by anyone but Bowcock's employees.

'I'm taking a big risk Billy, there's hundreds want this job,' Colin said as they turned into Parkgate, so Billy tried to reassure him his dad would get him some more orders from the Cleveland Bridge in return for this favour.

'There's five hundred men working there now and my dad knows which ones have bairns and the money to afford lemonade for them.' Colin dropped him on the corner so no one from the school could see him he said and when he spotted the police car he simply shouted 'Good luck' as he reversed the truck and set off back across town.

Billy rang the bell and a giant of a policeman opened the gate.

'Sorry son, we've got an incident on at the moment.'

Billy explained who he was and the officer replied, 'Don't worry son, we'll soon find your brother. I'm Inspector Harris, Harry Harris, and we've got men out searching the area, he can't have got far.'

A small woman in glasses emerged from behind the officer.

'This is Mrs Perkins, the head teacher, she is very worried too.'

Billy almost lost his temper almost shouting as he demanded to know how Billy had got out. Inspector Harris put his hand on Billy's shoulder, 'Listen son, the main thing is to find him so calm down.'

Mrs Perkins tried to explain that, as it was a fine morning, the children would read quietly outside on the veranda after assembly. This made sure that every child was breathing as comfortably as possible so that lessons and physiotherapy could start. Mrs Perkins was just about to explain further when Billy interrupted loudly, 'How did my Dave get lost?' Mrs Perkins looked alarmed, looked to the inspector for support and when none came simply admitted she had no idea.

'Somewhere between assembly and lying down on the veranda, David just disappeared. It seems the gate may have been open momentarily.'

Billy wanted to ask how this could happen but instead he just said he was going out to look for Dave himself. Inspector Harris took Billy to one side and explained he was welcome to join the search with his officers but there were some troublemakers turned up half an hour ago and he was sure Billy would not want anything to do with them.

Billy stepped outside the school and walked down the street, he did not know the area and tried to think what Dave might have done. He had decided to knock on some houses when he heard his dad calling him from the school gate. He ran back and Humphrey shook his hand, explaining he had been searching the school grounds for hours.

'Billy, those blokes over there, they say they've been sent to help you but they say they're from the Communist Party.'

'Alright dad, you stay at the school in case Dave is found and I'll go looking with the police.'

Billy had never seen his dad look so worried, normally his response to every problem was a hearty...'Right, let's get this sorted.' But today he looked older than when Billy had seen him six months or so ago. He knew he must find Dave for he feared his mam and dad would never recover from the shock if anything had happened to him. He strode towards the first house when a young man caught up with him, a short stocky lad with curly black hair peeping out from the side of his flat cap.

'Hold on feller, I'm Harry and Tom Stone asked if we could help you.'

'You know Tom Stone?' he asked.

'Well, I've never actually met him but Arthur here has, met him at the Party Congress in Manchester didn't you, Arthur?'

'That's right. He made a good speech on Spain and so I went and shook his hand and later we had a pint or two, as you do. Good comrade Tom, he rang the Federation office at the pit this morning asking for me. The bastard there pretended he didn't know me but luckily our marrer Harry had just called in and said he'd get me.'

Billy looked amazed but he shook their hands and asked if they had time to help search for his brother.

'We've got all day now Billy, well till our lift picks us up at six, we're on the night shift.'

They started knocking doors and Billy ran to the corner to check the street name 'We're in Morpeth Avenue,' he shouted to the others who had begun knocking on doors.

Arthur was talking to an old man who had answered the door and Billy passed him overhearing the older man say, 'Daft idea, putting them bairns in the bloody cold all day.'

Billy tried a few houses but had no replies, though he could see Harry in conversation with a young girl over the road. He waited for Harry to finish and then for Arthur to catch up. Harry reported that the girl had described a young lad who had difficulty walking going past the house with a teacher last week but had not seen him since. They turned into the next street; Arthur could not resist showing off to the younger men.

'Nice town Morpeth, that's where that Suffragette come from, you know the one that got killed at the Derby.'

Billy had no idea what he was talking about but he asked him if he had found anything out.

'Not really,' Arthur replied. 'But I reckon we might, they're all happy to talk, odd considering we've just come off the shift.'

Billy looked across and noticed there was a black coating still visible on Arthur's face. 'Never really washes off,' said Arthur.

They started in the next street Billy took the first house and he was pleased to hear the door open, if only as far as the lock chain allowed.

'What do you want?' said the woman inside. Billy explained and, as soon as he mentioned Dave, the door opened wide and a woman in a dark blue jumper and a pink apron splashed with moisture stood there.

'Is that little Dave Stainsby you're asking about, Et Stainsby's lad?'

'Yes, it is,' replied Billy. 'She's my mam.'

'I'd never have recognised yer, Billy, haven't seen yer since you went down south. Yer mam misses yer though, how is she?'

'She's not good I'm afraid because our Dave is missing from school since this morning.'

'Poor thing she must be worried sick, I missed her at chapel on Sunday, our Susan was poorly.'

With that she let out a call of "Fred, come quick" and a man swiftly appeared, still in his vest with his braces over and a large pipe clamped in the left side of his mouth. Fred grasped quickly what was needed explaining that he knew most people round here and would be glad to come and help look. He told the woman to iron his shirt quickly but she said there was no time and just to put his best jacket and scarf on. He came back as told and Billy and he started to knock doors together, Fred still puffing smoke after every call.

It was clear Fred knew almost everyone in the street, those that answered whether men or women wanted to chat but Billy helped Fred away explaining they were on an urgent search. As they came down the drive of the end terrace, they saw Inspector Harris had pulled up and was talking to Arthur, Billy crossed the road to see what the police now knew. Arthur was protesting that they were just helping Billy try to find his brother.

'If ever I need help from Communists, I'll phone Joe Stalin meself, now clear off or I'll arrest you both.'

'I don't care if they're Communist, Labour or what. If they help find Dave, I'd even have Tories. These two have done more than the police so far,' Billy shouted.

Harris looked furious and for a moment Billy thought he was going to arrest the Fishburn men. Instead, he turned on his heels and as he drove past, he stopped and said, 'I want you two out of town by this evening.'

Billy saw him stop further up the street and talk to Humphry who had decided to join the street search. Billy waited for his dad and explained that the men were miners who had come to help because they knew friends of his in London.

The men carried on knocking doors, in this stretch several houses gave no reply but they were suddenly interrupted by a call from the street corner and they turned to see Fred's wife carrying a baby, trying to run towards them with her pinny flapping in the breeze. Billy was closest and he noticed she now had on a blue flowery pinny which looked brand new clean, as he reached her, she blurted, 'Billy, I've just had an idea, might be nowt but there's a lass called Barbara who lives alone in the next street but her mam lives next door if you understand.'

It was clear Billy didn't understand so she went on, 'She went to the school before she got too old, friendly soul, bless her, but she can't really manage on her own, so her mam checks on her, helps her cook that sort of thing.'

Humphry had joined them and said he knew Barbara Tipstock as Et had babysat for Mrs Tapstock years ago after her husband got killed in that accident at North Road works. Billy and Humphry told the others and they all decided to try the next street so as not to get separated. They turned the corner and there a hundred yards away Billy saw a familiar figure. Dave was stood next to a punch bag on a wooden stand making it swing in a wild arc and trying unsuccessfully to hit it again as it swung back. The punch bag was held in place by an ill-dressed young woman who had her foot on the stand. Dave had on his head a black peaked cap which Billy recognised as a train drivers hat and this looked incongruous against the large bright red boxing gloves he was wearing.

Dave was concentrating hard and when Billy said, 'Whoa Dave, are you trying to be the next Joe Louis?' the boy swung round and with a whoop of delight jumped straight into Billy's arms. Billy could hear him wheezing badly and loosened his grip; getting Dave to stand still and not talk.

Dave coughed a little and then said, 'I'm alright now Billy.'

Billy asked Barbara if Dave had eaten any lunch and she said he had some bread and cheese and a cup of orange. Humphry thanked Barbara and said Mrs Stainsby would be over to see her later that week, he took her next door and Billy could hear Mrs Tapstock's shock and Humphry reassuring her that no one would hear of it. Dave waved goodbye to Barbara and asked Billy if he could come round to practice boxing again.

'Maybe,' Billy replied. They walked slowly away, Dave gripping his father and brother tightly by the hand and soon asking for a "one, a two and a three" through the air. It was Humphry who said that Inspector Harris and Mrs Perkins had no need to hear where Dave was found. Billy knew that his dad had a lot of respect for the police, indeed had volunteered as a special just after Billy was born, so he was pleased Barbara was not going to get into trouble. He lifted Dave up and told him to say that he was found in the street by Billy and his dad and not to mention the boxing. Dave agreed and skipped down the street forcing Billy to skip a little alongside. He stopped at the corner house where Arthur and Harry were resting on the wall.

'Cheeky little bugger,' Harry said with a grin. 'Causing all this fuss. We'll expect to see him in the Young Communist League soon to make up.' Billy replied that he would see what he could do. The story of the King's horse came back to Billy so he asked Arthur to explain.

'Just before the war,' Arthur explained. 'She wanted the vote so she threw herself in front of the King's horse at the Derby and was killed.'

'Suffragettes,' Harry added, 'like Sylvia Pankhurst.. But don't encourage Arthur anymore, he's read every history book in County Durham twice, the libraries can't keep up.'

'I don't go on,' Arthur insisted. 'Not unless folk ask, for as Marx said to change the world you need to understand it.'

Billy could tell this was a regular topic of banter between them and added, 'I doubt Darlington figured much in the history books anyway.'

'Well, that's where you'd be wrong Billy. For example, when Edward abdicated and ran off to France with that American, he couldn't find anyone to marry them. Step forward the poor man's vicar from Darlington, Jardine his name was, popped down to France and married them even though the church had banned him. Seen a picture in the paper of him at one of those posh French houses alongside the Duke.'

'Chateau,' said Harry.

'Bless you,' chuckled Arthur and Billy smiled too.

'I'll never forget these lads; I'd better go home with Dave but can I give you the money for a pint?'

'What spend Party funds on boozing, definitely not,' replied Arthur.

'I thought you said Billy was a Party comrade, Arthur, fought in Spain and the lot.'

'More like fought outside the Spanish City in Whitley Bay,' laughed Arthur.

Billy assured them he would pay every penny back and said this was real socialism in action. They shook hands and then the miners tickled Dave one last time and strode away with that familiar low hanging gait towards the town.

Moments later Billy, Humphrey and Dave were back at school and soon Dave was excited to be sat in a police car, he begged the driver to put the siren on. The driver forbade it so instead Dave arranged himself high on Billy's lap so he could see the whole journey. As the driver slowed along Louisa Street at the end of each road of terraced houses, Billy strained to see if anyone from Dodmire was passing by.

At Thirlmere Road, he spotted Freddie pushing a wheelbarrow and before Billy could stop him, he had wound down the window and shouted, 'Freddie, I've been arrested for murder.'

Billy quickly wound the window back up, but from the front seat Inspector Harris said, 'He's a bright lad for to be going to Salters Lane.' Billy did not bother to explain instead leaving it to his dad to say that Dave was indeed as sharp as a tack.

At the house, Dave rushed into his mother's arms only to be asked, 'What have I told you about wandering off, Dave?'

Billy stepped over the newly washed step, noting that the weekly tasks were being observed come what may and heard Humphry ask Inspector Harris in for a cup of tea. Billy said he would put the water on but was relieved to hear Harris say he must get on and he was pleased the force had been able to help. Dave insisted on standing on the step and waving the car away until his dad said, 'You'll be king one day, our Dave, with all that waving.'

Et responded that she had never heard of a King Dave, which Billy thought was odd from a woman who read the Old Testament every night before bed.

Billy was in the pantry, searching for the King George V coronation tea caddy, when he heard a knock on the door. Humphry opened it and there was Freddie.

'Hello, Mr Stainsby, my dad wondered if you'd like some of our briquettes.'

Humphry could not suppress a smile for Trevor Sawyer was the last man likely to help out a neighbour indeed usually Freddie was sent round by his mam to borrow a cup of sugar or some milk. Humphry knew that look of hunger though, a lean look almost pleading through the gap in the boy's teeth. By the time he had returned with some bread slices laced with margarine both boys were examining a couple of the briquettes.

'He makes 'em with special mortar mixed with coal dust, Billy, and they really explode in the fire like cannonballs.'

Humphry picked one up and agreed they were very fine, 'Imagine Bony getting one of those in the gut at Waterloo,' he laughed.

Once Freddie had finished his bread, he was politely ushered out as Et said it was time for a bath and an early night for Dave. Billy realised he should stay the night to check all was well and he promised Dave a new bedtime story if he had his bath in time.

Now the worry over Dave was over, Billy could see Humphry looked calmer. 'Pleased we found him, eh Dad?'

'It's not just that son. Didn't have time to tell you the good news, I started a new job last week. Those Public Assistance buggers can leave me alone now.'

Billy remembered a letter his dad had written him two years ago, just after he moved to London, when the investigators were due, they had been asking about where Billy was and how much his dad's war pension was and it was clear his dad was expecting a reduction. He had gathered last summer that the Ministry of Labour had taken over the means tests as the local council was not doing what the government wanted, his dad saying something about they wanted all councils to do their dirty work, like those so-called Labour councillors in Newcastle had. It was the only time his dad had ever criticised anyone in the Labour Party, or indeed mentioned politics, to Billy save the time Humphry had returned from a protest march in Durham over the Means Test and told Billy and his mam there were men there from all over, from Sunderland to South Bank.

Billy did not want to spoil the good day and simply asked, 'So it's alright now dad, you can make ends meet?'

Humphry agreed and lit his pipe, though he added, 'It's been hardest on yer mam, didn't always eat enough, but we'll get by now.'

Billy told his dad about his new factory job. 'Progress chasing eh Billy,' Humphry replied. 'I like the sound of that.'

Next morning there was a written message for Billy on the sideboard, Colin Dennis was loading up at the back of Crown Street and had to make a delivery to Piercebridge, if Billy could be at the library for eight o'clock, he could drop him on the road south. His mam insisted he have a boiled egg and toast and despite Billy's protests, for he knew it was the last egg in the house, he had to give in. Luckily Dave came down in his pyjamas, sat on his lap, and Billy played aeroplanes with him, zooming most of the egg into the empty hangar of Dave's mouth.

Billy walked up the street with his dad, they said nothing but at the top Humphry shook his hand and thanked him for finding Dave then, as Billy watched, Humphry crossed the road and joined the ant like procession heading for Cleveland Bridge. Billy thought it odd that these men who would work together all day and then meet up later for a fives and threes league match or, in summer, play cricket or flat green bowls, barely acknowledged each other in the early morning as they walked singly towards the works. Billy turned and walked into town past St John's Church where, one Sunday, he had once paraded as a Boy Scout and his mum and dad had deserted the Methodist Church for a day to watch him struggle in the wind with a massive Union Jack.

Billy smiled as he wondered what Tom Stone would think of that although he remembered hearing one of the mothers at work telling Grace about a folk group in Camden which she was thinking of joining her children to, seemed to be a peace rival to Baden Powell from what Billy could remember.

Billy crossed the Stone Bridge, noting that the Skerne seemed to have shrunk again during the recent dry spell and that someone had thrown an old pram into the middle of the river where a shiny mallard preened itself whilst resting on the handlebars in the early June sun. Billy turned right into Crown Street and, as he was early, went to look at the queue of girls waiting to clock in at Peases Mill. He did not recognise anyone although his mam had worked there before she was married which had meant that when he was little and in a pram a walk into town would be interrupted every hundred yards or so as someone from the mill stopped to pass on all the news. Billy did not want to miss his ride so went back to Crown Street and looked again at the memorial stone to WT Stead.

The only picture the family possessed of Billy's paternal grandfather showed him smoking a cigarette and standing next to this stone in his working clothes as if he had just installed the memorial. Perhaps he had for Humphry had passed the stone with him once and told him he was proud the family was associated with such a brave journalist who had "put the Northern Echo on the map."

Later, Billy had discovered that Stead had another claim to fame having taking a cruise on the Titanic and drowned after giving up his lifejacket to another. From across the street, Colin honked his horn and Billy could see the crates of lemonade glistening in the sun on the back. Billy quickly jumped in and

Colin explained he was on the village run as stocks of dandelion and burdock, limeade and ice-cream soda were dangerously low in Gainford and Staindrop.

'It's my favourite run, Billy, I can stop at Rachel's for a cup of tea and a cuddle.'

Billy remembered Rachel Harrison who had briefly attended Dodmire and so he asked if they were getting engaged. Colin explained that they wanted to but Rachel's dad had built up a big farm at Cleasby and when Rachel had mentioned she liked him had replied he would not be giving his farm up to the pop man.

'See, Rachel is an only child so I think he wants her to marry a farmer with a bigger farm, but she says she'll win him round soon. I hope so or we'll be twenty-five before we get wed.'

As they reached Merrybent, Billy asked to be dropped off so he could hitch down the main road. He thanked Colin and wished him well with Rachel. Billy could smell the manure from the farm where he had worked picking potatoes as a child, he had hated farms ever since and did not envy Colin one bit. He watched a pheasant strolling nonchalantly across the road, hoping that it would not meet a violent death as usually cars and trucks raced past quickly here. Billy reached the far side and tried to thumb a Ford as it passed but the male passenger held his nose as they passed.

'Bastard snobs,' Billy said aloud. It was now a beautiful day and Billy took his jacket off and stood for a while gently twanging his braces as the warmth of the sun changed his mood. All was well at home and now he was on his way back to see Brigid, hoping she might agree to a date as soon as he plucked up the courage. Grace had told him Brigid liked him but that she was not looking for a fiancé she had left Ireland to avoid that. Billy had thought this over many times wondering if Brigid thought herself too good for factory workers. He knew that several men at the factory had asked Brigid out and all been refused, John had told him that she was the best-looking girl in the factory, Grace excluded of course, and he had better get a move on if he wanted a date.

Billy undid his boot and removed a stone; he was holding the boot in mid-air when a lorry pulled up some twenty yards down the road. A voice called back, 'Are yer looking for a lift young fella, gan in quick.'

Billy hopped towards the lorry and was hauled over the canvas barrier and into the truck.

'He'll nivver make a centre forward for the Toon, not with no boots on,' said a very young squaddie.

With a silent inner sigh, Billy realised he was facing hours of football talk as there were six Geordie soldiers in the back and sure enough the talk soon turned to how much Newcastle were missing the throw-ins of Sammy Weaver and the merits of selling him to Chelsea.

'Had his best years,' opined a voice from the front. 'We made two thousand pounds profit an' all. By the way lads, I'm going to see if that nice Mr Hitler wants to buy Stewy for sixpence.'

They all laughed and even more when Stewy, the small lad who had first greeted Billy said he couldn't speak any German, 'That's English and German ruled out then, we'll have to form a Jarrow army so you can speak the lingo, Private Stewart.'

Billy started chatting with the friendliest of the soldiers, Bobby, who told him they were off to Woolwich barracks on a secret mission.

'Make a change from square-bashing round Catterick,' said Stewy and then whispered a little too loudly to Billy. 'We're off to guard the King.'

From the front came a rolled-up sock flying through the air but Stewy was ready and headed the item straight out of the back of the truck.

'Stewy that's my auntie's best knitting you've just wasted. I can hear everything up here and you're on extra duties tonight for helping the enemy.'

'I've never helped Sunderland in my life,' retorted Stewy, causing a further explosion of laughter.

Soon the truck pulled up in a lay-by. 'Right lads we're near Tadcaster so anyone who wants to piss on Yorkshire here's your chance.'

They all jumped down and Billy went over to the older soldier who had thrown the sock and thanked him for the lift.

'No worries son, why are you heading for London?'

Billy explained that he had no choice, it was the national government that forced him there. He was surprised at the response.

'That Ramsay-fucking-MacDonald was a right traitor,' was spat out.

'I'm Corporal Peacock and I like loyalty son.'

Billy replied that the men seemed in good spirits but the corporal replied they were just boys, knew nothing yet. Later in the journey Bobby one of the soldiers quietly explained that the corporal was one of the last who had seen active service in the last war.

'We found out he fought at the second battle of the Somme when he was just sixteen, his twin brother was killed in the Black and Tans, all the lads would storm a trench for him,' whispered Bobby.

The lorry rumbled on and some of the soldiers dozed, as they drew nearer to London the only soldier who had not spoken, a thin and undernourished looking lad asked Billy what London was like.

'Have you never been?' asked Billy.

'Yon lads nivver been to Newcastle, Billy, his mam only let him go to Blyth on his own for the first time last week and he's lived half a mile away all his life,' said Bobby.

The lad looked crestfallen so Billy tried to cheer him up with tales of Piccadilly and Mayfair. Billy realised he should soon jump off so when Stewy said again he was going to guard the King, Billy could not resist.

'For weeks London has been buzzing with the problem, lads, for the King and Queen are very unhappy at the feeble size of the chips being served with their fish. Afore I left there was even talk of a special squad being sent doon from Tyneside to cut some proper chips for their majesties.'

It took a while for the leg pull to sink in and all were laughing when Stewy chimed up, 'I'll cut some Seaton specials for Georgy any day, he was so brave taking over when his brother packed up.'

'Sod off, Stewy,' Billy and Bobby chimed together, causing more laughter.

Billy jumped off at Mill Hill telling them where to contact him if they had any leave and shaking the corporal's hand. They had made good time without any further stops and it was only late afternoon and even warmer than earlier. Billy decided to walk to Cricklewood and he put his cap back on to shield him from the sun. He was thirsty and stopped at the Welsh Harp pub for a glass of water, the landlord seemed reluctant to serve him but Billy said he was coming back later with a large party of thirsty birdwatchers. Maybe I will one day thought Billy for he knew the reservoir behind had a big tern population in spring, for Tiny Bennett walked there most Sundays with his binoculars and had invited Billy to join him.

It was two minutes to six on the office clock as Billy reached the factory so he thought he would wait for the shift to come out. Tom was first out dashing off to an aggregate meeting so Billy gave him most of the money back and briefly explained how Dave had been found. Before he had turned round, Brigid shouted, 'Billy,' and ran across to him hugging him tightly to her and asking how his brother was. He managed to blurt out that Dave was safe but Brigid showed no sign of letting him go and he put his arms gently round her back. Several workmates were gawping at them when Brigid opened her eyes.

'Damn you Brigid,' said Molly, recently arrived from Carlow. 'I thought Billy was going to be my beau.'

The group of women giggled and wandered off to the bus garage. Brigid said she had been so worried about little Dave, who sounded just like her nephew Seamus in Ballylickey "who lights up every room he enters."

'That's Dave to a tee,' replied Billy and started telling her how Dave had opened the police car window. Billy explained about the hitchhike with the army and suggested that they had a quick drink. Brigid seemed reluctant but eventually said she would but needed to get round to see Mary soon, for she was popping out to a meeting with Tom and needed the children watching for a couple of hours.

'The sacrifices you make for the Party,' said Billy smiling. They caught the bus to the Crown with Billy explaining about the Geordies obsession with football and Brigid trying to explain the rules of hurling in return. Once inside the Crown they found the saloon bar least crowded although a showband was tuning up on stage. Several smartly dressed men were in the corner, crowding round two young women dressed in identical red blouses and matching lipstick. Billy assumed they were extras from the studios, for they stood out from the greyer figures occupying the stool and spaces near the bar. Brigid found two brown stools in the empty centre of the room and Billy brought over the drinks.

Brigid remarked that they looked like two figures caught on the Titanic refusing to leave their drinks and Billy was about to tell the tale of his grandad when Brigid continued apologising for embarrassing him in public.

'I don't know what made me do that Billy, I've only ever hugged my big brother before, you'll get endless ribbing from those work lasses now. I made a fool of myself.'

Billy could see she was genuinely upset so he responded by saying he had not minded, did not care what the girls thought for he enjoyed the affection and indeed she had permission to hug him anytime she wanted. With that, he put his right hand lightly on her knee but Brigid reacted with fury, swiping his hand away, almost shouting as she said she was not that kind of girl and putting on her coat she walked swiftly to and through the saloon doors.

Chapter 4
A Pot to Piss In (1938)

Mr Willans had left home that morning feeling agitated as he seemed to more often these days. He could just about live with the fact that he and others knew war with Germany was coming and yet the government seemed incapable of understanding this. He often complained that Neville Chamberlain, who was an engineering manager like himself, seemed incapable of seeing the main threat to the country and he had told his wife so this morning, 'Too busy with his plans to clear slums and make life harder for those of us who have to deliver a profit. I think he needs replacing, he's forgotten what his job is.'

Once again, he had received no reply from Judith, who was busy combing little Alice's hair. He tried again, speaking louder, 'Churchill is the man for me, knows how to fight wars and win. This is the time for men of action not social reformers.'

Judith had heard the first comment and had tried to indicate she did not want to discuss the issue by her silence. Alice was struggling to be free and she could see that Henry, who had recently insisted on dressing himself, had his tie on back to front.

'Please Charles; I don't want the children upset with talk of war. I have had enough wars for one lifetime. If you want to be useful, show your son how to do his tie up properly.'

Mr Willans stood up and announced he would teach him later. He put on his coat and said he would need to work late tonight as they had a huge order to complete. Judith tried to say she would bring him some supper but the door had slammed before she had finished her sentence. Willans strode down Dartmouth Road gripping his brolly hard, he did not like being contradicted at home. He knew some of Judith's Women's Institute friends were active League of Nations types, as if that could stop a man like Hitler. Further on though he remembered that Judith often talked about her father who had been killed in France and thought that, like all women he knew, emotions were more powerful for her than the facts. He thought of her more fondly and decided not to discuss politics with her again, it was not for women role to have to worry about such things.

He strode on towards the factory, now looking forward to reading The Times and thinking it may be time for another letter on the subject of war preparations. He would do his bit today and that order for carburettors would be finished and woe betide anyone who stood in his way, including that Bolshevik foreman he had to rely on.

As he turned into the works, he saw in the office entrance Grace and Amy. He only knew Amy by name as he never forgot anyone who had slighted him or challenged his authority, 'Morning ladies, shouldn't you be at work? Amy, isn't it? Why are you standing here?'

'We can't work, we've nowhere to piss,' Amy responded.

Willans was shocked, he had never heard a woman use such coarse language before. He knew he could not allow this to pass.

'You sit there Amy and I'll deal with you when I have time. Now ladies please return to work or their will be trouble.'

Grace tried to explain that they had been sent by all the women that the toilets were blocked and nothing had been done but Willans decided he was not going to listen.

'Get back to work now you two ladies or there will be consequences. We have an important order for the military and it will be finished today. Mr Stone will look into the matter later; he is the union shop steward.'

'He's got somewhere to piss though,' Amy responded.

Willans knew that he could not let this pass for it was a direct challenge to his authority. Once word got out then discipline would start to break down and today's order would never be delivered.

'You're dismissed Amy. Please leave the building.'

No one moved. It was as if they were all shocked by Willan's words, including him. He could not back down so waited for Amy to leave.

Grace decided there was no point arguing and, in any case, Amy was not supposed to have spoken for they knew Willans disliked her.

'Come with me Amy, we'll see what the women think.'

They turned and walked out without another word. Willans decided to let things lie a moment. It was a pity Tom Stone was visiting the Midlands factory today for he would have ensured Amy left quietly. If necessary, he could let Stone sort it out tomorrow, the best thing for now is to ensure all managers kept production at a maximum. He walked through to his office and asked his secretary to ring Billy and get him to tell all managers there was a production update meeting at ten. He then asked for a cup of tea and opened The Times, he had had quite enough disturbances already today.

Billy was not at his post to take the call. John had run to tell him the news about Amy. He had followed John back to the installation plant where Amy was in tears and being comforted by Brigid. The usual clatter of machinery was silent and around a dozen women stood all of them shocked at what had happened to Amy.

Billy overheard, 'She's not a bad lass really. Just got a tongue in her head like a lot of us.'

An older woman known by all as Nana simply said, 'She's not upset for herself, it's her mam back in Ireland feeding six kids who relies on what Amy sends home. It's not right.'

There were murmurs of agreement. Brigid suggested they send a delegation to Mr Willans and threaten to strike if Amy was not given her job back. They all agreed but Grace told them he would only talk to the union and Tom Stone was not here today.

'He's part of management really anyway,' said a voice from the back.

'Billy goes to the union meetings in Edgware with Tom, he could go to see Willans.'

All agreed and teams were sent round to tell everyone what was happening. After half an hour they all came back, nearly all the teams reporting that all women were prepared to strike but that some of the men said they would not.

'Some of them said they were in the Amalgamated Engineers Union and would only strike if the union told them to. In any case they don't think any women are in the union.'

Grace spoke up, 'It doesn't matter who is in a union, I've never been asked to join, have you John.'

John had to admit that Tom recruited him the day they started but he also said Willans needed teaching a lesson and he would be joining the strike if needed. 'He can't run all the machines by himself, can he?'

Brigid said she would go with Billy as Grace and Amy had already been brave enough to do so.

'We must show him we all stand together or he won't back down,' she said. John also said he would come for Willans needed to know that all the workers were together on this.

Billy was pleasantly surprised Brigid had volunteered for she had hardly spoken to him since she had left the pub some months ago. They asked everyone to stay where they were so that they could report back what Willans agreed.

They knocked directly on Willans door and walked in without waiting for a reply. Willans had a pen in his hand and his writing pad was resting on an open newspaper.

'Get out,' he shouted. 'Wait until you're summoned.'

Brigid simply told him that the matter was very urgent and could not wait.

'We'll get the problem with the lavatories attended to, now go back to work.'

Billy explained that it was not just the toilets they were there for but he had been elected to say on behalf of the union that Amy must be reinstated.

'Tom Stone is the union representative, so we'll have to wait until tomorrow to see what he says,' Willans replied.

'I'm afraid that won't do with respect Mr Willans. Either Amy is reinstated immediately or we'll be calling a strike.'

Willans knew he could not back down. If the works manager was forced to back down, where would it lead? He also knew that any strike would not be popular with the board. He felt he could not show any weakness.

'I'm afraid I cannot reinstate your colleague; she has been insolent and defiant and used language today which was unbecoming of a member of the fair sex. As to going on strike I would think very carefully, for there are plenty out there who would love to work for the good wages and conditions this factory provides.'

Billy said he did not think making threats was a good way to proceed. He offered Mr Willans a final chance to agree that Amy would get her job back.

'I'm afraid I can't,' Willans replied.

They turned and walked out. John clapped Billy on the shoulders, 'You were brilliant, kept calm and just told him straight. You too, Brigid.' Brigid too said she thought Billy had handled him just right, 'Mind he's all talk and no britches though,' she added causing the men to laugh.

'You look happy,' said Grace as they joined the women still gathered at the workshop. More workers had arrived in the area and there must have been over two hundred eagerly waiting for news.

'Brigid, John and I put to management that the summary dismissal of Amy was unfair and that if she was not given her job back, we would strike. Mr Willans refused so now, on behalf of the union, I ask you are you prepared to strike?'

Every hand went up and Billy noticed that Amy was almost overcome when she looked round the room at the sea of hands she had to dab at her tears. Billy announced, 'We simply cannot have our fellow workers and those that depend on them victimised in this way. Amy raised a legitimate grievance that all workers must have access to lavatories and we cannot allow her or anyone else to be picked on in this way. We will strike from tomorrow morning; I'll be coming round with details later. If anyone has any problems with managers today, send for me, John, Grace or Brigid straightaway.'

Willans was not seen all day. As she often did Amy had shared her sandwiches with Brenda, Willans' secretary, who looked after her frail mother and often did not have time to bring any food with her. Usually, Brenda did not share any information at all about the company but she told Amy that Willans had a meeting with his managers. As she had been serving tea, Brenda heard Willans say, 'We cannot allow a bunch of women to tell us how to run our factory,' and that all present had cheered.

'I was very surprised to see Tiny Bennett cheering, always thought he was better than that,' added Brenda. Amy gathered that Willans had spent the rest of the morning writing a letter to The Times and Brenda smiled when Amy said, 'Fat lot of good that will do.'

After their lunch break had finished, Amy was also able to report to Brigid that Willans had also had a telephone call from one of the board members and Brenda had heard him say that he would ensure there was no interruption to production. Brigid had smiled and said, 'We'll see then Mr Willans.'

Billy and John wanted to arrange a picket line for the next morning at 7.30 when work commenced but when they told Brigid she argued that was too late, some would already have gone in and the workers needed to "ambush the managers" with an early picket.

Billy had been reading up on Irish history and asked, 'Will we need snipers?' but Brigid did not smile. Instead, she said Billy should go round every worker and tell them quietly to assemble at a quarter past six at the bridge near the entrance.

After work Brigid walked back to her digs and thought about the events of the day. She liked Amy, who could make her laugh, and reminded her of Maureen with her cheeky comments and fear of no one. Grace had told her Amy was very friendly with the younger men and had had several boyfriends since joining the factory, even causing a fight between two of the men after one caught her kissing a rival by the duck pond in Gladstone Park.

That would be typical of Maureen too thought Brigid, though she could not imagine Maureen standing up to managers for her philosophy was, as she had told Brigid many times, 'Enjoy yourself, don't worry about anything, you're only young once.' Brigid liked both their company partly because she realised she was a very serious person and it was nice to relax sometimes. However, whilst she wanted to support Amy she did not want to become too involved and hoped to step back a little now the strike was taking place. Tomorrow morning, she decided she would ask Grace to talk to the management if necessary for although Grace was quiet, Brigid thought she too had a resolve to achieve what was right. As she reached the shop and turned to open the door, she was shocked by a man's voice behind.

'Stand still Brigid, don't turn round or I'll arrest you. You lied to me in Willesden Green nick and I don't like that.'

Brigid recognised the voice and turned her head but a stick pushed her cheek hard and forced her to face forward.

'You will be deported back to Cork unless you provide me with information. I told you last time I don't like Fenians and I won't have you bombing and murdering over here.'

Brigid wanted to rub her cheek but knew it was best to do and say nothing.

'I want you to mix together with all your Fenian and Papist girlfriends and find out what they know, what their boyfriends, their brothers, their fathers know. I want names by next week and what those names are planning to do and where. Understand?'

Brigid knew there was no point arguing. 'I'll see if anyone knows what you're talking about.'

'Not good enough. Names and places, one week.'

She sensed him leaving and leant forward and unlocked the door. Her cheek was very sore and she could feel a bruise developing, she ran some water over the corner of a towel and pressed it to her face. Brigid felt calm, this is what they wanted as she had suspected, an informer. She would need to report this.

Suddenly the strike seemed unimportant but she decided to go straight to bed to nurse her cheek and think about what to do next. Usually, she was early to wake up but she set her alarm clock for four thirty just in case, so she would have time to gather her thoughts.

Next morning, to Billy's amazement, there were dozens of women at the bridge even though it was just turning six and a light drizzle was falling. Grace was issuing instructions on how to picket to women in groups.

'Hi Billy,' she said with a smile. 'Good of you to come.'

John was already there too and Billy recognised his handwriting on two placards proclaiming…'An injury to one is an injury to all.' Grace asked the women to move to the factory gates and form up in lines of ten outside. There were too many to fit on the pavement and so Grace asked the first two rows to move to Mora Road to picket the side entrance. As more and more women arrived, they flanked the main rows so that it was impossible for anyone to enter from the side without passing several pickets. Grace made a short speech explaining that everyone would be asked to join a union over the next week but, faced with the attempt to sack a colleague for asking for simple provision of lavatories, they would be striking until Amy was reinstated and lavatory provision guaranteed.

'And Willans must unblock the lavs himself,' shouted someone causing laughter and from the back of the crowd several women singing a repeat of the line,' make sure your umbrella is upside down.'

'Pennies from Heaven,' laughed Billy, 'if only that happened.'

Billy told John was amazed to see Grace taking this leading role and asked John where she had learnt how to do this. John explained that they had gone to a Unity Campaign meeting on Spain and heard James Maxton and Harry Pollitt and Nye Bevan.

'Grace and I somehow got sat on the front row, I think it was by mistake and Grace started talking to the lady sat next to her. I was sat next to a bloke called Bill Mellor, but he was too busy talking to others. Anyway, turned out that Grace was talking to Jennie Lee, you know the Scot from the ILP, and I couldn't hear but seems they talked about Spain and all sorts, Jennie even told Grace about her visit to France to see Trotsky a few years back. Anyway, Jennie invited Grace to tea the week after and she met all sorts of ILP people there, she couldn't stop talking about it.

'So anyway, Grace and |I went to meet two of these she'd met last night. They live in Highgate so we went to The Flask. They wouldn't let us buy a drink all night, said if we were striking, we'd need the money. Gave us some good advice about striking though, Grace had been talking all the way back about unity of demands, good morale and good discipline.'

'She's certainly got that,' said Billy smiling. 'She terrifies me.'

'No one here has ever been on strike before but we look like veterans,' John replied.

A few men had arrived for work, Tiny Bennett among them, and they hung around the bridge clearly unsure what to do. Tom Stone, who had only got back from Coventry late last night, met the smaller picket in Mora Road. He asked what was happening and was told they were striking until Amy got her job back and most of the pickets were at the main gate. Tom was astonished and asked what Amy had been sacked for. No one there was quite sure but Jean, one of the older women there, said she had heard that Amy had told Willans to 'piss off.' Tom ran to the top of the street and, as he turned the corner, he saw Brigid and Billy about to pass him.

'I'm away one day and chaos ensues,' said Tom.

'Blame that idiot Willans,' replied Billy. 'We went to see him about the lavatories being blocked and he sacked young Amy.'

'Everyone is very angry Tom,' Brigid added. 'We won't go back until there are working lavatories and Amy is reinstated.'

Tom asked if it was true Willans had been insulted but was assured by Billy he had not been.

'Probably no one in his house uses the word piss, but that's how we talk. He just got pompous and angry and sacked Amy for nothing.'

Tom asked them to come to the main gate with him but Brigid said they had to brief Jean and the other girls and check they were all right. Billy said Grace could answer any questions he had.

Tom was amused and pleased at the sight of Billy and Brigid walking and talking together but when he turned the corner he stood still in shock. Lined up in rows with their flank protected were at least two hundred pickets and he could see that apart from John, who was now in the second row, everyone was a woman. At the front was Grace stood on a wooden box and telling everyone that no one had gone into work and that, if necessary, they would stay there all day until the factory closed.

'Here's the union,' shouted a voice and all turned to look at Tom and some began cheering. Tom raised his arms and said he would need to speak to Grace and find out what had happened, explaining again he had been away visiting yesterday. Just then Mr Willans turned the corner after Tom and, on seeing the picket, told Tom to order the women back to work. Tom hesitated but Willans said, louder than he meant to.

'That's an order, Mr Stone.'

Tom had not replied when those closest to him who had heard Willans started shouting, 'Don't do it Tom,' and then the cry spread across the picket lines. After a while Tom stood on the vacant wooden box and asked for quiet.

'That's one of my favourite chants,' Tom said to laughter, 'so thank you. I didn't realise I would get such a welcome back from Coventry.'

'Did you see Lady Godiva, Tom?' shouted a voice from the back to more laughter.

Tom said that he had not yet caught up with what had happened yesterday and needed to speak with Mr Willans and with Billy. He suggested that Mr Willans be allowed into his office and that he would then come back to talk to them.

No one moved but, sensing that the mood had softened a little, Tom stood in front of Willans and asked the pickets to part. Slowly they edged their way through and Tom had to unlock the gates as it seemed the pickets had persuaded old Johnson, who had worked at the factory for half a century, to come in later that morning.

Inside Willans was furious, talking of Bolshevism and the ungrateful women who had been taken on by a company that liked to move with the times. Tom listened and ignored demands that he go outside and order the women back to work. After Willans subsided, Tom explained that he had no more authority than Mr Willans to tell the women what to do, they were not in a union and they were not eligible to join the Amalgamated Engineering Union. Tom suggested that the lavatories be fixed that morning and that they promise to hold a disciplinary enquiry into Amy's behaviour in which she could be represented. Mr Willans reluctantly agreed but said that he expected Tom to deliver that message and make clear that, if there was no return to work that day, more disciplinary action would follow.

Tom realised he was in a difficult position. The extra money as a foreman was useful and covered the rent, if they did not have the money they would have to move and he would have to reduce his subscriptions to the Party. On the other hand, he could not allow the Communist Party to be seen to support management and he needed to keep his position as shop steward. He tried to sell the idea agreed with Willans to the men gathered at the bridge but to his surprise Tiny Bennett told him that a random sacking for no reasonable reason was not acceptable.

Willans could sack anyone in future if they let him succeed. The men around him concurred and he heard a murmur from the back that starving a family just for a little bit of cheek was outrageous. He looked to see who had said this and was amazed to see old Johnson.

'You support the women striking, Dusty?' he asked.

'I do,' said Johnson, 'I've given my life to this firm, everyone works hard in hot conditions especially the women and we need to show Willans and the directors that we cannot be treated like dirt. That Amy keeps her sisters and brothers alive in Ireland and she should not be sacked on a whim, it's inhuman.'

This speech had general support from all the men around so that Tom abandoned the idea of calling an AEU meeting, in any case, he would have Billy and John arguing against him and he had hopes Billy would join the Communist Party soon.

Tom stood on the box again and spoke to all the pickets, he had a deep booming voice and could probably be heard in the bus garage as well. He explained that the lavatories were to be fixed that morning and thanked the men who had supported their colleagues.

'Good old Dusty,' shouted Amy and Dusty waved to her.

'Watch it, Dusty,' shouted Mairaid. 'She's looking for a new boyfriend.' There was laughter and Tom seized the moment to explain that the firm had agreed that Amy should have a proper disciplinary hearing next week.

Brigid stepped forward and indicated to Tom to pull her up alongside him. 'All those who refuse to go back to work unless Amy is with us, put your hands up,' she shouted. Every single hand in front of her went up and across at the garage all the men, bar a handful, put up their hands. There were loud cheers and two of the younger women lifted Amy up to acknowledge the support.

'I will tell the company what has been decided,' Tom announced.

As he made his way through, a voice from the side shouted, 'Which side are you on Tom?' and he could hear the buzz of discussion this caused as he re-entered the gate.

Willans was furious. 'This is what comes of trying to have it both ways, Mr Stone, you're either with the firm or with the rabble outside.'

'Indeed,' replied Tom, 'I resign as foreman and am going back to join the strike.'

Outside Tom made his announcement to loud cheers and Grace asked all the women to stand firm. She understood from Tom that the AEU did not allow unskilled workers to join and so she determined to find a union for all the women to join. She went round all the strikers explaining this in small groups and making sure no one wandered away for they had now been standing outside for over three hours. Grace was wondering how to keep everyone involved for she knew many would want to go home early if there was to be no work. She was about to discuss this with Billy, Tom, John and Brigid when she noticed Willans had stepped outside the gate. She walked quickly over to him and asked him if he needed to talk. Willans explained that he had no one to type a letter he needed to write and could he borrow Brenda for ten minutes. Grace stepped inside the gates with him, for she feared some of the wilder women might insult him or worse.

'You mean Brenda is on strike, Mr Willans?'

'Yes, I suppose so, she isn't here, in fact there is only Mr Eastwood and I and neither of us can type very well,' replied Willans.

Grace asked him if the workers agreed to let Brenda help him it would resolve the strike. Willans replied that he hoped so, if the workers were reasonable.

Grace came out to look for Brenda and had to walk round to the side picket to find her. She had never spoken to Brenda before and so they crossed the road to talk. When Grace explained Willans' request, Brenda exploded, 'Can't type very well, they wouldn't know one end of a typewriter from there, you know what.'

They both burst out laughing and Grace said she had never known a secretary would join a strike. Brenda explained she knew what was right and wrong and sacking Amy in a fit of temper was plain wrong.

Within half an hour, Brenda emerged with a letter and gave it to Grace. Grace read it carefully and shared it with Billy, Tom, John and Brigid. John thought it too harsh and suggested they reject it but Billy said that it conceded the main point that the lavatories be fixed and Amy be reinstated and the threat of disciplinary action. If there was a repeat of the insulting behaviour which undermined management was one they could ignore for they could strike again if that happened. Brigid was concerned for Tom but he stated that he no longer wished to be foreman.

'I see it is against my principles,' he said simply.

John could not be persuaded but he accepted the majority view that they should declare the strike a success and return to work, 'Especially as some of the men cannot afford to lose a day's wages.'

Grace bit her tongue at this and simply said, 'It's a great victory and shows we have to be taken seriously.'

Somehow Grace, Brigid and Amy shared the box for a second and when Grace announced, 'We have won, Amy is reinstated and the lavatories will be fixed.' The cheering was so loud Grace had to signal for quiet.

'We have stayed solid and united, remember that everyone and thanks to the men who have supported us.'

This time a chant of "Dusty" went up and soon a chant of "Tiny", as if two football teams were being supported and the two men had to wave across to the women. They all then streamed in to work, Amy once again being carried shoulder high with chants of 'Amy, Amy' as they passed Willan's office.

With Tom no longer a foreman and Eastwood and Willans hiding in the office, Grace felt it safe to spend the rest of the day touring the works and ensuring everyone was informed. She heard that no one had ever done anything like this before and sensed a feeling of exhilaration from most of the women. Some wanted to join a union and Grace promised to find out how they could. From the men there was less enthusiasm, some complaining that they had been barred from working and all because "some lass couldn't keep her coarse tongue to herself."

Grace knew that the men swore at each other endlessly when they were in the pub, but she knew they felt that was never done in front of women and they did not expect or like to hear such language.

'It's not right, women are there to be respected and bring up the little ones,' said one man.

Grace later told John it seemed that some of the men were resentful of women working at all and it was a miracle they had got them out on strike. Grace realised that everyone had been up very early and needed a rest after work but she suggested that those who wished to could meet at The Crown later at nine and have a celebratory drink. Jean was one of those flushed with success.

'Is Willans buying?' she asked. Billy asked Brigid if she was going but she replied she had some "home business" to attend to.

By the time Billy arrived at the pub, a full-scale ceilidh was underway, there were thirty or so women from the factory there, most of them dancing with their husbands or other women and, to his amazement Billy saw Tiny Roberts in the corner supping a Guinness and tapping his feet. Billy realised that some had been there some time, John almost fell over as he reached to shake his hand and when Amy was lifted on to a table to declare 'I love you all,' she was only prevented from falling off by two strangers.

As the band played an encore and the bar closed, Grace told Billy she had better walk John home as he was quite drunk. Billy said he could do that but Grace pointed to Amy

'I was wondering if you could escort our Amy to her digs up Cricklewood Lane, she's quite tipsy and I don't like the look of those two fellas.'

Billy went over and Amy put her arms around him and kissed him. The men walked away and Billy said he would walk Amy back to her digs. She found her coat and put her arm through Billy's and once they got outside, she seemed less disoriented and told Billy she always liked being out in the night air, especially on a warm evening. They set off up the Lane, saying good night to various couples who were turning into Elm Grove and Oak Grove, until they reached the railway station.

'Let's go and watch a couple of late trains Billy, I love trains.'

Before Billy could answer Amy had turned left clambered over the barriers and was heading towards the steps, Billy had no choice but to follow. They went onto the platform and Amy grabbed Billy's hand and pulled him into a shelter and sat on his lap. Billy hoped there was a night guard who had seen them but it seemed the station was deserted with only a lamp further down the platform illuminating the pavement edge. Amy was kissing Billy on the neck and she paused to say, 'You are my hero Billy, you saved my job today.'

Billy tried to reply but Amy kissed him again and her tongue was in his mouth preventing him speaking. Billy had never been kissed like this before and he was quite enjoying it, Amy after all, he thought to himself was his age and quite a good looker. After a while though Billy became alarmed, his trouser zip was undone and Amy was stroking him. He pulled away a little.

'No Amy, just kissing,' he said.

'That's all I'm doing,' she giggled and added, 'This is your reward for being a hero.' She bent her head and he felt her licking his cock and soon gently moving her head up and down, causing his member to swell and then her head seemed to bob like a cork on a stormy ocean.

'You don't have to Amy,' he groaned but she did not hear and soon he came, trying to avoid her mouth with little success. He stroked her back and they sat there in the quiet holding hands, whilst Billy resisted Amy's attempts to put his hand inside her blouse.

Next morning Billy had had to go into John's room to wake him and John complained all the way to work about his headache. 'I'm never going to a pub again, I swear,' he repeated and only later in the morning, whilst Billy was chasing parts in his workshop, did he seem to have recovered a little.

'If you think I'm bad go and see Amy, the girls have had to put her in a storeroom for a sleep and hope Eastwood or Willans don't go in. She told Grace she didn't know how she would have got home last night without you and you were a perfect gent.'

Billy was relieved for he had dreaded the ribbing the other girls would give him if Amy told tales and worst of all he knew Brigid would disapprove, just as they seemed to be friends again. He waited for Brigid after work but everyone passed by and he asked Jean, who seemed to be one of the last out, if she had seen her.

'Went home early, Billy, said she had a headache after yesterday.'

Chapter 5
Uncle Pat's Funeral

In fact, Brigid had been intercepted by two men two days ago on her way to work before and told to meet them today. The men had asked her for a light and when she stopped the taller man bent down and whispered that they had a message from the Army Council for her and she had followed them across the Broadway behind the railway cottages before they explained that "a senior figure" wanted to meet her but they would need to take precautions so she should be ready outside the bus garage on Wednesday at four. Brigid had been given no proof who the men were, but she recognised the Kerry accent, and reasoned that if it was a police agent trying to trap her, they would simply have arrested her on the street.

It was a very warm June day as Brigid waited by the bus stop. She had simply told Grace she had a headache and needed to leave early, usually she would have found Tom but now the only foreman was Eastwood and she did not want him to know anything about her. The number 16 bus stopped and Brigid had to explain to the woman behind in the queue that she was waiting for a friend and would get the next one. She lifted her head to face the warm sun and thought again, as she had for two days, who she might be meeting and what their message might be. She could feel her own excitement rising, for many times since coming to London she had felt she had been forgotten about and apart from a few letters from her mam telling her the Whiddy news, had heard nothing official about what was happening in Ireland.

She had gathered from some of the newer Irish girls in the factory that some IRA men had gone to fight in Spain against the fascists, Frank Ryan was one of them Amy had reported and Brigid had recognised his name. After ten minutes or so, a small woman wearing a large hat that covered the front of her face, approached her and asked if she was Brigid. The woman gestured for Brigid to walk away from the garage with her and, without saying a word, turned left into Gladstone Park Gardens and walked on down the street. After passing twenty or so of the new houses, she abruptly stopped and opened the door of a brown car indicating that Brigid should get in the passenger seat. Without a word the woman walked off in the direction of the park and the driver, immaculately dressed in a dark suit, black tie and dark trilby pulled over his face reached into the back of the car and handed Brigid a black hat and a veil.

'Put these on,' he said. 'We're going to Uncle Pat's funeral, let me do the talking if anyone asks.'

They drove back through Cricklewood and up Cricklewood Lane and at the top Brigid was surprised to see green woods and as they turned down another lane, trees almost stretching onto the road on either side.

'This reminds me of home,' Brigid said.

The man did not respond but after negotiating a narrow gap in the road apparently caused by an overlapping public house, signalled right to cross the road and pulled up alongside an entrance gate.

'Straight ahead, sit on the third bench on and wait. You won't need the hat now.'

Brigid handed the hat back, with some little regret for it fitted her perfectly, and thanked the man who did not reply. She walked on along a country path and found the bench and when she looked round the car was still there. She sat on the bench and looked out at the view, a fine meadow stretched ahead of her and a young couple with a picnic laid on the grass at the bottom of the hill, were standing up and he was flapping at a bee or other insect that had disturbed his companion. In the far corner two green birds were picking at the ground and Brigid was fascinated by their red markings, she watched them for a while, until from the trees behind a large thin dog emerged, forcing the birds to fly for the trees and the dog raced up the hill as if in pursuit of a hare.

'Lovely whippet that,' said a voice from behind.

Brigid sprang up and exclaimed. 'Conan.' And turning she saw her brother dressed in a black suit and tie and holding his hat. He stepped round the bench and embraced her and they stood for a moment until he said, 'Better not attract any attention, and let her go.'

Brigid looked at him and seemed to examine his clothing until she said, 'So you are going to Uncle Pat's funeral as well…' and he smiled. He pointed to the bottom of the hill and they set off, not speaking until they crossed a tiny stream and Conan pointed to a large tree to the left and they sat down behind it out of view to anyone using the path.

'I'm afraid the Special Branch are looking for me again, Brigid.'

'I'd be disappointed if they weren't,' laughed Brigid.

She felt a little guilty not asking straightaway about the family at home but she was desperate to confess her stupidity in drawing police attention to herself. She told of the police interest in her and did not spare the details of singing in the Old Bell. She told Conan she had sent a message through the agreed contact to him but had received no reply.

'Ah no, there's been a few changes in the network over here, not everyone is still reliable.'

Conan was silent for a moment. 'So, they keep asking about Sean Russell, anyone else?' Brigid replied that she had not been asked for any names and they did not seem to connect her with Conan as far as she knew.

'I call myself Brigid Doherty now and though they say they know I am a Fenian bomber and suchlike they haven't said anything about you or anyone else.'

'I think they're on a fishing trip with you, seeing if they can frighten you in to acting as a spy, they've done that many times,' he looked hard at Brigid. 'Perhaps you could feed them some titbits and then send them on some wild goose chases?'

Before Brigid could answer he told her the Army Council was planning a campaign of disruption in England later in the year. He said Special Branch was probably aware something was planned but so far, they had no details so later nearer Christmas perhaps Brigid could pass on some information which would put them off the scent.

'You know the type of thing, met a man in a pub, didn't know his name, overheard him say Brixton prison was next, that sort of thing.'

Brigid was overjoyed that Conan had trusted her with a role and immediately said she would. Conan said a war was coming in Europe and it was time to disrupt the British, and force them to negotiate a free Ireland.

'Now Dev has got Queenstown back off the British, he thinks Chamberlain is a pushover, but we need to force them to quit once and for all. Dev is trying to break us with arrests to sweet talk the British but we'll be hitting them where it hurts, electricity, railways but no civilians of course. That's all I can say but they know Sean Russell so you could drop his name a little.'

Brigid wanted to ask so many questions but Conan said he must leave in five minutes so she just replied, 'Well de Valera refused to arm the women in 1916, didn't he, so I'll be pleased to do my bit to prove him wrong.'

Conan told her a little about home, it seemed he had been on Whiddy recently but Brigid knew better than to ask him about his movements. It seemed their sister Agnes had been abandoned by her husband.

'I know he's up working in Sligo and, he doesn't know it yet, but soon he'll be sending his entire wages home to feed his bairns. Agnes knows it's for the best and Annie sees her every day and her oldest girl helps Agnes a lot with the younger children and Annie says they are more like sisters than aunt and niece.'

Conan confessed he had not told their mam he was coming to London, 'She can keep a secret of course but I couldn't have carried all the socks and gloves she'd have wanted me to bring.'

Brigid laughed and was pleased to hear all was well. Conan asked her where she was working as he had heard domestic service did not suit her. Brigid thought she could detect a grin on his face as he said this but she simply described the factory work she was involved in and the strike. Conan listened but was clearly unimpressed and suggested she keep a lower profile, 'The best agents are those no one notices.'

Conan explained that he believed Ireland had one last chance to free itself and they must remain focused. He clearly had no sympathy for the "social radicals" as he called them.

'Half of them who went with Paedar are Communists of one sort or another, we need to focus on Ireland, this is our chance, Brigid.'

He stood up and suggested she stay put for ten minutes and asked her if she had money for a bus home. Brigid thought this odd but then Conan produced two five-pound notes in his closed fist.

'For use as necessary,' he said, 'in the cause of Ireland. I'll make sure you have a new contact soon in case of urgent matters.' Brigid embraced him again and he kissed her head lightly and with a brief 'God keep you safe', he was gone.

*****

It seemed the strike had somehow made working the long hours at the factory more tolerable so that there were fewer groans about the repetition of the tasks or the heat and dust. Tom was back in the section testing speedometers and, whereas he had previously had to ensure everyone was working as required, he relished returning to a job requiring his skills and in which he did not have to concern himself with whether each section was keeping to production. Best of all he no longer had to attend the meetings with Willans in which hours were lost poring over targets and outputs.

He told Tiny one lunchtime that Mary had been "like a rock". She had supported his decision to join the strike and they had decided to keep the flat if she could get some part time work.

'I find I've more time for Party work too,' Tom said, perhaps forgetting that Tiny had never shown any interest in politics.

'It's a busy time, we are campaigning for a pact with the Soviet Union against Hitler and we have got lots of progressives working with us. Lots of young people joining too, which reminds me I must see how Billy is getting on with his classes.'

Billy was, at that moment, sat eating his lunch on the pavement at the side of the factory and poring over the sheets he had been given. Tom had suggested he join the classes on Marxist theory run by the Party and he had readily agreed, catching two buses down to a small meeting room in Clerkenwell. The class had already been going for several weeks and so he had been given some papers and asked to introduce what he had learnt at the beginning of the class. Billy was a fluent reader but he had never spoken at a meeting studying anything and he could feel the anxiety rising even though the class was not until tomorrow. Grace walked by and said John had been sent on an urgent errand by Willans and could she join him for lunch.

'Only if you can explain dialectical materialism to me,' Billy joked.

'Oh, my dad studied Marx and many others, it was his hobby sort of. Made us all learn this, *'No one steps twice into the same river, for what occurs in the next instant are never the same as the first'.*'

'Is that by Marx? Can you say it again and I'll write it down.'

Grace explained it was not by Marx but by a Turkish philosopher called Heraclitus, who lived in the Greek empire. Marx did not invent dialectics, the theory of everything in a constant process of change, but he borrowed it from Hegel. Trouble was Hegel believed perfection had been reached in the Prussian monarchy.

'That sounds convenient,' laughed Billy.

'Oh, my dad would have loved that comment, he used to say never trust anyone who receives a government honour.'

Grace explained that Marx developed the ideas of many others, including left Hegelians like Feuerbach, who had tried to apply dialectic ideas to the material conditions in the world today.

'Of course, Marx went much further, suggested that capitalism itself was just a temporary phenomenon and would be replaced, got him into a lot of trouble, that did.'

Billy was grateful, it seemed the texts he had been reading suddenly made sense. He told Grace this and said, 'The last question is a quote from 'The German Ideology'.'

'Let's be having it then,' said Grace.

Billy read the passage, 'In revolutionary activity, change of self-coincides with change of circumstances.'

Grace thought for a moment. She suggested that the strike was a good example.

'Why look at some of the friendships that have struck up since the strike, people who didn't even talk to each other before.'

She thought some more and suggested that Marx meant more than just this possibly, that if communism came about then everyone would be changed for the better as no one would be exploiting anyone else.

Grace unwrapped her sandwiches and offered one to Billy, who politely declined.

'Cheese and Branston pickle,' she said. 'My absolute favourite.' Billy was envious for he was tired of meat paste and Spam and decided to invest in some chutney, as his mam insisted on calling it.

He asked Grace how her dad knew so much about philosophy. She replied that he was self-taught as far as she knew before they had to move to London, when he joined some radical discussion groups.

'So, you weren't born in London then?'

'What you thinkin' of, my boy. I dun cummin from 'ere,' said Grace with a straight face.

Billy laughed, 'I thought you had a country twang underneath but I was too polite to say.'

'It's nothing to be ashamed of,' said Grace. 'We are fighters our family, dad had to come to London for work, no landowner would give him a job.'

'Where?' Billy asked.

Grace explained about a big strike in Norfolk before the First World War by agricultural workers, one of many that had taken place in the county. Her dad had been a voluntary organiser who went out on his bike every night organising, her mam had said she only saw him between two in the morning when he got back and six when he went out to work.

'So where were you born?' asked Billy.

'Trunch,' Grace replied, '1 April 1913.'

Billy could feel the force of the look she was giving him and he managed to keep a straight face and reply, 'Some places have funny names though; my dad knows someone who comes from Pity Me.'

Grace explained that the farmers had held out for months against the strike for wages in Trunch and St Faith in 1910 and after that her father couldn't get much work though the union leader George Edwards, who later became the first Labour MP in Norfolk tried to help and gave him a job in the union for a while.

'I was born then but my dad, Arthur Leeder, was gassed in the war and he wasn't well enough to work in the fields after. He said if the revolution came to Britain it would happen in London so he was moving and he got a job in the ticket office at Kilburn station with the London and Metropolitan, that's why we ended up living round here. He knew Sylvia Pankhurst and all sorts of people when the Communist Party was founded. His lungs never really recovered and he died just after the General Strike.'

'You were very proud of him weren't you,' Billy replied.

'He always made me laugh too,' Grace said. 'He said he taught me words by singing union songs, and whenever I came into the room until I was eight or so he would start whistling *'Dare To Be A Union Man, Dare To Stand Alone'*.'

Billy smiled and said it was no wonder Grace had been such a good organiser. He said there were still two things that puzzled him and Grace detected a smile on his face. Grace expected a joke about April Fool's Day but instead Billy said, 'Where is Trunch?'

Grace pretended annoyance but explained it was a village near the Norfolk coast, so close to the sea.

'We once walked to Cromer, my big brother Israel carried me on his shoulders most of the way there and back, and we went roller skating on the new pier.'

Billy was no wiser but pretended to know of Cromer so he could tease Grace a little.

'My second question is, if you were born in 1913 which cradle did you snatch John from?' Grace laughed out loud and said she had never thought of that but if John wanted a younger fiancée he only had to say.

'No chance of that, he's been like a lamb with two tails since he met you,' Billy said smiling.

They munched their sandwiches and then Grace told him she thought John was an example of what Marx was talking about, for he had never been interested in politics before. Billy agreed and said it was the fight with the Blackshirts that seemed to transform him, John had talked about it for weeks afterwards.

'Now he's one of the best trade unionists in the factory,' Grace replied and Billy noted a hint of pride in her remark. Billy said he was very surprised to hear John had met Jennie Lee for he was sure John would not have known what the Independent Labour Party was a year ago. Grace agreed and said she had wanted to go to the rally and so John came, Tom Stone was on the door so he wangled us some seats at the front, she smiled as she said it seemed Tom wanted to recruit them all into the Willesden CP branch.

Billy said that he read the Daily Worker and enjoyed the classes but there was so much he did not understand, especially why so many Bolshevik leaders were being tried and executed.

'Well Jennie Lee doesn't have a good word to say about the Communist Party, she had a friend who went to fight in Spain but died in a Communist prison, Bob I think she said his name was. Seems the Communists in Scotland made her life a misery too.'

Billy mentioned John's comment that Jennie Lee had told them about meeting Trotsky.

'Yes, I made a note after meeting her, the ILP had sent Jennie and another member to meet Trotsky. He was staying by the coast near Bordeaux but Jennie said he was not able to appear in public for the government had forbidden it and he was being watched by the French Communists who wanted him expelled from France. Jennie said he had been ill and they could only speak for twenty minutes or so at a time but he urged them to support a planned conference in Paris considering the establishment of a new international to replace the Comintern.'

Billy said he needed to understand more why the Communist Party hated Trotsky so, for he had thought he was one of Lenin's most trusted Bolshevik leaders. Grace said she too was mystified but thought it would be no good asking Tom, she and John were going to find anyone who disagreed with the official line and try to find out. Grace knew that the ILP was opposed to the purges in the Soviet Union for she knew, from the meeting with ILP members, that the ILP conference had voted against defending the trials with only two votes in favour.

'And, whilst we're talking, there's something else I have to find out,' said Grace.

'What is going on between you and Brigid?'

Billy answered truthfully, 'On that we can be absolutely clear, absolutely nothing, I'm afraid.' Grace gave him a sympathetic look and determined to see what she could do on that front too.

*****

Brigid had always loved Christmas as a child, when all the family would gather at the farm, and she would end up with numerous girl cousins sharing the bedroom and often her bed and, in the dark, someone would start shrieking at a find in the stocking Santa had left. Thinking back she realised that there was little in the stockings, some fruit and nuts and perhaps a little wooden doll her father had carved but she could still recall the sheer excitement of those dark early mornings and the sense of the feast and the songs that would follow after church, always including a toast to the memory of Donal Cam O'Sullivan Beare and a regret from uncle Martin that Whiddy was not what it was and soon there would be no one left on the island.

This year she had been invited by Mary and Tom to join them whilst the children opened their presents and to stay for lunch, Mary had apologised that they could not offer her an overnight stay for her cousin had moved out and they had needed to let the room to an old couple.

'Odd pair,' added Mary. 'Never seem to come out of their room and they seemed alarmed when I suggested we share Christmas dinner.'

Brigid was looking forward to watching the children open their presents and told Grace about it at work. Grace was pleased for her and they shared memories of Christmas in hard times, Grace remembering another strike year, just after the war, when her father had little food but had carved a wooden instrument, like a flute, from an old boxwood tree trunk that had fallen at Castle Acre when he worked there in spring and he had been allowed to bring some of the wood home.

'I never play it anymore but it is the most precious thing to me.' Grace added that she and John had been talking about Christmas too and had wondered if they might invite a few friends to Grace's lodgings.

'Trouble is we'd have to be quiet, as my landlady is quite strict and John says his Mrs C is probably a fascist and wouldn't appreciate trade unionists turning up.'

Brigid thought for a moment, it would be great to have friends round at Christmas and, having moved to new digs following the incident with Special Branch, she now had a small room in one of the railway terraces opposite the factory. Only last night Mrs O'Leary had mentioned that she and her husband would be away in Liverpool for Christmas and if Brigid wanted to cook dinner for a few friends that would be fine.

'You're the tidiest lodger we've ever had, Brigid, and it's good to have a God-fearing Irish woman lodging with us, someone we can trust.'

Brigid told Grace that she and John would be welcome for Christmas dinner but it would have to be in the evening or she would burst. Grace laughed and said she wished she had Brigid's figure for every time she looked at a scone her waistline expanded.

'Don't be silly,' said Brigid. 'Why, even Eastwood told Tiny who told Billy that you were the best-looking woman in Cricklewood.'

'Burgh,' spat out Grace. 'That creep,' which caused Brigid to laugh.

Grace said she wished she had beautiful glossy hair like Brigid and her slim figure and Brigid replied that she wished she had Grace's cheekbones "just like a film star" and her beautiful brown eyes. They laughed and Grace said the factory was lucky to have two such talented women. Grace had lent Brigid a copy of The Ragged Trouser Philanthropists during the strike and was impressed when Brigid said she had finished it. Brigid said she had enjoyed it for she knew all about poverty in Ireland but the descriptions in the book were an insight into English poverty.

'I don't know why but the details stuck with me, like Easton off to work in the dark three hours early because his clock had stopped and he couldn't afford another or Mrs Linden spending hours making clothes from old material which would fall apart because they couldn't afford anything new. And the debt the English were all in, we were never in debt.'

Grace said she was pleased she enjoyed the book and Brigid promised to return it then Grace said, 'I thought Ireland had a famine and people were often hungry.'

Brigid said that was true for the English had stolen all the land and they kept the price of food high but on the island all their furniture was years old and had been well made by grandfathers so they never had to buy anything. The bed my sisters and I slept in was the one my great grandmother was born in when the famine was at its worst.

'That's what struck me most about the book, as soon as you were out of work the debts mounted and the women starved themselves to feed their children. There was never a way out for the poor.'

Grace said she had read Tressell's book when she was twelve and so could not remember much detail now.

'I read it in two days because my mam had bought it for me, she couldn't really read herself and it was the only book she ever got me. I had to explain the basic story to her but I remember how hard that was, there were so many parts to it.'

Brigid agreed and suggested that next time they read a book at the same time and meet for a cup of tea to discuss it properly. Grace was delighted and asked Brigid if she had a good Irish history book they could read. Brigid promised to think about which book would be best and try to get a copy before Christmas. Grace asked if it would be alright to invite Amy to the Christmas meal, 'She's had such a tough time and she's always good for a laugh.'

Brigid agreed adding that Grace was to make sure Amy did not bring her latest boyfriend along. Grace promised adding that she and John had already invited Billy for Christmas dinner so Brigid reluctantly agreed he could come too.

The week before Christmas was bitterly cold and it snowed for two days, leaving the streets covered in a thick fall and the factory conditions intolerable for some. Billy was still chasing the orders around the factory and he did not mind going into the engine sheds, which had just a thin corrugated iron roof and no sides at all.

'Dunno how you can go outside in this cold,' said Amy.

Billy responded as he usually liked to, 'At the age of three, I was dressed in a pair of trunks and played all day on the sands in a howling North Sea gale at Saltburn. After that, the North Pole would seem warm.'

Amy had smiled fondly at him, but Billy pretended not to notice. On the Friday before Christmas Eve though Billy could not stand the bitter cold in the sheds, several women and men were trying to finish an order dressed in hats, coats and gloves but Billy could see they were suffering and he was worried about one of the men, a new worker called Charlie, whose teeth were chattering and who could barely open his mouth to speak. He asked all the workers to join him in the nearby speedometer room, where there were braziers keeping the temperature up. Billy asked Tom to join them and soon it had been agreed that no one could work in the engine sheds in these conditions. They were about to send a delegation to speak to Eastwood and Willans when Brenda appeared, distributing notices by hand. Tom read one and announced to all that the company was closing for Christmas with immediate effect, due to the appalling and dangerous weather conditions, and in recognition of the dedicated service of all staff normal pay rates for the day and Christmas Eve would apply to all staff, 'Who report for work as per contract on 27 December.'

'Well,' said Tom. 'Extra paid holiday, just think what we would have got if we had gone on strike.' Charlie had warmed up sufficiently to speak fluently again and he shouted, 'Three cheers for Mr Willans,' and could not understand why no one responded.

Brigid was delighted with the news and gathered together John, Grace, Amy and Billy and discussed plans for Christmas Day, everyone was to have a single present so no one would feel left out and she would allocate them all names as to who bring a present for. Billy volunteered to go back to Smithfield to buy a chicken and Amy said she could provide the spuds and the greens. They all agreed to bring beer and sherry and Grace said she would find a Christmas pudding somewhere.

Next morning was Christmas Eve and John woke Billy early as he had decided to accompany him to Smithfield as he had never visited a meat market. It was a long journey on three buses and it was seven o'clock by the time the bus stopped at Aldersgate and they walked to the market. Along the road were lorries and carts loaded with cow and pig carcasses and as they reached the gates John had to hold his nose for the stench was overwhelming.

'It takes some getting used to,' Billy said, 'but most of them that work here started young, sons follow fathers and have been coming here since they were little.'

John took out his pocket watch again, as Billy had noticed he liked to do regularly, and announced it was: 'Only ten past seven, it seems like the market has been going for a while.' Before Billy could answer, John was knocked forwards by a tall man carrying a huge dead pig over his shoulder. This man had on a white tunic which was stained at the front with dried blood and buttoned at the top, on his head was a white cap also stained at the side.

'Never even said sorry,' grumbled John but Billy explained that once you were carrying a pig or half a side of beef you could not really see on one side. Billy said that these tunics were copied from the doctor's aprons at St Bart's hospital, he had been given one already bloodied when he arrived four years ago because his butcher said it would get him used to the smell.

'It was the worst three months of my life,' Billy said. 'Getting up at two, carting dead animals around for hours and then the accident.'

John knew Billy limped as a result of what had happened in the market but Billy had never explained and John decided not to ask. Billy suggested John walked round the meat market and they could meet in the west market where the poultry was. John did walk round quickly but cut short his visit as he was feeling sick. He crossed to the adjacent market and found Billy talking to a stall holder underneath dozens of dead chickens hanging from metal hooks.

'That was quick,' said Billy. 'Don't like to see where your sausages come from?' John replied that he did not mind that but the smell was unbearable and he was almost retching.

'Much nicer in 'ere,' said the stall holder who was dressed in a shirt and tie and wearing a wide brimmed hat with a blue band around the base. Billy introduced the man as Reg and said he had been very kind and took him to hospital after his accident, even organising a collection for him. John could see Reg was blushing and his pink cheeks contrasted with the blue hat band.

'Well,' said Reg. 'I know what it's like to be on your own, old man got Spanish flu in the war, came home kissed my mum, she was dead by teatime and he died at the weekend after. I was thirteen and the oldest of five, got a job here straightaway and been here fifteen year and more, met the missus in the cutting yard one morning, we were frozen so we cuddled up for warmth.'

This made John smile and Reg asked where he was from.

'Leeds,' he replied. 'A proud Yorkshireman, me.'

'Well, if it's so good up there, why you all coming to London,' joked Reg.

'I didn't want to follow the family business,' said John.

'No work Reg, so my dad asked me to come on a government scheme to help you Cockneys out,' said Billy.

'Well, that didn't work out, did it?'

'No,' replied Billy. 'And when my dad lost his job, the Means Test people gave us a hard time, claimed I was earning enough for the whole family.'

'I could have told 'em you weren't,' Reg said.

Reg asked Billy if he needed a bird for Christmas and Billy said they had come to buy one. Reg reached under the counter and brought out a huge chicken.

'I keep my best ones under here,' he said. 'And for special customers Millie, my missus, makes her special stuffing.'

Reg brought out a small earthenware pot wrapped in a cloth and handed it to John. 'Should be enough for this beauty, about a ten pounder, I reckon.'

Billy said that the bird was too big, there were only five of them for dinner but Reg insisted and said they could eat it on Boxing Day and the next day too in that case. He insisted they take the bird and refused payment, 'Extra compensation,' he called it saying they had so many orders from hotels it was already a bumper Christmas and he only asked for the pot to be returned in the New Year. Billy and John shook his hand saying it was the best Christmas present they had ever received and Billy put it in the straw shopping bag Mrs C had lent him.

John had suggested they visit St Paul's Cathedral afterwards but Billy said they would not be allowed in carrying such a large dead chicken and so they went back to the bus stop. John looked at his watch again so Billy asked where he had got it. John handed it over and Billy carefully inspected it, seeing on the back an inscription "National Agricultural Labourers Union 1891".

He handed it back and admired it, 'Grace gave it me for a Christmas gift, it was her uncle's and I promised to keep it with me for ever.'

On Christmas Day, Brigid was pleased to see it had stopped snowing and as she stepped out to walk to Tom and Mary's flat, it was much warmer than it had been when she had returned from midnight mass. The church on Dollis Hill Lane had been nearer and she was not surprised to find it packed, for everyone went to church, except those with small children and there had been one or two small ones asleep in prams alongside some of the pews. Still, it was a trudge through slush and Brigid only had her best shoes for this weather and they had little grip, halfway down Ashford Road an old man already drinking from a beer bottle took a tumble and Brigid had struggled to avoid falling over whilst helping him up.

He thanked her but when she wished him 'Happy Christmas' he did not seem to understand.

By the time she reached the flat, she was tired with the effort of keeping upright and she was almost sent flying as Mary opened the door and Patrick jumped up and gave her a big hug.

'I told you Aunty Brigid would come if you were good and only opened your stockings when mummy said,' Mary laughed.

Brigid asked had they really done that and Mary said they had heard nothing until five thirty so that was thirty minutes improvement on last year. Tom was still in his dressing gown, holding two teddy bears whilst Emily dressed them.

'Ah,' said Brigid. 'The fearsome Communist agitator converting the teddy bears to world revolution.' Tom grunted and said the bears had a much better grasp of the proletariat than some so-called Marxists he could mention.

Mary laughed and asked Brigid through to the kitchen, 'Take no notice Brigid, he went to a meeting with Jimmy Maxton yesterday and he hasn't stopped grumbling yet. Have a cup of tea?'

Brigid nodded and commented it was still cold but then declined the offer of a drop of whisky. She explained it could be a long day as she was cooking supper for friends later and she did not want to burn anything through being drunk.

Brigid enjoyed helping with dinner and managed to avoid eating too many roast potatoes and helped tire the children out so that by four o'clock Patrick had fallen asleep on his father's lap and his sister was having an extended nap in the bedroom. Brigid said she had better get going for she had her own dinner to cook but thanked them for their hospitality, 'Seeing the children meant a lot to me, for my own nieces and nephews are back home,' she said.

Tom gently moved his son's head onto a cushion and gave Brigid a hug expressing the hope that Christmas would see peace and the Western powers would join a pact with the USSR. Brigid thanked him again and said, 'There's going to be war Tom, I know it. Ireland has its chance.'

The ground was even more treacherous Brigid thought as she walked carefully home. The snow had iced and eventually she had enough of slipping and joined others walking along the Broadway, one man wished her 'Nollaig shona dhuti' which made her feel that today she would rather be round the kitchen table back on Whiddy. When she had telephoned her mother that morning, she had only been told that Annie and Agnes and all the children were there, she hoped Conan was there too to carve the meat. Mary had asked which church she went to midnight mass in and she was able to answer honestly that it was a new church, St Mary and St Andrew, with a beautiful Italian interior. This had pleased her mother who replied that it was lovely to hear the faith was spreading in London.

She had only been in the house a few minutes and was just about to set the fire when she heard the rap from the doorknocker and let in John, Grace and Billy. Brigid said the chicken was the largest she had ever been asked to cook and she unwrapped the cloth covering the pudding Grace had ordered from the Irish bakers in Kilburn, 'Smells just like home, we're going to have a feast.'

They all busied themselves lighting the fire, peeling the spuds and sprouts and gutting, cleaning and salting the chicken. With the table set, they sat down and John opened a bottle of beer and filled two glasses as well as pouring sherry for Grace and Brigid. Brigid declined instead opening herself a beer and pouring it saying, 'It's Christmas, we always drank beer on Christmas Day.'

Brigid was telling them about Tom and the teddy bears when they heard a knock on the door. John opened it and there was Amy, dressed in her Sunday best, but panting as if she had been running.

'No need to run Amy, all tha' works bin done,' John said loudly so all could hear.

Amy came in and sat next to Billy on the sofa. She apologised for being late saying she would cook the dinner to make up. Brigid said she would help as she knew how to operate the cooker which was a new one. Brigid could see Amy was still agitated and asked her to join her in the kitchen but Amy said she wanted to tell them all something. It appeared that Amy had gone to the afternoon service with Brenda in Walm Lane.

'I've never been in a Protestant church before, I hope I'll be forgiven but Brenda had no one to go with as her friend has gone away for the holiday.' It seemed they had walked back towards the factory and decided to have a port and lemon in the Cricklewood Hotel.

'We were amazed it was open, I've never seen a pub open on Christmas Day but there was some sort of private party going on and somehow, we got served, Brenda said it was because we looked so respectable and no one would suspect us of being gate crashers. Anyway, we sat at the only table and got talking to this man.'

'No Amy, no boyfriends, remember?' said Brigid.

'He's not a boyfriend, Brigid,' Amy snapped back. 'He's a German.'

Now they were all were paying attention, Amy explained that he had just arrived having walked through Holland, 'Says he is a Communist and the Nazis are murdering Communists in Germany.'

Billy confirmed that was true as he had read about it in the Daily Worker.

'More likely he's a Nazi spy,' said John. 'Let's get the dinner on, I'm starving.'

Amy said it was up to the others but she believed the German and she thought they could invite him for dinner. Grace agreed and pointed out that even if he was a spy, so long as they did not mention the factory they did not have any secrets to give away. Grace could see from Amy's expression that, if he was a spy, Hitler would soon be well aware of the progress of speedometer production, but still her curiosity was aroused.

'I've never been out of England and I've never met anyone who isn't English,' she said, quickly correcting herself 'or Irish. I don't know much about Germany but I know Christmas is a very special day, I wouldn't want a stranger alone just down the road when we've more than enough food.'

That seemed to swing it for everyone and it was agreed that Amy, Grace and John would go back to the pub and only invite the German if they believed he was genuine. It was only twenty minutes later that they returned and introduced Helmut, a small man of about forty, thought Billy, who had on a pair of round glasses which only just framed his eyes. Brigid shook hands and she went into the kitchen to show Amy how to use the oven returning to hear Helmut describing how he had escaped.

Brigid sat down and as this created a gap in conversation, she asked Helmut where he came from.

'Well really I'm from a petit-bourgeois background,' he laughed. He took a wallet out of his jacket pocket and took out a creased and grainy photograph. He explained that it was the only photograph he had left as he had needed to put his wallet under his foot inside his boot when some Dutch police were carrying out a border search. He held the photograph up and explained this was the family shop in Wilhelmshaven and his mother and father could be seen in their shop aprons. He passed it round and Amy asked what the shop sold. Taking the picture back he translated.

'Drugs, Paints, Colonial Goods and Birdseed, what you call in England a general store,' he added. In response to their questions, Helmut told them of conditions in Germany and Austria as far as he knew. He said that many social democrats had fled to avoid arrest, but they had been refused visas by the British government, returned over the borders and arrested by the Nazis or shot. He was adamant that Hitler had also ordered the execution of Austrian Nazis just as he had had killed Strasser and the others in the Night of The Long Knives. He described the hunting down and execution of Communists often in the street or the certain death of a prison camp such as Dachau in Bavaria.

'Many comrades were sent there, some I knew from the revolution of 1918, one I remember marching with, we were both sixteen, singing *'Der Rosa Luxemburg reichen wir de Hand'.*'

Helmut glanced around and detected that none of his audience knew anything of what he was describing.

'It is Christmas; you are so kind to share your dinner and hospitality. One day when the Nazis are defeated and I return you must come to visit me in Germany and I will return your kindness.'

Billy said he would like to hear more and would like to meet Helmut again soon but now it was time for some Christmas traditions from England, Ireland and Germany. He asked Helmut to begin and the older man explained that in Germany presents would already have been exchanged yesterday and the Christmas tree would be the centre of the room.

'That's what we'll get you for a present,' said Amy. 'Because we've got a present each to open.'

Brigid objected that they would be nowhere to buy one, every single shop was shut.

'I'll be back in ten minutes,' Amy said. 'If John will come and help me.' Amy kept her word and John carried in a tree almost as tall as himself. Everyone was pleased until Grace pretended to be stern.

'Where did you steal that from, John Wood?' she demanded.

'No one will miss it,' replied John. 'The factory is closed tomorrow so we can sneak it back over.'

There was laughter and Brigid said she knew she recognised it from somewhere, 'It's got a few paper lanterns on, maybe we could add a few stars or something.'

They agreed to open their presents, Billy passed round more beers and sherry, and they all started unwrapping. Billy had drawn Brigid's name from the hat passed round and he was pleased to see her face light up when she opened her present box.

'It's a St Brigid's Cross,' she exclaimed. 'I left mine hanging in the farmhouse at home, to remind them of me and bring them luck. Thank you whoever thought of this, I'll keep it above my bed.'

'We have one at home too,' said Amy. 'It protects the house, for St Brigid made the first cross centuries ago.'

'It's also said that Brigid could turn water into wine as well. I'll try that later if we run out.' Everyone laughed and she smiled and looked across at Billy as if to say thank you.

When the presents were opened only Amy was underwhelmed, for she did not want an apron as she did not like cooking and had only offered today because it was a special day. As hers was the last present opened, she hid her disappointment by saying she would go and check on the chicken and, coming back, announced she had put the vegetables on and dinner would be ready in fifteen minutes.

They busied themselves trying to make Christmas tree decorations from the discarded wrapping paper, there was some swapping of paper involved and Brigid who had made a chick out of yellow paper reluctantly shortened its tail and leant some to Helmut. When it came to reveal the decorations there was John's castle, the chick, Grace's Silver Star, Amy's shamrock and Billy's football. Helmut was the last to reveal and he simply said, 'I hope you don't mind,' opening his hand to reveal a perfect hammer and sickle on a red background.

'Not at all,' said Billy. 'That will go on the top of the tree,' and he reached up and dislodged the paper angel which was looking somewhat bedraggled as it had been soaked in the rain last night.

'Workers of the World Unite,' said Billy and they all raised their glasses.

Amy and Grace went to check on the food. Amy told Grace the chicken had been in two hours so that it would be ready in ten minutes. They turned down the heat on the vegetables and John and Helmut were instructed to set the table. Grace opened the oven door and poked the chicken with a fork, it was hard and she told Amy it was not ready.

'Oh no, but I've roasted it for ten minutes a pound like the recipe says,' Amy exclaimed.

'It's meant to be twenty minutes a pound,' said Grace. 'How big is the chicken?'

Grace went through and told the others the dinner would take much longer as it was the biggest chicken she had ever seen and she had worked on some farms as a girl. Amy came in and said sorry but John just said it would taste even better when ready and opened some more drinks. Grace did not add that the cooking would take another two hours, instead suggesting they played a game of rummy and Brigid found some cards in a drawer only asking that everyone treated them with care.

After several rounds of rummy and whist, John went searching in the drawers of the front cabinet and found a set of dominoes. Strangely no one but Billy had played the game before and John explained it was "very big in Leeds" and after some jeering, silenced them by declaring it was 'a game of the working-class, not like the bourgeois card table games you all seem to like.' As a guest, Helmut knew better than to expound on the probable aristocratic origins of all games. The novelty of the game amused them, with the usual allegations of cheating by Amy whenever she found herself blocked and her disgust when Grace started a game with a double six and made her pass her move.

'That would never be allowed in Ireland,' she complained, storming off to check on the cooking.

When she came back, she said the meal would be ready in half and hour only to receive the unanimous response that: 'That would never be allowed in Ireland.'

Grace knew the chicken needed a further hour or more, so she suggested they abandoned the game and each of them could sing a song from their area.

'There's no Londoners here, so we won't have to sing Roll Out The Barrel,' she laughed.

Billy made sure everyone had a full glass and said, 'In honour of Amy and Brigid, here's a toast to Ireland,' and showing off he raised his glass and said, 'Slainte mhath,' and they all replied.

'Slainte mhath,' said Amy. 'And here's a song from the fair town of Cork.'

Amy sang the song with a beautiful soprano but it stilled the mood of the party, particularly as no one could pick the line 'of my own lovely Lee.' Everyone clapped loudly though but they asked for a song with a chorus.

'Billy, you must know that Geordie hymn,' said John. Billy said he did but he was not a Geordie, thank you very much.

Soon they had learnt the chorus. 'Oh me lads ye shud ha' seen us gannin' and Helmut managed to join in with "gannin" along the Scotswood Road, to see the Blaydon Races.' After two verses, Amy had them all stood up and linking arms in a line so that when the final chorus ended there was a hug in a circle.

'My,' said Helmut pretending to be exhausted, 'not like a German Christmas,' and asked for a quieter song. Grace volunteered a sea shanty from Norfolk and they all settled down as she taught them the chorus. 'In this windy old weather, stormy old weather, when the wind blows, we all pull together.' Grace explained that the song was about a ship off a beautiful place spelt Happisburgh and its lighthouse but this was pronounced Haizeborough.

'Why,' asked Amy but Grace just said, 'It's how we speak in Norfolk.'

When the song had finished, Helmut asked what a conger was and this provoked an argument over how long such an eel can be. John declared the argument silly and said he had a story to tell them but first they must fill their glasses.

'It's a very sad song,' warned John. 'With a powerful lesson.' He taught them the chorus 'On Ilkla Moor Baht'at' which Helmut declared impossible and took to drumming the chorus with a spoon. Everyone joined in with gusto and Brigid enjoyed it so much she insisted on singing all the verses again.

'Then we shall have to bury thee,' she said at the end. 'How sad.'

'I think you mean hen us'll ha to bury thee,' John said. 'My ma always felt sorry for Mary Jane,' he added.

'I know why,' said Brigid. 'I expect Ilkley Moor is very beautiful.'

John said he did not know as he had never been. 'We weren't a family for going on trips, though I had an aunty in Mytholmroyd, I used to go and stay with. Funny place, big smoky factories and everyone wore clogs.'

Amy said it was Brigid's turn to sing but John said that was ruled out, for last time she sang he got punched in the face by a huge Irishman. John continued the story adding that if the dinner was not served soon the Special Branch would be round and the prison kitchens would be closed on Christmas Day so they would all starve. Brigid added, 'That would be allowed in Ireland.' Amy said would they mind singing just one carol, for she had liked them ever since she was a child and that morning in church, they had sung In the Deep Midwinter which was her favourite. Helmut said he was not religious but every German child had to learn a beautiful song and he would teach them it if they liked, after all he had learnt Geordie and Yorkshire and whatever Grace was singing. They laughed and agreed.

As soon as Helmut began in a slightly wobbly tenor 'Stille nacht, heilige nacht,' Amy said, 'Also my favourite' and hummed along. Helmut agreed to write down the lyrics and they all gathered round.

'Durch der Engel,' said Billy. 'Good to hear old Friedrich gets a mention.' After they had sung Helmut said, 'That would not have sounded out of place in the Lutheran church in Oldenburg.'

'Now I'm hungry,' he said, the meal was delicious and Grace and Amy looked pleased when they were toasted by all. By the time the pudding had been eaten and the last of the sherry drained, they were all pleasantly tipsy, except Amy who had collapsed on the settee and was snoring loudly. John and Grace offered to help her home and Grace had to help her on with her coat and hat. Helmut was also putting on his coat when Grace asked where he was staying the night. Helmut said not to worry he had walked across Holland and would soon find somewhere warm. Grace took Brigid through to the kitchen and whispered, 'Could he sleep on the settee? Perhaps if Billy slept in the armchair, just in case.'

Brigid hesitated, not wanting to complicate matters with Billy, but also aware that she could not spend the night alone in a house with a man. It was all agreed and Helmut thanked them again saying that tomorrow he had some contacts in the East End he could look up. After John, Grace and Amy left, Billy started to run the sink to wash the dishes. Brigid protested that it could wait until the morning but Billy insisted that they do it now.

'My dad always used to say if the meal is great, wash your plate.'

Brigid gave him a stare and Billy conceded he had just made that up but it was true he had always helped his dad wash up straight after dinner, 'It's a man's job up north,' he said. Brigid could not say if her dad has ever washed up but she had certainly never seen Conan or any of her uncles do so. She announced that there was enough milk in the larder to make some cocoa before bed and to leave some for a cup of tea in the morning.

After everything was clean and stored away according to Brigid's instructions, she brought three cups of cocoa into the front room and settled in an armchair, remarking that it was a comfortable chair and they must not let her fall asleep in it. She asked Helmut how he spoke such good English and he explained that he had been good at languages at school and English was his favourite, eventually he held a post lecturing in English literature in Munich.

'I love Shakespeare and I was allowed to teach my course without much interruption by the authorities. I lectured on Measure for Measure every year, 'We must not make a scarecrow of the law, setting it up to fear the birds of prey'.'

Helmut realised Brigid and Billy may not have studied Shakespeare.

'Anyway,' he said, 'The Nazis grew in strength and the Brownshirts attacked the university. Courses were closed including any humanities not taught in German or not about Germany. I had to leave Munich in a hurry.'

Brigid wanted to ask more about how Helmut had escaped but Billy said he could not understand how the Nazis had come to power in Germany for he had read how the Communist Party there was the biggest outside Russia. Helmut explained that the Nazis won six million votes in 1930 because of the economic crisis and the panic of the wildgewordene Kleinburgeriurger, the small bourgeoisie who feared economic ruin and communism in equal measure. The Communist Party stuck with Stalin's Third Period idiocy that the social democrats were counter-revolutionary and no alliance with them was possible. The Nazis took advantage on the streets and eventually they arrested Thaellman, the Communist leader, and thousands of others.

'I met Ernest Thaellman once after a meeting in 1927, he wanted to discuss Shakespeare of all things, and this was before I became a Trotskyist. He was quite knowledgeable about literature but then he told me of the time the anti-Communists, Organisation Consul, they were called, threw a bomb into his flat five years earlier. Luckily his wife and daughter were not injured and he himself was out at the time, but he did not learn the lessons from their killing spree when the Nazis became stronger and the whole working-class has paid a huge price.'

Helmut was silent, as if remembering too much. Brigid wondered if it might be time to say goodnight but she decided to tell Helmut about the fighting against Mosley she had witnessed and how the Blackshirts were defeated.

Helmut did not respond so she stood up and touched his arm when Billy said, 'But it doesn't make sense what you're saying, why would a Communist Party refuse to fight Hitler if they knew their leaders and members would be murdered or imprisoned.' This seemed to stir Helmut who told them of Trotsky's analogy of the bulls driven to a cattle market.

'When the butcher arrived later one of the bulls suggested combining to jack up the butcher on their horns. Some of the other bulls, educated by the Comintern, replied that the butcher was no more an enemy than the cattle dealer who drove them there. The bulls suggested they could deal with the latter afterwards. The Comintern bulls declined replying that they would not fall for a trick, by bulls of the left, to protect their enemies. You bulls are social butchers yourselves, they declared, and refused to close ranks against the butcher.'

'I'm sorry to be so melancholy,' Helmut said. 'You're the first people I've spoken to about it in months. Now I think it is time for some sleep, thank you both for a wonderful Christmas, I will never forget your kindness to a stranger.'

Brigid went upstairs and found some old army blankets in a cupboard and brought them down to the men.

'First one of you two awake, lights the fire,' she laughed, 'Goodnight.'

Billy did not sleep well, the armrests of the chair poked into his back, the temperature fell so he could see his breath and the blankets were not enough. At about three, he thought about lighting the fire but did not want to get Brigid into trouble with her landlady, he knew this was a convenient and comfortable lodging and, even better, he knew there had been no police callers to the house. He wondered about what Helmut had said and decided to ask Tom Stone about it.

Eventually at six, he got up and raked the ashes and, seeing that Helmut was still asleep, quietly removed the ashes tray and prepared and lit the fire. When the fire started to blaze, he put on some coal from the bunker and the fire calmed, Billy knew this was the worst part of fire lighting in a cold room when the initial heat died down only to gradually seep back. He shivered for a while until the first flames licked through the coal and then stood with his back to the fire allowing it to warm his legs. Helmut woke with a "Guten Morgen" and said he would put the kettle on. Billy followed him into the kitchen and found the milk in the pantry.

'Did you ever meet Trotsky?' he asked.

Helmut said he had not but he had heard Lev Lvovich, Trotsky's son, address a crowd in Berlin the day Hitler became Chancellor. Helmut said he knew there were Trotskyists in London and he intended to try to find them today. Billy said that if he did, he and Grace would like to meet them. Helmut promised he would be back soon to see them. They poured the tea and Helmut called Brigid. They sat in front of the fire awhile and then Billy said he ought to get back to his digs for Mrs C would be sure to know he had not returned and she was a worrier he thought. Helmut too said he had to travel across London and needed to get started or he would be back begging for a bed again.

They assured him he would be welcome and Billy and he left together. Billy asked him if he needed a loan but Helmut replied some docker comrades in Antwerp had given him some English money and so international solidarity was still alive. They parted at the side of the factory, Helmut striding away along the road, avoiding the brown slush on the pavements, apparently intent on walking across London.

Chapter 6
Bombs and Raids (1939)

Brigid had left work a little early to buy some cough medicine for Mrs O'Leary along the Broadway. She had told Grace where she was going but had not informed either Mr Eastwood or Mr Willans as Grace had advised her not to bother…'or it'll give them the impression they are in charge,' and, in any case, Brigid had kept her dealings with management to an absolute minimum since her meeting with Conan, not wanting to draw further attention to herself.

In truth Willans rarely walked the factory floor preferring to delegate this to Eastwood. Unfortunately, Eastwood simply did not seem to have sufficient presence to convey any authority, he would appear in the corner of the workrooms and ask if all was well and seemed content with a grunt at best in reply. It seemed management had somehow lost control and many workers preferred to ask Tom Stone about work matters and problems.

Consequently, in order to complete reports to the board, Willans would need to ask Tom in for a morning tea to discuss progress on various targets. Neither of them mentioned the odd situation, for it suited Tom to have contact with all the workers and, in any case, he was a realist who, shared the same view as Willans that war was coming and production must be kept up. Once he had found Willans with his head buried in The Times.

'Living space, Lebensraum, it all means the same thing Tom, invasion and conquest by the Nazis.'

Tom had replied that a pact with the Soviet Union was essential to show Hitler he would be resisted. Much to his surprise Willans replied that he was probably right but Chamberlain was living in cloud cuckoo land, 'Only one thing Hitler will understand, force.'

Brigid meanwhile was enjoying the unexpected February sunshine and leant against the clock at the top of Anson Road allowing the afternoon sun to warm her face. Her thoughts turned back to Whiddy, wondering how her family were and then the unexpected heat on her face triggered a memory of that hot summer when she was seventeen and working the fields and all the talk was of McGowan's prize pig and how it nearly died of sunburn after he went to market early and left it in the wrong field all day. A smile involuntarily formed on her lips and soon she shook her head as if to clear the smile away lest any passer-by took her for an eejit.

Brigid remained in a good humour, why not though she thought, for it was Saturday and Amy was taking her to a ceilidh in Kentish Town tonight and tomorrow she could have a lie-in before church and maybe a walk in the fresh air later if the weather stayed warm. She stopped to look in the window of Grodzinski's and, on a whim, went inside. The cakes looked delicious but she limited herself to a small challah loaf and decided to see if Mrs O'Leary could be tempted to share it over a cup of tea. She strolled back along the Broadway, noticed that the morning shift would be over and saw most of the shift gathered outside the factory gates. She spotted Nana across the road and hurried across to speak to her.

'It's not another strike, is it?' she asked.

'No,' replied Nana. 'It's just folks minding others business. Nothing like police cars to attract a crowd, have a good weekend, Brigid.'

Brigid could tell Nana was in a hurry and so walked on a few more yards until she could see that a dozen policemen were blocking the entrance to the railway cottages and behind them were police cars, a Black Maria and, stood between the car and the van, she could see the bald head of a man in plain clothes and immediately recognised him. Brigid turned around and pulled up her coat walking as quickly as she dare without drawing attention to herself. As she walked, she wondered what to do next.

Conan had not arranged a contact for her as he had promised but she reasoned that she must be the target for this police raid. Unless she fled, she would be arrested and even if she could put that off for a few days she would have more time to think up some realistic false information to reluctantly give the police. She turned right into the residential streets and walked up and down long parallel roads until she decided she would call on Mary and the children and see what Tom knew.

She had been walking for half an hour and it was still warm, then she remembered the bread in her shopping bag and reached in and tore off a chunk tasting it first then chewing the sweet tasting bread and realising she had never had bread quite like it. Turning into Chichele Road, she approached Tom and Mary's carefully looking round again to see if she was being followed and reasoning that Tom would have had plenty of time to get home by now.

It was Mary and Patrick who opened the door and Patrick immediately wanted to know what was in her bag. Brigid said if he had been good at school, she would give him a slice of special bread. Patrick ran back into the flat and produced a drawing of a cat with the words Very Good Patrick and a silver star stuck next to the comment.

Mary laughed, 'He got this today and he's been dying to tell someone, even wanted to go to show his aunty in Kilburn. He gets a few of these for drawing but I'm waiting for one on arithmetic,' she laughed. Patrick had gone to tell his sister and Emily came bursting in straight into Brigid's arms.

'My, you weigh more every time I see you, young lady,' Brigid laughed. 'Are you sure you have any room for aunty Brigid's special bread.'

Mary gave her a quizzical look. 'Challah, from Grodzinskis,' Brigid said and Mary mouthed the word posh and said she had always wanted to go in there and she and Emily admired the cakes in the window, wondering which would taste best. They sat down at the table and Mary buttered some slices. The children tentatively nibbled theirs but Emily declared, 'I don't like it.'

'I do,' say Patrick. 'Can I have yours?' Mary went and buttered some bread for her daughter.

'There you are, soda bread, your favourite,' and Emily reluctantly handed her challah to Patrick.

'Peace in our time,' said Mary, then added, 'Sorry not something to joke about.'

Brigid explained that she was not just on a social call as there had been some sort of incident at the end of the morning shift and was Tom in. Mary said Tom had rushed in, kissed the kids and rushed off to a gate meeting at Whitton and James factory in Hendon where electricians had walked out over non-payment of travel allowances.

'He did say that there was a police raid though and some IRA man was led away, there were some bombs in tube stations that morning and people were injured at Leicester Square, I think he said.'

Brigid did not know what to think but decided she was safest staying put and she asked if it was alright to help put the children to bed. Mary was delighted and told the children aunty Brigid was going to read the bedtime stories after their supper.

It was half past eight when Brigid left and she assured Mary it was only a short walk home, without telling her exactly where she lived. She wondered if Tom knew anyway and might link the raid with her. She was grateful for the dark and avoided the lamps of the Broadway, walking alongside the factory until she was opposite the terraces. There was no sign of any police presence across the road but she decided to cross further up the street to avoid being too visible. As she approached her lodgings she kept looking round and, seeing no one, she let herself in.

At first, she thought no one was in, for Mr and Mrs O'Leary would often be sitting in the armchairs by lamplight, she knitting for her grandchildren in Liverpool and listening to some classical music on the radio and he studying the racing form before he left for his night shift guarding the goods yard at Acton depot. Brigid walked over to the fire and using the poker she put some old newspaper on the embers sparking a new light.

'Oh, Brigid, thank goodness you're here, I thought they were blaming you too and I could never have forgiven myself. Never, never …oh my poor Diarmuid, where have they taken him, he wouldn't harm a fly.'

Mrs O'Leary was curled up in the large armchair Billy had slept on at Christmas. Even with only the light of the fire, Brigid could see she had been crying and now, normally such a bustling energetic woman, she seemed helpless, coiled up like one of the tiny half-finished jumpers she carefully wrapped round her needles each evening. Brigid told her to stay there and she would make some tea and then they would make a plan.

Brigid walked through to the kitchen and, trying to reach the paraffin lamp, her leg caught up in some netting and, reaching down, she realised the drying rail had fallen from the ceiling and she felt the still damp shirts that belonged to Mr O'Leary. Carefully stepping over the clothes as best she could in the dark, she reached and lit the lamp and was amazed at the sight before her. The tin bath was piled on top of the chairs as if a bonfire was being prepared and every cupboard was open, the pantry door had been smashed and pans were scattered on the floor with sugar, salt and other cooking substances sprawled across the shelves.

Quietly so as not to disturb Mrs O'Leary, Brigid picked up the tin bath and set it again on its nail on the wall and she was just about to pick up the chairs when she heard a scream from the front room. Rushing through she saw Mrs O'Leary sat upright and pointing at the door.

'It's a knock,' she said apparently terrified that the police had come back. Brigid could see no alternative but to open the door for it was not possible to see the space outside the front door from any window. Brigid reasoned that if the police had come back to arrest her, she would refuse to talk until she had a suitable tale to mislead them and, in any case, it might be Mr O'Leary being returned. Brigid opened the door a little and was surprised to see the priest from St Anne's and alongside him Amy.

'Excuse me,' said the priest. 'Are Mr and Mrs O'Leary at home.'

Brigid invited him in and explained that Mr O'Leary had been taken by the police and he went over to Mrs O'Leary and said, 'I'm sorry for your pain, Roisin, it must be a mistake for we know Diarmuid is a God-fearing man.'

Brigid left them talking and took Amy through to the kitchen. 'Did you come together?' asked Brigid and Amy explained that she had met Father Dunphy heading this way and he had told her he was exhausted from running about all over Cricklewood comforting families whose men had been arrested that day.

'He did say that Mr O'Leary was the least likely to be involved in the evil bombings but you could never be absolutely sure about anyone.' Amy surveyed the damage as she spoke and commented that the police must have believed bomb-making equipment was in the house.

'Blimey Brigid, you certainly know how to draw trouble.' Brigid resented this comment but she did not respond simply saying it would be a blessing to Mrs O'Leary if they tidied the kitchen up a little. As they did so, Brigid wondered what Amy had meant and asked her what she had heard.

'Oh nothing, I'm sorry for saying that, it's just that I remembered at Christmas John said you started a fight simply by singing.'

Brigid responded by saying that John sometimes liked to exaggerate and she preferred a quiet life. As they swept up the salt and tried to rescue the sugar, Brigid mentioned that she would be grateful if Amy did not mention the Christmas Day in the house as Mrs O'Leary thought that only a couple of girlfriends had come round for a quiet meal.

'They don't drink or anything,' said Brigid. 'And I don't know what they would say if they knew a German had been in their house.' Amy promised and said she would prefer a quiet life but sometimes words just came out of her mouth and caused trouble. Brigid looked down at her sweeping the salt into the dustpan, 'And sometimes that's good, look what you did to Willans.'

'Who?' Amy responded and they both laughed. Brigid asked Amy if her family had been affected by any of the violence in Ireland and Amy simply said her father had taken up with General O'Duffy and he had been badly beaten up in Cork when she was eighteen.

'He never recovered really and died the next year,' Amy went on. 'I was the eldest of six and my oldest sister was only eleven. We had nothing and no one in Tralee would help us because they knew my dad was a Blueshirt so I heard there were jobs here and it seemed best to come and send money home. I miss Tralee though and my ma and the little ones, I want nothing to do with politics though, it only leads to suffering.'

Brigid explained that she really could not leave Mrs O'Leary that evening and did Amy mind. Amy said she would stay and help for if she went to the ceilidh alone, she would be sure to meet a boy and then her boyfriend would get jealous.

'Which one?' laughed Brigid and Amy put her hands over her face.

'Oh Brigid, how could you say such a thing.' They both laughed but were then interrupted by the priest coughing at the door.

'I've several more visits to make so I'll say goodnight, please try to be good quiet company for your landlady Brigid.'

'Yes father,' they replied together and Brigid took him to the door. Brigid explained to Mrs O'Leary that Amy was a friend who had come for Christmas Day and would it be alright if she stayed for a while. It seemed the conversation with the priest had revived Mrs O'Leary and she stood up and shook Amy's hand saying that any friend of Brigid's was always welcome and before they could stop her, she walked to the kitchen saying she would make them all a nice cup of tea and, on seeing the damage, burst into tears saying, 'Why have they done this to us?'

Brigid helped her back to the chair and sat holding her hand between her own whilst Amy said she would finish making the tea. Gradually Mrs O'Leary stopped crying and blowing her nose on a handkerchief and tucking it back in the sleeve of her cardigan she said she must be strong for Diarmuid needed her to be. It seemed that the police had forced their way in as they had returned from shopping and handcuffed Diarmuid and pushed him straight into a police van. One of them, in plain clothes, had asked her had she been in Birmingham recently and when she said she had he had shouted through the house 'another of the Birmingham gang, search everywhere,' and then she heard the sound of drawers opening and things being thrown on the floors.

'I tried to explain that our daughter lives in Digbeth and we just go to see our granddaughters there, but he just said don't worry they were searching there too and to shut up unless I wanted to be arrested too. Now I'm worried my son-in-law might be arrested just because we visited, he's a good man Sean is, even if he is a Kerry man as Diarmuid likes to joke.'

Brigid listened quietly and when Amy brought the tray in with a teapot and three cups, she told her that they were talking about Kerry and so she told Mrs O'Leary about Tralee. Mrs O'Leary looked at Amy and said she was a good-looking lass and asked had she ever been the Rose.

'Oh no,' laughed Amy. 'There are much better lookers than me, Mrs O'Leary.'

Mrs O'Leary responded that they must call her Roisin and thanked them again for staying with her. She asked Brigid if she could get the biscuit tin down but Brigid had to tell her it had been opened and all the biscuits eaten or smashed and Roisin commented that she thought some of the policemen looked hungry. Brigid went upstairs to inspect the damage and she put back drawers that had been thrown on the floor and managed to replace the mattress on the double bed in the larger bedroom. When she went back down, she heard Amy promising to ask around at church next day to see what had happened and how to find out safely where Diarmuid was.

They talked some more and Roisin took out pictures of the grandchildren and then said she hoped Diarmuid would be home next weekend when they were visiting. Brigid said the police were probably just on a fishing trip perhaps because they had some link from the bombings with Birmingham and they knew Diarmuid had visited. Brigid did not say that the police may have picked this information from a friend who knew but simply said she thought Diarmuid would soon be home. As Roisin seemed much calmer now, Amy said she would go home and leave them in peace but would call round tomorrow after church.

As Brigid stepped out to say goodnight, Amy asked her if she would mind not mentioning Tralee again, for she did not want anyone to link her to her father as what happened to her father was well known and some of the attackers were IRA men she had heard. Brigid promised she would never mention it to anyone, but she did not add that she knew about the attacks on the Blueshirts for Conan had once had come back in a good mood, possibly worse for wear, from Cork saying O'Duffy's boys had been chased around the town and knew not to come back. Brigid made a resolution to be very careful though what she said around Amy for she knew well that those who complained that they were not interested in politics often turned out to be informers or worse.

Chapter 7
The Obvious Irishman

Billy and John were playing a game of whist with some lodgers from next door when Mrs C knocked on the door of John's room and asked to speak to Billy.

'It's your sweetheart again, Billy,' John whispered causing Billy to throw a cushion at him and the younger Irish boys playing with them to shriek with laughter and suggest it was time for them to leave, one of them winking excessively as he stood up. Billy waved his knuckles at them as he stood up and went outside.

'I'm sorry Mrs C,' he said, 'If we were making too much noise.'

Mrs C said she liked to hear men enjoying themselves, it reminded her of the café in the square at home, but there were two visitors to see Billy and John and she could not let them into the house. Billy asked her to wait and he went back and asked John to come with him, telling the boys the game was over and Mrs C would let them out the back just in case. They went downstairs and Billy asked if the men were in uniform.

'No,' replied Mrs C. 'But one of them is definitely a German, said his name was Helmut. Those Germans are evil people.'

Billy decided to say nothing more, he had assumed the police had called so he simply told his landlady that they would not cross her doorstep. They opened the door and saw Helmut accompanied by a taller man of about the same age as Helmut but with a shock of thick black hair which matched the dark overcoat he was engulfed in.

'Comrades of the heroic trade union struggle, I greet you again from Germany,' said Helmut. John stepped forward and offered his hand but Helmut embraced him reaching across to shake Billy's hand.

'It is great to see you both again, I have been briefing Hamish here on the struggle in your factory.'

'Well done comrades,' said the older man. 'I understand the Stalinist manager tried to break your strike.'

Billy explained that this was not the case and in fact Tom had stood on the picket lines and resigned as a foreman.

'Though I am interested in understanding more about why Tom and the Communist Party support the executions of Bolsheviks.'

Hamish realised that the two younger men had little knowledge of world events but like many young workers he met they seemed keen to learn more. He spelt out his view to see their reaction.

'It is the leading British Cper, J R Campbell who called us Trotskyists, the Friends of Hitler who the labour movement must vomit out. This because we will not support British imperialism in its war aims and do not recognise the so-called democracy of the ruling class. We stand for the interests of the working-class against the bourgeoisie in every country. We defend the Soviet Union but we do not refuse to fight the class enemy at home. It was Stalin and his agents like Campbell and Harry Pollitt here and the rest of them who refused to unite the German workers against Hitler, now they try to do the same here.'

Billy had never heard such a view and he did not immediately respond. John though said, 'Of course we must fight the bosses, if there is a war we must look after ourselves and not allow the bosses to trick us.'

Billy nodded surprised again at how John's views had developed, and for he knew John was not one to simply agree with the last person he heard speak. They decided to find a café to continue the conversation for Hamish said that too many good Communists he knew in Glasgow had spent too much time drinking and arguing and not enough time intervening in the labour movement. Billy said he had seen the great temperance campaigns which had swept through Darlington and he agreed drunkenness was a curse.

'Comrade,' replied Hamish. 'I do not oppose drink on those terms at all. The crusaders for abstention, the Methodists and all the other Lutherans, want workers to abstain so that they will work harder for the capitalist bosses and demand less wages, instead looking to God for their reward after their death.'

Billy thought back to his years in Sunday school and wondered how much he had understood of what he was being taught and why.

'Come, young comrade,' Hamish continued. 'I will explain to you why the poor man is not at the rich man's gate because it was ordered by a God.'

It being Sunday night and late there were no cafes left open in Cricklewood but John said they would be welcome at the Railway Club where two shop stewards from the garage were on the committee and had joined the factory picket. They walked round to the club and John saw Ted Johnstone, one of the stewards, playing snooker. He came round and offered to buy them all a drink but when John explained they only needed a quiet corner to discuss politics, Ted opened the office and said they were welcome to stay as long as they liked, explaining he was on a winning streak but as soon as he lost, he would come and join them. After he had left Hamish asked if Ted could be trusted and Billy replied that he was a very good union organiser but he had never heard him express a political view.

'Let's hope he pots the black by mistake next shot,' smiled Hamish. 'He sounds worth talking to.'

The discussion covered such a wide range of topics including the defeat in Spain where Hamish said the support of the Comintern for the bourgeois democrats had limited the efforts for a General Strike in France and a successful socialist revolution in Spain.

'Stalin sees every conflict as a means to strengthen the Soviet Union so long as his partnership with Chamberlain and Co is not disturbed. This means every worker seeking revolutionary change is an enemy and Stalin will use murder at home and in Spain to ensure no one challenges his line.'

Billy asked again about Trotsky and Hamish replied that comrades in the United States had to guard Trotsky in Mexico because the GPU, Stalin's secret police, had orders to assassinate him. Hamish described briefly the founding of the Fourth International in Paris the year before which, he said, was necessary because the Comintern had become an agent of counter-revolution.

'So, all the followers of Trotsky in the world are united,' said John. 'We'd better join up, Billy.'

Hamish explained that whilst he supported the Fourth International his group had not yet been recognised as an affiliate. This was because his group, the Workers International League, had not agreed to merge with other groups in Britain.

They could hear the club closing and some loud dispute outside seemed to promise a fight, Ted Johnstone came in and apologised explaining that he had won every game and the rule of the club was that you stayed on the table until you were beaten. It was clear to Billy from the look on their faces that they did not believe this but Helmut simply said they would call again and let Ted know in advance.

*****

Amy was one of the first into St Agnes church the next day and talked to anyone she knew about the bombings. She learnt from her next-door neighbour that the bombings at the underground stations were on Friday and that dozens of suspects had been arrested over the weekend. The priest, an older man than Father Dunphy, gave a sermon in which he urged anyone who knew anything about the "terrible bombings", which he said were against God's word, inform the police immediately.

Afterwards Amy went round to see Brigid but there was no news, Mr O'Leary, had not been seen and it seemed Mrs O'Leary could find no one who knew where he was but that the police had told her she would be notified in due course.

The following day Tom was called in for tea as usual by Mr Willans. Willans began by asking Tom if he thought any of the workers were involved in the bombings. Tom was very surprised and asked why Willans thought this possible. Willans asked Eastwood to share the Daily Mail with Tom pointing to the story under a headline 'Revolvers Issued to 100 CID men.' The story told of large amounts of explosives stolen from factories and searches of IRA sympathiser's homes.

'There was an arrest of an IRA man across the street on Saturday,' said Eastwood. 'I wouldn't be a bit surprised if that troublemaker Foley who caused the strike was involved, or that other agitator O'Brien. They both come from Ireland don't they?'

Tom was taken aback that Eastwood regarded Amy or Brigid as possible suspects and said so. Most of the Irish people he knew, and there was a huge number in this part of London, were good trade unionists and would not take part in violence. He promised to keep his ears to the ground but he had heard nothing suspicious and the stocks were checked every morning and evening and nothing had ever been stolen, not so much as an alarm clock.

'Funny you should mention that,' said Eastwood. 'For this report says the police are investigating a clock which exploded at Tottenham Court Road.'

Tom kept this conversation with management to himself but he did think back to Brigid's comments that Ireland could be free. He agreed that Ireland should be a free nation but they had discussed it in the branch last year and they did not support attacks in Britain in which workers could be killed. He would just listen to see if anyone knew anything but he would need Party advice as to what to do if he discovered any involvement.

The next day Eastwood and Willans asked to see him again which was odd because they had set the weekly targets already and nothing had happened to interrupt the work yesterday. This time Eastwood was more forthright indeed Tom had never heard him speak so much.

'Mr Stone,' he began. 'Yesterday the trial of the twelve IRA men at Bow Street heard that Special Branch have got hold of the S Plan, the secret IRA plan to attack us. It seems the IRA want all British troops to withdraw from Northern Ireland or they will wage economic warfare against us.'

Tom wondered why he had been called in to hear this.

'They are cunning Mr Stone,' said Eastwood raising that day's copy of the Daily Mail and reading:

'Mr McClure, prosecuting, said that the S Plan advised operatives to avoid looking like the Obvious Irishman.'

'And what does that look like, Mr Eastwood?' asked Tom.

Eastwood refocused on the paper and announced, 'Cap Worn Rakishly, Green Scarf, Hands in Pockets and wearing a Trench Coat.'

Tom glanced at Willans but he seemed to be taking this seriously.

'So,' he replied, 'I should keep a look out for anyone wearing their hat straight, with a blue scarf, and their hands by the side of their jacket.'

'Exactly,' said Eastwood. 'And good luck.'

*****

The whole factory had been talking about the explosion at the canal. Brigid had listened carefully to Mairaid who lived in Harlesden and whose brother had been cycling to work along the canal when the bomb detonated.

'Our Pat was dead lucky,' Mairaid explained. 'another hundred yards and he'd a been blown up.'

It seemed that the target had been an electricity pylon but no one was quite sure although Mairaid had heard that the IRA had intended to blow up the road bridge over the Grand Union. Amy was shocked too and said she could not understand why Harlesden was attacked when so many Irish people lived there.

Tiny heard that and soon there was several men speaking loudly and above them Tiny shouting, 'Any IRA bastard should be strung up.'

It threatened to get out of hand until Amy shouted herself stating that she hated all violence and did not want anyone to be injured, English or Irish. This settled the commotion although Tiny had the last word saying that any he expected anyone who knew or suspected anyone to report it to the police straightaway.

Brigid felt she had no one she could trust to talk to about the situation. Conan had not arranged a further contact and even the police had apparently forgotten about her, even though she was living as a lodger with Diarmuid O'Leary who had been released after three days and warned he would be deported to Ireland if his name came up again. He had not spoken about his arrest but Roisin told Brigid that he had been questioned about his relatives in Liverpool and Birmingham but he had refused to give any details beyond what the police already knew.

The police had threatened to get him sacked from the depot in case he allowed bombers access to the railway terminal but, when he turned up for work, he was only given a warning for failing to report he was ill. Roisin told Brigid that some of the family in Liverpool had strong views but, even though she and Diarmuid opposed all violence and just wanted a quiet life, they were not going to allow family members to be put under suspicion.

Later in the shift Grace asked Billy round for tea as she wanted to find out what Helmut and Hamish had said. Grace explained that John had told her some of it but his listening skills were sometimes affected by excitement. Billy said nothing in reply but when he heard that Grace had persuaded Brigid to come as well, he was delighted. The four of them walked down Larch Road, Grace explained she had a room in a house of "young ladies," as her landlady liked to call them.

Grace said that John had never dared to come in but she had explained they were having a young people's prayer meeting this evening and the landlady, one of the wardens at the Baptist church, had offered them use of the front room. Grace said to lock their hands together if she came in. They turned into Ivy Road where Grace lodged, a man walked past them and a few yards on, called back.

'It's Brigid O'Brien, isn't it?' Brigid was alarmed but tried not to show it.

'I'm sorry, I don't think I know you.'

The man smiled and said, 'Well, you were probably ten when we last met. You must remember my uncle's wedding, we played in the woods for hours afterwards.'

'It's Martin, is it?' asked Brigid. 'You were the one my dad carried on his shoulders whilst he was dancing?'

'Well, I was probably eight at the time, my uncle's wedding, wasn't it? We had a fine time of it, playing in the Atlantic Pond for hours.'

Brigid stepped forward and gave him a hug and he explained he had just arrived that afternoon although Billy noticed he did not say from where. Brigid introduced him as a relative but she could not explain exactly what relation he was. She excused herself from the prayer meeting and asked Billy to explain tomorrow what had been said.

'Prayers I imagine,' said Martin to which Grace replied that the best bit was the gossip between the prayers.

They waved farewell and hoped to meet Martin again. As Brigid and Martin walked away together Brigid suddenly realised what she had done and apologised for giving his name away. Martin said it probably did not matter as he would not be in England long but, in any case, they should not stay together in the street. He asked where they could meet later for a quiet drink away from prying eyes. Brigid thought and suggested the Carlton Tavern which was the other side of Kilburn.

'Perfect,' said Martin. 'I've some business round there afterwards.' They agreed to meet at seven but Brigid asked Martin to make sure he was early or 'every waster in the pub will be bothering me.' They parted and as she set off back to her lodgings Martin called, 'Conan sends his love.'

Brigid was excited to meet Martin and looked forward to hearing all the family news from Cork and she went home to change first and put on some lipstick so she would look "presentable" as her dad used to joke every time they left the farm for a family outing. Brigid thought of her father often and it was pleasing to anticipate spending time with someone who remembered him, for since meeting Conan last year she had no relatives in England. As she waited to spy the bus turning out of Cricklewood Garage, Brigid also reflected that Conan rarely spoke of their father but had never explained why.

The Carlton Tavern was a rebuilt pub that had been destroyed by German airships in the first war and it attracted a mix of clientele, on Sunday worshippers from St Augustine's and in the early evening those returning from work on the Bakerloo line to Queen's Park. Tonight though, as Brigid entered, there were only two men at the bar and as she looked beyond them, she saw Martin in a quiet and darker corner and she waved. He came across and asked her what she would like to drink. Brigid asked for whatever he was drinking and soon he was carrying a pint of stout back for her and, raising his own glass, toasted the family.

'Here's to my second cousin, Martin,' she said. 'The first time we've ever had a proper drink together.'

Martin smiled, 'Well apart from the time you spilled orange juice down my clean white shirt at that party.'

'I did not,' protested Brigid and Martin said he must be mistaken and it could have been a third cousin.

Brigid relaxed and explained that on the bus here she had worked out that they both had the same grandfather although he had died before the turn of the century. They toasted him, although neither could remember his name, and then they toasted their parents and all the Walsh and O'Brien family they could remember. Brigid toasted the horse last and Martin said he was still healthy as he had visited Whiddy last summer.

'I heard from your ma that you'd been leading a strike.'

Brigid explained what had happened, carefully keeping Amy's name out of it, for Ireland was a small place where everyone knew their history. 'So, Conan had been home then, is he still there?'

Martin drew a breath and hesitated and Brigid sensed bad news. 'He's not dead, is he?'

'No not dead, Brigid,' he replied. 'But captured.'

'Where?'

Martin explained that Conan had been unlucky to be caught in a random check at Holyhead.

'It seems some chemicals were found in the cargo on the ferry crossing and the police were alerted. Conan would have been on the right boat for sure and he would never accompany the materials himself anywhere, seems somehow the lorry had been held up and the chemicals loaded on the next boat by mistake. There's been an investigation but it just seems to be a stupid error. All the passengers were held and Conan was one of seven men held for further questioning. The next day the declaration of the government of the Republic was issued and then the bombing campaign started.'

'So, Conan's been in jail since mid-January?'

Martin explained Conan was being held in Walton Jail and had been there two months. 'They think he might be someone important to us but you know Conan he will not say a word and no one else will. He has been loyal.'

Brigid had dozens of questions but Martin simply said the army was looking after the family back on Whiddy.

'No one needs to know where he is, Brigid, no one. Understand? Your mam is used to not seeing him for months and she'll have read the news about the bombings or the priest will have condemned it in Bantry. The less she knows the better.'

Brigid asked if she could go to visit Conan but Martin said she would probably be arrested if she did.

'In any case, we want you to undergo training Brigid. Will you?'

There was no hesitation. 'I came to England to serve Ireland, I thought I'd been forgotten.'

Martin stood up to leave, he leant across to hug her and simply said, 'It's best if we leave separately. I'll be in touch.'

Chapter 8
A Not So Popular Front

'Chamberlain has recognised Franco; we are in league with the murderers of our Spanish comrades.'

No one answered John. It was if the fall of Madrid and the news of arrests and many fleeing which were filtering through had numbed them all. Billy leant against a large willow tree in the grounds of Dollis Hill House and gazed across to Wembley, just about seeing the shape of one of the towers through the low cloud. He wondered if Darlington would ever play there, probably not he thought, smiling. Neither will Grimsby Town this year he thought remembering having heard the lament of one of the engineers in the finishing room who was a school friend of a Tipperary man George Moulson. Moulson the Grimsby goalkeeper had been injured in the semi-final at Old Trafford and with only ten men they had lost to Wolves.

'Billy, did you hear John?'

He had to admit he had been thinking of football and apologise to John. Grace said John believed we are in league with Franco.

'We?' queried Billy. 'Those Tories don't speak for me, peace in our time, give me strength they'll be at war with Hitler this year and they'll expect us to fight for them.'

'And will you Billy?' asked John.

'Course I will, I'll be storming machine—gun posts day after day.'

John looked across at Billy and Billy raised his left leg up saying, 'After me miracle cure by the priest.'

John laughed back. 'I'd like to see that maybe Brigid could arrange it.'

'Is that where she rushes off to after work?' asked Grace. 'I didn't realise it was religion she doesn't say as much to me as she used to.'

John agreed that Brigid had gone a little quiet recently and Tom was asking him yesterday if he thought Brigid was involved in the bombings.

'Worried about his babysitter being arrested, was he?' said Grace. 'I don't think Brigid would ever get involved in blowing up innocent people.'

No one disagreed but neither Billy nor John said anything in reply. If he was honest, Billy knew he was not sure what Brigid was involved with but he felt he knew for certain she was a serious person prepared to commit to her beliefs.

John broke the silence saying it was a big question whether to fight in a war against German workers. Grace agreed and said no one should want to kill anyone but the fascists were ruthless and how were they to be stopped.

'Is that what your friend thinks?' asked Billy. Grace knew he had heard about her tea with Jennie Lee.

Grace said she was very surprised to receive such an invitation and it was very odd to have a waitress serving them. It seemed Jennie was quite used to eating out, especially since she married that young MP.

'She seemed to know everyone in that Lyons place in the Strand, she even knew the waitress was called Nellie.'

'I thought she was known for her independence,' said Billy. 'I'd heard she had a lot of affairs.'

Grace said the marriage was about two equals and Jennie had made her squeal with laughter when she described her cooking skills as non-existent and said she had no intention of improving. Grace said she did not know about others but Jennie had told her she had loved another older married man but he had suddenly dropped dead and she had not even been able to go to the funeral.

John and Billy did not know what to say, neither of them had ever discussed such a topic with a woman and they had never met any woman who was prepared to talk about it.

'I expect she's happy to be married now, I mean if she wants children,' said John.

'She doesn't,' Grace replied. 'And she knows how not to have any.'

Billy who always enjoyed Grace and John's company was uncomfortable discussing this, for John had told him he wanted to marry Grace and settle down by the sea somewhere after the war. He considered bidding them goodnight but instead he said, 'I hear her husband Nye Bevan was thrown out of the Labour Party.'

Grace said that was a disgrace for he had been speaking at the meetings calling for a Popular Front government and he and Stafford Cripps had been expelled without being allowed to give their reasons to the National Executive.

'What about Jennie? Is she still in the ILP?'

Grace said she was but that the ILP was declining and Jennie was still furious with Jimmy Maxton for congratulating Chamberlain over Munich.

'I had the impression Jennie and Nye were in favour of rearmament now but certainly Jennie wants to be an MP again and is hoping the ILP will be allowed to re-join Labour.'

Billy said he found it odd that Helmut and Hamish were in agreement with joining the Labour Party.

'If those who advocated joint work with the Communists and independents in a Popular Front are thrown out, why would the Labour Party allow those who want the working-class to seize power be allowed in?'

John agreed that this was a good question and probably the only way to answer it was to join and see what happens. Billy agreed and said he was thinking of joining the Workers International League too he was not sure if he agreed with everything they said but the Trotskyists seemed a good bunch more united and prepared to discuss issues in a friendly way.

John said that Hamish had told him that was not true, there were all sorts of stories of attempts to unify the British Trotskyists which failed because tactics had not been agreed. John said Hamish told him that some lies had been spread by one faction against one of the WIL leaders, Ralph Lee, it was alleged that he had stolen the strike fund of some South African workers.

'Apparently the story had been spread by the South African Communist Party and after letters from trade union leaders there arrived praising this Ralph Lee, some people were disciplined for spreading the story.'

'One thing's for sure,' said Grace. 'If you join the Trotskyists, you will no longer be Tom's blue-eyed boy!'

Billy said he was not but Tom was a good man in many ways especially since he gave up being foreman.

'He practically runs the factory even though he's not being paid, everyone says he is very fair and looks after everyone, probably why there's rumours of new managers being brought in,' said John.

'However,' said Billy. 'I cannot understand how he can support what Stalin has done in Spain, killing fellow socialists is beyond me and ever since the first day I read about it I cannot believe that the stories about great heroes of the revolution are true or that they should be shot.'

Grace agreed and said she found it sad that someone could be so wedded to the view of their organisation that they could adopt the strangest policies, 'How can Tom spend so much time calling for an alliance between Chamberlain and the USSR, when Chamberlain and the Tories hate the workers of this country and, as John said, were so quick to recognise Franco?'

Billy said he needed answers to these questions too and thought if he joined the WIL he might get them, even if he found it was not the organisation for him. John and Grace said they must all keep discussing like this and sharing their ideas and they all agreed.

'So, you might be off to Dublin then?' asked John.

Billy was unsure what John meant so he explained that Hamish had told him the leaders expected to be arrested in the event of war so several had gone to Dublin, he could not remember all the names but Gerry Healy and Jock Haston were two he mentioned.

'Apparently Jock is working with James Connolly's daughter, Nora, and they have recruited quite a few republicans,' Hamish said. Billy assured them he would not be going to Dublin he needed to keep sending money back home, his dad was out of work again.

'Phew that's a relief,' John said. 'I don't know who would be more upset if you left Tom Stone, Brigid or the love of your life, Mrs C.'

Just in time, John saw Billy coming and jumped off the bench and ran past the house and down the hill towards the synagogue. Billy soon gave up the hopeless chase shouting, 'Just you wait till I get you home, John Wood.'

Chapter 9
Don't Breathe a Word

Grace saw Billy leaving and caught him up at the end of the road.

'Where are you off to in such a rush, Billy?' Billy explained he was getting a lift from Willesden Green station from his WIL comrades.

'It's one of our street meetings down in Putney and we've been winning recruits there from the Hammersmith factories, I was down last week and there were over two hundred there crammed underneath the bridge. We've heard the Communist Party is sending a contingent tonight to try and disrupt the meeting, so we are going again to protect the speakers.'

Grace was tempted to ask to come, she knew she wanted and needed to be more politically active but she was not sure how to achieve this. Billy was always off somewhere to join or support a strike or attend a street meeting and Brigid too disappeared straight from work. Grace had not asked Brigid about this but Amy had been going to Hyde Park on the bus after church on Sunday and had spotted Brigid talking to a man in Maida Vale and then walking arm in arm with him. Amy of course immediately asked Brigid about this on Monday but Brigid said he was just a friend from County Offaly and they were only holding hands to avoid suspicion.

When Amy told this to Grace and John at the tea break it was clear she believed Brigid had a boyfriend but perhaps he was a married man from back home and Brigid did not want anyone to know and refused to tell Amy his name. Grace thought she knew better and told John later that Brigid had meant she did not want the police to suspect them. Irish men and women were being arrested and deported following the bombs at Kings Cross and Victoria stations and John also wondered if the police would remember Brigid soon. As Billy said goodnight, Grace resolved to ask if him tomorrow if she and John could come to the next meeting.

Brigid had been annoyed that Amy had spotted her with Peter Barnes. He was lodging at Warwick Avenue and said it would be safer to meet on the street away from the lodgings in case the police decided on a raid. Peter was ten years or so older than Brigid and he told her he had been in the army since he was a teenager but had volunteered for this campaign as he was fed up shovelling coal and staring at the bog marsh every night. This had made Brigid laugh and she had said she too had been fed up watching the sea passing her island and going somewhere interesting.

'I feel so alive in London,' she said. 'Somehow you seem like you're at the centre of the whole world.'

As she took his upper arm, she had felt his taut biceps which confirmed his job as a steam-raiser back home. Brigid knew Amy or Maureen would regard Peter as a handsome man worth getting to know but, even though she could see what they meant, she could not summon up any interest in him beyond their shared tasks. Instead, they briskly discussed the orders he had been given.

'It's urgent for tomorrow night,' Peter said. 'Can you manage it?'

Brigid asked what she had to do and Peter told her of a hardware shop in Edgware where he had bought electrical wire in big quantities and no questions had been asked. Peter said that most of the hardware shops had been visited by police and warned to report any Irishmen buying such items.

'We need flour bags urgently, Martin says, and it might be easier for you to get them.' Brigid agreed she would try and was already thinking of an alibi concerning her work in a bakery just in case.

'I'll meet you here at six tomorrow then,' Peter said, 'you can just hand them to me as you walk past.' Brigid agreed and was about to walk away when Peter leant over and kissed her cheek. She did not react and he said, 'Just in case the Brits are watching.'

'What is the equipment for?' she asked not wishing to acknowledge the wink if that was what it was.

'The British Empire is under attack from powerful enemies and we have our chance,' Peter responded. 'But I don't know where this bombing is aimed for, better not to know Brigid, just in case I'm caught.'

Next morning Brigid was up early as usual and on the bus north by eight o'clock. She had never been as far as Edgware but as she got off the bus at the garage there she saw the tube station and, just beyond, the hardware shop Peter had mentioned. She walked past to check it was open and went into the grocers next door to buy some apples and pears so she could place them in her shopping bag to cover her next purchase. This was her first active operation and, although she was quite calm, she desperately wanted to hand over the bags safely to Peter that evening without either of them being caught.

As she entered the hardware shop, a bell tinkled from above the door and a boy dressed in a smart brown overall rushed up from the back of the shop. Brigid looked at him from under her headscarf and saw his large quiff, brushed back and held in place as if he had his own Brylcreem vending machine under the counter or perhaps his mam was still smartening him up for his first job.

'Good morning missus,' he said, 'You're up bright and early, our first customer today. How can I help you? Does your husband need something?'

Brigid explained that she was doing a lot of baking that week to help out friends and she needed quite a few flour sacks. The boy looked puzzled and said he was sorry he would need to go and ask his gaffer adding needlessly that this was his first week in the shop. Brigid told him you would usually find them with the other empty sacks for sale and the boy brightened saying they were in the corner. She followed him and found a large stock and said she would take ten if that was alright. He counted them out and helped fold them tightly into the large shopping bag she had brought and she carefully placed the fruit on top. He gave her the change and as she was leaving an older man a few strands of white hair on his head emerged from behind a bead curtain which seemed to contain a desk.

'Have you served the lady, Edward?' he asked.

Brigid responded, without looking at the man, that she had all she needed and it was very good service and she would be back soon. As she glanced back at Edward, she could see the smile on his face.

Outside Brigid carefully took the receipt out of her purse and put it firmly inside one of the sacks. As she sat on the bus to Cricklewood, she smiled at how she had managed to look older by wearing Roisin's old gabardine and headscarf. At least it had worked with young Edward and she would have loved to hear his description of the lady he had served though she hoped Special Branch would not be asking him. Her mother's saying, 'There isn't a man alive who can't be puffed up and distracted by a little flattery,' suddenly came back to her.

Why her mam used this phrase occasionally was never clear for Conan was the only man in the house for ten years and he had no room for flattery or indeed much use for conversation in general. Peter had heard that Conan had been deported back to Dublin but whether he had been released or imprisoned by de

Valera he did not know. Brigid would like to know more but she had no contact details for Martin and, in any case, all republicans were under watch and only essential business could be conveyed. Still, Brigid reflected, playing tricks on the male ego and male assumptions could be useful on active service whether it was pretending to be a meek married woman or an object of desire. She smiled as she thought of herself being described as the Irish Mata Hari though that ended very badly.

As she thought again about men who seemed to like her such as Billy and others, she wondered again why she could not feel anything for them in that way. All through her teenage years she had listened to Maureen gush about this man or that from Errol Flynn to the ferry operator to Whiddy but she had never found any of them made her blood rush. She chuckled to herself that perhaps she would make her mam happy by becoming a nun or maybe an old spinster who lived in the family home cooking and cleaning to her last day. The shout of 'Cricklewood Garage' from the conductor below ended her contemplation and she waited to leave the bus last hoping no one would recognise her on the street.

It was a relief that Roisin had gone out and she knew Diarmuid would be asleep after his shift, she had rarely seen him since the arrest, even at weekends he seemed to spend more time at work and, if he was home, he seemed to sleep a lot either in bed or in the armchair next to the wireless set. Last week Roisin had said the experience seemed to have knocked the stuffing out of him a bit and he was still shocked that a law-abiding man could be arrested just for being Irish.

Still Brigid took the stairs gently, as if she was playing sardines back in the farmhouse with her cousins, and once in her room she stored the flour bags under her bed, reflecting that this very spot had been searched by the police only a month ago. She replaced Roisin's coat and scarf and put on her factory cap in her usual manner, leaving several strands of her hair uncovered as if they were making their own bid for freedom.

On entering the factory, she passed Mr Eastwood but he barely noticed her nor that she still had her coat on, she was pleased to spot Tom next and explained her landlady was ill and she had needed to go to the chemist for her and would need to leave a little earlier. Tom asked if in return she could baby sit for a couple of hours the next evening explaining that Mary and he wanted to hear Harry Pollitt who was coming to speak to the Willesden branch about his new pamphlet.

'You'll have to be strict with Emily though, she's being going to Irish dancing and would practice all night if we let her.'

Brigid laughed and told Tom she had loved dancing as a girl and would practice her sidesteps in bed after the lamp was put out.

'It's a wonder you didn't fall out of bed judging by the energy Emily uses up,' Tom said.

Brigid said she was looking forward to it and seeing what Patrick had been up to. As an added thought she asked if Tom would tell her what Mr Pollitt said at the meeting and Tom replied that he would adding that he had never heard him called mister by anyone. Harry, insisted Tom, was a son of the working-class and had no airs at all and everyone liked him as he could and would talk to anyone and he was the hardest working Communist he had ever met. Brigid said she would like to hear him speak one day and Tom said he would happily take her next time there was a rally.

It was raining as Brigid left the factory that afternoon and finding Roisin baking bread she asked if she could borrow her raincoat as she had to meet a friend. Roisin agreed and said she could borrow the blue headscarf that she sometimes wore to church. Brigid protested that this was too much but Roisin insisted that it would keep her beautiful hair dry and would suit her blue eyes. Brigid thanked her and was indeed grateful, for once again she could pass for middle-aged in this outfit and it was a different disguise to that worn that morning. As she boarded the number 16 bus Brigid could feel a shiver of anticipation, this time she decided against riding upstairs and found a seat next to the door just in case she needed to escape.

As they accelerated down Shoot-Up Hill, Brigid remembered her uncle Sean showing her a book of photographs of the Easter Rising when she was seven or so. One image had caught her imagination, Molly Childers, with a rifle and ammunition box next to her on the yacht running guns to the Volunteers from Hamburg. Brigid could visualise the photograph now although she had forgotten the name of the yacht and the other woman pictured. Brigid smiled to herself as she wondered if a picture of her gripping a shopping bag on a bus would ever inspire anyone. The rain had stopped as she got off the bus and to the left, somewhere over Regents Park she could see the faint remains of a rainbow and she suddenly remembered her dad saying that many colours in the rainbow were invisible but God made sure that the green of Ireland was seen right in the middle.

Yesterday Peter had suggested just passing in the street so as not to arouse suspicion and so she was relieved to see him striding along the pavement to meet her and she rearranged her shopping bag and umbrella in her hands so he could pass on the right-hand side. As they passed, he did not even glance at her but simply lifted the bag off her fingers and strode on. Brigid kept going until she reached the corner and then whilst refolding her umbrella glanced at the disappearing figure of the young man from Offaly. Brigid watched for a moment but could see no police agents following him or watching and so she walked on further pleased with herself that the mission had been accomplished and hoping more would be allocated to her. As the sun was now shining, she decided to walk on and thought she might look for some playing cards or other small gifts she could send to Annie's children.

Mary had welcomed Brigid apologising that the children were still getting dry after their bath and would Brigid mind emptying the tin bath out, 'Best to use a large pan, even when empty, it's a really heavy thing to move.'

Mary was apologising for being late but Brigid just took her arm and gently led her to the coat hanger telling her to go or she would miss Mr Pollitt's speech. Brigid then allowed Patrick to help empty the bath which he did with great care and she smiled as she saw him carefully weighing the water until he was sure he could carry the pan to the outside drain. Emily meanwhile was showing off her dancing and eventually collapsed into Brigid's lap so tired that Brigid immediately lifted her up and carried her to the sink to clean her teeth and tucked her up in bed. Within two pages of her Goldilocks book, Emily was asleep and Brigid was able to help Patrick finish emptying the bath and pretended to let him help lift it. He told Brigid he was "nearly eight" and so was much stronger.

Brigid agreed and after a couple of stories he too was turned over in bed ready for sleep. Brigid tidied up and washed the dishes, then switched the radiogram on just in time for some music by Charlie Kunz. Brigid had heard Amy telling Grace that Charlie lived close by on Dollis Hill Lane but she had then no idea who he was and she was surprised to hear such a famous musician lived locally.

Brigid was tired and curled up a little in the armchair until she was woken by the sound of the lock turning and Mary saying, 'Oh Brigid, have they tired you out?'

Brigid assured Mary the children had been as good as gold and had gone to sleep quickly.

Mary saw the tidy kitchen and told Tom to get the whisky out for, she said, Brigid had been cleaning-up, emptying the bath and reading stories all after a hard day's work for that slave driver Willans. Tom served the drinks and told Brigid all about the meeting, how Harry had a new pamphlet out called "How To Win The War."

Tom said this showed how right the Communist Party was to press for an agreement between Britain, France and the Soviet Union.

'First unite the peace-loving countries then we stop Hitler,' Tom finished.

Brigid sipped her whisky and simply said she was pleased they had enjoyed the meeting although she was not sure how peace-loving she thought the English were. Tom would usually reply with a long explanation but instead he sighed and slapped his thigh.

'I nearly forgot Brigid, I meant to tell you as soon as you came round. Just as I was leaving today three plain clothes police called to the factory, luckily Willans and Eastwood had left early for a meeting with the directors. The police, Special Branch I think, wanted a list with addresses of all the Irish workers at the factory. I managed to persuade them I did not have access to the files but could bring a list to them by ten o'clock tomorrow.'

'How many will be on the list?'

Tom explained that he was hoping to just tell the police without Eastwood in particular having any contact with them.

'Otherwise, Eastwood will just pick out people he doesn't like, Amy, you and others from the strike and the police will probably visit you first.'

Tom said he would tell Willans after he had done it but he would have to give him a copy of the list.

'I'll put them in alphabetical order, I think there will be at least forty.'

Brigid thanked Tom and said she would go round the factory first thing telling everyone what might happen. She wondered whether to tell Tom a fib that she had moved address, for she dreaded Roisin and Diarmuid being visited again but decided against it, even though her link with the house would mean she would be a suspect and, at least, taken in for questioning.

Tom was not at the factory when Brigid arrived next morning and no one had seen him, she assumed he had already left for the police station with the list. First, she sought out Amy, explained that the police were just harassing all Irish men and women and if Amy just told them she knew nothing about the IRA and was not interested in politics she would be fine. She made Amy swear not to start chatting to the police, they were not friends and anything she told them would get other innocent people into trouble. Amy seemed to understand so Brigid did not mention Peter Barnes hoping that Amy would not mention that to the police.

Brigid worked her way through the factory quietly talking to anyone she found who was Irish or at least of Irish descent. She had known that the government had been deporting people on suspicion of involvement in the campaign but she was surprised to find that everyone she spoke to knew at least one person who had been arrested. A small man called Jimmy who worked in the tool shop told her he had been in the big pub in Harlesden on Sunday when the police raided it, blocking doors and questioning everyone before they let them out.

'They took my mate Hugh away, no idea why for he's in the pub every night after work so when would he get up to any bombing? I've never heard him say a word about politics, horses yes, he loves a bet but never politics.'

Brigid explained that he should not mention Hugh or the raid or even being in the pub for the police would then link him to a possible conspiracy.

'They seem to be deporting who they like now, just on Hoare's signature,' Brigid said and Jimmy replied, 'I don't like it over here but I need the wages.' A sentiment Brigid heard several times that morning. As she finished her round, she passed Tiny enjoying a cigarette break.

'You seem to have time to chat today, want a Service?' he said.

Brigid said she had better get back to work and Tiny replied that she only seemed to have time for the Irish. She explained that she was only telling people their names and addresses were being given to the police by the company so that if they were stopped and questioned, they would know why.

'The sooner they catch these bastards the better,' Tiny said. 'Blowing off people's legs and smashing up the waxworks, for what?'

Brigid decided not to argue but simply repeated that she was simply giving people a warning so no one was upset, for there was no one in the factory involved.

'We don't know do we Brigid, that's the problem,' replied Tiny.

As she walked away Brigid saw Billy, Grace and John in a heated conversation and said to them, 'When the boss is away, the mice will play, eh?'

'Stalin has signed a peace pact with Hitler, Brigid, we can't believe it but it seems to be true, all the papers are reporting it. Have you seen Tom?'

Brigid said she knew he had a message to run but she assumed he would be in soon.

'Why would Hitler want a truce with Communists,' she said. 'It doesn't make sense.'

Billy replied that was why they wanted to speak to Tom. In fact, Tom was not in fact in the factory that morning he was busy recruiting for the Communist Party all over London and he had taken John to an early morning meet with Party shop stewards from the AEU near Hammersmith bridge. Tom regarded John as an ideal recruit who had an instinctive class consciousness and was brave and, he believed, had an instinctive international loyalty to the Soviet Union. On the way by bus, Tom had told John about the record Party recruitment underway, the strength of the Party in the factories and Trades Councils and the new policy on how to win the war against the fascist Hitler.

When they reached the hall John was impressed to find over a hundred men there, as they spoke, they introduced themselves as shop stewards from various big engineering factories and talked about the fight for an alliance of the democratic states and the need for a pact between the democracies of France and England with Stalin to ensure the fascist Hitler was defeated. From reports given of various local meetings it was clear that the Party was recruiting fast and Tom leant over and told John now was the time to join for "history does not wait for stragglers". John said nothing about this but commented on the impressive attendance and made careful notes in a notebook of which factories were represented.

Afterwards Tom said they should get breakfast and suggested they walk up to Shepherd's Bush. It was past nine o'clock and John wondered if they should be getting back to the factory but Tom explained that Willans knew they were out all day visiting suppliers and negotiating increased deliveries.

'I told him you were coming with me as we needed to train more men just in case anyone is called up for the war. Could be more money in it for you John, Willans seems to have forgotten the strike now we're all agreed on the need to defeat Hitler.'

John asked why Willans and Eastwood did not carry out the factory negotiations after all was not that the task of management.

'Frankly John,' replied Tom. 'Eastwood couldn't negotiate his way out of the bog and Willans spends his day composing letters to the Times and Telegraph supporting Churchill, though I don't think he's ever had one published. They're both happy to let me get on with and I can recruit to the Party when I'm out and about.'

As they reached the café, Tom pointed out the new football stand at Loftus Road.

'I was there last year when Herbert Morrison opened the new stand, sadly Rangers lost to Palace so that spoilt the day a bit,' said Tom. John knew nothing about any sport so just nodded until Tom mentioned Queens Park Rangers being on the up again, he made a mental note to ask Billy about them just in case he ever needed a favour from Tom. They finished their English breakfast and, as Tom wiped his plate with some of the remaining bread, John followed suit.

'Always think that's the best bit of a fried breakfast, gives your stomach a lining against the cold I always say. Somehow can't get the kids to do it and Mary always tells them it's a disgusting habit.'

They left the café and Tom said the next call was to Acton depot as delivery of some essential parts had been held up on the railway and he needed to find out why. He suggested they cross the Scrubs to walk off their breakfasts and they passed the prison before stretching out across the scrubland. Tom said it used to be infested with snakes Mary's friend grew up over there and her dad was bitten by an adder once.

'Nasty bite but he survived apparently.' John kept his eyes on the ground just in case and he thought of Armley park where he played as a boy in sight of the prison. He decided not to mention this to Tom, somehow, he thought a life in the prison service was not ideal background for a Communist. They walked on along a huge hedge masking the prison and on the far side they heard a woman calling her dog, it looked like a terrier of some sort thought John and it bounded up to her obediently. Otherwise, there was no one on the scrubland and they walked along the huge hedge shielding the prison and Tom remarked on the numbers of sparrows sitting in and out of the hedge.

'Spuggies all over the place here,' he said. 'I expect not many care to walk near the prison so the birds are left in peace.'

They turned a corner heading north and saw a man in a gabardine looking at the prison through some ancient binoculars, probably army issue from the last war. John asked him if he was checking there were no escape ropes visible but the man just laughed and handed the binoculars to him. John looked in the direction the man was pointing but could see nothing, 'There just above the white line at the top of the tower,' he said and sure enough John refocussed and saw a pair of yellowish legs and then the bird itself staring out across the Scrub.

'Peregrines,' the man said. 'Fastest bird alive and living here amidst all this muck.'

Tom took an interest and watched the pair of birds for a few minutes asking the man what the birds ate.

'They hunt pigeons and smaller birds mostly but last week I saw one of them kill and eat a crow. There are several pairs in London, I could watch them all day, and I saw another pair on the House of Commons last week.'

Tom joked that there were plenty of crows to eat there but the man just took his binoculars back and strolled away.

'Solitary types these birdwatchers,' Tom remarked. 'Get obsessive about anything rare and chase around the country after birds.'

John just said he was glad to have seen the falcons and might get himself some old binoculars too.

'Don't tell Willans though,' Tom said, 'He'll want a pair to spy on us from his office.'

John was so surprised by the joke he laughed too loud making Tom laugh in return.

'Time to get over to Acton young John some railwaymen's heads need banging together.' John walked on thinking to himself there was a decent human being inside Tom but still mentally bracing himself for the Party recruitment session he knew was coming.

The meetings had already lasted almost three hours and Tom decided he had gained enough assurances from the rail companies that problems with supplies were temporary and the metal required would start arriving promptly in Cricklewood. Tom had finished by saying that there was a war coming very soon and any more delays would hamper the fight against Hitler. Everyone present seemed to agree bar one of the Great Western Railway managers who said he thought Hitler would back down. Even so they all agreed, after Tom insisted, that they would meet again in a month to review the situation. Tom left the meeting in high spirits and, breathing in, smelt the familiar sweet smell of biscuits wafting over from the McVie and Price factory.

'The greatest Scottish export after whisky and haggis,' Tom said. 'It's making me hungry again. I suggest we go for a pie and a pint in the Junction if that's alright with you, John.'

It was already past three and after the long meeting and the walking on a sunny day John could think of nothing better. They ordered two steak and kidney pies and took their pints on to the canal side tables. A barge was passing under the bridge and a little girl waved to them from the top of the hatchway and John waved back. Tom said the canal was a fine example of capitalist development which had halved the cost of coal in London last century but that capitalism quickly moved on and now the railways had taken most of their trade.

'Still this time the capitalists have left some beautiful walking and boating routes behind instead of their usual despoilment and poverty. Although I'm not sure the navvies who slaved to dig the canals would see it that way if they were still alive.'

They discussed the history of capitalist development a little for John had been reading Marx and wanted to test his understanding. Tom steered this onto the need for the majority class, the proletariat, to take power and for the Communist Party to become strong enough to lead. Tom said the Party in Britain was approaching thirty thousand members and they were represented in nearly every major workplace with hundreds of shop stewards and district secretaries.

'Now's the time to join John for the war against Hitler will change everything in this country.'

On this point John agreed and seemed to satisfy Tom by agreeing to come to a local meeting soon. Tom said how much he regretted Billy becoming one of the splitters trying to divide the class. John just said firmly that Billy was his best mate and he was not going to criticise him.

They left the pub at four and Tom said they could catch the bus back to Cricklewood and he could report to Willans before he left for the day. As they waited at the bus stop, they heard a cry of 'get those bastards,' and walking to the road crossing they saw about a dozen men chasing three others and punching them when they caught them. The three turned round and tried to fight back but one of them was knocked down and was being mercilessly kicked. Tom saw John race past him and they both forced their way between the attackers and the three men. Tom noticed that all the men, the victims included, were wearing coach builder overalls some mentioning Park Royal Vehicles and some with the AEC initials on. The fight had temporarily halted and John shouted, 'What's this about, why are workmates fighting?'

'Those Irish bastards are no mates of us,' shouted the largest of the men. 'They should all be strung up.'

He was a huge man and he tried to swing a punch over John to reach one of the three. John held him back and threatened to punch him back if he tried that again. There was another pause and this time an older smaller man stepped forward; Tom recognised him from a union meeting. 'It's Charlie Price, isn't it?'

Charlie could not remember Tom's name but he said, 'These Irish bastards have gone too far now, they've blown up shoppers in Coventry today, innocent people killed.'

John said whatever bombing had happened was wrong but not every Irishman could be blamed, it would be like blaming every Englishman for Neville Chamberlain. Tom sensed the heat of the moment had temporarily subsided and whatever the merits of John's argument it had confused some. He said they would be taking the three workers away to safety and everyone could think about events a little. He helped the stricken Irishman up and suggested they walk slowly away towards Harlesden. The three men agreed and they set off slowly, only the larger man called after them. 'Murdering Irish, get back home.'

The five men walked back towards the Jubilee Clock, a Black Maria screamed past in the direction of the Junction Arms. The youngest man who had been on the floor and had blood dripping from his nose said they should go to the Green Man together and get cleaned up and no one would attack an Irish pub. Tom and John saw them in and refused the offer of a pint instead catching the bus back to Cricklewood.

It was Friday and leaving time at the factory and everyone was streaming out, Tiny came up to Tom and said there had been some bad feeling since the news from Coventry arrived and several men were saying they did not want to work with the Irish anymore.

'Not sure I do either, Tom,' Tiny added.

Tom ignored this comment and soon they were met by Grace who gave John a hug and asked what had happened. John explained the attack in Park Royal and Grace said they must make sure Brigid, Amy and the others were safe going home. They found the two sheltering in the tool room with Billy standing guard.

'Eastwood came round telling everyone the radio had reported a young boy had been killed in the Coventry attack and everywhere IRA supporters were being attacked in the streets,' Billy reported.

'Some of the workers went home early together for safety but Brigid said she was not afraid and would not be bullied out and Amy insisted on staying too.'

They all agreed to stay in the factory awhile and then escort Brigid and Amy across the road to Brigid's lodgings, 'This sort of mob reaction only lasts a few hours usually until everyone gets to the pub and boasts about it,' John said, 'I've seen it in Leeds when crowds gather outside the prison sometimes.'

Grace wondered why John was at a prison but thought it better to ask him privately and she said she would join them to make sure Brigid and Amy were safe. After half an hour the factory had emptied and they crossed the highway and Brigid, having discovered she had forgotten her house key had to knock and a slightly flustered Roisin opened the door. Brigid simply asked if they could come in and Roisin stepped aside ushering them in with a greeting and, for Amy, a brief embrace.

'You're all welcome but I'm sorry you've caught me in my pinny, I've just baked a sponge cake and now I've got people to eat it all. Diarmuid come and help me serve the tea.'

Diarmuid who had been snoozing with his copy of The Sporting Life over his face, blinked and asked what was going on. When Brigid explained about the bombing and the attacks on Irish people, Diarmuid sprang into life and said they must all have a cup of tea immediately. Brigid followed him into the scullery and explained that none of the factory workers had been attacked but that Tom and John had broken up a beating near the canal. When Roisin explained that she had been baking to music all afternoon and Diarmuid had been picking which greyhounds to lose money on so they had not heard the news.

'Sounds like a bomb has gone off in the town centre in Coventry and killed some passersby.'

Roisin said that was terrible news for she had an aunty in Coventry herself who liked shopping.

'Was it the IRA Brigid?' she asked. Brigid said that was unlikely for their campaign had only hit transport and power targets adding that she understood the aim was to get the British to remove all troops from Ireland.

'That'll never work,' said Roisin simply and sliced the cake onto plates handing them to Brigid. In the front room, Diarmuid was pouring the tea and handing cups round. They sat for a while eating and no one seemed to know what to say.

Tom complimented Roisin on the cake and said it reminded him of the cake shop where all cakes were two pence a slice but this one was threepence, when a customer asked why, she replied, 'That's Madeira cake.' No one laughed but John managed a groan and then had to explain the joke to Amy.

Brigid thanked them all again and said she was grateful to have such friends and she accepted Grace's offer to call for her before the Saturday morning shift. As she was leaving Grace remembered Amy and that she had moved recently to Colindale so Roisin suggested Amy could stay the night for safety and, as Amy quickly agreed, Brigid did not want to mention the raid on the house only six months ago.

The sunrise brightening the bedroom always caught Brigid by surprise whenever she had forgotten to pull the curtains fully together and she half opened one eye and, before drifting back to sleep, realised an arm was draped across her chest and a warm body was snuggled into her back. A memory of her little sister Agnes sharing her farmhouse bed to her came and made her smile but then she realised it must be Amy who Roisin had insisted share the bed saying, 'Plenty of room for two little ones.'

Gently Brigid peeled the arm away and turned around slowly, anxious not to wake Amy. She looked at Amy for several minutes and could see why so many were attracted to her for she had the high cheekbones and long black hair men liked. One strand of hair had stuck to her forehead so Brigid gently lifted it back into place and gently kissed Amy's forehead.

Brigid rolled away in silence until, almost inaudibly, she heard Amy whisper, 'That was nice.'

Brigid had made some porridge before Grace arrived and insisted, she ate some. 'For you are our security Grace and we need you to be fit and strong.'

Grace replied that she reckoned the three of them could look after themselves and they were laughing when Roisin came downstairs.

'Summer porridge,' she said, 'we might as well be back in Limerick for that's all we ever had to eat.'

Amy said, 'Porridge, that's posh,' and made them all smile.

Brigid knew Roisin was worried though and promised to do the shopping for her when she came home at lunchtime then she added, 'And I'll pop back at eight to make sure Diarmuid's safe and sound.'

Roisin looked relieved and simply said, 'You are a blessing from God, Brigid, a blessing from God.'

The three women left for work and as they reached the factory gate Grace said, 'Open sesame, for St Brigid of Whiddy is here.'

Brigid was thinking of a witty reply when she spotted Billy and John who suggested they have a catch up in the yard.

'Tom's dictating letters from yesterday and said to only disturb him if there was a problem, Eastwood and Willans have gone on a jolly with the owners, a shooting weekend up north apparently.'

Grace said Eastwood would enjoy shooting peasants. They all laughed, 'Watch that Grace she's sharp as a tack today,' Brigid said and put her arm around Grace and John as they walked.

A small group of workers saw what was happening and followed amongst them Nana and Dusty. Nana demanded to know what John had found out about orders for it had been a quiet week and everyone knew Nana had several mouths to feed. John told them Tom had insisted the railway improved delivery for he had months of work piling up for want of parts and, anyway, Tom said that if war came, they would have more orders for tank parts than they could handle.

Nana said it was a pity they did not make gas masks for they were being given out everywhere and all her grandchildren hung them up at home as if they were Christmas stockings. Amy asked if Nana was going to send the children away to the countryside if war was declared and she said she would not so long as she could feed them all. As with the meetings yesterday there was a general resignation that war was coming and Amy said she was thinking of joining the ARP.

'There's hardly any men joined though Amy,' said Nana to laughter but this time Amy replied sharply that she should give it a rest for everyone knew she was only jealous.

At that moment Tiny turning the corner and seeing the group asked loudly if they were on strike and why had no one told him. Billy said there was no strike but in the absence of any managers the factory was under workers control and they were just checking there was enough work to keep Tiny out of mischief.

'Cheeky buggers,' Tiny retorted. 'I'd like to see any of you do my job.'

Tiny told them his news that he had gone for a drink last night in the Queens Arms and there had been police cars screaming up and down after nine o'clock.

'They've caught one of the Coventry bombers when he returned to Westbourne Terrace, one of the police narks came in later and said he'd heard the house was full of bomb-making equipment.'

There was a general murmur of support as Tiny gave his account. Grace suggested that any idea of punishing all Irish people for the actions of a few bombers would be wrong and they should agree to work normally with everyone. Everyone agreed and several volunteered to spread the message around the factory. As they dispersed, Billy noticed Brigid facing the wall in the corner as if she was praying to a statue he wanted to go over but hesitated and when Brigid turned round he just waved.

*****

It was Saturday evening and Billy was attending a WIL meeting at the headquarters near Kings Cross station. John had asked to come for as he told his friend he wanted to hear what the splitters had to say before he joined the mass Communist Party. Billy knew it was sometimes hard to understand when John was being ironic for as Humphrey used to say, 'Yorkshire folk like speaking in riddles.'

Humphrey had once been wronged in some way by a tradesman from Batley and he usually liked to add, 'There's a reason all of Yorkshire like that saying there's not so queer as folk.'

On the way to Northdown Street Billy had explained that the discussion that evening was to be about the counter-revolution in Spain which led to Franco's victory. When he heard that Helmut was leading the discussion John was pleased, for he had taken a liking to the German and had asked Billy where Helmut had got to with Billy only able to say he was touring the country giving talks. John told Billy about a letter he had received from home, as usual his mam wanted to know when he was coming home to visit and John said he was hoping to persuade her to come to London and stay a couple of days.

When Billy suggested he could easily get a couple of days off to go home John replied he did not regard it as home anymore and Billy knew not to ask more. John said the letter had saddened him for one of his school friends had been killed in Spain.

'I couldn't understand it Billy, when I saw Kevin last, he never mentioned Spain but mam said he went with some friends to join the International Brigade. I rang her as soon as I got the letter but it seemed he was killed last autumn. Mam doesn't like politics at all she only knew he had fought at Ebro and was killed afterwards. Of course, mam thinks it was a stupid decision to go, thinks we have enough problems here to sort out and says Kevin's mam is heartbroken. His mam was a kind woman, gave me tea sometimes and she really was proud of Kevin.'

John tailed off and for a moment Billy thought he was about to cry. Billy simply said there may be someone at the meeting who could explain about the battle and what happened afterwards. They turned left and John was shocked to enter from a yard an old decrepit building which inside was dominated by an old printing press and beyond which were stacked copies of Youth for Socialism. A few old wooden chairs were already occupied and Billy had crossed the room to speak to an older woman seated behind a table. John picked up a leaflet entitled "Fight War Plans" and was reading a passage attacking Labour and Communist leaders for supporting a war for profit when the woman called the meeting to order.

'Good evening comrades, my name is Hetty Richardson and I'll be introducing the political discussion tonight. For those who don't know me, I live in Tower Hamlets and have been speaking to local members of the Communist Party about Stalin's pact with Hitler. Instead of our scheduled discussion on Spain, we've decided to discuss the crisis in the Comintern tonight of which, of course, includes Spain. Helmut is detained with important work in Glasgow but will be able to join us next month.'

John was disappointed but during the round of introductions he described himself as someone who hated fascism, came from Leeds and had taken part in the strike against unfair dismissal of a women worker. Hetty thanked him and hoped he enjoyed the meeting. There were about a dozen people present and with the exception of Hetty, all were under thirty in John's estimation. Both from their self-descriptions at the start and from their physical appearance John could tell that these at least were not the 'bourgeois and petit-bourgeois Trotskyists' that Tom had described. Hetty was talking about Stalin's treachery to the international working-class through the treaty with the Nazis. She urged the meeting to counter the lie that this had anything to do with securing peace, for fascists were the tool of the capitalists to smash workers organisations.

'It is a disastrous continuation of the policy of Socialism In One Country and the Popular Front with capitalists which has already led to defeats and thousands of deaths of Communists and socialists in Spain.' Hetty ended by describing the opportunities for the world Trotskyist movement in which many class-conscious workers will be asking how can the official Comintern parties sign a pact with fascism.

'It is our opportunity to win these comrades over to the Fourth International,' Hetty concluded to loud applause, 'Go to it.' After a brief discussion on the talk, there were reports on finance and organising opportunities and on the street meetings being organised and those Communist Party street meetings they would intervene at. John was not surprised to hear Billy volunteer for several of these next week, for he rarely saw him in the evenings back at the digs.

On the way home on the top deck of the bus, Billy told John that Tom would be in a terrible crisis for he had wanted to sign up for the British army to fight Hitler but Mary had pointed out that he was too old. John said he had Harry Pollitt's pamphlet on how to win the war at home and was going to read it tomorrow then ask Tom some questions.

*****

At the same time as the men returned home, Brigid had found someone who knew what had happened in Coventry. Brigid had spent the day and much of the previous night wondering if Peter Barnes was the man arrested and, if so, whether the police had traced her too. She remembered that Martin had said he was leaving England soon after their meeting and even if he was still here, she had no means to contact him. Brigid calculated that if the police were on her trail, she needed to know in order to flee and she needed to know quickly.

Brigid knew there was a risk in going to Kilburn but felt the risk was greater if she waited to be arrested. Avoiding the pubs she had previously visited she visited the Colin Campbell and then the Earl of Derby where at the bar, an older man asked where she was from and insisted on buying her a drink gesturing to a table with five others around it.

'We're all from County Cork too.'

Seated at the table, Brigid was introduced and realised she had joined three married couples all of whom seemed to be from Midleton, a town Brigid had never visited. Tales from home were soon being told and after Brigid had shared the cost of another round with Sinead and her husband Fionn, Sinead proposed a toast to 'Sean O'Shea and the heroes of Clonmult,' revealing that her great uncle was one of those shot in cold blood by the Black and Tans afterwards.

Brigid said that those men were celebrated across Ireland and she had attended a commemoration in Bantry as a young woman. This prompted another toast to Bantry and Fionn ordered a round of whiskies, 'Had a win on the gee-gees today,' he explained. This time the landlord came over with the drinks asking what all the celebrations were about.

'Have one yourself Jimmy we're remembering Ireland's heroes.' Jimmy pulled up a stool and laughing said it could be a long night for his brother-in-law was injured on Bloody Sunday. After toasting "the heroes of Mitchelstown" Sinead asked Jimmy what he had heard about the Coventry bombing. Jimmy looked round to see if anyone could hear and then as he was about to speak, he asked who Brigid was.

Assured by Fionn that she was one of ours from Bantry, Jimmy asked who ran the ferry there. Brigid replied that it was nearly four years since she had left but Patrick Finnegan had been running it then. This seemed to satisfy Jimmy and he told them he had heard it was an IRA operation that went wrong, seems someone panicked and left the bomb on a bike in the town centre. Jimmy knew that a young fella from Meath, called Barnes had been arrested and was being held in Paddington. 'The High Road is swarming with cops and agents, seems they think the whole unit planned it from here.'

There was a silence and then a thick set woman at the end of the table still dressed in a shawl although it was summer said that it might be better to lie low for a week as she did not want to be in a police cell again.

'They don't clean them properly and their tea tastes like shite.'

Everyone laughed and Sinead said she thought Deidre was right and maybe they should drink up and let the heat die down for a week. Brigid saw the opportunity to leave and promised to see them all again soon and Sinead told Brigid she worked at Rolls Razor so maybe they could meet in Cricklewood after work one night. Brigid walked down the bar and had just entered the Ladies toilet when four uniformed officers came through the door and ordered everyone to stay where they were. Brigid stayed inside and locked herself in a cubicle.

After a few minutes she heard a scuffle and a man shouting, 'I said every one out of the bogs and that includes you,' and a second later an order, 'put him in the van.'

'Yes sergeant,' said a voice back and then the clump of boots seemed to be inside the toilet.

As a girl Brigid had been taught by her brother how to hide in the outside toilet by locking it and standing crouched on the toilet seat and she breathed in as his voice murmured, 'Things I do for King and Country,' and she heard the heavier breathing and the crash of what she assumed was a truncheon on the floor as the sergeant looked under the cubicle doors. It seemed that another policeman was at the door now for the sergeant got up saying, 'You breathe a word of this outside and I'll have you, understand?'

'Yes sarge, just checking you were all right,' and Brigid heard the sergeant groan as he got up and then the sound of two sets of boots leaving. Brigid stayed crouched for as long as she could, then slowly let her legs dangle and after a while gently unlocked the door and peeked outside. The pub was empty but she realised there was a back entrance along the corridor and took it, entering into an alleyway and then into Priory Park Road. Brigid thought carefully for a minute and decided against walking or catching a bus along the High Road, instead she set off through the side streets and took the long route home.

As she walked her head was filled with thoughts going through the possibility that the receipts from the flour bags had been found, whether or not the young boy in Edgware would remember her, would Roisin be identified in her hat and scarf and would they raid the house again and finally, whether Amy would be questioned at work and unwittingly reveal details of the Peter Barnes meeting and location.

By the time she was striding past the Victorian mansions of Brondesbury Park, Brigid had decided there was little she could do to prevent any of the possible scenarios and, feeling the effects of the drinks with Sinead and the others, she resolved to go home and get a good night's sleep. As she approached Midland Terrace, she was cautious however trying to make sure there were no police watching the house and then peering through the gap in the curtains. Brigid knew Diarmuid would be out on his shift and by now Roisin would probably have gone to bed with a cocoa, a small whisky and her copy of The Tablet.

For safety, she gently knocked on the door and was surprised when Roisin opened it in her dressing gown and explained the milk was on for the cocoa and would Brigid like some. Brigid decided she would and was reassured that Roisin mentioned only the worry Catholic mothers were having about evacuation and whether their children would receive a good Catholic education in the countryside. Brigid said she was sure the church would make arrangements and said goodnight as she climbed the stairs.

Brigid lay on the bed fully clothed and sipped her cocoa but her mind kept racing through the police search she was sure she was connected through the flour bags to the Coventry bombing and with such a public outroar the police would be under pressure to make more arrests and would be following every possible lead. Brigid knew she could not rest until she had done something to reduce the risk and eventually decided to write a note to Amy reminding her not to chat to any police and deliver it to her house. Grace and she had been invited to tea by Amy last week and Brigid was sure she could remember the house opposite a small park.

Brigid wrote a short message. 'Remember to keep mum, Amy. Love, Brigid' and put it inside an envelope which in turn was placed in the lining of her coat. Quietly Brigid slipped out of the door and set off north towards Burnt Oak and was relieved to find there were few pedestrians for at nine o'clock on a warm Saturday night people were either at home or comfortable in the pubs and clubs and cinemas of Cricklewood or Kilburn.

The sun was setting and there was an orange glow to the west and Brigid closed her eyes as she walked, for some reason remembering the sunset over Whiddy when she and Annie had stayed out late near Kilmore lake counting the oystercatchers and Conan was sent to find them. She smiled at the memory of being sent to bed without supper and resolved to take up Tiny's offer of a tour of the local reservoir for she missed the space of open water. Brigid turned right at Montrose Avenue and soon turned left walking alongside a park.

For extra security she waited across the road for a while alongside a battered sign saying Silkstream Park and watched to see if the house was being observed or if she had been followed. Satisfied she crossed the road and in the cover of the doorway took out the envelope and posted it as quietly as she could. As she reached the gate, the door opened and Amy said, 'Brigid come in, what a wonderful surprise.'

Amy explained she had decided to lie low although it was odd to be at home on a Saturday night, for she usually went dancing.

'Still I've got a little drop of whisky left over from last Christmas, will you have one with me, Brigid?'

Before she could answer Amy had walked over to the sink, reached two glasses and poured two very large whiskies. She offered one to Brigid saying, 'How wonderful you're here, Brigid,' and Brigid leant over the outstretched arm intending to kiss Amy on the forehead but as she did so Amy stretched up and kissed her mouth. Neither pulled away and they stood there kissing as best they could whilst holding the drinks behind the others back.

*****

Early Sunday morning the sun poured straight into the room and settled on Amy's face waking her. She looked at the time. 'I'd normally be on my way to church now but I'm not sure God would want me now.'

Brigid thought for a moment and said, 'I'm sure God will forgive us but I'm not sure about Father Romilly.'

They both burst into laughter and when one stopped the other would start again until eventually Amy put her hand gently on Brigid's mouth and lay her head on her shoulder.

'You don't regret coming here, do you, Brigid?' she asked.

'I've never felt happier in my whole life,' Brigid replied.

Chapter 10
'We Will Have to Fight Another War in 25 Years'

Eastwood was making a rare tour of the factory, and as usual, he only spoke to a few people he knew, for even the most obedient worker now referred to him as Pudgy. In fact, Eastwood was neither overweight nor small, indeed like Willans he was over six feet tall and was known to walk to work from Golders Green every day. Despite his bearing which Grace had once reminded her of a "poor man's Anthony Eden' Eastwood failed to make an impression.

In quiet moments in the factory, or when they were just bored, workers would invent stories about him and one day Mairaid had joked that no one had ever taken his Boop-Oop-A-Doop-Away. This had spread gradually around the factory until any appearance by Eastwood would lead to the tune being whistled and once Charlie, who had quickly realised Eastwood was to be treated with disdain, had been spoken to by Tom after singing *'You can feed me bread and water,'* so loudly that Eastwood and Mr Willans had heard and complained. Tom later told Mary he could barely keep a straight face as he told Charlie that all references to Betty Boop were banned. Despite this the whistling continued and soon the nickname Pudgy emerged, though many workers who had never seen a Betty Boop cartoon did not know why.

Despite this underwhelming impression Eastwood created, as it was a Friday and sometimes announcements about weekend overtime were made, most workers were watching him to pass to see if there was an announcement. Sure enough, as he left the drill room Tiny announced that work would stop in ten minutes so everyone could listen to an important BBC announcement. The directors had ordered enough radios for every workshop but so far, they had never been turned on. Willans had agreed with Tom that the radios would be a good thing once the war started for everyone would realise how important it was to work hard for the war effort. Tiny though struggled to get the radio tuned and they only heard the last pip. Lionel Marson announced some wavelength adjustments and someone joked that they would never get the pips now. The laughter died down quickly as the words 'Germany has invaded Poland and has bombed many towns' were heard and Tiny said, 'That's it another bloody war.'

As the list of Polish cities being bombed was read out John said he had never heard of any of them but Tiny simply replied that it would be London next. They all listened in silence until Hitler's speech was reported and the pact with Russia mentioned. Tiny turned the radio off saying, 'You can never trust a Communist,' adding that everyone must go home and follow all instructions from the government.

Brigid decided to visit Mary, Patrick and Emily in case the children were being evacuated tomorrow. When she knocked on the door there was no answer and she was about to leave when the door opened a little and the worried face of Patrick peered round.

'Mummy's sick, Aunty Brigid, can you help?'

Brigid went into the flat and found Mary slumped on the sofa, dabbing her eyes with a handkerchief with Emily alongside holding her arm tightly. Emily did not jump up as usual but just waved her hand whilst her brother sat down on the other side of his mother. Brigid said she would make a cup of sweet tea and when that was done, she handed it to Mary and explained to the children they should go and play quietly whilst mummy and aunty Brigid talked and then they would all make supper together.

Emily asked if mummy was better soon could they make a sponge cake and Brigid promised they would and, before he asked, promised Patrick he could scrape the mixing bowl with a spoon. He let go of his mother and held Emily's hand as they went to their bedroom. It was a very touching sight and Brigid suddenly thought what wonderful children they were and wondered how her real nieces and nephews were.

They both sat there in silence a while until Mary said she felt so stupid crying over nothing and she was so sorry. Brigid waited until Mary added that she and Tom had had a row the night before and they never had rows.

'Has he absconded?' she asked.

Mary said nothing then she laughed through her tears, 'Absconded Brigid, we're married not signed up to military servitude.'

Brigid laughed too and leant over to gently push the untouched mug of tea upwards to Mary's lips. Mary took a sip and grimaced saying she had heard of sweet talking someone but that tea was the most disgusting she had ever tasted.

'Now you see what county Wicklow is missing,' Brigid retorted and made a drinking motion for Mary to take some more.

Instead, Mary stood up, drying her eyes and walked into the bedroom to check on the children. They were building towers with some cylinders Tom had brought home from the factory and Brigid heard Mary tell them they would be making a cake in a few minutes. Mary came back in and said they should have been on the evacuation train that morning at Willesden Junction but she just could not bring herself to send them.

'They're too little to be going to a farm in Northamptonshire without me, when we went to the rehearsal on Monday at the school it was different but I did not sleep last night with worry and this morning I couldn't take them.'

'Just couldn't,' she added.

Brigid did not reply but sensed that Mary needed time to compose herself. After a few minutes silence Mary got up and washed her face in the bowl, drying her eyes on a tea towel.

'Every bloody tea towel has got Lenin on it. Tom got them at a Daily Worker fair says they were cheap. I'd just like a picture of the Wicklow mountains to remind me of the times we used to climb Djouce when we visited grandma Childers near there. It's so beautiful Brigid, you can see for miles across the mountains.'

Brigid said she had never been there but in her opinion all of Ireland was beautiful. Feeling that Mary was looking more composed she asked whether she might not get into trouble with the Party for being disloyal to Lenin. Mary laughed and said Brigid had a funny idea of the Communist Party as if they were all spoilsports and no one was allowed to disagree.

'You're mixing us up with the Catholic church, Brigid.'

Brigid could not resist. 'You are guilty of blasphemy Mary Stone, at least we're allowed a drink not like those Protestants. I don't think half the congregation of St Agnes would come if they couldn't go over to the club afterwards.'

Brigid asked what the Party thought about the evacuation of children and Brigid replied that this was what the row with Tom had been about. She said Tom had come in late from a Party meeting and had obviously had a few drinks and would not listen to her worries saying Party members had to set an example and be at the front of fighting the war against Hitler.

'You can imagine what I said, Brigid, why should little Patrick and Emily be at the frontline of the war.'

When he left this morning for a factory meeting at the Royal Ordnance, the children were still asleep and he just kissed them and said he would miss them terribly.

'He'll be expecting them to be gone when he comes home.'

Brigid reached for the handkerchief but Mary went on, 'He's a good father, always has been, I know he loves the children as much as me.'

Mary paused and took a breath. 'He's having arguments in the Party, I know, he wants Hitler stopped at all costs.'

Brigid said she agreed with that but she couldn't understand why that deal with Hitler had been agreed.

'Neither can I,' Mary said. 'And I don't think Tom can either.'

Brigid went and got the children and they made a Victoria sponge with Emily allowed to let the flour drop through the sieve like snow. Mary told Brigid quietly that Tom objected to the Victoria label and always called this cake Kollontai cake though she always told him that if anyone made cakes in the Kollontai household it would be her husband. Brigid did not know who Kollontai was but helped make the tea and read the children a story once they were in bed. As she got ready to leave, Tom was still not home but Mary assured Brigid they would sort the matter out and if bombing did start soon, she would find a way to get the children out.

As Brigid left, Mary gave her a hug and said she was a good friend. 'But you won't tell your Trotskyist friends what I said about the pact, will you?'

Brigid said she would not tell anyone she was for the freedom of Ireland and she did not care about anything else.

*****

At the factory Tiny had become the daily source of news on all aspects of the war and as the factory had rapidly expanded production there were now two thousand or so workers spread across the site. Tiny was now the foreman responsible for training and Billy was his assistant and also had an enhanced role progress chasing the whole factory. Other section leaders and foremen would complain loudly if Billy had not visited with the latest news by the end of the day. Billy only knew that Tiny had befriended some American journalists and they had a drink most nights and Billy knew he also visited the Naval and Military Club in Piccadilly sometimes. Tiny had never explained how he had become a member or how he afforded such fees and generally he liked to tease Billy by divulging no personal information whenever Billy asked.

Amy had discovered Tiny had a birthday at the time of the strike and they had held a toast in which Tiny said he was "forty-five and too old for birthdays" which Billy surmised meant Tiny would have served in the First World War. Exactly where and at what rank Tiny would never say although Tom reported once that Tiny had told him Winston Churchill and TE Lawrence were the greatest men he had ever met.

This day Tiny had important news and Billy went around as usual telling all who wished to listen about the German plane attacks in Scotland and further details of the tragic sinking of the Royal Oak at Scapa Flow. It took Billy much longer to get round for everyone had questions about what U boats were and why Scapa Flow had not been defended and in the finishing shop, an older man who Billy did not know stated that the Royal Oak was a jinxed ship whose officers had mutinied and been court-martialled ten years ago. Billy picked up a mood of anxiety at the huge losses on the ship, several workers remarking they had sons in the navy but most interest was in the German air attack and whether Billy though it was the start of the invasion.

Billy often reflected that it was odd that a Trotskyist was entrusted with spreading the war news and even odder that Mr Willans and Eastwood required him to pass on the news at four o'clock each day in their office. Billy did not mind for Brenda always gave him a cup of tea afterwards and usually a chocolate biscuit wrapped in silver paper from the director's biscuit tin. They had a daily joke as to whether Eastwood would say that of course he and Mr Willans knew the news thoroughly but it was important to hear what the workers were hearing or some such comment, most days Billy would emerge with his thumbs up and Brenda would try not to laugh.

Later that evening Grace and John had arranged to meet Billy for a drink. John said that at least all that Anderson shelter digging he had helped with had not been wasted and the real war would now begin. Grace joked he now had the muscles of a bodybuilder and if he carried on, he would soon be in a circus as the strongman. Billy said that nothing would get him into one of those wet and smelly cold shelters, he was going to run to Willesden Green underground and shelter on platforms.

'And miss the chance of a night cuddled up for warmth with Mrs C,' John retorted.

Billy ignored that and said that Mrs C had told him she had been turned down for the ARP.

'Apparently foreign nationals are not allowed to join or do war work or anything, I heard Tiny complaining about his Austrian neighbours sitting in the autumn sunshine whilst he slogged his guts out.'

'He hates all foreigners does Tiny, a real member of the lumpenproletariat he is,' John commented.

Grace smiled and said that John had been learning sections of the Communist Manifesto by heart. John nodded and looked pleased and said it helped him understand things better. Billy said Tiny was a complex character who had supported their strike but seemed to regard the only good foreigner as one who supported the British Empire.

Grace remarked that the war, particularly now that it was becoming closer, was testing every workers political beliefs and patriotism and the defence of Empire was a big part of that for some workers, she had even argued with Jennie Lee last week who she said had now become a big supporter of the British war effort, 'This hatred for fascism is leading many on the left to follow Attlee in supporting the Tories, given a chance they'll have Labour in another national government, probably not with Chamberlain but more likely Halifax or even Churchill.'

Billy nodded agreement adding that the Communist Party was in the biggest crisis of all and it seemed Harry Pollitt had been sacked. Grace expressed surprise saying she thought he was their best speaker at the rallies she went to and a real working-class militant even if she did not support the Party line. Billy explained what had been said at the WIL meeting the night before that Pollitt had been sent a telegram from Moscow telling him that the war could not be supported and must be opposed as an imperialist war. It seemed Pollitt had hidden this telegram and then when others "like Stalin's man in England, Palme Dutt" challenged the continued support for the war the Central Committee had still voted for Pollitt's line until Dave Springhall came back from Moscow and told them the new one.

'Even then Pollitt and that liar Campbell voted support for the war and they've been removed, rumour is Pollitt is on his way to Moscow for retraining.'

Grace said she hoped that was not a euphemism for something else. Billy said Willie Gallacher had also refused the new line but had now recanted and was back in favour.

'Jesus Christ Almighty,' said John. 'It's hard to know whether Stalin or the Pope has the most power over the faithful. I'm going to find Tom tomorrow and ask him what's going on, there's no bigger supporter of the war than him.'

Brigid meanwhile had arranged to meet Sinead after work and she walked down to the Rolls Razor factory on the Broadway waited beside the clocking off queue and when Sinead emerged, still putting her raincoat on, it was agreed to walk down to Kilburn to Sinead's flat for a cup of tea.

'That work is killing me Brigid I even dream about razors and I'm bored out of my skull. What's it like at your place?'

Brigid said that it was much the same she was inserting parts in speedometers all day but she could ask the managers if they had any vacancies. Sinead said she would be grateful for she had heard the pay was better and then she said, 'Oh it's so great to be out in the open and the light and stretching our legs, let's not talk about work anymore.'

Instead, once they passed Kilburn station, Sinead bought some soda bread from the Irish bakers. The flat she and Fionn had in Dyne Road was decorated with the tricolour and a large map of county Wicklow on one wall and on the other a large photograph of James Connolly. As Sinead was busy in the kitchen, Brigid also noticed on the sideboard a framed picture with the Declaration of the Provisional Government covered in glass. Brigid closed her eyes and began reciting quietly.

'IRISHMEN and IRISHWOMEN In the name of God and of the dead generations from which she receives her old tradition of nationhood. Ireland, through us—'

Until a voice joined, 'Summons her children to her flag and strikes for her freedom.'

Brigid opened her eyes and smiled at Sinead.

'Ah trust Ireland to let a poet write its declarations. My dad used to say not bad for a Dublin man and made us recite it through on Sundays whilst having his weekly beer. I must have been six or seven when I could recite it in full.'

Sinead set down a pot of tea and offered a slice of bread, still warm from the shop, to Brigid. Taking a bite herself, Sinead said soda bread always reminded her of watching the ships load up with malt at Ballincurra, she and her sisters would bake in the morning and then walk to the harbour taking a picnic of bread and jam to eat when they got there. Brigid asked if Sinead was not worried the Special Branch might call and see all the republican images.

Sinead snorted with laughter, 'Why they're here every other week, I bake a loaf specially for them the gobshites.'

Sinead explained there was only Fionn and her, they could not have children and most of their families were back in Cork.

'I wouldn't really mind a free passage back, courtesy of the British.' Brigid asked if they were active in the military campaign and Sinead snorted again.

'If I was would I tell you, do you think?'

Brigid replied that she should have known better to ask but Sinead said she was only teasing for she knew exactly who Brigid was and indeed her cousin Martin had stayed a night in the flat just recently.

'Before you ask, Conan is safe and back in Ireland but not on Whiddy, I don't think.'

Brigid nodded, thanking Sinead and pouring the tea into cups whilst Sinead went to fetch some more bread.

'I'd better save some for Fionn,' she said. 'Or he'll claim the old republicans are being forgotten.'

Brigid said nothing until Sinead explained that Fionn had known Dick Barrett in the Cork GAA, played with him and joined the war against the Tans. Fionn had escaped from the Dublin battle but Dick was murdered on the orders of O'Higgins.

'I met Fionn when he was brought to our house injured and I treated his bullet wound, superficial through his arm really but I could tell he liked me to dress it every day. The stories he can tell, so anyway I came to London with him and we got married in the middle of the General Strike here, 7 May 1926. He was thirty-seven and I was twenty-two. He always says Conan reminded him of Dick, the two best quartermasters the IRA ever had he says, reckons Conan knows every arms dump and safe house south of Cavan and exactly what is in them.'

Brigid knew not to ask more about Conan but just told Sinead she was so grateful for news of her brother. Sinead replied that now Brigid had been in active service and proved herself then she was able to share some information and wondered if Brigid could help the campaign to demand murder charges be dropped against Peter Barnes and James McCormick, 'Who everyone knew had not even been in Coventry when the accident happened.'

Once again Brigid felt more questions would be regarded as suspicious by Sinead so she simply said she would do everything she could and then was surprised when Sinead asked what she thought about the bombing campaign. Brigid replied that she always supported the right of Ireland to fight the occupiers and the war with Germany gave a great opportunity. She was surprised when Sinead talked about the doubts she and Fionn had about the English campaign, how if they were on the Army Council they would have sided with Tom Barry's plan to focus on the north.

Sinead could tell Brigid was puzzled and so added, 'Don't get me wrong, Brigid, Fionn and I are loyal, we have our doubts about Sean Russell who doesn't listen to anyone but we still follow orders.'

Brigid said she had no doubts on that score at all, she did not want to admit that she knew nothing about Tom Barry's plan or the other matters and so simply repeated that she wanted to help on the Peter Barnes campaign adding that she was grateful for news of Conan who had always looked out for her, 'A bit of a mix of brother and father,' she added.

Brigid refilled Sinead's cup and wondered why neither Conan or Martin had never discussed what was happening in the IRA with her. Sinead changed the subject asking if Brigid knew the Englishman with the limp who worked at Brigid's factory and was always selling his paper at the tube station. Brigid said that must be Billy and described the strike and how Billy had supported it. Sinead replied that Brigid better have a word with him and stop him trying to recruit IRA men in the Kilburn pubs, 'The army had to drive some of those Marxists out of Dublin recently and you might remind him of that and what happened to Tommy Dunne when he went back to Ireland.'

Chapter 11
The Wench of Bliss (1940)

Roisin had been fussing all day and insisting that Brigid took the extra blanket and some pots from the kitchen. Brigid knew Roisin was upset and so accepted all the gifts, carrying them outside to the cart. When Roisin suggested they would need the bulky chest of drawers from the landing, Brigid put her foot down pointing out that pushing that up Dollis Hill would break the boy's backs.

'Besides,' she added. 'Where would Diarmuid keep his old racing papers. He might start losing on the horses because of me.'

Roisin smiled but then said she could not understand why Brigid had to move for there was plenty of room for both she and Amy to stay. Brigid put down the vase she was carrying and put her arm around the older woman's shoulder explaining again that with the bombing campaign continuing Amy should not be on her own and it would not be right to disturb Diarmuid with yet more chattering women.

She put both her arms around Roisin and hugged her, 'You've been like an auntie to me, Roisin, and I promise I'll call in after work every day for a chat, make sure you have the kettle on.'

This cheered Roisin a little but she said again that she had always wanted a daughter and Brigid was exactly the daughter she would have wanted. Brigid replied that in that case she assumed there would be freshly baked biscuits with the tea.

'Not likely,' laughed Roisin. 'Not on two ounces of butter a week. Even the priest will have to do without.' Diarmuid was having his usual Saturday snooze after his walk to the friend who accepted bets but this seemed to wake him.

'No biscuits to dunk in my tea, bloody hell the Nazis have gone too far this time.'

Brigid and Roisin burst out laughing and Brigid promised to give her allowance to Roisin. Amy promised too, 'It'll be good for our waistlines, won't it, Brigid?' The others had arrived inside but only Grace heard the remark and put her fingers to her lips so only Amy could see. After further goodbyes and thanks, they filed out and John and Billy took a handle each.

Diarmuid offered to put his boots on and help but Billy shouted back, 'It's Ok leave it to the English,' and was then too far away to hear Diarmuid's reply.

Grace and Amy walked behind the wagon as the men pushed it along Dollis Hill Lane, from time-to-time Brigid who was steering from the front came round and helped push the cart over an incline. As they passed the park, they hit a steeper hill and one of the porters from the park café was recruited to help. Grace and Amy were walking some yards behind and Grace said she was pleased to hear Amy had enjoyed the book she had lent Brigid.

'We've both read it twice,' said Amy. 'I don't think I understood it properly even the second time but it was good to know others felt the same for each other as I feel for Brigid.'

Grace was pleased for she thought she had taken a risk lending Brigid. She told Amy that although many famous women loved each other, Emily Pankhurst and Ethel Smyth for example, this love was not understood by many.

'I think even John and Billy would be amazed and perplexed,' Grace added.

Amy replied that she and Brigid had decided to keep it a secret, neither of them wanted to upset their families.

'My mother just wouldn't understand and she is precious to me.'

Grace replied that most people would not understand in her opinion saying that Queen Victoria did not believe women could love each other at all and that is why it is not legal. They managed to cross the large roundabout on the North Circular Road without incident although Brigid had to wave furiously at a car which came too close. The flat was upstairs above a newsagents next door to the large London Co-operative Store and Grace remarked that they had a cinema and a library too.

'It's really quite smart is Neasden and your own tube station too. You've gone up in the world you two.'

Brigid smiled and said she and Amy were as refined a pair of modern Irish ladies as you could hope to find why they had read the latest by Djuna Barnes and were just starting Homage to Catalonia by George Orwell.

Although it was now mid-afternoon and the sun was setting Grace suggested to John and Billy that they walked back across the park and take in the view of the sunset from Dollis Hill House. They set off with Amy challenging John to race and Billy going ahead to act as the finishing line. Grace and Brigid followed and Grace looped her arm into Brigid's.

'You are making Amy very happy,' Grace said.

Brigid replied that Amy was making her very happy and she was astonished to discover Amy's capacity for learning.

'Her face is in a book every spare hour, I don't think she has ever had the time before. I can barely keep up.'

Grace said she was pleased Amy had enjoyed Ladies Almanack.

'Enjoyed it is barely the half of it Grace, she quotes it every day. She calls me the Wench of Bliss.'

Grace looked away to hide her astonishment and then squeezed Brigid's arm saying, 'You really trust me don't you, Brigid?'

In return Brigid squeezed back and asked, 'Well what is John's pet name for you?'

Grace hesitated so long Brigid thought she would not answer until Grace said John liked to tease her gently about her country upbringing. Again, Grace hesitated and Brigid asked what the name was. 'It rhymes with pumpkin,' she said putting her hand over Brigid's mouth both to stop her laughing and to make clear that this was a secret never to be shared.

They caught up with Amy and the men who were arguing about the dead heat Billy had declared. Brigid suggested they think of something nice to do to celebrate the move.

'That's the pub then,' said John but Amy suggested going to Kilburn to see the "New Maureen O'Sullivan film at the Gaumont".

John laughed and said that what she meant was the new Charles Laughton film about a hunchback. They all agreed to go and when Grace said she had never been, Amy said the chandeliers alone were worth the ten pennies. Amy added that she wanted to support Ireland's biggest film star.

'Imagine being a Dublin girl like Maureen O'Hara and moving to Hollywood, how glamorous.'

They had reached the Edgware Road and, as the light was fading, they decided to catch an omnibus to Kilburn. On the top deck they spread out across the empty seats and Billy turned round to them with his finger to his lips.

'I want you all to imagine being a girl from Tralee who moved to Neasden, how glamorous.'

Amidst laughter Amy threatened to hit Billy but as she was seated on the inside next to Grace, she pretended she could not reach him.

At the cinema they bought their tickets but, as they had an hour to spare, they walked back to the Black Lion for a drink. Brigid and Grace went to the bar to order and Brigid asked Grace to keep an eye on Amy on Wednesday explaining that she was going to Birmingham early with Sinead and others to hold a prison vigil for Peter Barnes and James McCormack who were due to hang at Winson Green.

'Amy has been to all the meetings and street stalls to try and get them reprieved and she wanted to come on Wednesday too, even her mam had heard about it back in Tralee, there's been huge campaigns all over Ireland. It is so cruel to hang people for a bomb that exploded when they were not even there and no one intended to kill anyone.'

Grace asked if she expected to be arrested and Brigid replied she did not know but she had managed to persuade Amy not to come just in case. They went back with the drinks and found Billy explaining how the WIL was apparently making gains in Liverpool and elsewhere but not recruiting as many Communist Party members as they expected.

'Pollitt was busy this winter explaining that he had been wrong and had underestimated imperialism, whether he believed this or not, and so many Communist Party members accepted the change in line, particularly as they focused their efforts on defending the USSR.'

Grace asked if this meant Billy was friends with Tom again and Billy said that for now, they had the same opposition to the imperialist war but when Hitler turned against Stalin then he believed Tom would be back supporting the war. Brigid said she had rarely seen Tom whenever she had called to see Mary and the children, he seemed to be out at meetings every night.

'Mary is just glad to have kept Patrick and Emily at home, nearly all the women at the factory have their kids back now, Nana says her lot have come back from the farm looking so much healthier than when they went, she says she might move out to Sussex herself after the war is over if she can afford it, she has a sister in Worthing and she thinks the children would love being near the sea.'

*****

Billy had already been woken by the sun warming his face through the skylight, but he was enjoying a snooze knowing that John would already be up in the next room and he would hear a knock on the door and receive a cup of tea twenty minutes before the shift began. He had once asked John how he managed to rise so early and was told his mother came from a long line of market traders and he reckoned it was in his blood to be up and about at dawn.

'It was one of my ancestors who was driven out of the temple by Jesus himself,' John had once claimed loudly at the factory, unfortunately just as Eastwood was passing and took offence, telling Tom not to allow blasphemy on the factory floor.

As Billy dozed, he was disturbed by a much gentler knock on the door than usual and soon this was followed by a soft voice asking, 'Mr Billy, can you help me please?'

He pulled on his trousers and when he opened the door was surprised to see that Mrs C was already dressed in her coat and the green flowered headscarf she always wore to go out shopping. Billy could see from her anxious look that something was wrong and he promised to be down in two minutes. He splashed his face and underarms with water put on his shirt and boots and ran downstairs. He knocked and went into the living room and from the kitchen Mrs C offered him a cup of tea which he declined. He had only been in this room once and was trying to establish what had changed until as Mrs C walked in, he realised that the large tapestry map of Sicily had been taken down and was folded in the corner. Now that he could see her in a clear light, Billy noticed that she had been crying.

'What is it Mrs C? Have you had some bad news?' Mrs C burst into tears and Billy moved forward to hold her, she sobbed on his shoulder and he could feel his shirt becoming damp.

'Everything has gone wrong Mr Billy, everything.' Billy held her a while after she had stopped crying, 'I'm so sorry Mr Billy, you are all wet, I could get you one of Ernesto's shirts to wear today.'

Billy had only seen Ernesto once or twice and as he could not speak English, they had just nodded. Ernesto was as muscular as a heavyweight boxer and he told Mrs C that he would look like a ghost in one of her husband's shirts. This made Mrs C smile and she walked into the kitchen to compose herself and when she came back, she had a towel for Billy and a plate with a cake and some jam.

'Please eat something, Mr Billy.'

Billy was hungry so he sat down and spread the jam on his cake and ate it declaring it delicious. Mrs C told him that Ernesto had been arrested in April and sent to a prison camp in Douglas. Billy did not know where Douglas was but he let Mrs C explain, 'All the Italian men have been arrested by the government in case they support the fascists.'

She said that she had promised to look after the family restaurant but now it had been attacked and damaged, she felt she had let Ernesto down.

'Will you come with me this morning, Mr Billy, my friend and his granddaughter Greta are coming in his car soon.'

Billy promised he would come but it took a while to extract the full story from Mrs C. Yesterday that oaf Eastwood had toured the factory announcing that 'The Eyeties had joined Hitler but it will do them no good.'

It seemed that Italian owned cafes in Soho had been attacked by a mob last night and she had heard windows had been smashed and more trouble was threatened. On hearing this Billy went back upstairs and asked John to come too. John agreed but asked what they would tell Eastwood or his foremen.

'I'll go and tell him we were defending people against racialist attacks,' said Billy. 'Without mentioning they were Italians.'

The older man was driving the car and he opened the door for Mrs C to get in and then opened the back door for Billy and John.

'I'm sure Greta will be pleased to share with you both,' said the man.

Billy climbed in and sat next to a young woman dressed in a cream plaited skirt and a blue padded top and with her long dark hair Billy thought she could have walked straight out of one of the smart restaurants in Rome he had seen on Pathe news. The young woman introduced herself as Greta and shook both Billy and John's hands.

'It is so kind of you both to come and look after Benedetta,' she said.

On the journey to Soho, Greta explained that she too was part of a family that owned a bakery but as that was in Clerkenwell it had escaped attack. It seemed that her grandfather was an old friend of Ernesto and they had gone to school together in Syracuse in Sicily and opened their first restaurant there.

'My Rinaldo worked there when he was only twelve,' said Mrs C. 'Such a good cook, better than his mama.'

Billy said he was sure that however good it could not taste better than the cake he had earlier. Mrs C turned round and smiled and said, 'This is the finest and most polite Englishman I have ever met, Greta and his friend John, of course.'

John doffed his cap and Greta asked where he came from. 'Yorkshire,' said John proudly but Greta simply turned her palms up and looked quizzical.

'It's south of County Durham,' said Billy causing Greta to lift her palms even more and break into a grin.

Billy told John later that when her eyes sparkled with the joke he knew he believed in love at first sight. After the men explained where Leeds was, Greta asked what cakes Billy had eaten.

'They were panini buns,' said Mrs C and Greta added, 'Sicily's finest made by Benedetta, the best Italian baker in London.'

Billy asked if he could call Mrs C, Benedetta in future for it was such a warm name that suited her. The mood had lightened and Benedetta said she would be making a special caponata for Billy and John once they had secured the shop.

'Greta and you Nonno must come, a real Sicilian meal.'

Nonno grunted and said he would bring his friscaletto so they could have a real Sicilian celebration. Before Billy could ask what this was, Benedetta said her Rinaldo had been conscripted and was in Africa, 'He does not want to fight, I know; we have never liked fighting.'

As the car drove on towards Marble Arch, Benedetta explained that Ernesto had been sent with many others to Liverpool and then to the Isle of Man.

'There are all sorts there, Billy, fascisti, Nazis and many who have fled from Hitler.' John made a brusque interruption.

'Is your husband a fascist, Mrs C?'

If Benedetta was insulted, she did not show it but turned round and explained that Ernesto was not political at all, he was the gentlest of men who missed Sicily.

'He loved to recite Dante and his favourite phrase was 'tu lasceria ogre diletta piu caramente,' which is about leaving what you love. He once told me the thing he hated most about Mussolini was his stealing of "la vision dell'Alghieri," for that terrible dirge.' Greta explained that Ernesto meant the fascist anthem, Giovinecca.

'I hate to think of Ernesto without music, surrounded by fascists,' Benedetta said.

The mood in the car had darkened again and as they pulled into Frith Street Greta said despite the attacks last night there would be many of the Italians who did indeed support Mussolini and they would not necessarily be friendly to the English, especially English socialists.

'Enemies all around then,' said John. 'Perhaps I should have brought a spanner.' Benedetta said there was to be no fighting they just needed to repair any damage and protect the café.

As they got out of the car it was clear there were no troublemakers around but everywhere was the sound of hammering and sawing wood and of glass being swept up. The windows of Benedetta's café had been smashed and as they stood outside, John pointed to a sign in the next-door café which read: "This is a Swiss owned restaurant. No Italians or Germans work here". Greta smiled and said they had done the same in Clerkenwell, her shop was now a French owned business although no one there could speak French.

When they stepped inside the shop a fierce argument was being conducted in Italian between several men, it involved a lot of shouting and Billy could make out the occasional reference to Il Duce. Benedetta gestured to John and Billy to come outside and explained that the fascisti were supporting Mussolini, others think he is a buffoon for joining the Germans and Ernesto's partner, Andrea, is arguing that Italy had it made and was selling to both sides and now it is a disaster.

Andrea offered a cigar to Billy who declined but John took one for he knew Tiny liked a quiet smoke. John said he would smoke it later after he had helped clear up. Andrea leant over, which seemed a strain as he was dressed in a tight fitting but immaculate blue suit and said, 'I speak English very badly but Mussolini is an ass. I want to weep when I think of Mazzini and his followers who died to create Italy and now this buffoon is in charge.'

He added that the argument would soon subside there was no need to worry, protecting the businesses would unite them all. John replied by complimenting Andrea on his perfect English and said he was proud to help and was pleased to have met so many fine Italians today and would like to know more about Mazzini.

'Though please keep me away from the fascists or there will be trouble,' he added.

Andrea suggested that they board up the café until new windows could be ordered and then help others protect their shops. It took all morning to protect the shop fronts and whenever Greta came near, Billy was sure to be hammering nails or lifting planks of wood.

'I'm going to tell Eastwood how to get you to work harder, Billy,' John joked as Greta approached.

She seemed to have misheard or misunderstood for she said that they had worked very hard indeed and she wished all Sicilian men would spend less time smoking and arguing and more time working. In turn Andrea and Benedetta heard this last remark as they came out with two trays covered in bread and olives and various dips.

'It is siesta time,' said Benedetta as Andrea returned again with chairs for everyone and finally with two bottles of red wine. As a glass was given to John, Andrea poured a little into his glass and asked if he would sample the wine. John had never drunk wine before and looked around desperately for help until Greta said, 'Sniff the bouquet, John and swill a little around your mouth.'

John tried his best but found the wine bitter and vinegary and he spat it out.

'Excellent,' clapped Benedetta. 'Our wine is famous, full of berries. Quick, Andrea, pour our guests a large glass.'

They sat in a circle talking about the attack. Andrea said he thought it was just a few drunken soldiers and it would not happen again. Greta disagreed she said her cousin had telephoned from Edinburgh last night and had sounded terrified. Hundreds had been arrested and some of the Italian men had been injured in the fighting. Billy said that settled the matter, he and John would be staying the night and he was going to call his comrades to come too.

Andrea was worried that if there were too many of them a major fight might occur, so it was agreed that Billy and John would stay and only call for help if needed. Greta said that she would cook everyone pasta con le sarde for they had a fresh delivery of seafood that morning and she would arrange for it to be brought over.

'Sounds delicious,' Billy said, 'And we will wash it down with English beer, which John and I will provide.' Greta had noticed that neither man had touched their wine but said nothing.

The afternoon passed with further boarding up of cafes and shops and then they sat down again in the evening sun to eat. Nonno asked if his could be saved for he intended to stay the night too but had to give Greta a lift home first, tomorrow early he would give John and Billy a lift so they did not get into trouble at work. Greta shook hands with John and thanked him and then thanked Billy saying she would arrange for some blankets to be sent over later and how lucky Benedetta was to have such wonderful and helpful tenants and that she would never forget their kindness. Billy said it had been a pleasure and thanked Greta for the meal. He leant over so the others could not hear and asked if they might meet again. Greta leant up and gently kissed Billy on the cheek saying that it would not be possible for her husband would not like it.

Chapter 12
An American in London

Brigid had not heard from Maureen in a while and so she was delighted to receive a phone call at work. Maureen of course had put on her thickest west Cork accent and simply told Brenda that there was an emergency at home. Brenda was suspicious but decided that it would be an excuse to stretch her legs find Brigid and stop for a chat with Amy on the way back. Brigid dashed to the office and through the glass partition could see Willans' reading his newspaper and pretending not to see her. Maureen was excited and told Brigid about the huge bomb in Hackney and wanted Brigid to come over and see her and the site. Brigid agreed to come over on Sunday but made Maureen promise they would shelter if there was a bombing raid. Brigid told Amy later that Maureen had never been so excited as the day the milk cart got stuck in the school gate so that a whole war was sure to be heaven for her. Amy laughed and said she would like to meet Maureen, 'To find out the truth about the naughtiness Brigid O'Brien had got up to as a girl.'

Amy said that war was one of those events that changed everyone in some way and sometimes in a good way for…'without the war, I would never have fallen in love with you.'

They risked a small hug, breaking the rules they had agreed on and Brigid said she would go over on Sunday whilst Amy was in church thanking God for their meeting.

'I think God approves of our love, Brigid.' Brigid did not comment but promised to invite Maureen to come for lunch soon.

The bomb had made a huge crater and Maureen insisted that Brigid take a good look. Brigid reluctantly leant over and as she did so she felt a heavy shove in her back and had to windmill her arms frantically to save herself. Maureen helped to pull her back and simultaneously yelled, 'Watch yerself yer big bastard,' at the man behind.

It took a moment for Brigid to settle herself, straighten her coat and recover her composure but when she did look round she saw a huge man, at least six and a half feet tall, dressed in a stylish cream gabardine which opened onto a muscular chest covered in a blue polo neck and tapering down to long grey trousers ending in polished black brogues. As Maureen pointed out later, over a half pint of Truman's in the Bird Cage, he was the best-looking guy she had seen since the war started.

'If not ever,' she had added.

For now, Hank puffed an apology. 'Sorry ma'am I didn't mean to push you but there was pressure from behind, are you OK?'

Brigid said she was but that did not stop the flow of regrets from the man which only concluded when he asked if he might buy them a drink.

'Yes,' replied Maureen before Brigid could speak. 'My local is just down there in Columbia Road.' On the way, Hank continued to apologise and explained that he was out exploring and using his camera for the first time as he had only arrived in London two weeks before. Maureen hogged the conversation asking endless questions and, noticing the leather case on Hank's arm, asking if he would take their photograph.

Once they were settled in the snug, for the saloon was full of noisy market traders, Hank went to fetch some drinks and Brigid reminded Maureen that she had only got engaged to Frank three weeks ago. Maureen appeared not to hear, or at least she did not reply, for her eyes were fixed on the man at the bar. He returned and sat next to Brigid and dinking their glasses he toasted.

'Two beautiful Irish girls, far from home.' Maureen returned the compliment toasting "handsome Americans" much to the dismay of Brigid.

The awkward silence that followed was only broken when the man introduced himself as Hank and explained he was attached to the American embassy in Grosvenor Square. Maureen pressed him for details but he would only say his work was classified and they were watching the enemy. Maureen loudly blurted out.

'We've found us a spy, Brigid,' so that two men glanced at them and Maureen was apologetic.

'I'm sorry, I've never met a spy before.' Hank smiled and put his fingers to his lips. 'It's our secret,' he replied softly. 'If it gets out, I'll be back across the pond in no time.'

After half an hour, Brigid thought she had better remind Maureen of her shift.

'Damn it's half past, I'll be in trouble if I don't go now, I was late yesterday.'

Brigid could see her friend's disappointment and so suggested they might meet up with Hank in London and she could let Maureen know. Hank agreed and took Maureen's hand and kissed it.

'Au revoir Madame, until we meet again.'

Now they were alone they chatted freely and Brigid was keen to discover something of America. Hank spoke about his home town in Illinois and Brigid decided to be straight about it and confess she had never heard of Peoria and was not sure where Illinois was.

'I have a cousin from Fermanagh who lives in Brooklyn,' she said, 'but we only ever got one postcard from him which showed a railway above the streets.'

Hank smiled and said he had never heard of Whiddy island either but he had met a man in Washington DC a few weeks ago who came from Wexford. Brigid asked if Hank's parents still lived in Peoria and Hank paused as if trying to remember. Then he said quietly, 'Ma and Pa were mown down by hired strike-breakers in the big strike of 1913. I was only nineteen and it was kind of hard to take.'

Brigid expressed her sympathy and told of her own father's death when she was only five, Hank wanted to ask more but sensed Brigid did not want to tell more.

'Well, that's all very cheerful,' he said. 'We've only known each other five minutes and soon we'll be making ourselves blubber.'

Brigid laughed and Hank said he had nearly knocked her into a deep bomb crater and now depressed her, she would probably never want to meet another American again.

Hank disappeared in search of a "washroom" and whilst he was gone Brigid realised, from what he had just said that he must be well over forty years old, she had assumed he was a little older than her or possibly thirty at most. When Hank returned with two glasses of whisky, she protested that she never drank so early but she took a swig and studied his face. There were a couple of faint elephant ridges on his forehead but otherwise he had the fresh complexion of a younger man. Brigid must have smiled at the memory of her Aunt Catriona pretending to wave a trunk at Brigid every time she frowned so that Hank asked if she found his face funny.

'Oh no,' said Brigid quickly. 'It's just that you have such a young face,' and Hank interjected. 'For an older guy.'

They smiled drank up and Brigid got up to leave and, once outside, said the strong breeze reminded her of the wind across Bantry Bay. Hank said they might smell Peoria soon for after the sewage came his dad did not take him fishing anymore.

'He loved to go to Senachwine Lake but it was ruined like the whole of the Illinois river and it really saddened him.'

They walked down towards Shoreditch station and on the way, Brigid asked again about the strike. 'We were all in it,' said Hank. 'Four of us in the family worked at Avery Implements and the strike took off in May. Most of the Wobblies organisers turned up and my dad helped pay the lodgings of the agitator, Jim Cannon. They became friends and I went to his wedding to Lisa, they had less than twenty dollars between them.'

Brigid was listening carefully and realised that name was familiar.

'Is that James P Cannon?' she asked. Hank looked astonished and asked how she knew of him. Brigid explained she had a friend Billy who talked about him and that she knew he was a Trotskyist leader in America.

'Yeah, he's carrying the flame now as Trotsky is holed up in Mexico,' said Hank adding that he would like to meet Billy if possible. Hank scribbled down a telephone number and handed it to Brigid who said maybe Hank would like to meet Billy in The Crown.

'Royal huh,' said Hank and Brigid shouted back, 'No way,' as she headed for her platform.

It was two days later that Maureen was surprised by the sound of a car horn behind her as she and Lottie left the factory. Turning round she saw a beautiful plum and green car slowly moving along the kerb beside them.

'Look, it's a Roller,' said Lottie but Maureen had already noticed the driver, 'Hank, what are you doing here?'

Hank pulled over, introduced himself to Lottie and explained he was hoping to take Maureen out to supper in a perfect little pub he knew.

'Oh no Hank, I can't go out to supper like this, I've got oil in places you wouldn't believe.'

Hank smiled and said he would take Maureen home so she could freshen up and change if she wanted to. Lottie insisted on joining the short ride up Bethnal Green Road and in his mirror, Hank could see her waving to her workmates as she passed. Lottie was reluctant to get out and wanted to fetch her mother to see the car but Hank said he was in a hurry and Americans hated missing their food. He handed Maureen a parcel with the words Post Exchange stamped on, and inside was a delicate pink scarf and a pair of nylons.

'You couldn't look more stunning Maureen but these are just a thank you for letting me take you out.' Maureen thanked him and rushing in to hide her blushing face, said she would be 'ten minutes.'

Maureen quickly washed in the scullery bowl and thanked God she had a clean blouse and underwear to go with her only blue skirt. Carefully she caressed her stockings over her legs taking care not to catch them on her finger nails. Whilst coating her nails she admired her legs in the mirror. *Betty Grable, eat your heart out,* she chuckled to herself. She rubbed her shoes on the blanket but they were simply too old to shine up properly so she hoped her new scarf would distract people from too close an examination of her footwear. Back in the front of the car and as excited as when she was six at Christmas, Maureen wondered where they were going.

'West End, ma'am?' Hank asked and she replied that would be perfect.

Soon they were passing Green Park and Hank parked in Queen Street. He asked if she would like a stroll to see where the King lived but she replied, 'No thanks, that doesn't interest me, besides I'm hungry and I'm on the arm of a handsome American.'

They walked to Sheperds Market and Hank pointed to a sweet little corner pub called The Grapes.

'Modest looking, I know, but fantastic food and there might be someone famous at the bar. Inside it was quiet and above the bar was a sign saying, "For Service Please Ask Sylvester".'

A barman in an unusual silver apron soon appeared from behind a mirror and exclaimed, 'Why Mr Trotter sir, what an honour to have your company, American gentlemen and beautiful women always welcome here.'

Hank returned a warm greeting and asked for a bowl of oysters and a bottle of the usual.

'Of course sir, oysters and champagne it is,' replied Sylvester and Maureen caught his wink to Hank. Maureen did not care and she supposed oysters could not be much different from the mussels her father brought home from Skibbereen market. Nor did Maureen worry much about sex, she usually enjoyed making love so long as she could not get pregnant and, she reasoned, a mature American would make a nice change from the occasional pimply boy she shared a silent bed with, keeping as quiet as possible so as not to wake the landlady.

Hank enjoyed showing her how to open oysters, squeeze them with lemon and swallow them whole. Maureen tried a couple but found them too briny and had to wash them down with gulps of champagne.

'Hey steady on,' Hank laughed. 'Or you'll get tipsy.'

Maureen apologised and said the champagne must be expensive but Hank said not to worry, everything was on the US government expense account. Maureen did not want to say she did not like champagne and would prefer a milk stout so she was relieved and amazed when the steak course arrived and presently Hank asked if she had spotted anyone suspicious in the bar. Maureen had to reply that she was enjoying her meal so much that she had not noticed. Hank told her not to turn round but the couple drinking gin and tonics were MI5, probably trying to work out who she was and, more importantly, who she worked for.

'You mean I'll have a file in British intelligence,' Maureen whispered and Hank had to admit this was likely especially when they discovered she was from Cork. Maureen pondered this awhile and Hank apologised but Maureen said it was quite glamorous really and she had nothing to hide. Maureen talked a little about life on the farm at home and how she knew it was not for her and besides she had two brothers who could manage easily.

'This is the sort of evening I always dreamt would happen if I came to London.'

She asked how Hank had known where she worked and Hank confessed to asking at the Bird Cage about the beautiful blonde. A lot of them knew you and one of them, seemed a bit drunk, claimed to be related.

'Oh no, cousin Hoisin, he'll be blabbering to ma straightaway, he seems to think he has a duty to watch over me. Be careful what you tell him Hank..'

He promised never to visit the Bird Cage again, 'Why would I, now I've found you' and he took her fingers and kissed them. Maureen responded by leaning over and kissing him passionately on the lips and when she had finished said, 'Put that in your file, Britain.' Hank smiled and said she was the most refreshing and beautiful person he had met in ages, he paused and asked if she would like to come back to his flat for Bourbon.

Maureen asked what this was and said she would, adding, 'And after perhaps you will make American love to me.' They left hand in hand and Maureen turned and winked at Sylvester who waved back.

Together they strolled across the road and into Belgrave Square, they paused for an embrace and Hank then guided her into one of the buildings, past a sleepy concierge and into an elevator until at the first floor they got out and Hank unlocked the door and, as she was ushered in, she felt his hand at the top of her leg.

'Hey mister,' she said, trying to mimic his accent. 'I was promised a Bourbon and I don't want to ladder these new nylons.' Hank disappeared into the kitchen and she could hear ice clinking into glasses. When he emerged carrying a tray, he was astonished to find Maureen draped across the armchair, most of her clothes neatly stacked on the table. He offered her a sip of Bourbon and she pulled a face so he put the tray down and picked her up and kissing her said, 'Holy Jesus, I thought you Catholic girls suffered from tremendous guilt.'

He carried her through to his bedroom as Maureen murmured, 'I never really listened at Sunday school, did I miss something?'

Afterwards Maureen lay on the bed watching and listening as Hank gently snored, in a quiet and gentlemanly way she thought, and she propped herself up to admire his torso with its tufty chest hair starting to turn white. She gently peeled the damp condom off him and carried it to the waste bin. He was still asleep so she ran the bath and soaked in luxury adding whatever was in the tiny bottles to the water. When she was dry and dressed, he was still asleep so she found a pencil and left a note 'thanks—lovely meal and company x'.

*****

Mary told Brigid that Tom had not been happy since he realised he was too old to be called up.

'He's been grumpy for weeks, keeps repeating that he's fitter at forty-three than half the twenty-year-olds he knows.'

Brigid smiled and said in any case Tom would be given exemption for without him production at the factory would be in chaos and John had wanted to go and fight too but Tiny had said he was essential to the tank production and persuaded him not to for Tiny says, it would take two years to train a woman to learn what John knows.

'A lot of men undervalue us, don't they, Brigid?'

Brigid had to agree saying it was the same in the republican movement and Mary said the same about the Communist Party from what she had seen.

'Somehow the men are always too busy to look after the children,' she added.

Brigid said she thought the Communist Party was opposed to the war and so why did Tom want to join up.

'Oh, he's loyal to the Party, of course and won't join the LDV but he doesn't like being officially classified as older.'

Mary paused for a moment and thinking she had been over-critical of her husband added, 'Tom's a wonderful father though and often says keeping Patrick and Emily home was the right decision.'

'He's an outstanding man for admitting he was wrong at all,' Brigid said laughing. 'Very few of them do.'

Mary had taken on a cleaning job at a large house on Bishops Avenue next to Hampstead Heath and had to work Saturday afternoons. Brigid and Amy had volunteered to look after them when Tom was at a meeting which was nearly every Saturday. Today though Amy was shopping in London for her sisters and brothers in Tralee and so when Mary had arrived home with her usual fresh scones, she realised she had one too many.

'Save one for Tom,' suggested Brigid. 'And put some jam on.'

'That's rationed too isn't it, I've only got half of a tiny jar of Chivers strawberry left.'

Brigid said she and Amy had agreed to give up jam as it was too fattening but they had a jar of Hartleys left and she would bring it next week. Mary was grateful but said she would have to steam the label off for Tom had banned Hartleys as he did not like their advert as the First World War soldiers favourite in the trenches. Brigid looked bemused and Mary said, 'Oh yes we've got plenty of political principles in this house, that's why I'm scrubbing floors for the posh folk!'

Later that evening Amy and Brigid entertained Grace and John for supper. There had been regular broadcasts on the works radio about the evacuation from France and Brigid said she had mixed feelings for she was always glad to see British forces defeated and scuttling away by sea but she did not like the look of the Nazis either. No one liked to ask Brigid about the IRA campaign which seemed to have come to an end so they got to discuss their friends and when Grace mentioned Helmut, John said Billy had gone to Newcastle for a meeting

Helmut was speaking at and had promised he would pass on their good wishes. Grace said Billy was always at a meeting these days, dashing off after work most nights and all the weekend.

'He'll never get a girlfriend that way,' said Amy. 'It's a shame for he is the nicest fella' and she almost added if you like men but caught Brigid's stare before she did so. John had told them all about the night in Soho and how one of the men they had worked with that day called Bosco had drowned on the Arandora after the government arrested him the next week and imprisoned him in Liverpool and then tried to send him to Canada.'

'I heard about that,' said Brigid. 'Over a thousand men drowned and many of them were Italian and German who had opposed Mussolini and Hitler. The British government just doesn't value human life.'

John lightened the mood by adding the detail of how Billy had been crushed to discover Greta was married.

'Was she good-looking, this Greta?' asked Grace.

John fell for it. 'Oh, she was very beautiful, could easily be a film star.'

The silence was prolonged until John realised his mistake and added, 'Like any of the fine women here tonight.'

Grace had made a pretend show of leaving the room and John was forced to go after her so that Amy had the chance to squeeze Brigid's hand. When Grace came back holding John's hand, she asked what could be done for Billy, surely there was a woman somewhere in the factory who would not mind Billy being so politically active. Brigid said that Tom had brought a new girl round late yesterday, her name was Martha Long and she was starting on Monday.

'Tom said something about she had just moved down and was another socialist for the ranks,' Brigid reported. 'And I have to admit she seemed attractive enough.'

'Operation Billy and Martha starts Monday,' Amy said. 'Top secret, hush-hush, you all know what to do.'

The next day John, who was eager to hear about the Newcastle meeting, had arranged to meet Billy off the train. It was a sunny Sunday and Grace suggested they took some sandwiches and had a picnic in Regents Park. They found a large beech tree to shelter from the sun and Billy opened the beers he had brought.

'Mustn't drink too much beer,' said Grace. 'It must be nearly ninety degrees now and it'll go to our heads.'

Billy told them about the open-air meeting in Biggs market, 'There were some great speeches by new comrades I hadn't met, Roy Tearse, Jock Haston and Dan Smith and there was a woman comrade from Binns department store in Sunderland who made a great speech about the shop assistants union conference she had been to at Easter.'

Grace asked what had happened and Billy explained that the union conference had carried a motion describing the war as an imperialist war for the defence of British and French colonial possessions and therefore as a capitalist war the working-class had no interest in supporting it.

'It was a woman comrade from John Lewis in London who moved the resolution and the Communist Party voted for it, it caused a sensation in America.'

John asked about Helmut and Billy said he was fine except he was hiding from internment, probably in Scotland but he did not say where exactly. He had come down in a van and they had met later last night, Helmut had remembered Christmas well and made me swear never to reveal he had sung a religious song. We had a good discussion and Jock told us about his time in Ireland with Ted Grant, they had won over some Irish republicans to socialism and had received a death threat from the IRA.

'No wonder they came back,' said John but Billy replied that Jock agreed they had made a mistake thinking they would be arrested here and closed down by the government.

'As Jock put it, our immediate task is to pose a big enough threat to the imperialist war effort to make the state take notice.'

Grace said it was obvious Billy had been impressed and Billy replied that he had been but there were really only a handful of comrades actually living in Newcastle and Roy had asked him to consider moving up there. They both looked at Billy but he said nothing and simply stretched out putting his coat across his face. Grace looked across to the edge of the zoo and mentioned that all the poisonous snakes had been killed when war was declared in case they escaped in any bombing.

'They often get escapes though I've heard,' said John, causing Billy to sit up quickly to find Grace and John laughing.

Chapter 13
Mr Rude

When Brigid met Grace and her new friend Martha at clocking-out on Saturday lunchtime she was delighted to hear they were going swimming next morning and she readily agreed to join them. If there was one thing Brigid missed in London it was the sea and skinny-dipping with her friends after school. Next morning a thin sun was up and Brigid arranged to meet Amy later in the park for lunch as Amy could not swim and did not want to spoil Brigid's fun. Brigid started early and was one of the first in the Lido and was soon swimming fast in the kidney shaped pool, she imagined she was racing Conan again and wondered where he was now.

By the time she stopped to rest, she could see the Lido had filled up with every bench occupied and across the pool Grace was waving and she walked round drying herself as she went. The warmer weather after a wet August so far was bringing family parties and Brigid decided it would be too crowded for more swimming. She sat for a while with Grace and Martha and heard the familiar Scouse traces in Martha's account of why she was in London. John arrived and they talked some more with Brigid asking where Billy was.

'He was meant to come but duty calls, they've murdered Trotsky and there is an emergency meeting.'

Once Brigid had dried herself and changed, she excused herself saying that, she was a country girl at heart and needed some space away from crowds on her day off.

'Good to meet yer Brigid, maybe we can have a bevvy after work one night?' asked Martha and Brigid said she would like that.

She walked up the bank towards Dollis Hill House and turned to see the view with the Wembley Towers bathed in a creamy haze about two miles away, she and Amy had promised to walk there just to sample the atmosphere outside next time there was a big football match. Brigid smiled to herself at the thought of how Amy had to experience everything she could, it was sometimes hard to keep up with such an enthusiast for life itself. Brigid sat on the bench alongside the pond, she had arranged to meet Amy here and she put her bag with the wet swimming costume under the bench and her gas mask alongside her for suddenly the threat of bombing was real and the factory had been buzzing on Friday with news of the bomb which fell in Harrow.

Gazing across the pond she saw a flash of black and white alight on a tree on the small island on the pond and disappear. Brigid realised the bird must have gone into a hole in the tree and kept her eyes on the tree for several minutes until she heard a voice.

'Excuse me,' it said. 'But would you mind terribly if I sat here and pinned my hair. You see I've walked a few miles today and somehow, I've lost a hairpin.' Brigid turned and saw an extremely tall young woman with a blue hat in her hand and she instinctively took a hairpin out of her own hair and handed it to the woman.

'Thanks awfully,' said the woman who Brigid now realised was in full military uniform. 'We've got the afternoon off and I just wanted to find some green open space. I miss the countryside so much.'

Brigid agreed and explained that she was watching the tree because a bird had flown in and she wondered what it was. The young woman asked if she may watch also and Brigid nodded, indicating the bench. She sat down and said, 'My name's Felicity,' but Brigid did not reply so after a while Felicity explained that she had been brought up on the coast in Holkham village and was used to riding the beaches which stretched for miles to Hunstanton.

'Of course, the land is very flat but we used to meet at the Earl of Leicester's place, Holkham Hall, wonderful deserted beaches there we could ride for hours. I remember once when we were younger the Princesses came to stay, the younger one Margaret was quite naughty and the Queen Mother told us all off for following her and hiding in a wardrobe.'

They continued to look at the tree Brigid realised she was talking to a member of the British armed forces and an aristocratic one at that and felt she needed to explain she did not know England outside London.

'Were you born here?' asked Felicity and Brigid replied she was born in Ireland.

'Oh, I'm afraid I don't know anything about Ireland, we weren't allowed to talk politics at the table you see.'

Brigid did not see but Felicity carried on talking saying that last night at dinner in the mess one of the girls was telling a rather risqué joke and was overheard by the sergeant who told her that Mr Rude was not invited to supper.

'I got into trouble for laughing but you see that is exactly what mother used to say to us at home except it was tea not supper.'

Before Brigid could reply Felicity tapped her on the shoulder and pointed to the tree where the bird had emerged and was climbing a little up the trunk. Brigid could see it had a flash of red on its head and Felicity leant over and said, 'Greater Spotted Woodpecker, we used to see them all the time in Holkham woods.'

The bird flew off and Brigid said she had never seen a woodpecker before, had never heard of them in Ireland, and thanked Felicity. Felicity said she would have to be going for she only had a pass until four o'clock, she stood up and Brigid asked which regiment she was in.

'Well, you see, I have been quite bold and decided not to join the FANYs. Most of the girls from the balls were joining but Diana and I, that's my elder sister, decided we wanted to see the world and so we braved the interview with Lady Cholmondeley and joined the WRNS. Such a mixed crowd, I'll say, in our billet in Finchley.'

Felicity hesitated and put her hand to her mouth, 'Oh no, I shouldn't have told you that.'

Brigid smiled, 'Don't worry, your secret is safe with me. Although I don't think the Wrens are Hitler's top target are they?'

Felicity replied that it was very strict and now the bombing had started they were only allowed out with a special pass on Sundays and she had to be back by three.

'Everyone else is too scared but Diana and I managed to sneak out last Thursday night and went for supper at Claridges with our brother Reginald. It was scrumptious but I don't know when I'll be back there, the food in Finchley is not as good I can assure you.' Brigid laughed politely and hoped Felicity got back in time.

'Oh yes I'll manage, after all the marching I've been doing I could reach Windsor Castle in time for tea.'

Felicity laughed and thanking Brigid for the hairpin marched off for a few yards before turning to wave.

Brigid watched the woodpecker fly off and was wondering how easy it would be to befriend British soldiers and get useful information from them. She had not received any contact from anyone and, apart from a couple of small explosions in March, either the bombing campaign had been called off or the movement was regrouping, so she made a mental note to meet Sinead next week to find out. Just then Amy arrived having climbed the hill from the other side, she sat on the bench and asked who that beautiful soldier was that Brigid had been talking to.

'Oh, I'm expanding my contacts in the English aristocracy.'

Brigid squeezed Amy's hand hidden behind the gas mask holder and explained how the other half lived.

Chapter 14
Brighton Outing

Tom had stopped providing Billy with the Daily Worker months ago, indeed the two men barely spoke, but every day at work John found a copy by his work table. Occasionally he would find Tiny glancing through it and Tiny would usually put it down immediately muttering that it was nonsense. John had heard the news from Billy that Trotsky had been murdered and his death had been reported in the newspapers on Thursday. John read in the Daily Worker that day that Trotsky's secretary, Franck Johnson, had attacked him with a pickaxe. By Friday the Daily Worker was reporting Trotsky's death and John read the article headed "A Counter-Revolutionary Gangster Passes" aloud to Billy and Grace that evening.

'It's grim reading Billy,' said John. But Billy insisted "the lies" be read out.

'With the passing of Leon Trotsky, the counter-revolution has lost one of its outstanding organisers and demagogues.'

'Stop,' said Billy. 'Just tell me who they say murdered Trotsky.' John found the passage.

'The various Trotskyist sects, throughout the world waged fratricidal war against each other and the recent attack on Trotsky may well have been an incident in that war.'

Grace and John could see the anger in Billy's face but he simply said, 'After a failed attempt Stalin has finally succeeded in murdering the leader of the Red Army and the lie machine is at full strength.'

He picked the paper up and glanced at it, 'I could have guessed it was that wretch JR Campbell.'

On the Saturday shift John asked Tom if he thought Stalin's agents had murdered Trotsky. Tom replied that it was probably a rival Trotskyist behind the murder.

'But whoever did it has rid the world of an enemy of the Soviet Union.'

John said nothing but simply looked at Tom that seemed to Tom to express both disbelief and sorrow. Tom sensed, at that moment, that John was one recruit he would never make.

*****

As it turned out Operation Billy and Martha proved unnecessary for, on the first Friday in September, Martha told Billy that she was missing the sea badly and asked if he would like to come with her to Brighton on Saturday. John was amazed when Billy told him and reported to Grace that he knew Billy was supposed to be leading an intervention by the WIL at a Communist Party rally in Hyde Park on Sunday.

'He must have reported in sick,' said John. 'Let's hope there are no Trotskyists having an ice-cream on the seafront.'

Billy met Martha at Victoria station at nine, as they passed through to the train, they were stopped by an ARP warden who asked them to produce their gas masks for inspection. The warden told them there had been recent bombing raids in Brighton and asked if they really needed to travel. Martha replied it was urgent family business, their mother was ill but they would be coming back later that afternoon. The warden, who although only thirty or so had a paunch as well as a moustache which made him look much older, smiled at Martha and said it was a pleasure to meet two young people so devoted to their mother. Once on the train Billy looked hard at Martha until she said she only told harmless fibs when she was excited. Billy said he was pleased to be going to the seaside too and hoped it would remain sunny.

'Of course, it will, Billy,' she replied. 'I wonder if it will be as exciting as Blackpool.'

Billy had never been to Blackpool as his dad used to say it was a waste of time crossing the Pennines just to get soaked with rain but he asked why Martha liked it. Martha said the three of them, her mam and dad, used to go three or four times a year when her dad was working.

'We loved it all, the performers, the Irish Sea to swim in and a bevvy on the pier. Dad said he was descended from an ornamental dancer and insisted she had had married his grandad but mum said that was only a family story. Even though

Dad once produced an advertising poster signed by one of the swimmers, Louisa Webb her name was, mum still did not believe it.'

Billy was enjoying listening to Martha but he wondered if she ever paused for breath, he had never heard speech so fast and the Liverpool accent made it more difficult for him to follow. He interrupted to ask what an ornamental dancer was and Martha obliged with descriptions of women in tanks of seawater drinking tea underwater and performing acrobatics.

'They were a real hit on the piers apparently but they had died out by the time I started going.'

Billy changed topic asking if Martha was born in Liverpool and she replied that she was and her dad was but her mum was a Suffragette from Manchester. Billy said he thought that was where the Pankhursts' came from.

'Too right, Billy, my mum was born in Cheetam Hill and we used to visit me gran there when I was little. Anyway, before the First World War, mum was locked up for smashing windows and when she got out, she went straight to a local meeting where Winston Churchill was campaigning to keep his seat. Sylvia Pankhurst was there and kept asking if he would support votes for women. Churchill was so annoyed he asked her on stage to ask the question and then made her sit on a chair at the back whilst he told the crowd he never would support votes for such unruly people. Sylvia would not be quiet of course so the Liberals locked her in a room and mum and others went round the side and squeezed her out through a tiny window. Mum always laughs when she tells that story.'

'Churchill was a bad one then and a bad one now,' Billy opined.

'Oh, don't get me started, he'd set the bizzies on his own mum that one. Sent a battleship, a bloody cruiser up the Mersey in the big strike, then he turned the police on the crowd that was out to see Tom Mann speak, we call it Bloody Sunday in Liverpool, my dad worked in the docks with one of the two lads shot, Michael Prendergast his name was, shot in cold blood by one of the Hussars sent in. I forget the name of the other fellow but they were doing nothing except being on strike. My dad had a big role in the National Union of Dock Workers and my mum was in the Women Workers Union at Myfield Sugar Works. My uncle Jimmy had to have stitches after the bizzies attacked them for nothing, he used to show them to me when I was little, right across his scalp they were.'

The train stopped and Martha paused and smiled at Billy.

'Sorry,' she said. 'I do rattle on sometimes.'

Billy said it was great listening to her and it was clear she came from socialist royalty. This pleased her and she leant across and touched his hand. As the train moved off, she noticed the green view outside and asked Billy where they were. Billy said the last station was Haywards Heath and Martha said perhaps they could come there another time and go for a walk and a picnic. Billy said he would like to and they sat in silence a moment admiring the view.

Soon there were in Brighton and there were troops lined up on the platform waiting for a train, Martha was walking a little ahead and as she passed a soldier issued a low wolf-whistle. Billy caught up just as she turned and said loudly, 'Don't ask for what you can't afford,' to the offending soldier, causing his mates to laugh at him.

Martha walked off telling Billy she knew how to look after herself, there were some men back in Clayton Street who crossed the road to avoid her and her mates. Billy said he was duly warned but Martha replied by taking his arm and squeezing it. Again, just past the ticket barrier were two ARP wardens who were warning people of the dangers of bombing raids. Billy asked how many raids had happened and the warden told him it was regular now; a train had been bombed on another Southern line two weeks ago and even a brewery had been hit in Brighton.

Billy assured the man they would listen carefully for warnings and make sure they knew where the shelters were and discovering that the brewery was nearby, he asked Martha if she would like to see. Martha agreed and, having asked for directions, they walked past a large church which the ARP warden had called the Cathedral. It was clear that Tamplins brewery had taken a big hit and, as it was the first bomb damage they had seen, they stood looking for a while. An old man with a muscular black and white dog on a lead came close and Martha bent down to stroke the dog.

'Not many folk will do that,' the man said. 'Staffies have a bad name with some but she is a real pet of a dog. We come out early these days to avoid the Nazi bombers, don't we, girl?'

Billy asked about the brewery but the man replied it was not as bad as it looked saying the Albion brewery was closed and only used for storage.

'Not much beer lost, I reckon,' he said tugging on the dog lead and heading towards the church.

Martha had kept her arm in Billy's and now tugged him away saying she could smell the sea. They reached the front and Martha said, 'Let's go down to the sea, it always makes me feel better.'

They walked down the steps to the beach crunching the pebbles Martha remarking that the beach was not sandy like Blackpool beach and there was nowhere for children to build sandcastles. Billy agreed saying that we should feel sorry for the poor southerners if this was the best they had. As they reached the incoming tide Billy stumbled and Martha had to grab his coat to prevent him falling over. They laughed and Billy put his hand in Martha's. They walked on until Martha found a candy floss stall and bought one to share. She fed pieces to Billy who soon had a pink moustache.

Martha laughed and took out her hand mirror to show him and then stopped his hand as he reached to clean his face instead saying she was not letting good candy floss go to waste and, pulling his head gently towards her she licked his moustache and then his lips until her tongue was in his mouth. They kissed again and then Martha asked why Billy did not have a girlfriend. Billy shrugged not knowing what to say and Martha said, 'Well you've got one now, Billy Stainsby.'

Billy was pleased and put his arm around Martha who said that sheltering like this reminded her a bit of the Dockers umbrella near home. She explained that the Liverpool docks had an overground railway and everyone would shelter underneath when it rained hard.

'I used to take dad his sandwiches and was allowed to sit there with him sometimes, mum said he spoilt me, because I was an only child.'

They sat in silence for a while and watched some young children being pushed by a youth on a swing roundabout. Martha asked Billy if he had any brothers or sisters and Billy, surprised at being asked about himself, explained about David and recounted the dash home to find him.

'I haven't seen him since January though, he'll be twelve next month and I must get back to see him.'

They got up and walked on hand in hand along the promenade towards Hove until Martha said, 'So your little brother is a bit simple then.'

'I don't think so,' replied Billy. 'Just different and the sweetest brother you could want.'

Martha was not sure if she had offended Billy so she squeezed his hand and Billy squeezed back. At Billy's suggestion they turned back towards Brighton in search of some lunch. Soon they were sharing a pasty and looking out watching the waves, Billy said the sea was alright but the waves seemed a bit insipid compared to the North Sea and Martha repeated, 'Poor southerners,' causing them both to laugh.

They strolled through the lanes of shops but Billy noticed Martha was not really that interested in clothes or jewellery and suggested they wandered back to the station and found a pub. Martha insisted on buying and they took their pints of bitter to a table in the corner, Billy offered his pork scratchings to Martha who pulled a face and pretended to be horrified. Billy laughed and made a point of crunching some in his teeth.

'Not much of a pub,' Martha said. 'It's Saturday afternoon and no one is singing, not even a piano in sight.'

Martha said if there was no music it would have to be politics and she asked Billy why he would not fight in the war. Billy was surprised but said his leg would probably prevent him being accepted but his organisation did not oppose members joining the forces for that would be a good centre for agitating against the war. Martha replied that of course she knew she could not trust the Tories but now there was a coalition it was vital to stop the fascists and then defeat the Tories afterwards. Billy said the war was simply two capitalist economies fighting for dominance and the brutal British Empire was not something to defend.

'You're wrong Billy,' Martha retorted loudly. 'Why even Nye Bevan and Jennie Lee support the war now.'

Billy had heard about Bevan but he was surprised at the claim about Jennie Lee and made a note to check with Grace.

'I could never support Churchill in anything, he hates the working class, I thought we agreed that earlier,' retorted Billy.

Martha agreed they had but said circumstances change. 'I read in Tribune that last week Bevan said Churchill was the unchallenged leader and spokesman of the British people.'

Billy was doubly surprised that Bevan had said this and that Martha knew it and he did not. Martha sensed his hesitation and said, 'I think fascism has to be fought first and, on this, the Labour leaders are right, I mean your lot don't even belong to the Labour Party. Lenin will be turning in his grave about that for back in 1920 he persuaded Sylvia Pankhurst that working in the Labour Party was essential for Communists.'

Billy said nothing for a while surprised again at how much Martha knew and Martha in turn seemed to have decided she had won the argument and sipped her beer with a triumphant satisfaction. Billy though said that the way to fight fascism was for all the working-class to unite and oppose their rulers and this included German workers.

'Nazis,' snapped back Martha but Billy carried on saying that if Bevan and the other social democrats had declared for Churchill then they had put British capitalism and its survival ahead of the international working-class, what Lenin called social chauvinism. Martha interrupted saying anyone could see there was a difference between supporting a war between two imperialist nations in the First World War and, by the way, she would have supported Keir Hardie in opposing that and the current fight against a fascist movement that was killing trade unionists and socialists.

'Why Grace told me you spent last Christmas with a German socialist who told you all about the Nazis. I've never met a single German and I know they have to be stopped now.'

Billy sat glumly staring at his empty pint glass and eventually asked, 'Would you like another?'

When Martha said no so there seemed to be no alternative but to head for the station. The Victoria train was due in three minutes and whilst they waited Billy tried again arguing that only the international working-class was could defeat fascism and capitalism.

'International, Billy Stainsby,' Martha retorted scornfully raising her voice so that even the ARP warden fifty yards down the platform looked up, 'International? Why your tiny group of so-called Trotskyists wouldn't even join the Fourth International. I reckon Trotsky would be turning in his grave at you lot.'

They boarded the train in silence and Martha dumped her handbag in the adjoining seat, leaving Billy to sit behind. When they reached Victoria station the clock was striking four and Billy was about to suggest a cup of tea and cake when Martha, clearly still angry, said, 'See you Monday, Billy,' and walked off.

Billy caught the Cricklewood bus, went upstairs and tried to nurse his disappointment. He had really liked Martha and wondered what he had done wrong. He brooded on why he had never had a girlfriend and now he had got one he had lost her within hours. He had never really understood why Brigid had rejected him and, apart from the time a drunken Amy had to be resisted, no one but these two had ever kissed him. He still managed to smile to himself thinking he could not count the time Janice one of the girls at the bottom of his street had kissed him and run away when he was eleven in some stupid game the girls were playing.

As the bus reached the factory, he heard the sirens and looking out he saw people sprinting in every direction, even the old people were trying to run. He jumped off the bus and could hear the thudding of bombs which seemed to be getting closer. He dragged his leg as fast as he could down the street and into and through the house out into the garden and into the shelter. Only Mrs C was there, somehow, he still could not call her by her first name, and she was clearly very frightened.

Billy said nothing but put his arm around her and she picked up a cushion she had brought with her and closed her eyes, resting on Billy's shoulder. He wondered where John and Grace were, he knew that they had planned to go shopping but he did not know where. He hoped it was not near the river where he had thought the bombing was heaviest.

Mrs C had stopped shivering and seemed to be asleep, Billy could feel the burning sensation on his face from the Brighton sun, it had been the warmest of late summer days and he desperately wanted to splash some water on his face. There was nothing in the shelter except the two of them, although it was cool, and he did not want to disturb Mrs C.

He could not rid himself of his thoughts of the day, twenty-four years old and never had a proper girlfriend. He sat there staring at the corrugated iron, feeling very sorry for himself. He could still hear the dull thuds from the bombing raid and he moved slightly to see the watch on Mrs C's wrist. It was just ten to six, he wondered if the bombers would go home when it got dark and then realised this was absurd.

Billy and Mrs C had both dropped off and were woken by the all clear sounding and within seconds John appearing at the shelter door.

'It works then,' John said for he had done most of the digging of the shelter.

'Bit noisy, but nice and cool,' Billy replied. They set to work adding a layer of soil to the top of the shelter whilst Mrs C made a flask of tea and some sandwiches. John explained that Grace had gone home when they got off the 16 bus in Cricklewood and they were supposed to meet up later but the siren had gone after about ten minutes. He had started running but met Roisin and Diarmuid walking back and escorted them home.

'Their shelter was better than ours, Billy, so crack on. Brigid told them that Tiny was giving out tips on how to grow food on the top of the shelters and they were worried about their potatoes all through the raid, we need to grow some too.'

It was still very warm and a couple of sugar seeking wasps disturbed John and he tried to swat them away then rested on his shovel.

'Billy, I almost forgot mate, how did the date with Martha go?'

Billy had been dreading this moment, he thought for a moment, and replied that it had ended badly adding that "irreconcilable political differences" meant it was never going to work. John was in characteristic blunt mode.

'You mean she didn't fancy you?' Billy snapped back.

'Look John it's none of your business. I know she fancied me and I liked her but we had a row on the way home. It's over and I don't want to discuss it.'

As the bombing had continued the factory had closed on Monday so it was the following day that groups of workers stood around in the workshops discussing events. Usually by now any groups gathering would be broken up but, mysteriously, no one from management was around. The factory had expanded so quickly that there were now many new managers each it seemed more eager than the rest to ensure their section was working to capacity at all times. Eastwood had been sacked, or moved, no one was sure but somehow Willans still sat in his office and conducted meetings. Tom Stone had been moved to a machine job and had lost all his ability to approve leave and had been given a personal warning by Willans against spreading any anti-war ideas in any way.

A circle of workers gathered to discuss the bombing in Tiny's work space and Grace and John were holding hands glad to see each other safe, whilst Amy and Brigid told of the horrible conditions in their basement shelter and the man from next door with terrible wind who stank the shelter out.

Tiny was telling how he had been to Loftus Road on Saturday, 'Great game three all against Clapton Orient until it was called off due to bombing,' and when Amy quipped that was lucky for the Hoops everyone laughed.

Grace asked where Billy was and John said he had been sulking all yesterday after his date went badly.

'Oh no,' Amy said. 'The plan has failed,' explaining that Billy's friends thought Martha was perfect for him.

They all agreed to meet again at ten at Tiny's space for as Amy pointed out, 'The bosses need Tiny more than ever, he can fix anything, teach anyone so he'll never get into trouble.'

Tiny turned away to look out of the window mumbling something about his dad teaching him everything he knew until he exclaimed, 'Look, lovebirds at eight o'clock.'

They rushed over to see Martha with her arms around Billy's neck across the street and Billy gripping her close at the waist.

Chapter 15
Old Russia

Hank recommended the golubtzi or the variniki but he soon discovered that Brigid did not enjoy riddles.

'What are they Hank?' she snapped. 'You know we don't know.'

She looked across at Maureen and noticed for the first time a new necklace of dark brown stones.

'You don't mind if I tell your boyfriend off, do you, Maureen?'

Hank laughed and said Brigid knew how old he was and surely, he was too old to be called a boyfriend. Brigid knew Hank had cornered her knowing full well she would not call him Maureen's lover or some such.

Maureen though was a little put out for she knew that Brigid did not approve of her seeing Hank and she would be due a reminder of her fiancé Frank next time she and Brigid were alone. Maureen did not care about that for life had been a bit of a drudge before Hank came along in his Bentley. Maureen looked forward to Hank's visits and treats and she had not come to London just to work in a factory and write faithful letters to an absent soldier.

Besides she now regretted becoming engaged to Frank and, if she was honest, she could barely remember his face clearly and his last letter had been so dull with its talk of "settling down in a nice terrace house in Beckton" that she had not been able to raise the energy to reply yet. Frank was in the desert somewhere in Africa was all she knew but his imagination did not seem to have been stirred in any way judging by his letters.

'Oh, come on you two, don't spoil the adventure by bickering,' she exclaimed.

Brigid apologised and Hank explained what the dishes were and they agreed to have one each and share.

Maureen leant back in her chair and smoothed the linen tablecloth taking her time to survey the customers. The tea room was filling up now and she noticed how well dressed some of the women were with long feathers protruding from elegant hats and several fur wraps draped across shoulders despite the mild late autumn weather outside. Maureen explained to Brigid that she had been pestering Hank to take her somewhere that might contain spies, double agents or anyone else with something to hide. Brigid lightened a little more and remarked it was the perfect place for plotting with its dark corners barely lit by small oil lamps.

'One could see Karamazov drinking champagne in here or perhaps Dostoyevsky conducting one of his affairs in the far corner.'

Maureen knew Amy and Brigid were spending their evenings reading books and supposed these were Russian writers. A thought confirmed when Brigid asked, 'But why has Hank brought us to this corner of old Russia?'

'Don't look but the reason just walked in,' Hank replied. 'Admiral Nikolai Wolkoff, Tsarist Naval attaché and the organiser of White Russians in London. This is his daughter's tea room but he seems to be supervising it again.'

Brigid waited a few moments then glanced over her left shoulder. Unable to see because of a huge samovar which had been placed on the table behind her she stood up disturbing two elderly ladies behind her. Brigid made a show of removing her black cardigan, apologising and saying how warm it was in the room whilst viewing a silver haired gentleman leaning against the wall by the door and waving a matching cane in the air whilst explaining some point to two men in military uniform. The man waved at Brigid causing her to sit down hurriedly. Hank appeared not to notice but pointed out Wolkoff was talking to two Polish pilots who were probably Sikorski supporters.

'They hate both Hitler and Stalin and are not sure which one is worse.'

'I feel like I'm being spied on already by everyone in the room,' said Maureen. 'This is the most mysterious place I've ever been.'

Brigid sometimes despaired of Maureen reflecting to herself that a girl from Skibereen would find most places mysterious. Hank explained that it was possible that some spies were in the tearooms today but there were more likely to be working for the Soviets, or possibly the Nazis.

'There might be some MI5 here but I know a lot of them and there is no one here I recognise.'

'Unless they're in disguise,' said Maureen who looked offended when Brigid and Hank laughed.

Hank leant over to kiss Maureen, who responded more passionately than he expected her to so that he did not see the young waiter hovering behind him until a plate of caviar had been placed on the table along with plates and cutlery, three crystal glasses and a bottle of Russian vodka.

'A welcome from Admiral Wolkoff to our American friends and his beautiful lady companions. Long live Russia,' said the waiter.

Hank responded, 'Indeed. Please thank the Admiral for his generous hospitality.'

Hank turned and waved in the direction of the door, whispering to Maureen and Brigid. 'Of course, we may have different Russias in mind.'

Hank poured the vodka into the glasses, explaining that it was traditional to drink the first glass in one gulp.

'Za Zdarovye,' he said swallowing his drink and watching in amusement as the women followed suit. Neither would, on principle, show any sign of visual distress but Maureen later admitted her head started spinning as soon as the first glass was downed. Hank was now forking some caviar into his mouth and they both followed him; this time Maureen showed no restraint.

'It's like salty sheep shit,' she exclaimed.

Somehow Brigid kept a straight face and Hank said, 'I'll eat most of it, just pretend, I'm afraid it's an acquired taste.'

Their main courses arrived served in silver tureens with a double crowned eagle carved on each lid. Maureen had found something she liked.

'It's just like my ma's stew,' she said. 'Although she would never allow tasty meat to be wrapped in cabbage.'

Brigid asked Hank why the Admiral was running the restaurant again and Hank explained that his daughter, Anna, had had an affair with an American embassy official called Tyler Kent.

'Is that an offence now?' asked Maureen apparently worried.

'Not in itself of course but, and this is a secret never to be told, a few weeks ago both Kent and Anna were sentenced to years in prison for espionage, all hush-hush. I had to go to the trial to observe, the court windows were covered in brown paper.' Hank felt the need to reiterate.

'I could be sacked for what I've just told you, perhaps I shouldn't have but I wanted you to know the spying business has deadly consequences.'

The women both swore never to tell anyone and Hank relaxed saying, 'Turned out Kent had several mistresses, one of the others had a father who traded with the Soviet Union. Very odd affair all round, discussed it over a pint afterwards with an odd chap from MI5, unusual name too, Muggeridge. We were more concerned that Kent was sharing the ciphers between the President and Churchill, trying to keep us out of the war by leaking stuff.'

'But you're not in the war,' said Maureen.

Hank agreed that was the official position of the United States government. Brigid asked why the Nazis were interested and how they could keep a spy ring operating in Britain. Hank was a little surprised at having to spell this out to Brigid of all people, 'The Nazis want to keep us out of the war of course, this place is one of several where Nazi sympathy is strong, upstairs a nasty right-wing group meet and Tyler himself hated Jews.'

Brigid understood and realised that it was not just Tsarists she was sharing a room with but Nazi sympathisers or worse.

'I'd like to go now please Hank these are not my kind of people at all.'

Maureen was outraged at having to leave protesting that it was the nicest and most exciting place she had visited but Hank explained there was an unpleasant crowd in today and no spies he could see. He leant over and whispered to Maureen that they could come again if she wanted to. They put their coats on and Hank shook the Admiral's hand as they left, Maureen accepted a peck on the cheek but Brigid was through the door before Wolkoff could react.

Outside on the pavement a heavy drizzle was falling, driving into their faces as they turned into Cromwell Place. It was getting dark and umbrellas were up but Brigid saw a man across the road nod to another who was passing, this second man paused a few yards later and lit a cigarette whilst looking across the road at them from under his trilby. Brigid walked ahead wondering if this was a tail and why was he following them if it was. For the first time she began to wonder about Hank. He certainly knew a lot about workers struggles in America but if he was a socialist why work in the US Embassy as an intelligence agent and who was he spying on? Was it the Russians and Nazis or did he know more about her than she knew?

He certainly seemed keen to meet others In the factory so was he trying to infiltrate socialists here. He could, of course, have his own genuine socialist beliefs but these could be studied and learnt, that is what spies did. These thoughts occupied her and she decided to trust him for now, taking both Maureen and him by the arm and telling them she thought they were being followed.

'We are,' said Hank. 'Not very well though. It happens I'm afraid, let's split up and meet later at the taxi rank.'

He hugged them both and set off across the road and Brigid noticed Maureen's face was aglow as she linked arms with Brigid and walked down the street.

*****

Grace, Billy and John were discussing the new shifts introduced the week before which now stretched to eleven hours and a full day working on Saturday. Management had taken advantage of the bombing raids to stress the need for more production and it was hard to convince most of the workers to resist. Whenever the grumbles started someone like Tiny, or one of the other senior men, would talk about the war an

d how without the factory production our tanks would grind to a halt. Grace said that it would only take a spark to provoke the union members for most of the new managers lacked any subtlety at all.

'That Blunt goes round boasting how he drove buses to break the General Strike,' said John. 'And every one of them starts by Mr Willans says this and Mr Willans says that.'

Amy came past and told them about the two minutes silence at eleven for the police killed in the bomb at Salusbury Road police station, 'Apparently one of the specials was a cousin of Blunts.' When Brigid arrived too, she had news that several of the women were upset that Blunt was proposing this silence only for the police victims. Nana and her friend were neighbours of the stretcher bearer killed in the bombing of the ARP hut at Gladstone Park a month ago.

Grace volunteered to go and talk to the women and soon returned saying there would be no silence at all unless John and Francis were remembered alongside the thirteen police killed.

'Seems like several were neighbours of the wardens in Ilex Road and Dawpool Road, good men both, it seems.'

Billy suggested they call an immediate meeting and soon a crowd of a hundred were gathered in the inner yard. Grace and Martha were nominated to go and speak to Willans. They did so and returned to find that most of the crowd were still there, refusing instructions to return to work from several managers.

'Tributes will be paid to all the victims of the ARP and Police station bombs at eleven and those who knew John and Francis can say a few words and anyone who knew other local victims like the poor victims in Clarence Road can say a few words too. The factory will stop work for half an hour and Willans has asked the vicar and priest if they can come.'

There was no cheering but a murmur of satisfaction and several women came forward and hugged and thanked Grace and Amy.

'A small victory over management,' Billy said to John. 'Let's see if we can build on it.'

Chapter 16
Coalminers (1941)

John heard the knocking first, loud and insistent, and he glanced at his watch using the torch he kept under his pillow. It was 4.15am and as he struggled to wake up and get out of bed the cold hit him like a lightning shock. He was already fully dressed with an extra pair of socks on to keep himself warm under the blankets but his breath was visible through the gloom of his attic room as he reached for his coat. He wondered if the ARP had found a chink of light in the house or perhaps there was a gas leak as he scrambled down the stairs trying to balance on his toes so as to avoid waking Mrs C or any other lodgers. He opened the door to find a familiar face beneath a mop of thick black hair.

'Hi it's John, isn't it? Can I tempt you to a trip to Deal.'

The visitor, Jock Haston, explained that the Kent miners at Betteshanger pit were on strike and there was a meeting in Deal at ten o'clock. He went on to explain he had stayed over in Burnt Oak last night to borrow a car and suddenly thought Billy, and maybe John, would like to meet the miners and sell a few papers. John said he would come and he would go and wake Billy up. Mounting the stairs though he met Billy, explained the situation and they agreed to go. By the time they had put their boots on and come downstairs, Mrs C had invited Jock in and given him a scarf.

'If you're going down to the coast, it'll be freezing,' she said. 'Let me give you some of last night's pasta and bean soup in the Thermos, won't take a minute to heat up.'

Billy looked doubtful but Jock said he would love some and thanked her.

It was freezing cold outside and Jock had to hand crank the car to start it up.

'I don't think the heater works in this,' he said. 'So that soup will come in handy.'

They drove off and Jock explained the situation at Betteshanger where the pit had only opened after the General Strike and men victimised elsewhere had got jobs there.

'So, some good militants, they struck three years ago to protect pit boys from harsh treatment, now they are striking for extra payments for a tough seam.'

John was sat up front and said he did not know there were mines in Kent. Jock pretended to admonish Billy for not selling John the latest Socialist Appeal which covered the strike. Billy insisted he did and John said he was going to read it with Grace that evening.

'That's good,' laughed Jock. 'I shall report to comrade Ted what a good militant you are, for Ted often quotes Trotsky's saying that young workers are the vanguard of the working-class.' Billy knew what Jock was referring to for Ted had given a long speech on the tasks of professional revolutionaries at the last WIL meeting and Grace, who had attended as a visitor, thought it was directed partly at Billy for his Brighton trip.

Billy thanked Jock and said whatever Trotsky or Ted Grant thought, he needed his kip if he was going to be any use in Kent. He rolled himself up and lay down using a leather satchel full of papers for a pillow. As they drove on Jock quizzed John who was just describing the little he knew about the organised unions in Leeds, where he knew the Communist Party had a grip, when Billy woke up. It was still dark but Jock said he needed a piss so perhaps they would try some soup for breakfast. He pulled over and Billy said it was too cold to get out but where were they.

'Just outside Rochester, where Miss Havisham lived,' replied Jock but the reference was lost on his two companions. Instead, they drank the soup from the mugs Mrs C had put with the flask and Jock declared it delicious.

They carried on and Billy asked Jock about the British workers enthusiasm for the war. Jock replied that the war had thrown up the sharpest questions and, of course, no British workers wanted to see Hitler triumph, that was completely understandable and correct. The war though needed to be transformed into a workers war for socialism against both the Nazis and British imperialism therefore he had produced slogans for trade union rights for soldiers, control of the army units by Soviets of workers, mass air raid shelters to protect the working-class and so on.

As the bosses under Churchill, supported and abetted by Ernest Bevin and the TUC tops, would seek to destroy workers conditions, independent struggles like the Kent miners would grow and more workers could be won to the WIL.

'Makes sense to me,' John said. 'Workers must never give up their rights or we'll be trampled on.' John could not resist adding, 'Maybe that will convince Martha, eh John.'

Billy winced in the back seat, normally John would have earned a gentle punch for that remark but somehow the presence of Jock acted as a restraint from playfulness.

This Jock was a serious comrade thought Billy who expected them to miss work and travel to Kent at a ridiculous hour in the freezing cold just to sell papers. He was annoyed at John for mentioning Martha for this reminded Jock of his absence at the Hyde Park meeting and, more importantly, after Martha had called round the day after their trip and suggested that they did not discuss politics for a month they had been getting on well and he really liked her. There was an awkward silence for a while and then Jock asked, 'Who is this comrade, Martha?'

Billy jumped in quickly and said she was a good comrade and his girlfriend adding that she was an anti-fascist who believed in loyalty to the Labour Party.

'So, you went to Brighton to recruit a comrade Billy and fell in love.'

Billy did not answer so Jock continued, 'We all need love Billy, nothing wrong with that, I have my own too,' adding that he was not sure Ted Grant did though.

'He's in love with Marxism is Ted, probably sleeps with a copy of the Grundrisse under his pillow.'

Billy knew there was a dispute between Ted and Jock over the Proletarian Military Policy and so said nothing. After another silence, Jock added, 'As the Labour Party has closed down Billy perhaps Martha might like to come to a WIL meeting?' Billy felt obliged to agree to ask her and Jock asked when John's girlfriend was coming back.

'Grace is coming to the Willesden meeting on Wednesday,' replied John proudly.

'Excellent comrades,' Jock replied. 'We've recruited two aggregate members before we've reached Deal.'

They arrived in Deal just as the first light was appearing in the town and Jock pulled up alongside a small recreation ground. Jock explained that there was to be a mass meeting of miners at 8.30 to decide what to do about their leaders being arrested. They got out of the car and Jock recognised one of a small group of miners near the park gate.

'Brother Green,' he said. 'Good to see you again.'

The small muscled man shook Jock's hand and was introduced to Billy and John.

'Thanks for publicising our fight in Socialist Appeal, went down well with most of the lads to know our fight here is being spread.'

John was stood next to a miner called Ken Evans and admitted he had not known there was coalmining in Kent. Ken explained the Betteshanger pit had only opened after the General Strike which was lucky for many now in Kent who had been blacklisted after the strike.

'Had to walk from Merthyr with two lads and pretend my name was Ken, which it is of course,' he smiled.

Ken asked where John and Billy were from and on hearing Billy was from Darlington said he went there once as the Federation had a meeting at Redcar steelworks with the management of Dorman Long. Billy knew the works for some of his mam's relatives worked there and they sometimes had days at Redcar beach with the smoke from the steelworks blowing out to sea.

'Dorman Long that's a coincidence,' Billy said and Ken explained that the company owned the Betteshanger mine.

More men were arriving and John got the papers out of the car and started selling them, giving them away to anyone who had no cash on them. Soon there were several hundred miners there and John recognised some Yorkshire accents and talked to some men who had come from Wombwell. They explained that the men had gone on strike and three Federation officials had been imprisoned and most of the rest of the miners threatened with prison if they did not pay fines.

'See lad, they hopes to make all the miners frit to strike, but no one will go back, Will tha' Greeny?'

'Not a soul,' replied Green. 'Now give 'im a paper John and let him read what it's all about.'

'I'm not much of a reader,' came the reply. 'But this grand young fella from Leeds will tell us all about it.'

Green laughed and walked over to a small hill whilst other miners called for quiet. After a short speech about standing together Green called for a vote on whether to support the Kent Miners Association, continue to strike and to approach miners at Tilmenstone, Snowden and other pits to join the strike. John noted that every hand went up and there was a muted cheer. Billy and John sold papers for a while until Jock found them and suggested they find some breakfast in Deal.

Ken walked with them towards the castle and they found a café and enjoyed the "special" washed down with mugs of tea. They insisted on buying Ken's meal as he was on strike and in return, he offered to show them the town and then they could go up to Betteshanger to make sure the picket line was solid.

'If anyone is scabbing and I doubt it, they'll go in for the two till ten shift, one or two odd buggers on that one because they never see anyone else except their missuses six days a week.'

They walked along the sea front and, passing the castle Ken said it had been built by Henry VIII to keep the Spanish out.

'The Tudor wages weren't good and the men went on strike. Next day the supposed ringleaders, shop stewards I suppose, were thrown in jail.'

'Bloody hell,' said Jock. 'Don't give Churchill ideas.'

Jock drove them to the pithead where there were a dozen pickets round a fire and a hundred yards away about fifty police officers listening to a senior officer. When he had finished the officer walked towards them with two sergeants alongside him.

'Haston, this is your first and last warning. Get out of Kent and don't come back,' before turning round and walking back.

'Gentlemen you have met the Chief Constable of Kent,' Jock said. 'What a charmer.'

One of the pickets said, 'They're frightened of you Jock and of us. They know if they arrest us every miner in Britain will be out and their war will be over.'

Jock shook his hand and asked him if he would like a paper sent every week.

'Aye we would,' said his mate scribbling with a pencil on the back of an old envelope. 'Sends it to my house because Jack's mam wouldn't like him getting Communist papers.'

All the men laughed and Jack indignantly said his mam would be on the right side of the barricades when the time came. Jock had a word with Green, promising to come straight back as soon as anything happened and then they got in the car and drove away.

This time Billy sat in the front seat and John tried to catch up on some sleep. He asked Jock what he thought would happen next. Jock replied that it was a win-win for the workers movement, either Morrison or Churchill backed down and the message went out that workers could defend their rights and conditions or they arrested the miners and the strike spread across the coalfields and beyond. Either way Jock added he was putting his foot down and getting back to London before Ted Grant started the print run.

'Of course,' he said. 'Ted and I have our occasional differences but he's the hardest working comrade in the WIL and one of the best Marxist theoreticians we have in this country.'

They discussed the ban, just announced, on the Daily Worker and agreed this was the start of a government clampdown on anyone deviating from the Churchill line.

'Herbert Morrison seems just as bad,' said Billy and Jock agreed. 'A true agent of the capitalist class in our movement.'

Jock pointed to a newspaper just under Billy's foot and Billy retrieved it saying sorry but Jock replied, 'It's only the Guardian, just about fit to wipe your boots on.'

He told Billy to find the editorial and Billy did so, reading aloud that no one could censure Mr Morrison for his actions in suppressing the Daily Worker for "the paper has largely devoted its pages to derogatory accounts of Service conditions and to the encouragement of agitation amongst munitions workers."

Jock commented that the liberal imperialists as always put the Empire first, 'There is no principle, not even freedom of the press these people will not abandon to serve their masters.'

Billy asked if the ban was the reason for Jock moving to Dublin when the war started. Jock replied that it was but they had overestimated their own importance to the British state at that time but now with the Nazis about to invade all dissent would not be tolerated. Jock continued that the Irish sojourn had been useful though and he had made some useful contacts.

'It was a huge privilege to hear Nora, James Connolly's daughter, recall the night she visited her father before he was murdered in cold blood.'

There was a silence and then Jock laughed and said he had left Ireland when he heard the IRA had sentenced him to death for discussing socialist revolution with some of their younger members.

Billy remembered the warning Brigid had passed on last year about selling papers in certain Kilburn pubs but said nothing, instead asking if Gerry Healy had been threatened by the IRA.

'Sadly not,' Jock replied, this time not offering an explanation.

*****

John stopped to say hello as usual and thought Grace looked content for a Friday morning, considering she was facing a long March day over assembly motors that required constant attention. He wondered if the thought of the trip he had proposed to Richmond on Sunday was the reason for he knew Grace loved being by water and missed the sea and beaches of her childhood. He too felt the need for a change, the war was going badly and they were in a constant battle with management over the longer hours being required. His chances of breaking up the monotony of the job were being reduced as Billy was unable to come by so often and could not stay long as he had endless orders to chase.

John's regular trips to the lavatory were life-savers allowing a chat with Grace and Brigid along the way but now these were being curtailed, partly because Willans had taken to patrolling the factory urging people on but also because Tiny, who was now in charge of the two workshops, had recently become short-tempered occasionally snapping at John and others for simple mistakes. Yesterday Tiny had said aloud that he wondered if John needed to visit the doctors, for he seemed to be suffering from incontinence. A couple of women at the back of the shop had sniggered but John had not replied, not wishing to focus on the matter. After work though he sought out Tom to complain.

'He's watching me like a hawk, Tom. I don't mind the boredom too much but everyone needs a little break every now and again.'

Tom only replied, 'Leave it with me, John.'

Tom had received a complaint from two others about Tiny becoming rude and whilst no one would consider taking it to management it was clearly becoming an issue. Tom knew that with spring in full swing Tiny would be keeping his bird diary and so he sought him out after work and asked if anything unusual had flown in to the Harp. He received no reply and looking across at Tiny's damp eyes he thought he had never seen anyone look so lost.

'Fancy a quiet pint, Tiny?'

At first, he thought Tiny would refuse but after a pause, Tiny said quietly, 'I've got to tell someone Tom, let me buy you one.'

They walked to the Tavern and Tom suggested they sat in the snug as it was empty. Tiny came back from the bar with a pint of bitter for Tom and a lemonade for himself. They sat in silence for a while, sipping their drinks and then, without looking up, Tiny said he had never felt lower. Tom knew that Tiny had lost his wife to TB a few years back but he waited for Tiny to compose himself.

Eventually Tiny whispered, 'I've lost Eric, Tom, lost him.'

He paused and added, 'I don't know what to do, first Sheila and now Eric.' Tom looked across and saw that Tiny was shaking, his face was very pale and Tom tentatively asked if Eric was his brother.

'He was my son, my only child.' Now the sobbing started. Tiny's whole body seemed to tremble and tears and snot mingled together and dangled down on to the table.

'I'm sorry Tom, I'm sorry. You're the first person I've told.'

Tom produced a handkerchief from his pocket.

'Here, it's not the cleanest, had to clean some grease out of the drill after that new boy ladled too much in.'

Tiny did not smile but recovered a little and said, 'I'll clean the table with it if Mary don't mind.'

Tom nodded and then Tiny went to the gents and came back a little freshened though both his eyes were reddened and blank. Tiny told Tom what he knew which was very little. Eric was twenty-two, had joined the navy when he was seventeen, and had sailed most of the world. Tiny said he had been very close to his mum but could not make it to her funeral as he was in the middle of the Indian Ocean at the time.

Tiny repeated, 'Everything I have is gone,' twice, the second almost inaudible so that Tom thought the tears might restart but suddenly Tiny continued telling Tom that Eric had been killed when the Nazis bombed the Southampton near Gibraltar.

'Dozens of them killed Tom, they didn't stand a chance.' Tom waited but the silence grew so he asked quietly how Tiny was managing.

'I'm not Tom. Go home, sleep in the chair, keep waking, can't cook, can't eat, can hardly move. Come to work, snap at everyone. I'm lost.'

They sat in silence. Tom could not think of anything to say and so sipped his pint hoping that just the company would be enough. When he had finished, he said, 'I've got to get home to bath the kids, Friday night is get the tin bath down and they don't like the hair washing bit.'

He received no response so suggested Tiny come round for tea and lend a hand. Tiny stood up and put his coat on saying he would not be good company at the moment but would like to meet the children sometime. Instead of parting outside, Tom decided to walk home with Tiny back past the factory to the flats beyond the bus garage. Tiny did not speak until they reached the door.

'Thanks Tom, telling you has helped make Eric a real person somehow.'

After he had put the children to bed, he told Mary about Tiny and she immediately got a small pan down, ladled some of the hotpot in and tied it up with a clean tea towel and an elastic band.

'Poor fella,' she said, 'must be heartbroken; here take this round to him.' Tom protested that it was a three-mile round trip but Mary kissed him saying that both the hotpot and his wife would be waiting for him when he got home. Tom smiled and carefully put the pan in his rucksack and set off, it was dark by the time he got to Tiny's again and he stumbled over a step, just righting himself before the meal slopped over the sides of the pan. Receiving no answer to his knock he put the pan on the step.

Next morning, Tiny caught him at the door and returned the clean pan. 'Tell your wife it's the best breakfast I've ever had, please Tom. So very kind.' He walked quickly away desperate not to show his emotions again.

Chapter 17
Aurora

The Saturday morning shift always seemed to pass more quickly John thought and he was in a very good mood, looking forward to his day with Grace tomorrow. He had been in a torment all week wondering if the riverside would be a good place to propose to Grace, for he was worried about being called up and wanted to marry Grace but felt she may be too independent to want that. He had thought her acquaintance with Jennie Lee was the cause of this reluctance but even though Jennie seemed to have ceased inviting Grace to meet her, he knew Grace would make her own mind up. Billy and he had discussed these remarkable women one night with Billy concluding, 'Ugly oiks like us are lucky to have met Grace and Martha, one good thing to come out of the war.'

Unusually Grace appeared at his workstation just as John had these thoughts in his head. Grace looked excited and blurted out that she had been invited by her cousin Tony to stay with him. Tony had a new job managing a pub in Norfolk and there was a spare room she could stay in.

'I haven't been back in seven years, I miss it, do you think Willans would let me have a week off?'

John tried hard to mask his disappointment he knew Grace missed her childhood area in a way he had never missed Leeds. If he was honest, for though he often posed for fun as a proud Yorkshireman, he preferred London there were so many interesting people around and somehow, he felt closer to the centre of world events. He knew his mam and dad had done their best for him and he was grateful but he could rarely spend a day or two at home before the family chatter of how we had to defend the Empire and what a great man Churchill was depressed him.

It was over a year since he had visited and he told Grace she would not like his family as they were all Tories but Grace kept teasing that he was ashamed of her so that he had needed to promise they would visit this summer. Now he listened as Grace told him about a pub called the Buckinghamshire Arms which was near a town called Aylsham.

'My dad used to cycle over there recruiting, I'm sure that's the pub where the landlord had him arrested, how funny the family is now managing it.'

When Grace had gone, John told Tiny he had to see Tom briefly to sort out a small problem. He was pleasantly surprised when Tiny agreed and even more so when Tom promised to help.

'Oh, that's priceless that is, Willans just had two weeks off to gallivant up to Appleby, seems his brother-in-law had an accident at Haweswater, broke both legs and she couldn't manage the farm alone. I mean who even knew he had a mother.'

Tom had expected John to laugh but none came.

'Oh, you poor lovesick fool,' Tom said. 'You need to go as well. Just leave it to me, one of the managers owes me.'

He told John that Grace needed to make up some desperate family story and he was sure he could sort it. By the time the hooter sounded four days leave had been sorted and Tom told John, who told Grace, that she had a family emergency.

'Could be true,' said Grace. 'My grandad must be nearing ninety and he was injured back in the Mahdi wars. I should go and visit him.'

The Sunday outing was postponed and so, therefore, was the marriage proposal. On Tuesday they were on the Cromer train, which was crowded with RAF personnel of all sorts returning from leave. At Norwich even more got on and John gave up his seat to a chaplain with a handlebar moustache who discussed the weather with Grace. By the time they reached Cromer station the crowd had thinned and Grace held John's hand so tight he could feel her excitement. They had their kitbags searched at the station, Grace had remembered to hide the Italian label on the one Mrs C had loaned and they walked into town. They had a pot of tea opposite the town church and then walked through the graveyard where Grace spotted some giant bugloss bushes and told John they were her mam's favourite.

'She kept bees for honey and bees love bugloss.'

They strode on and paused to watch the fishing boats from the cliff top. They could see soldiers to the left of the pier exercising by leapfrogging in lines and then assembling for a tug of war. John wondered why such a small sleepy town was so heavily defended. They walked along the top, past the closed funfair below until Grace spotted the retirement home, a house painted lime green so that it stood out from its neighbours and with a small sign declaring it the Imperial Hotel and Rest Home.

'Just what grandad would have wanted,' laughed Grace and kissed John.

He suggested she went alone so as not to confuse the old man and arranged to meet in an hour. John was also excited to be by the sea, he was not going to tell Grace but this was only his second visit and he remembered being seven and enjoying the sheer joy of walking from one bay to another on a day trip to Scarborough with waves crashing over the barriers and soaking him. He decided to walk on the first pier he had ever seen and made his way down the steep steps.

Grace had wondered if her grandad would remember her but as she was shown to the hotel lounge a familiar face waved from a green covered armchair which, given his shrunken shape, seemed about to devour him. She bent down to kiss him and he looked pleased saying that he would have recognised her face anywhere.

'Such a beautiful girl should have been a film star. I told your mother many times it was lucky for Judy Garland she got started before they saw you.'

Although Grace had not seen her grandfather since she was sixteen, she knew to avoid reminiscing about the family, the old man hated trade unions and did not speak to his son-in-law for years, not even coming to his funeral. At one point as she listened to his memories, she realised he had now confused her with her mother and talked of carrying her on his shoulders to school. Soon the conversation turned to his military exploits and she went, as requested, to his room to collect his medals. The room was on the upper floor and Grace was pleased it had a wide sea view.

Returning she mentioned the view to the old man who appeared to be falling asleep and he sprung upright saying he had asked for a machine gun to be installed adding, 'I could still bring down a Jerry or two.'

Grace knew not to laugh and said she was sure he was still a good shot which led him to more memories of how the Maxim gun saved his life against the Dervishes.

'Devil of a place Ginnis,' he said, 'only that gun and bravery saved us from slaughter.'

Meanwhile John had reached the pier and realised it was being guarded by a single soldier who snapped to attention as John came close. 'No further son, the pier is closed to all civilians.'

Disappointed John walked to the side of the pier and admired the iron structure with a building right at the end facing the sea. John felt his trouser leg being tugged and looking down saw a small brown dog.

'Come away Louie, there's been no food there,' said an older man who was leaning on the rails looking out to sea.

The stranger told John the dog searched for food everywhere even though they fed him twice a day.

'He's a terrible chaser too, can't walk the beach to Overstrand anymore he chases anything Turnstones, Sanderlings, Black Backed gulls bigger than him, nothing is safe he even tried to attack a bull seal at Salthouse once.'

John said he had never seen a seal and the man told him he only needed to look to sea long enough and he would see one.

'Yes, you're in the right place here for seals, grey seals and common, see 'em at Wells and Blakeney or get a boat at Marston.'

The man said he had to get home for lunch and John held the dog's collar whilst he was put on a lead. He asked the man why the pier was closed and the man pointed to the middle of the pier.

'Not just closed but cut in half to stop Nazis landing on it.'

The man walked away with a doff of his cap and John descended to the beach looking out to sea as he strolled, looking for seals, enemy aircraft or ships but only finding a young couple splashing the cold water over each other as they paddled.

Grace was polishing her grandfather's medals from his campaigns whilst he complained that no medals had been issued for Ginnis. 'Not enough killed, even though a spear parted my hair.'

Grace had no idea which battle he was referring to but simply said it was a shame to be a medal short. When she offered to take the medals back to his room, he said he would like to sit with them for a while. Grace said she needed to meet cousin Tony but he did not seem to hear, murmuring only that it was "devilish heat, devilish" and so she gently kissed his head and left him with his memories.

She walked briskly down to the pier and John told her about it being cut in half which he thought was unnecessary. Grace replied that a German bomber had been shot down and landed in the town and that Cromer and the coast seemed to be an unloading spot for Nazi bombers trying to make it back to France and Germany. John said he was hungry and suggested that if they were to be blown to smithereens maybe the chip shop would be a good place. They walked up the narrow street with tall houses towards the church square; Grace was again holding John's hand which he knew she rarely liked to do in public and was a sure sign how happy she was to be here.

Suddenly Grace let go and started to run shouting as she did so that the last one to the chip shop had to buy the chips. John set off slowly in mock pursuit but suddenly as they reached the square up a narrow street, Grace halted as her way was blocked by dozens of children mobbing an older teenager who was giving out coloured stickers. Grace was bewildered but John said, 'It's a Glory Club meeting reminds me of one I went to on Woodhouse Moor when I was about six.'

Grace was still unsure until John took a pink sticker and gave it to her, 'God Is Love' it read and, on the reverse, 'Love Thy Neighbour as Thyself.'

'They'll be singing "Jesus wants me for a sunbeam next",' John added, making his way around the children.

They took their chips to the cliff top and sat there munching them and looking out to sea until John said, 'This is heaven, we make our own not the God botherers.'

Grace had a mouthful of chips and scraps and could not reply immediately. Then she said, 'Religion is the sigh of the oppressed creature, the heart of a heartless world, and the soul of soulless conditions. It is the opium of the people.'

John looked across, he knew it would be a quote from Marx, or possibly Engels or Lenin, and that Grace would know the source but he decided not to ask.

As arranged her cousin Tony was waiting for them at the Town Hall but she was surprised to see him standing with a uniformed RAF officer. Tony gave Grace a huge hug and then shook hands with John. He turned to introduce Jack who had opened the front passenger door indicating that Grace should get in.

'Jack is one of the officers billeted with us,' Tony explained. 'He comes from Cornwall and wanted a sniff of the sea so kindly offered to pick us up.'

As they drove along the flat and still wintry brown fields which did not seem to inspire conversation, Jack eventually said he could not discuss military operations of course but they were very busy and Grace replied that everyone knew what courage was being shown. They arrived at the pub just before dusk and John saw the walls of a grand house directly opposite. Tony said that John could sleep on the saloon bar couch after hours as there was only a single room available but Grace replied that they were content to share.

Down in the crowded bar John bought Jack a couple of whiskies and listened, supping his pint of beer slowly, as Jack talked of the family fishing business and unloading at Newquay after a night fishing, he was clearly missing being on the trawler with his brothers. At seven a whistle blew and the air force men slowly filed out with Jack and a fellow officer wishing them a good stay and then climbing the pub staircase.

Tony whispered, 'Poor buggers, them lads are off for their last suppers. Flying Blenheims over Belgium, it's a mugs game. Top secret and all but some of 'em won't be back in here again.'

It seemed most of the men were billeted at a grand house, Blickling Hall opposite the pub which the family of the late Lord Lothian had offered to the nation. 'But the nation doesn't know if it wants it yet!' laughed Tony.

The pub was empty now apart from two young women in the corner and Tony opened the front door to let the cool night air in.

'Land Girls,' Tony said, 'They say Lord Lothian has insisted on an armed guard on their room at night. They are working his vegetable patches and he only has them and old Walkley left.'

Grace suggested they invite them over but Tony said he did not want to get too friendly, he liked his job and did not want to be sacked.

'I'm an essential worker you see, providing accommodation and driving beer around to troop locations and I do not want to have to register as a conscientious objector.'

He told Grace it was a Johnson family characteristic always trying to work out what was right and wrong.

'I could not kill another human being but I've struck lucky so far and hope Summerskill and Bevin and all those busybodies don't give my job to a woman. Unusually I'm keeping my nose clean at the moment.'

Grace and Tony talked about their mothers, the sisters Johnson who begged and borrowed and organised food for families in the strike actions.

'Your dad is still fondly remembered round here Grace, and George Edwards too, people say your dad led the pelting of Sam Peel in the big strike.'

Grace had to turn away to wipe a tear away.

'I'm pleased people remember. I don't think that's true about the pelting though dad was not one for gestures like that. He hated the way the farmers behaved though cutting wages and all. They were brutes, some of them, used to strip little boys hang them up naked like dead cows and beat them with a paddle, just for being too tired and hungry to stay awake.'

Tony replied that after the war everything will change and no one will accept being punished for being poor. Big changes are coming.'

Later Grace and John lay holding each other in the narrow bed.

'It's so quiet here,' said John. 'Seems like the war has gone away.'

*****

As she left the factory Brigid was pleased to see Sinead again who was waiting by the gate.

'No fuss now,' Sinead said. 'There's Special Branch all over and Fionn and I just wanted a word.'

Brigid gave Amy a wave and saw the disapproving look on her face. They walked down Temple Road alongside the factory and then past Mora Road school and into St Michael's Road then a sharp left into Ivy Road where Sinead knocked on the door of a house. Fionn opened the door and gestured them in and, once inside, gave Brigid a hug.

'Not to beat about the bush, Brigid,' he said. 'We're leaving London and we just wanted to say goodbye.'

'You're going back to Dublin,' Brigid exclaimed. 'Why?'

Fionn hesitated but Sinead simply said they were not going to Dublin but further away where they could raise funds for the cause. Brigid had a flutter of envy for she too had often thought she would like to see America and Sinead, sensing this, said if you ever get to Boston or New York or Chicago just ask for Fionn, in any of the Irish bars. Fionn could see Brigid looking doubtful and explained that they had been asked to go to America to raise more funds for the army.

'Any veteran of the Rising is guaranteed a hero's welcome in America, we already have a tour planned for us by the Clann and Fionn is eagerly awaited.'

'I shouldn't have to buy a drink for at least two years,' said Fionn, licking his lips.

Brigid asked what the funds were for and Sinead explained that the army was much depleted in Ireland and de Valera was more vicious than the British themselves.

'He's terrified that the Brits will allow the Nazis to invade and he wants everyone to see he is crushing their enemy.'

'The campaign in Britain had failed badly and the negotiations with Germany had apparently got nowhere,' added Fionn.

Brigid had been disturbed to hear rumours that the IRA had been working with the Nazis and asked if that were true.

'It is Brigid and neither Sinead nor I supported that although it was born of desperation not support for fascism. Not even those of us who disagreed with his tactics would have wished Peadar to die on a U boat and be tossed in the sea wrapped in the Swastika. Awful.'

Brigid knew better than to ask how Sinead and Fionn were travelling to America but she remained quiet for a moment wondering if there was now any role for herself in London and whether she could be more use back in Ireland. She had spoken to her mam at the weekend and all seemed well at home, she had a new niece and she thought it would be nice to see her. Brigid never asked about Conan partly because the lines could be tapped and partly because she knew her mother would not know much. Sinead sensed this and said that Conan had been captured and was in Mountjoy, he had been sentenced to ten years but would be out, along with others, as soon as the war ended.

'Don't worry,' added Sinead. 'The movement looks after its families; your sister is well looked after.'

Brigid hugged them both and wished them a safe journey.

'Be sure to have a hamburger ready for when I visit,' she laughed.

'Oh yes with extra fried onions,' replied Fionn.

*****

'It's a day I will never forget,' Tom said. 'We could barely move for the heat and just sat indoors letting the kids play in and out the bath.'

Mary added that it was so hot that Tom had taken his socks off and splashed Patrick and Emily with his toes. 'And that from a man who would never even paddle in the sea at Skegness when we were courting.'

Tom grunted and said it was the hottest day he had ever experienced and made him realise he would never grumble about British weather again.

'I couldn't sleep a wink; it was unbearable and not just because of the news.'

'What news?' asked Brigid.

'That was the day the Nazis invaded the Soviet Union, two weekends ago, we only found out in the afternoon for Tom had no meetings that day and we were going to have a picnic in the park, but it was too hot to go out, over ninety degrees,' Mary explained.

Tom said it was a momentous day and the Communist Party had been proved right to demand a pact with Russia.

'Only six months ago the appeasers were still laughing at our rallies and now we can get them all out of the government. Harry Pollitt is back in charge and we will be backing the war effort, no more opposition to war production from me, the defeat of Hitler is everything.'

Mary whispered to Brigid that Tom had never been this happy for years for he was desperate to back the war.

'So, the Party is backing Churchill now?' asked Brigid out loud a little confused.

'We are all allies in the fight against Hitler and woe betide anyone who gets in the way,' Tom exclaimed.

Mary added that it probably meant Alan Bush would be allowed back on the BBC and she liked his concerts.

'My favourite though is The Lark Ascending and even more now when Vaughan Williams bravely spoke up for Alan.'

Tom agreed that when you are being witch-hunted you certainly find out very quickly who has principles.

Later Brigid discussed the tea time visit with Grace and Amy back in the Neasden flat.

'I can't understand how Churchill can be closing down the Daily Worker one minute and the next the Party is praising him to the hilt.'

Grace explained about the duty of the Communist Parties, as they saw it, to defend the Soviet Union at all costs and to support those who were fighting on the same side. Amy said she found Tom's politics bewildering, switching about every day, and she had thought Ireland was confusing.

'I'm sticking with literature,' she added. 'Where no one actually gets hurt.'

Brigid and Grace smiled at each other and Amy saw them, snapping that she knew they thought she was naïve. Brigid leant down and kissed her. 'Not naïve just kind and beautiful,' she said.

*****

Martha was nothing if not diligent in her pursuit of ideas and the correct orientation to issues and organisations and Billy told her so one evening as they sat warming muffins Mrs C had somehow managed to make, over the fire at Martha's digs. They had decided that it was impossible for them not to discuss politics but in order to avoid them having a 'fall-out' as Martha called it, they had agreed that if one of them was getting annoyed they could call out, 'Aurora' and they would stop arguing. Martha in fact had conceded that she had been wrong to champion work in the Labour Party for the party had closed down for the duration of the war and, she also conceded, that the attempt to suppress the Communist Party had been a disgrace. Billy had not known the answer as to why the WIL had not joined the Fourth International, mainly because he had not been involved at the time, and so he suggested Martha came to a meeting where he had asked for the question to be explained.

'You must think me an idiot Billy, just trying to recruit me like all the other groups do.'

'Aurora,' shouted Billy. 'You've fired the first shot, you Bolshevik.'

They laughed but when Billy explained that Martha could come for the first part of the meeting only and then leave, she agreed.

The Wednesday meeting was chaired by Hetty Keen, whom Billy knew and her husband Roy was giving the talk. He started by thanking Billy for raising the issue which he realised had been overlooked for new comrades who had joined since the founding conference in 1938. Roy stressed that the WIL was in support of the Fourth International and spent some time explaining why Trotsky had been right to declare the need for a new revolutionary international that put the interests of the world proletariat first. However, when Roy started to discuss the position in Britain in 1938 Billy and Martha soon started to lose track.

Who were the Revolutionary Socialist League was unclear and names like Harber, CLR James and others meant nothing to them. It seemed that the WIL refused to work in the Labour Party and had not seen the point of merging into one organisation where two different tactics were being used and had resisted this unity when James P Cannon visited London and tried to secure it.

'No point uniting and then having two completely different strategies in the movement, it would only lead to division and splits,' Roy pointed out.

There was talk of the WIL not having enough money to send anyone to the Paris founding conference as most of their members were unemployed and of a letter sent to the Conference by the WIL asking to be the British section or an affiliate not being read out. As Martha said afterwards it sounded to her like tiny organisations in which personal differences got in the way of a simple task to build a movement but at least the commitment to join the International was there.

'They needed someone to shout Aurora back in 1938,' said Billy leaning over to kiss Martha.

That was not the only reason Billy was in a good mood for he had been given two days off to visit home on Friday and Saturday, thanks to Tiny talking to Willans about it and he asked Martha if she like to see to the new Henry Fonda film tomorrow.

'Thought you said romance films were a sloppy diversion to keep the workers quiet,' Martha said, adding, 'course I'd like to go,' and looping her legs onto his lap she kissed him again before he could answer.

Billy was lucky that the new edition of Socialist Appeal, the WIL paper, was being distributed that weekend and on Saturday he hitched a lift in the military support vehicle to Newcastle from where several hundred copies were distributed on Tyneside and elsewhere.

'Churchill would have a fit if he knew Trotskyism was being spread by his army.'

The gruff corporal driving only said it was not Churchill's army and reminded Billy to tell no one or he would be court-martialled. It was midnight when he jumped off at Scotch Corner and walked the miles into Darlington the roads were empty of private cars now and only one convoy of army lorries briefly lit the road. By the time he reached Falmer Road, not without difficulty in the pitch dark and once hearing a warden shout to put his torch out, it was past three o'clock and the whole street was dark and quiet apart from the muffled noise from Richardson's joinery on Neasham Road which seemed to be working a night shift. Billy decided not to disturb the family and, though it was a cool night, managed to doze off wrapped in his coat in the bowling green shelter in Eastbourne Park.

He was woken at six by Harry the park keeper who opened the bowls house and got the fire going which Billy thought was good of him given that the last time they met, just after the General Strike, Harry had chased him and other boys for stealing apples from the nearby allotments. Half an hour later his mam had sat him in the chair opposite the coal fire, usually Humphrey's seat before work, and was fussing over him saying what Harry was thinking about not sending him straight home. His dad looked well and apologised for having to go to work and promising him a beer in the club later. Billy asked if he could go and wake Dave up but Et said he often slept in till eight. 'His chest plays him up at night, he was coughing after midnight last night.'

They sat together by the warmth of the fire, saying little, just glad to see each other, until Billy asked about the family in Redcar and South Bank and about his school mates.

'I didn't want to worry you Billy until I saw you but Colin was killed two months back in Africa of all places, some dreadful desert place. It was so very sad for Mrs Morris had been planning the wedding to Rachel for his next leave. Such a friendly and helpful lad Colin was and he and Rachel met at school, you know.'

Billy did know of course and he knew most of his friends had joined the Durham Light Infantry but he had never thought any of them would be killed. He asked his mam who else had been killed and she told him about Bert Exall, one of the apple stealing boys, who had died of wounds he got on Dunkirk beach. Billy closed his eyes and his mam stopped talking and leant over to touch his arm. He said a little silent prayer for Colin and Bert. He dare not open his eyes in case his mam saw a tear drop and he was grateful when he heard her leave the room saying something about breakfast.

He stayed there, eyes closed and remembered the walks his dad took with him on Sunday mornings when he was ten or so, usually they would go along the river Tees at Broken Scar or through High Coniscliffe to the Roman fort at Piercebridge but one fine Sunday they only walked through Bank Top station and his dad pointed out the terraced houses along Park Place pausing at the houses and shops and marking which men had been killed in the 1914-1918 war, thirteen in all. Humphrey remembered every soldier killed and where they had fallen, the tobacconist his grandfather had bought from every Saturday, the fellmonger, the crane driver and the chemistry teacher at the grammar school.

'Such a waste, Billy,' he remembered his dad saying, 'most of the young men in this street dead, we must never let it happen again.'

Billy opened his eyes and watched his mam return with two huge lumps of coal on a huge shovel. 'Here, let me do that,' said Billy and lifted each lump onto the embers of the fire. As he straightened, he took his mam in his arms for a moment, 'Fine lads gone, mam.'

They each sat on an arm rest of the chair watching the fire spark and enjoying each other's company. Et broke the silence.

'I was furious with your dad once Billy just after we were married and moved here, he'd spend every night walking the streets getting people to vote in the Peace Ballot. Now I realise he was right though and so were the millions who voted but Hitler smashed all that.'

Billy nodded but could think of nothing to say partly in amazement that Et had expressed a political view at all, the first he could ever remember, for she used to enjoy teasing Humphrey that there was a reason the ballot box was secret and refusing to say who she voted for. The silence was broken by the sound of coughing from the back bedroom and then a shout of, 'Is our Billy here?'

Billy was shocked when having climbed the stairs he saw Dave, partly because of the severity of the coughing fit which greeted him and took several minutes to subside but mainly because Dave who was now fifteen seemed to be exactly the same size or possibly smaller than when he had last seen him two years ago. When settled Dave did not give him a hug so Billy put out his hand and Dave shook it.

'Can we go to the river?' he asked.

'No problem, Dave, it's not far to the Skerne,' Billy joked.

'Not that smelly old stream,' Dave responded.

Et managed to get old Mr Connolly, from the corner shop, to give the brothers a lift to Blackwell in his van.

Dave seemed to have new energy and walked the few hundred yards through a wood to the river and then sat on a rock staring at the Tees as it flowed past. He pointed at two birds skimming across the river which seemed to be diving underneath the surface.

'Can those birds swim, Billy?' he asked.

'They can indeed they're dippers and they love a fast-flowing river, I think they eat something they find in the water,' Billy replied. Dave said they must catch fish but Billy did not think so 'more like freshwater shrimps, I think, let's see if we can find some.' Dave searched under stones but found only minute sticklebacks and then he lost interest and decided to search for skimming stones. Billy liked being out in the fresh air and they shared the eggy bread and flask of tea Et had given them for lunch.

'Why can't you stay in Darlington, Billy?' Dave asked and Billy told him to keep a secret that he was doing important work in London and could not leave at the moment. Dave looked disappointed and asked if Billy was fighting the

Germans and seemed happy when Billy said he was fighting evil people everywhere.

Chapter 18
Clear Out Hitler's Agents (1942)

Tiny was holding one of his impromptu war briefings and, as usual, had gathered a small crowd; this time numbering around twenty. Eastwood seemed to have instructed the managers to allow these briefings to occur, the rumour in the factory was that he thought workers would increase production f they heard the latest news. It was well known that what Tiny said was reported straight to Eastwood and occasionally Tiny would be summoned to the office to explain why he thought The Times reports were inaccurate and they usually agreed that some censorship was necessary to avoid despondency setting in. Billy was listening intently as Tiny spoke describing the Japanese advances in the east and quoting Churchill's view that the loss of Singapore was the worst disaster in British military history. Tiny said it was time for the Americans to take the battle to the Japanese. Tiny added that the Japanese were the most bloodthirsty murderers the world had seen and a voice from the back said, 'They bayonet our soldiers even after they have surrendered,' and Tiny agreed saying that he hoped everyone would work harder than ever today to defeat this evil.

'Let's get to it,' shouted the voice and there was some cheering as they all dispersed. Billy recognised the man as Gary Dobson, who had once knocked on his door before the war on a canvass for the Conservative party. Billy noted that as Dobson left, he was slapped on the back by Tom and the two of them left deep in conversation.

That evening in the Kings Cross office, Billy mentioned the incident to Jock Haston who summoned Ted Grant over to listen. Ted thought for a moment and said the ruling class was stirring up anti-Japanese hatred whilst ignoring the British record of murder in the same sphere. I think we should point this out that both imperialist nations use the same brutality.

'Billy, could you try and put a piece together for Socialist Appeal.'

Billy protested that he was not much of a writer but Ted said everyone should try and improve their skills and, besides, Helmut was arriving later and would be able to help, 'He knows the anti-colonial struggles so well.' Billy was relieved and returned to packaging the new copies of Trotsky's Permanent Revolution for the branches and support groups with Jock, who was helping, proudly telling him that his wife Millie Lee had typed every page onto stencils.

Billy was hunched over a typewriter by the time Helmut arrived and was struggling both for content and to get his thoughts down using his single finger typing.

'Billy Stainsby,' he said. 'A Marxist must know how to type, stencil and work a printer.'

Billy laughed protesting that it was alright for the educated sons of the German petit-bourgeoisie to lecture workers but there was little call for typing skills in Smithfield market. Helmut smiled and sat down at the typewriter confessing that he had learnt to type whilst producing handbills for the family shop. Billy explained the hatred for the Japanese expressed by his factory workers and suggested this needed to be taken into account. Helmut agreed and Billy suggested a headline 'British workers—remember Hong Kong and all these imperialist atrocities too.'

This seemed to give Helmut an idea and he went off to search in the box files stacked on the metal shelves against the far wall leaving Billy to draft the opening paragraphs. Billy started from the well-known atrocities of the Japanese against British soldiers in Hong Kong adding, 'And no wonder! It is our husbands, sons, brothers and friends upon on whom these terrible atrocities are being committed.' Billy admired his sentence for a moment and then heard a triumphant shout from across the room.

'Got them, comrade Billy, photographs speak a thousand words.'

Two grisly images of decapitated prisoners were held up and Helmut explained the first showed Chinese soldiers killed during the Japanese imperialist conquest of Manchuria.

'The British press and politicians supported the conquest, the hypocrites,' Helmut added.

He held up the second image. 'Only ten years ago this one, British murders of Burmese anti-imperialists, just as brutal as the Japanese and heads displayed in public to discourage others.'

Billy was typing now but Helmut was frustrated at the slow speed and complaining at having forgotten what he had said by the time it was typed he sat down and typed himself. Words flowed condemning the hypocrisy of Churchill who had helped the Japanese secure huge swathes of China and reminding readers of the British atrocities of General Dwyer in India and the context of the Burmese executions. He paused asking Billy to sum it up and Billy said, 'Look at these pictures. The method is the same.'

Helmut grunted approval and with a final clatter of keys brandished the finished article above his head.

'Ted Grant will be in tomorrow and he better not censor this, well done Billy I think we deserve a pint.'

The next day was Saturday and Billy had arranged to collect Martha and was surprised when he knocked to find the door opened by her landlady.

'Are you Billy?' she asked and when Billy nodded, she handed him an envelope.

Billy walked away from the house and opened the letter, inside was a short note telling Billy that Martha had to rush to Liverpool as her mam was ill. The letter was signed 'See you soon, love Martha xxx.' Billy sat on a wall and wondered what had happened, he tried to work out how old Martha's mother would be and reckoned she could not be over fifty and hoped therefore that it was nothing serious and Martha would soon be back.

Billy heard nothing for a few days, then a letter arrived from Liverpool. Mrs C handed it over and had an anxious look on her face as if she expected the worse. Billy climbed to his room and opened the letter.

Dear Billy

Mam has suffered a stroke, no one knows why, but she cannot speak and her body is shaking. Dad and I are in pieces and I have to, want to, stay here and look after her. I don't know if I will return to London but it will not be for a while, the doctor cannot say how mam will respond but it will be a slow process.

I love you Billy so please do not take this as a Dear John letter for that is the last thing I want.

Please explain to Eastwood and the others at the factory.

Love and kisses Martha.

Billy had read the letter a hundred times before he returned the next evening to Kings Cross, he had told Eastwood very little and even John, Grace, Brigid and Amy only knew Martha's mother was unwell. He tried to get enthusiastic about the new edition of Socialist Appeal which displayed his headline and Helmut's photos on the front page.

'Pity they don't put names on the articles,' said John. 'You could become a journalist after the war, Billy.'

Helmut pointed out that revolutionaries were being hounded enough without giving the government a list of who to arrest. When they had finished packing the copies for despatch and he and John were on the way home, Billy suggested a quick drink and once inside the pub he asked John to read the letter from Martha carefully. When he returned with two pints of bitter, John tried to reassure him that Martha did not mean to refer to a Dear John letter for Martha could hardly have found a new man in three days. Billy snapped back that he knew that and snatched the letter off the table. John put his palms up to calm him and said there were four words in the brief letter that were the most important and these were 'I love you Billy' and these were the real message in the letter.

Billy smiled at that and said the pub was very noisy and could John repeat the four important words, so John repeated them more emphatically and only when he had finished did he realise Billy had tricked him.

'Don't worry John, it's our secret, I won't tell Grace.'

John look disgruntled so Billy said he was a real marra, the very best.

'Now you're calling me a vegetable,' John protested so Billy told him he was the best mate a man could have and he had put his mind at rest over the letter.

'So, what is a marra, then?' John persisted and Billy took out his copy of Socialist Appeal pointing to the headline celebrating the victory of striking miners at Blackhall Colliery.

'Marra means sticking together, helping your mates, never crossing a picket line, that pit is near a seaside place called Crimdon Dene, where I taught our Dave to kick a ball when he was two or three, there were some miners bairns there who joined in and by the end of the afternoon one of the dads said we were all marras.'

John replied that calling something dene was a bit posh but Billy carried on saying it just meant anywhere with a small valley by a stream.

'I mean Crimdon Dene is near Hartlepool, how can it be posh? Anyway, we have half a dozen Denes in Darlington, along the Cocker Beck, nice little walk that is.'

They supped up and as they left John asked what was so wrong with Hartlepool. Billy tapped his nose saying that when he thought John was old enough, he would tell him about the sad fate of the Hartlepool monkey.

*****

Tom liked to stop for a chat with John and seemed to have given up trying to recruit him to the Communist Party. They talked about football, family and any subject which avoided political controversy and on this occasion, Tom asked if John was interested in art. John said he had learnt a little from Grace who had visited the National Gallery before the war.

'I'd heard all their pictures are hidden in a coal mine now,' Tom replied adding that he had tickets for an art auction on Sunday and wondered if Grace and John might like to go.

John asked if he would be expected to buy anything and Tom laughed saying he doubted John could afford anything but there would be free drinks and food. At lunchtime, Grace agreed she would like to go and said she would ask Brigid and Amy too. Brigid was very keen said it would make a nice change especially as Amy was busy on Sunday afternoons now helping with the Sunday school at Neasden Methodist church.

The auction was in Hampstead village and they decided to walk there up Cricklewood Lane and down the Vale of Health. Grace asked Brigid if Amy was now a Protestant but Brigid replied Amy had looked into it and decided all Christians shared the same belief adding that Amy was really pleased to be asked by one of their neighbours, as she loved children and spent hours planning the sessions.

'Amy doesn't want this spread about,' added Brigid. 'She doesn't want any trouble with anyone.'

John and Grace promised to keep quiet and in return John asked them not to tell Billy he had been to a Communist Party fundraiser or there would be no end to the leg-pulling. As they started down the hill John said he had been told the Vale of Health was called that because no one had died there in the Great Plague.

'Probably they were so fit from walking up this hill,' Grace replied. 'Careful not to drink too much free booze John or you'll never make it back.'

They reached the house in Willow Road just as a small crowd filed in, they waited their turn gazing at the strange house, which seemed to be three knocked together and was entirely different to its neighbours. A man behind them commented, 'It's an exciting experiment in itself isn't it, Erno really has produced a live-in masterpiece, don't you think?'

As they climbed the spiral staircase inside, he introduced himself simply as, 'Penrose, I dabble a bit in sculpture you know, perhaps you know my Captain Cook?'

'We're just beginning to explore art,' Grace apologised.

'Splendid,' said Penrose. 'I'm mainly a collector these days, perhaps you'd all like to come and see my Picasso one day, I don't live far away.'

Grace replied that they would like that very much and Penrose went off to get them drinks, returning shortly with a tray and four glasses.

'A good stiff G and T should get us in the mood to spend a little, don't you think?' Penrose said distributing the gently fizzing drinks.

Listening and watching in amazement John noticed that Penrose was immaculately dressed, his three-piece suit was clearly expensive and the buttons on his waistcoat were thrust forward as if to emphasise there was not a spare ounce on his frame. He asked what they did in the war and said, 'Ah, making weapons is not an option for us Quakers, saw some fighting in Italy in 1918, terrible times, we were driving ambulances you know. Came back through France and stayed, do you know it?'

Without waiting for an answer Penrose carried on the conversation. John had never met anyone from a public school to his knowledge and was amazed at the easy flow of words and stories.

'Anyway, this time round I've done a bit of ARP and now they've got me teaching camouflage, perhaps you know my best seller The Home Guard Manual of Camouflage?'

Brigid could not avoid laughing but realised to her horror that Penrose was serious.

'I know,' he said, 'I hope Max Ernst doesn't hear of it, I'll be cast out as a traitor.'

Penrose scanned the walls of the room, 'Anything you've got your eyes on, Bridget?'

Brigid usually corrected people, she hated to be called Bridget, but she let this pass. She too had looked at the paintings and could not find any she liked, she spotted one on the far wall and said she quite liked the colours on the leaf.

'Oh yes, good choice, I agree, Rita is one of our best for colour contrasts often pink and blue but here one is drawn to the burnt sun, bathed in blue.'

They moved across to the painting which was entitled Sycamore Leaf and Brigid remarked that she did not know what the white figure represented.

'Oh quite,' Penrose replied. 'The omnipotence of the dream, Breton called it the whole beauty of Surrealism, we could ask Rita if you like, for there she is looking thoughtful, rather stranded here in London now Denmark is occupied by the Nazis.'

Grace looked across to the elegant middle-aged woman in a cream two piece with a bright embroider rose in the button hole. Her hat though seemed to match no part of her with two balls suspended above a beret. Perhaps wondered Grace that is a Surrealist concept too. Penrose asked if Brigid would like to meet her but Brigid said she did not want to bother anyone and was alarmed when Penrose suddenly darted off.

'I think we had better scarper,' said John. 'We're clearly expected to bid and I doubt anything will sell for sixpence.'

Grace and Brigid nodded agreement and they turned to leave just as Penrose reappeared, accompanied by an open-faced man with, Brigid noticed, wonderfully full eyebrows.

'I am honoured to have three worker comrades at my house,' he said and John noticed a strong European accent similar to the two Polish women who had started at the factory last week. The man spoke directly to Brigid.

'I understand you are an admirer of the work of Ms Kernn-Larsen too. Would it be acceptable if I bid for it and then you would be able to admire it here any time you choose?'

He smiled at Brigid who said that would be very kind unless the painting was too expensive. 'Us Hungarians love a challenge,' replied Goldfinger. 'Oh yes we will build a Proletkult here in Hampstead yet.'

Goldfinger moved away with a smile and Penrose reappeared saying that Erno Goldfinger was notorious for provoking arguments for fun.

'Quite a single-minded genius though when it comes to his architecture, some call him the Hungarian le Corbusier, he also admires Lunacharsky and won't have a word said against him or the proletarian art movement. He will get the picture now as a point of principle.'

Brigid said she hoped she had not provoked unnecessary spending.

'Oh, don't worry,' Penrose replied lowering his voice and cupping a hand over his mouth. 'He has married the divine Ursula who has the tinned food millions behind her.'

Brigid looked puzzled so Penrose whispered, 'Crosse and Blackwell, though don't ever mention it.'

Before Brigid could answer the high-pitched chimes of a small bell being rung caused the conversations to cease and she looked up to see Erno with a golden bell in his hands.

'Comrades, the peal of socialism for we must come to the aid of our heroic Red Army battling the Nazi hordes and to the people of the Soviet Union. Aid to Russia is our cause bid generously and don't disappoint our distinguished auctioneer, Roland Penrose.'

There was a ripple of applause and as Roland introduced the first item, John suggested they leave. Outside John said that was a narrow escape and that he had never realised rich people could be Communists.

'Well,' said Grace. 'It's time for me to tell you about Savva Morozov, one of the richest factory owners in Russia, who was a founder of the Bolshevik Party.'

*****

Brigid had invited Grace and John over for Sunday afternoon tea and as they were welcomed into the flat, Brigid said it was time for their weekly poetry challenge and Amy was about to read her response and John said he would like to hear some poetry and Grace recognised the fib and patted his back gently so Brigid could not see.

'It helps us raise our eyes and thoughts away from the factory and the war,' Amy said. 'Each week we take it in turns to select a line or two of poetry and the other has to take the thought and match it with a line of poetry.'

Brigid explained that Amy sometimes matched it with her own poetry but Amy said she had found a beautiful Irish poem this week. Grace asked what the poem being responded to was and Brigid said she had found a stanza from Keats.

'Deep in the shady sadness of the vale,
Far sunken from the healthy breath of man.'

Grace said it made her think of a decayed wood and John that he did not understand the line about the healthy breath of man. Amy said that was the beauty of poetry in her view, each poem will evoke a different reaction. She recited from memory a line which, she said, matched her reaction to Keats.

'Somehow to lose my way I must contrive,

To lose my way, ignoring stars and sun, milestones and signs.'

There was a silence and then Grace said that she could see the link to both be alone and to seek to be alone and not just alone but a little lost perhaps deliberately so. Amy was delighted and said so adding that such a feeling of being lost would create a spark for writing, although that would be hard to achieve in Neasden sometimes. John was surprised and said he thought they liked their flat and Brigid explained that they did but their neighbour was proving difficult, picking fault with them and spreading tittle-tattle with anyone who would listen.

'What sort of tittle-tattle?' asked John but Grace interrupted to say that was dreadful and they must just ignore him meanwhile squeezing John's hand tightly and hoping he would not enquire further.

'He is annoying,' Brigid added. 'Yesterday he told us we were being unpatriotic and not separating our rubbish properly and said he'd found a tin can in our food waste. He was quite aggressive saying if Ireland was at war, then he thought every scrap of metal would be saved by us and maybe the Irish should be sent home.'

Amy said that they would just ignore him for everywhere there were bound to be silly neighbour disputes in her experience and she just wanted to be left in peace with her books, her writing and most of all with Brigid. Grace took the opportunity to return to the poetry asking Amy whose lines about losing oneself she had quoted. Amy held up a magazine with an image of a winged horse on the cover and the word Poetry above, explaining that one of the ladies at the Sunday school had heard her say she liked poetry and had brought her six magazines which were wonderful.

'The poem One in Dublin is in here,' she added. 'It's by Blanaid Salkeld, I love it and the poems in here are wonderful.' They left Amy and Brigid with a promise from Amy that she would recite one of her poems when they came for tea in return in two weeks' time.

As they walked home John said that he thought he and Billy should have a quiet word with Brigid's neighbour for gossip was one thing but this was getting out of hand and upsetting their friends. Grace said she did not think that would be a good idea for the neighbour could probably cause even more trouble.

'Just because they're Irish?' replied John. 'I don't think so.'

They were passing Dollis Hill underground station but it was very quiet and Grace asked John to sit down on a wall nearby. Grace took his hand in hers and said she was never sure if John had understood about Amy and Brigid. John looked at Grace clearly not understanding so Grace went on, 'Amy and Brigid are in love like us, they are lovers like us John and that is not understood or accepted by everyone.'

John was quiet for a while then he said, 'There are some evil troublemakers in this world, aren't there?'

Grace pulled his hand to her lips and replied that love frightens some people and that is why they must protect their friends. They walked down to the park edge and Grace said that in any case Billy was in no fit state to be challenging anyone just now, we better go and check on him. When they reached the lodgings, Mrs C opened the door before John had turned the key.

'He'll be alright John; I've had some ice brought up from the restaurant and the swelling around the eye has gone down.'

Bettina took them through to her sitting room where Billy was holding a damp towel over his eye. Grace asked what had happened and Billy said some Communist Party members had attacked him in Trafalgar Square yesterday where he was selling Socialist Appeal. Billy said they were selling their pamphlet "Clear Out Hitler's Agents," aimed at Trotskyists and got aggressive when they saw him.

'One of them, a woman I think, swung her umbrella and caught me in the eye and another punched me in the head and I fell.'

Grace said it was a disgrace that violence was being used to try and intimidate other political arguments in the workers movement. Billy said luckily that was what most of the crowd listening to him speak thought and they chased them away.

'Might have got a good kicking otherwise for I couldn't see out of my eye.'

Billy let the towel drop and revealed black bruising and a swelling turning purple over and around his right eye. Grace was shocked and said she was going to speak to Tom Stone about this.

'I shouldn't bother Grace, before I was attacked, I passed Tom selling the pamphlet in the corner of Whitehall opposite Nelsons Column.'

Chapter 19
White Lines Were Painted (1943)

'Three cheers for the Red Army,' Tom proposed and even Tiny joined in the cheering which brought workers running from all parts of the factory.

Tiny was forced to repeat his analysis, discussed at length in his club last night that the German surrender at Stalingrad could be the turning point in the war. Hitler had declared that the Nazi army would never leave the city but now some quarter of a million Nazis and Rumanian fascists were captured and the oil supplies to the Red Army were intact.

'Three cheers for the Red Army and comrade Stalin,' shouted Tom again but this time John replied with a shout of 'Stalin must stop shooting his own commanders and waging terror, victory to the working-class of the Soviet Union and the world.'

The workers were confused and the cheering was stifled this time, across the workshop Grace saw Tom glaring at John until one of the new managers Blunt intervened telling everyone to disperse so that everyone could support the brave soldiers with the best equipment they could have. 'Cricklewood must do its bit,' he shouted as the crowd dispersed.

After work Grace, John, Amy and Brigid went round to John's lodgings as Billy had been to Liverpool to visit Martha. Somehow Benedetta's living room had become a meeting place for the friends and Benedetta would fuss and apologise that rationing meant she had no real food to give them when everyone knew Sicilians were the most hospitable people in Italy. Billy was drinking tea in the corner of the room when his friends arrived and he said that Martha sent them her love and was sorry not to have said goodbye.

'Is she not coming back?' asked Brigid and Billy said she simply could not.

'Her mam was worse and needed caring for all day and her dad was not coping so Martha had to get his breakfast ready before seven and virtually force him out of the door to the docks. Her bit of Liverpool has been badly hit by bombing so although neighbours try to help, they've all got problems with overcrowding and feeding their own families.'

No one said anything except Mrs C who whispered something in Italian and crossed herself. Billy said they might as well know that Martha had said they should split up for even if Billy moved to Liverpool, she would be tied to the house nearly all of the time. Everyone could see Billy had not agreed with this but no one knew what to say until Brigid said she wanted to know more about Billy's groups views on Stalin and what John had said that morning. Grace could see this cheered Billy a little and said she would like to come too. On the bus home, Amy expressed surprise that Brigid was getting involved in politics again but Brigid said not to worry she only wanted to educate herself a little just as she was reading more books now she shared Amy's passion for reading.

'I was thinking last night how little I knew about the IRA leadership but I was prepared to help them. If I'd known they were working with the Nazis. I don't know what I would have thought for England's enemy is Ireland's friend but surely not brutes like Hitler.'

Brigid paused and, as the top deck was empty, Amy squeezed her hand and said she was sticking to poetry if Brigid did not mind and Brigid squeezed her hand back and said poetry was very important but in any case, Billy was a friend and it was obvious he was very upset at losing Martha and he needed his friends to support him.

'I'm not sure the Workers International League is good at mending broken hearts.'

*****

Hetty Keen lived in the East End and had invited Billy and "any contacts he had" to supper and a political discussion. Brigid, John, Grace and Billy walked the last two miles to Roman Road and knocked on Hetty's door which was opened by Roy who announced, 'Four more for the anti-imperialist united front discussion,' and ushered them into the flat.

There were half a dozen young people sat on the floor of the tiny living room including a young man in army uniform called Roger and Billy only recognised one from Kings Cross and when Roy introduced everyone it was obvious this was the first meeting for most. Roy worked on the docks and occasionally could procure food and other damaged goods so when Hetty appeared at the door from the kitchen wearing a flowered pinny she was able to announce, 'Irish stew is served, in honour of our comrade Brigid.'

They filed into the kitchen and received a plate of thick stew with dumplings and runner beans. Brigid declared it the best meal she had eaten since the war began and Hetty gave all the praise to Roy.

'For a cook is only as good as the ingredients and Roy somehow manages to find the occasional treat.'

Hetty went on to say that Roy had challenged one of Mosley's supporters on the docks before the war and beaten him in a fist fight outside Smithfield.

'It's never been forgotten for as the fascist slunk away, Roy shouted after him that this was the spot where Wat Tyler was murdered and no one would divide the working class here again. Even today some of the dockers exclaim, 'You want some, Wat,' whenever anyone opposes the union.'

Roy had disappeared into the kitchen, apparently embarrassed, and could be heard running the tap and filling the kettle to wash up. Brigid stood up and announced it was time to clear up and took her plate to the kitchen causing all the others to follow and soon the narrow doorway was blocked. Brigid announced there had been a decision of the Central Committee and Billy would wash the pans and plates, John would dry them and Roger would put them away.

John asked what the women comrades would be doing whilst the work was being done and Grace responded that the women would be holding an important theoretical discussion. Roy stepped forward and handed round some candles saying it would get darker later and announcing that 'the British imperialists have been bombing the German imperialists in Berlin at the weekend so we may get interrupted later. If we do, run for the underground station, it's the safest place for miles around.'

Billy asked if the government had built these shelters and Hetty said he must be joking and it was only when she, Roy and others from the tenants association had refused to move from the station platform that a campaign began. Roy reached behind the sofa and passed some leaflets round and Roger read aloud 'Over a thousand Londoners killed and four thousand wounded because the government refuses to build bomb shelters. The rich have sent their children to America to protect them but the children of the working class are being offered no protection.'

Roy suggested that they examine the nature of the imperialist war now the USA was fully involved and made some opening remarks about the rival imperialisms fighting for territory and influence. He indicated that the imperialists were trying to silence those opposed to the war and eighteen members of the Socialist Workers Party of America were facing jail sentences including Cannon the SWP leader and now entire print runs of The Militant had been destroyed by the US Attorney General. He mentioned the attacks in Parliament following Billy's article on British imperialist crimes.

'Comrades, everywhere they fear our ideas but we are growing in influence and our tasks are huge.'

John put his hand up and, just as he was about to comment, a familiar whine was heard and Hetty said the discussion would have to continue on the Bethnal Green platforms.

'Comrades follow Roy and stick together and we will try to continue in the station. Walk as quick as you can but there are old people and children also and it is dark now, so be careful.'

Outside it was calm and most of the group linked arms in lines of four with Grace, John and Billy linked with Hetty at the back. They started to walk briskly along the road keeping the line in front just in sight or at least in contact by talking as the blackout was in full force. Just then a huge booming noise was heard very close and the crowd started to run. Grace gripped John tightly as if to indicate a need to stay calm but it was no use, men carrying children broke their line and rushed past and soon everyone was running towards the station.

In front of them, Brigid stumbled over a small child and fell to the floor. The little girl, perhaps two years old, screamed in terror and when Roger braced himself against the crowd and helped Brigid up, he saw she had gathered the girl in her arms. Roger heard Brigid say, 'We'll find mummy' but then a huge pressure carried them forward and they were swept on barely managing to touch the ground with their feet.

The crush was frightening and Brigid struggled to keep the child's head protected whilst Hetty tried to stand behind and shield them. As they reached the tube Brigid saw John's cap above the crowd and shouted but at the steps there was suddenly a collapse and bodies were falling forward. Grace saw what was happening and managed to force herself away from the step and joined Billy in shouting warnings to stop or they would be a crush. Roy anchored himself to an entrance post and held Billy tight by an arm whilst Billy tried to pull people away from the crush, people were confused and one man took a swing at Billy thinking he was trying to stop him getting shelter. Hetty appeared alongside and she and Grace started to chant, 'Stop pushing, there's a crush,' and soon they were joined by others and eventually the forward crush of the crowd halted.

Brigid had walked with the child around the crowd and onto Bethnal Green itself where she sat on a bench trying to console the little girl who had not stopped screaming. Brigid could hear cries and screams from the tube and, after a while, shouts to get people out. Billy and several other men had formed a line down the first few steps to the tube and were helping pass children up to the top.

Grace was there and the first child she was passed was a gap-toothed boy of six. His fair hair was unusually long and flopped across his face but Grace realised he was not breathing and she hugged him close, carried him to an open space and tried mouth to mouth resuscitation. The noise from the station was deafening and soon Grace realised the boy was dead and she picked his head gently from the wet turf and began to cry.

*****

Next morning it was Billy who stirred first and saw the clock stood at ten to ten. He looked round and first saw Hetty sitting in the armchair staring straight ahead with a mug of tea resting on the arm of the chair. Billy could hear a gentle snore coming from the other corner and he looked round to see Roy laid with his mouth open and he got up to gently move Roy's shoulders so that the noise stopped.

He went over to Hetty who did not move and he picked up the mug and noticing the tea was cold and untouched said he would make a fresh brew and, receiving no reply, walked into the kitchen. As the kettle slowly boiled, he thought he would check the bedroom to see if any other comrades were there. He knocked gently and Brigid opened the door and said she would like a slurp of tea as she would need to find Grace and help her, for Grace had gone out again half an hour ago to search for John.

Hetty stirred and said that eventually after the ARP and police had chased them away round about four in the morning, they had come home but because Roger was in uniform, he had been allowed to continue helping and had knocked on the door an hour earlier.

'He'd been up the rest of the night and took bodies to the Salmon and Ball on stretchers. He came back with a warden and I made us all tea, the man said Roger had saved a baby on the steps. I don't know, I don't. Such a terrible waste.'

Billy came through with a tray of cups of tea just as Hetty was finishing and explaining that Roger had gone back to Woolwich and sent his love, 'He'll be on a charge he expects for a late return.' The clinking of cups woke Roy who stretched and grunted and sat up.

'Where's Grace?' he asked and Brigid explained.

'We must find her quickly,' Roy replied then told them he had some very bad news.

'I went out again an hour ago to Queen Elizabeth's hospital, the kids' hospital, John Wood was there amongst the dead bodies. I'm so sorry Billy and Brigid.'

*****

Grace had spent the last two days at Brigid and Amy's flat. None of them had wanted to go to the factory and they had talked about John until late into the night. Grace kept returning to how she knew John wanted to propose but she had always avoided giving him the chance and now it was too late. Amy and Brigid did their best to console Grace but there was little they could say and they were both relieved when Grace announced that she was going to work on Saturday saying that she needed to get details of John's family for she could not yet face going to Mrs C's. Amy promised to go with her but Brigid asked if it would be alright to visit Hetty for she too had been in shock.

Hetty was surprised to see Brigid for she had set the morning aside to get the washing done.

'Roy's leafletting at Bethnal Green so I thought I'd catch up on the washing,' she explained.

She went back to the mangle which was in the kitchen and asked Brigid to put the kettle on. Hetty continued to turn the mangle with one hand whilst checking that there were no studs still attached to the collar and gently easing the shirt through. Brigid started to help hold the shirts and said that she had not used a mangle since leaving Ireland.

'My big sister, Agnes used to turn and I used to feed,' Brigid said. 'And which of you emptied the bowl.'

'It should have been my big brother Conan,' Brigid replied. 'But he could never be found when the bowl was full.'

Hetty laughed and said he sounded like a typical man and quickly added that Roy was one of the best though.

'He sweeps the yard every summer and made the bed only three weeks ago.'

She could see Brigid was confused by this and added, 'I'm joking, Brigid, why only last summer he made us both a cup of tea.'

This time Brigid got the joke and exploded with laughter so that her full cup of tea slopped over onto the floor. Brigid apologised but Hetty said not to worry Roy would clear up the mess when he came home. They both laughed so much at this that Hetty had to put her hand up to signal a stop. When she had regained control, she looked across at Brigid.

'Your face lights up when you laugh Brigid, you really are a handsome young woman with those gorgeous cheekbones. I'm surprised young Billy isn't trying to romance you.'

Brigid went quiet and then said that Billy had recently lost his girlfriend who had returned to Liverpool to care for her mother. Hetty said she was sorry to hear that and started on the shirts again and Brigid was glad to focus on the task, together they emptied the bowl and then Brigid started to feed Roy's sock through. Hetty said it was clear that Brigid was expert at the task and Brigid replied that her mam had taken in washing from Bantry and so she had got used to helping with washing when she was about four or five years old. When the socks and shirts were finished and hoisted on the washing line above the kitchen, Hetty carefully extracted Roy's long johns and other undergarments from the sink into a small tin bath.

'I'll do those later for there are some tasks I wouldn't ask an Irish revolutionary to perform,' she laughed.

They sat down at the table and Brigid produced a brown paper bag from her coat and took out two slices of cake. 'The very best Irish apple cake rationing will allow.'

They sat there munching their cakes until Brigid said that it seemed wrong to be laughing and eating cake when poor John was just killed.

'I just wanted to see if you were alright Hetty, you looked so lost when I left you.'

There was a pause and Hetty said it was hard she wanted to focus on how angry she was at Herbert Morrison and his ridiculous sheds and them not giving a toss about the safety of East Enders at the station.

'That's what Roy has done, he's barely said a word about the deaths of people we know but he was up all night producing a leaflet, determined that Churchill cannot cover up this disaster.'

Brigid waited for somehow, she knew Hetty had something more to say and soon Hetty said that she was angry but also the last two days had been the worst of her life.

'I sat with Mrs Jones upstairs last night, suddenly she has lost her mother and brother in one night, and it's unbearable. One of the children that always said hello is gone and we've had to have a collection for the funeral and then there is poor young John, only came for my meeting, how must poor Grace be feeling?'

A tear fell down Hetty's face and Brigid brought her chair round and put her arm around her. They both wept now holding each other until they heard Roy open the front door and hang his coat up.

He called from the hall, 'Cops wanted to arrest us, there's a big cover-up going on, the bastards are painting white lines on the bloody station steps, bit fucking late.'

Roy entered the room saw Brigid and stopped, 'Oh, sorry Brigid, pardon my language, didn't know you were coming round.'

He saw that Hetty had been crying and asked, 'You alright love, terrible business Brigid so sorry about John, any news on Grace?'

Brigid explained that Grace was trying to find out the funeral details as John was from Leeds but she was very upset.

'Naturally,' Hetty said, 'no human being should have to bear such pain.'

Brigid said she had to be going as she had a friend to visit and Hetty said she would walk with her some of the way. Hetty did not want to pass the station just yet and so they parted with a hug and a promise they would arrange to meet again soon. Brigid walked on avoiding the guarded station and she felt it had done her good to cry for sometimes words were not enough. By the time she reached Maureen's digs, she felt ready for her friend's company. Maureen answered the door and apologised that she could not invite Brigid inside explaining that there was a wake in progress for her landlady's brother had died.

'Seems like a lot of poor souls died trying to get into Bethnal Green station during the bombing on Wednesday.'

Maureen suggested they stretch their legs and find a pub as it was too cold to sit outside so they set off up the Old Ford Road and Maureen explained that she and Hank had been in the West End and she had only learnt of the disaster at work the next day. As they passed Victoria Park Maureen learnt that Brigid had been caught up in the tragedy and pressed Brigid for details. Brigid said she needed a drink and so Maureen linked her arms with her friend and guided her left eventually entering the first pub they saw, the Lord Napier. Inside were a dozen men some studying the racing form whilst one group played dominoes.

Brigid sensed they were not welcome and suspected that possibly no women ever visited but, as she expected, Maureen went straight to the bar, greeted everyone and ordered two drinks. They took them to a corner table and Brigid told Maureen the news about John and for once Maureen was silent until after a long pause, she said she had always liked John when she met up with him in Cricklewood…'one of those people who seems to have hidden depths.'

Brigid agreed and they raised a toast to John and Maureen asked when the funeral was and Brigid explained about his family in Leeds and wondered how they were all going to get there. Maureen said that if she or Hank could help in any way then they would.

*****

Hank had arranged to arrive early to make sure they could get to Leeds by lunchtime. When Grace heard his single horn toot, she had already been awake for hours and had dressed quietly so as not to wake Brigid or Amy who were under army blankets on the floor. Brigid woke up with a start and quickly washed and dressed, Amy stirred and offered to make tea but Brigid told her to get her beauty sleep for an hour as they had to get started as Leeds was two hundred miles away.

Grace had been upset that Willans had refused to let more work colleagues travel to the funeral. He had been adamant that the days already lost and the impact of John's death had badly affected production already and had sent Blunt round with the message that John would never have wanted the war effort reduced with the Allies fighting on so many fronts. Willans had wanted only Grace to go but had eventually agreed she could take a companion and Billy and Brigid had agreed that should be Brigid. Billy had considered going anyway but he remembered he got emotional at funerals and, if that happened, it would not help the Wood family.

'I'll visit Leeds as soon as I can and say my own farewell to John, the best mate anyone could have,' Billy had promised Grace.

The worry of this negotiation had added to Grace's concerns that she had never met any of John's family and, as time had worn on, she had begun to wonder if John was ashamed of her. It had not helped that Tiny, intending to wish her well for the day, had mentioned that Yorkshire folk all distrusted strangers.

A thin sleet was driving into the windscreen and Hank glanced round to see both Brigid and Grace were asleep and realised he had been talking to himself for the last ten minutes. He checked the road for hitchhikers but there were none out in the cold and wet and then suddenly the weather worsened and he had to concentrate hard through heavy snow. He decided he needed a short stop and left the main road, soon driving into a town square and pulling to a halt. Hank got out and could see two young men challenging each other to a snow sliding contest across the square until one crashed into the side of a pub named The Queen to the amusement of his friend. Hank opened the back door and the blast of cold air woke the sleeping women who stepped out and exclaimed about the cold.

'Oh Hank, have you been driving in this whilst we've been asleep. Come on we must get you a nice warm drink.'

Brigid surveyed the scene, nothing seemed to be open, and it was too early for the pub to be open so they crunched across the snow barely able to see for the lack of lights and the snow.

'Christ, where are we? It's worse than Cricklewood,' Brigid exclaimed.

Hank laughed and said they were in the heart of mining country, a town called Doncaster and they should treat the town with respect as it was keeping the army fed with coal. They spotted a light from a café and headed towards it and as they entered a blast of welcome heat and cigarette smoke hit them and Grace could see two large coal fires crackling on the far wall. The warmth had led several of the men present, there were no women, to discard their jackets and sit in shirtsleeves.

Hank had on a trilby and his dark overcoat and as he went in search of seats, Brigid thought he resembled a movie gangster disappearing into fog. Grace was dressed in her best funeral attire and made the mistake of inspecting the surface of a chair for any grime. An old man spotted this and called, 'Tha'll need clean chairs for the lasses' to a lanky boy serving at the counter and another voice added, 'And no wiping 'em with that filthy washcloth either Jonno,' causing laughter on several tables.

Brigid and Grace stood awkwardly not quite sure what to do until Jonno emerged from behind the counter with two new chairs. Hank thanked both the boy and the old man and the latter asked what an American was doing over here. Hank thought for a moment and answered he was involved in logistics. The old man seemed satisfied murmuring, 'Logistics, very important in mining too,' to his companion. After they had drunk their tea, Hank suggested they had better get on and stood up to leave. The old man got up and shouted aloud, 'Raise your mugs to the USA and these fine young Americans, over here on logistics.'

There was a cheer to which Hank replied that the American government thanked those producing coal for the war effort. In reply to a question Hank told the café that they were on their way to a funeral in Armley and several men wished them a safe journey. Outside the snow was falling again and Brigid pointed out they could barely see the imprints of their previous footsteps, just as they reached the car a young man caught up with them.

'Can youse givus a lift to Armley, I know the best way?' he asked Hank.

Hank agreed welcoming the company to help keep him focused. They set off and Hank discovered the young man was only sixteen and in reply to a question whether his father was serving the boy laughed saying his dad was in the unpaid army of His Majesty, serving twelve years for armed robbery. Sensing their surprise, he added, 'Don't worry, it's not a hereditary disease as me ma used to say.'

The boy told them to call him Scouse, everyone else in Yorkshire did, and went on to explain that his dad would have been hung but his victim had survived though he was now in a wheelchair.

'Me dad says he wouldn't have minded being hung but not with Big Barry, that's his accomplice who carried the shooter. See they hang 'em in pairs in Armley, the week me dad arrived Pierrepoint hung two together, one of 'em had battered a greengrocer and they say it was personal because Pierrepoint's dad was a grocer. Any road Barry's lost three stone in prison so maybe a double drop next time.'

He paused to laugh giving Brigid time to say they were on the way to a funeral and did not want to hear any more about death and killing. Scouse seemed to understand but within ten minutes he was chatting away again about prison food, the Vauxhall Road gangs he was involved in and how he was fed up visiting prisons. Brigid wondered if he suffered from some condition preventing him from hearing others or just a compulsion to talk, the opposite of her cousin Frances back home who barely spoke at all. Eventually Hank simply asked Scouse the way to Hall Lane, 'That's easy, right next to the prison.'

He directed Hank through Leeds, showing them the Town Hall lions, and on to the west of the city. When they reached the street, he asked to be dropped off and wished them well.

'Christ that's a relief,' Hank said. 'I thought we'd never get rid of him. I'm so sorry, Grace.'

Grace though was relieved they had got here in time, 'It's only an hour to the funeral, perhaps we had better go in,' she said.

The house had several men smoking outside, mainly visible through the sleet by the faint glow from the end of their Woodbines. Two of the men stepped over to inspect the car and Brigid noticed that they each wore identical caps, with the snow forming a white wall on their peaks as if they had all been given a ribbon of promotion. Hank asked the first man if this was the funeral for John Wood, for they were his friends from London.

'Better he'd nivver bin forced to go there,' said the first man walking away.

The second man stepped forward taking off his cap and tapping it on his leg.

'I'm sorry that's our John's younger brother Dennis, he's taken it hard. Thank you all for coming, we knew John had some good friends, you must be Billy, and I'm Ron, John's older brother.'

Hank explained who he was and why Billy would visit later, he took Ron aside and explained about Grace. Hank turned and saw Grace and Brigid being covered in snow and asked if they should wait in the car.

'Of course not, I'm a rude bugger me, come in and warm up.'

Ushering them into the house Ron said, 'So you're the Yank chauffeur today, Hank, good of you to bring the lasses, bonny pair, aren't they? John always had girls interested in him.'

Hank had laughed at the chauffeur comment and said perhaps he should have a peak cap like Ron and Dennis.

'Government issue I'm afraid,' said Ron, 'we've had prison warders in the family nearly a hundred years. Poor John was the first in the family ever to leave

Yorkshire, didn't fancy the prison life, can't say I blame him. Dad was a warder for forty years and Dennis and I just followed him.'

Hank asked which prison they served in and, after Ron had introduced Grace and Brigid to his sister Dot, he showed Hank through to the back garden. Looming above the garden, through the snow, were two turrets as if a small castle had been built there.

'Armley Jail,' said Ron with obvious pride. 'Keeping Leeds safe for a hundred years, it's the same model as Pentonville but we don't let 'em escape like the Cockneys do.'

They went into the back sitting room and found Grace and Brigid being introduced to a small squat woman who was wearing a black felt hat with soft rims which accentuated her plump face. Mrs Wood introduced Grace and Brigid to her friends and relatives, announcing them as John's London friends and when Hank reappeared, she said it was a great honour to have an American ally visit them adding, 'My late husband would have been so proud.'

She seemed overcome with this so Dot asked if anyone needed more tea and conversations restarted. Grace, Brigid and Dot managed to find a quiet corner in the kitchen. Dot told them the family history, how John's dad had died of a heart attack whilst on prison duty ten years ago and it had been a real struggle since. Brigid asked if Mrs Wood knew Grace was John's fiancée and Dot looked surprised and said that if she did, she had never said anything.

'John was her favourite, we all knew, and she was heartbroken when he moved and, although he wrote often, he rarely came home. Dennis was one of Mosley's men and he and John could barely stay in the same room together, it's why John moved to London.'

Grace was learning more about John than he had told her and, though she tried, her face betrayed her anguish. Dot noticed and added, 'Mam never told us much of what was in her letters from John, she kept them in a locked box under her bed. He would have told her about you, Grace, I'm sure, but she might have thought it would mean John would never come home again or she was not going to let Dennis and Ron know, she knew they didn't like their brother.'

Dot paused then added, 'I liked John, but I was only eleven when he left and now, I'll never get to know him.'

She could not help a tear falling and the three linked their shoulders together with their arms. They stood silently for a moment and Grace then thanked Dot as it had helped her understand a lot, Dot was about to reply when Ron came in and said they all needed to stay strong for John's mam and it was time to get to the church as traffic might be held up.

Brigid was relieved when the funeral ended, she had never liked funerals, not even the republican funerals back home which ended with shots across the grave. Looking round the bare interior of Holy Trinity she missed the brass and golden gilded statues of the Catholic churches, whilst here the greyness of the light on the pale pillars and the dark brown of the pews created a gloom which echoed the dark uniforms of the warder's guard of honour. The service had been unbearable, if only the assembled state servants knew John had been associating with Irish republicans, and Trotskyists.

At least in Cork and Kerry everyone, including the priests who might ritually denounce violence, knew exactly why and how the young man had died even if the rebel songs were only sung after the service. Here though the vicar had talked of someone who had attended Sunday school, sung as a treble in the choir as if John's life had ended before he became an adult and John's name was simply inserted into a prepared script. Grace firmly stepped out of the church and into Boar Lane, immediately needing to put up the umbrella Hank had found in the car boot.

The snow was falling straight down now, thicker than before, and she could just see Dennis and Ron ahead, seemingly arguing with the undertaker. Ron came over and said he was sorry but the hearse could not get up the hill to the cemetery and the burial would have to be postponed until the weather cleared.

'If you don't set off for home soon Hank, there's a chance you'll get stranded, the churchwarden heard the Home Service weather warning and the snow is going to continue all night.'

Hank thought for a moment and said it was so dark now that it would be against regulations to drive back to London today.

'I can't risk a diplomatic incident,' he joked. 'And I must have the car back tomorrow night. I suggest we find a hotel for the night and set off early tomorrow.'

Brigid leant over and said she could not afford a hotel and in any case her flatmate Amy would be worried where she was. Hank asked Grace if she could think of anything as he could probably claim expenses for three hotel rooms provided his field report on Leeds was good enough. Brigid said she would ring Mrs C and ask Billy to let Amy know. Brigid went to find the vicar to ask to use the telephone and Mrs Wood came over to Grace and took her to the side.

'I'm so sorry you can't come back to the house for some tea, I so wanted to talk to you. John told me all about you in his letters.'

Grace felt a huge relief. 'I'm so glad Mrs Wood, I did wonder.'

'Perhaps I shouldn't say but he said he was going to ask you to marry him but he wasn't sure how you would have replied.'

'I'd have said yes, I loved John.'

Mrs Wood held Grace in an embrace and whispered, 'We've lost the one we loved most.'

They parted without a further word and soon Hank was suggesting they make a move. He moved the car into a roofed space next to a shop and said he hoped it was not far to a hotel. Ron directed them along Boar Lane and Brigid and Grace sheltered behind Hank as the snow now blew straight into them.

'It helps to have a big fella around sometimes, huh,' shouted Hank as he wrestled with the umbrella.

They reached the square and Hank made out the railway station and headed there, spotting as he did so the Queens Hotel. A man in a maroon coat was stationed at the door and handed them a clean towel each and a clothes brush to share. Brigid and Grace went to the washroom, as Hank called it, and he went to enquire about rooms. When they emerged Hank was waiting holding three keys. 'The last rooms at the inn,' he said adding that he needed a Bourbon and he would meet them in the bar at seven if that suited. They agreed and Hank told them dinner was booked for seven thirty.

Brigid went with Grace to her room and to their amazement there was a maid lighting a fire in the hearth. The girl turned and asked if there was anything else madam needed.

'Oh, please just call me Brigid and this is Grace.' The girl looked confused but managed to explain that they were only allowed to call guests sir or madam.

'Or miss if they are girls,' she added. Brigid apologised and said she would not want to get anyone into trouble. The girl said there was a drying room downstairs and if anything was damp, she could take it there, it would be dry in an hour. Grace said that was wonderful news and could she collect some things in a moment as they had not really come prepared for snow. The girl left and they both took off their jackets, skirts and blouses and neatly stacked them. Grace then opened the bathroom door and called for Brigid to look.

'I've never stayed in a hotel before,' Brigid said. 'Would it be alright to have a bath in the morning before breakfast?'

Grace picked up two large white towels and said she was certainly going to, in fact she was going to have a basin wash now, and it would warm her up. The girl returned and collected the clothes and Brigid realised she could not now go to her room until her clothes returned.

'I'd like you to stay please,' said Grace. 'I don't want to be alone.' She offered Brigid the towel and said, 'Go ahead and use this, there is a week's supply in the cupboard.'

Brigid took off her petticoat and her brassiere saying, 'This snow has got everywhere, I'm hanging these by the fire,' and soon Grace could hear the splash of water and Brigid called out that the water was piping hot. Brigid came back into the room rubbing the towel across her shoulder blades and suddenly shouted, 'No.'

Grace turned to see Hank had opened the door and stepped inside, now standing still as if unable to move. Brigid quickly moved the towel to cover her breasts. 'Get out,' she shouted and only then did Hank turn away and apologise through the door saying he had only wanted to check they were comfortable.

Grace said he should have knocked and they would see him in the bar as arranged. She looked at Brigid who was shivering with anger,' no man has ever seen me without clothes,' she said, 'I hope he never tells Maureen about this.'

Grace replied that it was typical of Brigid to think of her friend straightaway. 'I'm so sorry that happened, Brigid, you've been such a friend to me today.'

The women sat quietly saying little and Grace began to doze in her chair, so Brigid covered her in a blanket. Brigid was enjoying the fire which calmed her and she began thinking back fondly to the farmhouse and the songs her father would sing on dark winter nights and how Conan would be sent out to the woodshed for logs with her dad saying, 'You don't want the girls to get ambushed outside.'

Once when he was about ten, Conan had argued that girls had to learn not to be afraid of the dark too but his dad did not reply or even look at him until he had no choice but to fetch the logs. Brigid remembered suggesting they brought more logs in during the day but her dad had smiled at her and said Conan needed to learn that the dark was a soldier's friend. Her memories were interrupted by a knock on the door and a soft call, 'Your clothes are ready madam.'

Brigid noticed the clothes had been ironed and were still warm and she reached into her purse for some change and thanked the girl. Grace had woken and Brigid hurriedly dressed and said she would visit her room and come back shortly.

It was half past six when Brigid returned and suggested they go downstairs for a drink if Grace was able to.

'I think that big American owes us that,' Grace replied and Brigid smiled at her and said she was sure John would never had wanted too much misery on his behalf adding it was a great Irish tradition to toast those that have gone.

They reached the bar which was crowded with people hiding from the weather but they soon found Hank who was regaling a group of men gathered in a circle, some joke with the punchline 'The Canadians of course' set all the men laughing. Hank quickly ordered them a drink and said hotels were great places for meeting new people and one of the men, already quite drunk, said it was a great place for meeting beautiful girls. Grace ignored this and looking round asked if anyone knew why they were in the Ivanhoe bar. Hank, it turned out had studied Sir Walter Scott at school and soon was telling of Robin of Loxley who some said was the first socialist.

Brigid said it was a shame that the English had to have a Scot make up their outlaws for everyone knew the real outlaws were Irish such as Billy the Kid. The discussion got louder with Brigid loudly claiming Jesse James as Irish and telling of the exploits of James Frenemy and the Kellymount gang. Hank protested strongly that Brigid was claiming half of America as Irish, and the argument had grown so loud that the bar manager, dressed in a bow tie, asked them to keep it quieter. Grace suggested they went for supper and the three of them excused themselves.

Hank seemed calmer away from his companions and, suddenly remembering, apologised again for his intrusion.

'It's forgotten, Hank,' said Brigid. 'I was disappointed for you've always shown us respect but I can't forget your huge favour today. That was an awful drive and now you are buying us dinner.'

Hank thanked her and said he was glad to be able to help and the dinner and hotel was not on him but on President Roosevelt. Brigid said it was the first time she had ever stayed in a hotel and as her beer arrived, she proposed a toast, 'God Bless America.'

Hank said perhaps they should toast John's memory too but Grace said she would never ever forget John but could they not toast him. Brigid leant over and touched her friend's arm and asked Hank if he would get into trouble for the expense of the trip. Hank was relieved at the change of topic and said not to worry as Johnson, one of the men he had been talking to in the bar, was a mine owner and had promised him a briefing over breakfast. Hank said his report on the security of the coal supply should be easy to write after that.

Grace noted that Hank had revealed the sort of work he was doing for the first time and, as he had ordered two more Bourbons during the meal, she wondered what else he may reveal. As they left Hank suggested another round and soon the waiter appeared with two more beers and another large spirit. Hank began a long story about his visit to the Grand Canyon and Brigid was content to listen until Grace said she could drink no more, was very tired and would they mind if she went to her room.

Brigid insisted on going with her and Hank said he would escort them to their rooms as a gentleman should. They took the lift and as she reached her room Grace turned and thanked Hank, saying she could not have come if it was not for him and giving him a kiss on the side of his cheek. Brigid proceeded to the next door and simply said, 'Thank you Hank, goodnight.'

As she closed the door behind her, she was driven forward by the force of Hank pushing the door as he said, 'I need a goodnight kiss too,' and took her head in his hands, lifted her head up and forced his tongue between her lips. Before she could react, he lifted her whole body and carried it to the bed and he was ripping at her underclothes saying he had always wanted her. Brigid was trying to hold his arms back but realising it impossible said, 'Not like this Hank, let me help.'

He loosened his hold and, as he moved to the side, she slipped from under him and regaining her footing quickly moved to the fireplace. Hank stood up and she shouted that if he came closer, she would scream but he did not seem to hear and moved towards her unbuckling his belt as he did and saying nothing. As he came near, Brigid swung the poker hard in his face and he grunted as a crunching noise followed by a spurt of blood across his shirt sent him staggering backwards. Brigid was just as shocked as Hank, who stood there holding his nose with blood streaming down and seemed to realise he could not continue, turning for the door muttering something about the crazy Irish.

Brigid closed the door and locked it and stood shivering with shock and staring down at the large blood stains on the blue rug and the trail across the light carpet to the door and wondered, incongruously, if it could be cleaned. She breathed in and out regularly to calm herself and noticed a speck of blood on her blouse sleeve and scrubbed at it at the sink until it was gone and she could try to dry the area with a bath towel. Suddenly she thought of Grace and worried where Hank had gone so she picked up the poker and quietly unlocked the door and peered into the corridor.

Along the line in the corridor, she could see drops of blood heading away to the left towards the stairs and she ventured out and knocked hard on Grace's door and her friend soon appeared and seeing Brigid's face, wet with tears, ushered her quickly inside and locked the door. Grace poured a glass of water for her friend who drank it quickly and they sat there not speaking for several minutes until Brigid said she would describe what happened if Grace promised not to tell another soul.

Grace nodded and Brigid said, 'I don't want Amy or anyone to know. Hank tried to force himself on me, he would have,' she paused. 'He wouldn't listen, unless I'd hit him, he would have raped me, Grace. I'm so sorry.'

Grace took Brigid in her arms and gently wiped her face saying it was Hank who would be sorry and they should call the police. Brigid became agitated and sat up straight.

'You promised Grace we will tell no one,' and Grace reassured her that she would never mention it to anyone. They discussed what to do next and Grace went out to see if she could find out where Hank was, looking first in the bar but there were only a few men left there and not finding him she rang the bell at reception. A small older man appeared and Grace asked if he had seen her companion, the tall American. The man looked at Grace carefully and said that Mr Trotter had left about half an hour ago.

'I don't want to get involved madam or alarm you,' he added. 'But your husband looked like he had been in a fight or an accident and he was holding a hotel towel to his face.'

*****

It was two weeks later that Brigid was surprised by Maureen at the factory gate after work and she could see immediately that Maureen was worried.

'Have you seen Hank since you went to Leeds?' she asked immediately and Brigid said she had not but she was on her way to call on a friend and Maureen could come and they could talk. On the way Maureen explained that she had telephoned the factory but they had refused to let Brigid come to the phone so she thought it would be quicker to come.

'I was going to send a telegram but thought they might not deliver it, so I've taken a day off.'

They crossed the road and knocked and Roisin was delighted to see them saying that Diarmuid would be disappointed to have missed her for they had been talking about her that very afternoon. Maureen was introduced and Roisin said that all the best-looking girls seemed to have left Ireland and went off to make some tea. Brigid quickly explained that Hank had rushed off from the funeral and she assumed he had driven back to London adding that he had not told them why he was leaving. Maureen seemed even more worried and Brigid asked her if she was in trouble but before she could answer Roisin returned with a pot of tea on a tray.

They chatted for a while until Brigid explained that Maureen had come over from the East End with some family news and she wondered if they could just have a moment to discuss it. Roisin said she needed to make some sandwiches for Diarmuid for his shift and they were welcome to use the front room as long as they liked. As soon as the door closed Maureen said that she was not in trouble, she was always very careful but she was worried about Hank and what might have happened to him.

'He's probably on a special assignment, he was working on something whilst he was with Grace and I and it's probably top secret.'

Maureen seemed unconvinced so Brigid reached over and took her hand, 'You're really fond of him aren't you?'

Maureen said she was and she was missing him, she'd broken off her engagement and she hoped Hank might propose to her. Brigid struggled to continue talking about Hank, she did not want to have to think of him a moment longer and now she was finding Maureen absurd. She managed a final assurance that Hank would be in touch as soon as possible but she and Grace had agreed on the train back from Leeds, that Hank was almost certainly married already and probably had a family.

Besides Grace and a friend had gone to the pub in Shepherds Market two nights before and spoken to Sylvester and some Americans there none of whom had seen Hank and they assumed he had been posted, probably back to the States. Grace thought Hank might have requested a move fearing Brigid had gone to the police. Grace said it showed how little Hank knew if he was supposed to be a spy but she did not tell her friend that Hank had once described Brigid as possessing a fearsome beauty and of being a woman as firm in her principles as any woman he had met.

Chapter 20
Joe Louis

Billy had been selling Socialist Appeal in Leicester Square for two hours and the light was starting to fade, he had started the sale tired after a busy morning shift so he sat on the pavement, opposite to where the statue of Eros had been, whilst he summoned up the energy to travel to Kings Cross and help with the production of the next edition. There were only an old couple of Communist Party members who had bothered him accusing him loudly of being in the pay of the Nazis and he smiled as he thought that if it were true Hitler's hourly pay rate was very poor. He had enjoyed a couple of discussions with passing soldiers regarding whether Mussolini was finished and Italy would soon be out of the war, they had friends who had been fighting in Naples when news of Mussolini's overthrow had reached there and reported that most Italians hated Mussolini and wanted the war to end. Just as Billy was getting up to go a voice asked him if he knew where the Bouillabaisse Club was and as he looked up, he saw a black GI with his hand out and took it and was helped to his feet.

'My name's Edward,' said the soldier. 'And this is my buddy Malcolm we're a bit lost and in need of some jazz. Any idea where New Compton Street is, buddy?'

Billy offered to show them and they set off up Shaftesbury Avenue as Edward explained they were on weekend leave and had come from Checkendon in search of music and dance. Billy had to confess he had never heard of Checkendon and had never been to a jazz club so Malcolm said, 'Reckon we can sneak a white boy in, Edward?' and they both laughed.

Billy was a bit concerned, 'I won't have to dance, will I?'

Malcolm laughed a reply, 'Don't worry everyone knows white boys can't dance.'

Edward knew Malcolm was so excited he had not noticed Billy had a limp so he explained that Malcolm had been on so many charges from the MPs that this was his first weekend on leave for months.

'We're cooking for the battalion mostly and Edward has peeled more spuds than a man can stand.'

A few steps further and Billy heard a trumpet solo drifting out of a red lit club door. The doorman was reluctant to let Billy in but Edward said, 'Don't worry he's a brother,' and slipped something into his palm. Inside it was dark and they found a table next to the dance floor and within seconds a waitress was on them and Billy had ordered three beers.

Edward remarked loudly, 'A white waitress, wow my ma would think the Kingdom had come.'

There was a sergeant on the next table who had overheard and leant over to Edward and said, 'No smart remarks son or you'll be out, just drink your beer and relax.'

Malcolm had been tapping his feet since he arrived and glared at Edward in disapproval. Soon though he had persuaded a partner to join him on the dance floor. The men smiled at his line of chat offering to teach her the jitterbug and Edward said Malcolm had missed female company during his leave bans for initially, after a few days in Checkendon, he only had to walk into the Four Horseshoes to be surrounded by locals. Billy asked if there was any hostility but Edward explained the white US soldiers had upset the village by shooting up the weathervane so they seemed to have moved elsewhere.

'Just as well,' he added, 'because any trouble and the MPs always take the white soldiers' side.'

Billy asked Edward where he came from and Edward told him he was from New York.

'Harlem of course, though I was born in the slums of Greenwich.' Edward told him of the shock of the journey across the Atlantic. 'We knew that if the boat was torpedoed, we black troops would never get out from the bottom of the ship, whilst the white officers were lounging in the pool and the bars on deck, as if they were on a cruise.'

Billy understood a little of the bitterness of his new companion and said that now that everyone was in the army ready to fight things might improve.

'Guns,' snorted Edward. 'They'd never give us any guns, we're here to fly balloons and get bombed.'

They sat in silence for a while and then Malcolm returned during a break for the band. Billy asked if most of his 320th battalion were religious and Edward said they were and back home he had gone to the Episcopal Church four times a week, including twice on Sunday. Edward seemed unsure that Billy had believed him for he quietly recited: 'Man that is born of woman hath but a short time to live and is full of misery. He cometh up and is cut down like a flower.'

Billy interrupted to say he now knew Edward had learnt his Scriptures and Edward told they had found a white man who did not know the Book of Common Prayer.

'For Chrissake, Edward, they playin' Don't Fence Me In, I ain't got time to talk about religion.'

Malcolm got up and was soon dancing again.

'Take no notice of that Billy, he's a good man just a bit excited, like I was when I first courted Merrine. We getting married as soon as I get back.'

Billy congratulated Edward and they watched Malcolm dancing until Billy remarked. 'He's a good dancer for such a big man.' Edward agreed adding that Malcolm was well over six feet tall and suddenly remembering a story.

'When we passed through the port at Felixstowe there was a drunk there who grabbed Edward by the collar and called him a name, another guy told the drunk to leave him alone or there would be trouble and then he shouted out.

'We've got Joe Louis here, the man who defeated the Nazi Schmeling. It was chaos then everyone wanted Malcolm's signature and the whole platoon was halted until a sergeant threatened to arrest anyone who obstructed the troops. We laughed all the way to our billet, but don't mention it to anyone, after a few days Malcolm threatened to punch anyone who called him Joe again.'

Billy said he had been in the meat market when the second Schmeling fight took place and worked stopped when it began and people crowded around radios and Edward added that the whole of Harlem was on the street listening and when Schmeling threw in the towel you could hear the cheering on the Staten Island ferry.

'Every black man in America was cheering Louis and some white boys as well.'

Billy said he knew little about the history of mistreatment of black people in America and needed to learn more admitting that Edward was the first black person he had ever spoken to. Edward laughed and said such a conversation, in such a club, could never happen in America. Edward said if he had time tomorrow, he was going to try to find Dr Harold Moody for his work against discrimination and his League of Coloured People was known about in Harlem. Billy produced a copy of Socialist Appeal and wrote his address on it.

'Look me up if you ever have leave in London again,' and Edward promised that he would and pulling Billy's arm said, 'Now it's time to find some dance partners.'

Chapter 21
Fare Thee Well (1944)

Tiny would admit to himself, though not to anyone who asked him, that he always looked forward to his monthly meetings at the club in London. Partly he liked to know the detail of the war plans and the options being discussed for he knew this sustained his energy in the long working days but also, he saw it as a remembrance and tribute to his son, he wanted him to know that the Axis powers were being slowly beaten back and that his death had not been in vain and his father was keeping abreast of the war and encouraging everyone to work hard. Last night there had been a fierce discussion as to whether Churchill was right to insist on the Mediterranean war being prioritised against the insistence of Stalin and Roosevelts on a landing in Europe.

Tiny continued his weekly reports on the war to his workmates, he still enjoyed tea with Eastwood to discuss the war and the occasional pint with Tom, but he found them ill-informed as if they were chess players who only knew how to move the bishop or the rook but could not see the strategy behind the whole game. It was for these reasons that he had taken to giving separate reports, usually during the short break for lunch, to Grace and Billy. Grace in particular he found well informed and it was hard to disagree with her analysis that the war against Hitler was essentially won and it was only a matter of time before Kharkov was recaptured by the Red Army and the Germans were driven out of Rome and Kiev and probably the Crimea.

'It is a race for territory and influence and exploitation of resources between the Allies,' Billy added. 'We workers have no interest in the US capitalists and Churchill imposing their rule on us.'

Tiny countered that he had heard that Churchill had been outmanoeuvred by Stalin and Roosevelt and the invasion of France was being planned. Grace countered that it was not surprising there was this rivalry for the Americans were the strongest power now in the war and they would want their own access to resources like oil in the future.

'That means loosening the grip of the British Empire in Africa and India, perhaps,' Grace concluded.

'No wonder Churchill wants the status quo returned as soon as possible.' Tiny countered that the Empire had brought prosperity to England and Churchill was right to defend it.

'We'll never agree,' laughed Grace. 'But it is good of you to pass on the thinking of your military pals. It reminds me of my grandfather still reliving what he regarded as the glory days of his youth.'

Tiny protested that he was not that old and Billy agreed, adding though that Tiny was the only man he knew who had actually ridden a penny-farthing. This made Tiny laugh and he said he wished he had met the US soldiers, Billy had told him about.

'Maybe I'll borrow my mate's car and we'll go and see them when the weather improves, I should think Checkendon is a nice day trip, my aunt used to live out at Stoke Row just after the last war and we used to go walking in the Chilterns there.'

Billy agreed and as the hooter sounded and Billy and Grace left, Tiny thought it was time for some peace and quiet and a good think and, given the recent bitter January weather, he thought they would certainly be redwings at the reservoir on Sunday.

'And no one else,' he said aloud to himself with satisfaction.

After work Grace had asked Brigid to come for tea in Cricklewood for apparently Grace had discovered a new tearoom that 'worked wonders with the rations.' They strolled along the Broadway arm in arm as if they were on holiday and Grace appeared to have her eyes closed as she said, 'I'm imagining that winter sun on my face in Hunstanton.'

Brigid replied, 'Even better I'm on Dunmore Head and I can feel the sea mist blowing against my face.'

They stopped for a moment, facing what was left of the winter sun, as if savouring the sea air as a breeze wafted through their hair blowing strands across their face. A dark-haired man stood next to them and asked them what they were looking at.

'An eejit,' Brigid snapped laughing and guiding Grace away.

They soon found the restaurant and Brigid ordered two Woolton pies with gravy and they were delighted to find the pies smothered in cheese when they arrived.

'Don't ask,' Brigid said. 'Just enjoy, it's my treat.'

Grace protested but Brigid said she had some news and wanted to treat her best friend. They ate quietly, enjoying the rich vegetable mix and the potatoes alongside, Grace knew better than to ask a question and simply said it was the best meal she had eaten since the war began. Only when Brigid had ordered two teas did she say that she and Amy were leaving for Ireland next week. Grace assumed she meant a trip to see families but Brigid said that Amy had accepted a job in a wealthy farmers home to educate her children and she herself had been offered a gardeners and odd job role.

'The fresh air will be a sweet change from that factory and those machines, I may never see another clock face in my life.'

Grace was quiet and Brigid said she would miss Grace more than anyone but she hoped Grace would come and visit. Grace promised that and asked why Amy and Brigid were leaving. There were many reasons it seemed, Amy wanted to write poetry and the house was only two miles from Inch beach which could inspire anyone and it was close enough to Tralee and her mother and siblings but far enough away also as Amy had pointed out. Brigid had her reasons too; she could make visits to Conan in prison in Dublin and see her mother and sisters again when she visited Whiddy sometimes.

'There's something else too Grace, something I've never spoken about in England. My dad was an IRA man, fought for Irish freedom and was murdered in the reprisals by the Free Staters, we've never had a grave to visit. It's near Tralee and I want to spend some time there, maybe help put up a memorial to remember the heroes who never surrendered to the British.'

There was a silence, Grace did not know what to say until Brigid added, 'I was only six when they shot my dad,' Grace leant across and put her arm around Brigid and wiped the tears away.

'There's something else Grace, I can't stay in a country where a man tried to force me to. To…'

'Sshh,' whispered Grace. 'I know, I know.'

*****

In fact, Brigid and Amy had been forced to delay their departure as a result of the ban on all but urgent travel to Ireland or 'Churchill's bullying of de Valera to try and force Eire to break neutrality' as Grace described it.

They almost lost their job offer as they had to make special requests for permits to leave for Ireland and only after all the priests they knew had signed supportive letters and Tom Stone had asked Eastwood for a personal reference did permission arrive.

Tom spoke at the farewell party that Roisin was hosting this Sunday evening praising Amy and Brigid as the best babysitters anyone could want and remarking to laughter that when Eastwood heard it was Amy that was leaving, he got out his fountain pen and composed a letter of support to Churchill himself. Diarmuid had managed to procure a bottle of Jameson and Bettina had brought extra cups and they shared out the whisky with Bettina explaining that the Jameson family were related to Marconi who invented the radio. Mary Stone whispered to Grace that presumably Bettina did not know Marconi was a fascist.

The party went well and Amy read a poem, Emily danced to loud applause and Grace made a speech. The toast 'To Ireland' had just been made when Billy arrived and, obviously elated, said he brought greetings from the Revolutionary Communist Party formed that very day.

'Oh Billy,' said Amy. 'Give us a hug, you always have to bring politics into it.'

Walking from the party along the street, Billy told Grace that though they never discussed it he missed John every day especially now when strikes were occurring everywhere against the employers.

'John would have thrown himself into that, he is such a loss, such a good friend.'

Grace thanked Billy for mentioning John as she rarely got a chance to discuss him as it seemed no one knew what to say to her.

'I'll miss Brigid a lot too, she and I came from such different backgrounds but she is my closest friend and the only person I was able to discuss how I felt about losing John.'

They walked on and Billy said it seemed to him that a gang of the five of them, thrown together by the war, had been broken up. Grace said that was what usually happened to gangs eventually but, despite everything she would not have missed meeting them all. Billy agreed and said good night and Grace walked on turning to shout, 'When's the next meeting of the Party then?' and receiving thumbs up signal from Billy in return.

Grace had heard that the Workers International League had merged with other smaller groups of Trotskyists and managed to get Billy to explain how a week later over a lunch sandwich. Billy said that once again the American SWP had been keen to have one section of the Fourth International but this time there had been agreement to build an independent party of the working-class opposed to Labour and hence the name of the new party. Billy said the real triumph had been recruiting more young workers to the WIL which had guaranteed it a majority at the founding conference. 'Although it seemed the Americans were hoping for more support for their positions.'

Grace had her doubts and wondered. Now the war was being won, were the working-class not more likely to turn to the Labour Party but Billy said the current wave of strike action meant workers were seeing through Labour and, he added, 'Through the strike-breakers-in-chief, the Communist Party.'

He finished by telling Grace he was probably going up to Huddersfield soon, as a strike of apprentices was about to start on Tyneside and more organisers were needed to spread the strike and persuade the striking miners to support the apprentices. Grace realised that Billy wanted her to cover for him and agreed to pass on a story of domestic need to explain his absence.

'At the current rate of action, I'll need to become a full-timer soon,' said Billy. 'But Jock says the rates of pay are a disgrace.'

It was two weeks later that Billy arrived back at work and was immediately summoned to the offices.

'They don't seem to believe my aunty was very ill,' he laughed afterwards with Grace before telling her of the arrest of Party members Heaton Lee and Ann Keen in Newcastle and Roy Tearse in Glasgow.

'They wanted to arrest Jock Haston but he was on a speaking tour in Scotland and they could not find him only after he had taken his kids to a show one night did he walk into a police station in Edinburgh.'

Billy said he had been to Parliament with Ted Grant to brief Nye Bevan and other Labour MPs about the arrests.

'We watched from the gallery whilst Bevan was speaking against the secret trials and imprisonment of our members, Richard Stokes Labour MP from Ipswich called Bevin "The Gestapo", it caused a sensation.'

The next evening Grace insisted on paying Billy for some leaflets for the rally against anti-labour laws and took them to the factories in Edgware explaining the issue to some women there she knew from the AEU. In the factory she worked every day to persuade women to come and on 9th May eleven young women left work early at five and walked to Conway Hall in Holborn to hear a packed meeting elect Jimmy Maxton, Sydney Silverman, Reg Groves and Bevan and others to the campaign committee.

*****

Tiny had suggested that the last Sunday in May might be a good day for the trip out to Oxfordshire and Billy agreed saying he had been offered some petrol coupons but Tiny said he rarely used his friend's car and he had just finished levelling a floor for him and so the loan of the car and the coupons he had were his payment. Billy offered to buy Tiny's beers instead and Tiny agreed. 'As long as it's only a few, I haven't driven a car for a while.'

The sun was already shining as they drove past RAF Northolt and Tiny pointed out it was the oldest military airport in Britain "even older than the RAF." Billy did not want to encourage the sort of detailed military history he knew Tiny could talk for England about, so he said nothing for a while. Then he unwound the window as far as he could and said, 'It's going to be up in the 80's today again, do you mind if I take my tie off.' Tiny let out a little laugh and said, 'That's exactly what my son Eric used to say, he hated ties and always said collars made him itch.'

Billy was surprised as he had no idea Tiny had a son and decided to await more details. Tiny asked him if Tom had told him what had happened so Billy just said he and Tom rarely spoke now, 'Ah yes, of course, political differences I suppose,' said Tiny. Billy nodded and Tiny told him a little about Eric who was a couple of years younger than Billy.

'I think you two would have got along, he loved the sea but we didn't see eye to eye on politics, last time I saw him he said he was going to vote Labour.'

Tiny went quiet and Billy said he wished he had met him. Later as they passed over the Thames at Henley, Tiny added that Eric was one of the reasons he wanted to meet the young American soldiers. 'Such a bewildering thing to be over here at such a young age I should think, fighting in a war they never expected a few years ago. I want to thank them personally.'

Billy thought it best to remind Tiny, 'I did tell you Edward and Malcolm are part of a coloured regiment, didn't I, Tiny?'

'You didn't,' said Tiny. 'But even more reason to make them welcome.' Billy could not resist. 'I thought you hated foreigners, Tiny.'

Tiny looked across at Billy in mock offence then smiled, 'Only when they do bad things. I'm really looking forward to meeting your friends Billy, I've seen some coloured soldiers in the West End but I confess I've never spoken to one.'

Billy agreed that Edward was the first coloured man he had ever spoken to and in fact he had never met anyone from outside Britain, except for a couple of Irish boys at school, until he left Darlington. Tiny said London was a real meeting ground and he had often envied Eric for his tales of foreign ports.

'Before the war he wrote me a card whilst he was in an African café in Lisbon and I had to look up where Angola was on the map in the club. He was playing a trick on his dad, I reckon so I wrote back hoping he'd dock in Luanda one day.'

Billy lifted his hands to indicate he did not know where that was and this seemed to encourage Tiny who mentioned how much he had enjoyed talking to Benedetta at the leaving party for Brigid and Amy.

'I knew there were Italians who were imprisoned for opposing Mussolini but, of course, there were many who weren't that political but just did not want to fight.'

Billy said Benedetta had been the most wonderful landlady to both John and himself and was more like a second mother to them both. 'She doesn't really get much news on her husband or her son; it must be terrible not knowing. I daren't mention anything but we hear reports that the Nazis were allowed to attack and almost destroy the Italian resistance fighters after the British General Alexander announced a close down of the Italian campaign for last winter on radio.'

Tiny said nothing in response, deciding it was something he had no clear information about but would discuss at the club next week. As they turned left for Checkendon he told Billy that this war had shown him that war was a complex political matter and there were many innocent victims on all sides. Billy thought about mentioning Helmut to Tiny but decided that might be a step too far for today.

Tiny stopped the car outside a pub called The Black Horse, it had a sitting area out front and a few older men were occupying a table in the shadow of the pub roof. Billy asked them if they knew where the US military barracks were and the oldest of the men replied, 'It be just round there like, but we ain't seen 'em for weeks, have we boys?'

One of the other men nodded agreement so Billy and Tiny followed directions to the track to the left of the pub and within fifty yards they turned a corner to find a barrier blocking the road and four armed sentries standing behind it. A large sign read Stop. No Entry. Billy walked towards the barrier and behind could just see the first of a row of corrugated iron sheds, which reminded him of his classroom at Dodmire school, affectionately known as the tin shed.

'Halt. Turn Round and Leave,' shouted one of the soldiers. Billy thought for a moment about speaking to the guard but Tiny was tugging at his sleeve and Billy decided to retreat, 'It's time for that pint you owe me.'

Tiny said, 'We haven't come here to upset our allies.'

They went back to the pub and as they passed the older man asked, 'They not coming out to play then?' and Billy nodded.

Inside the pub was cool and rather gloomy, with dark wood giving it the feel, Billy thought of a Wesleyan chapel. There were no customers and no one in the room so Billy rang the small bell on a leather-bound book at the bar. There was no response so they took a seat by the door and Billy said that Edward had found this pub very welcoming and the landlord friendly, 'That's if he ever appears,' said Tiny walking to the bar and ringing the bell again.

There was still no response so Tiny sat down again murmuring that it had better be a good pint after this wait. Eventually from the corridor behind the bar they heard a door open and a bass voice say, 'No need to be a ringing that bell, Geoffrey, you know I'm busy shoeing old Larry, don't want him to go lame does ye?'

A small man emerged wearing a large leather apron that covered all his body to his neck. He saw the two men and apologised saying it can be a busy job being the local blacksmith and publican at the same time. Billy offered to buy him a pint and he accepted saying it was hot work over the forge on a sunny day. The three took long swallows and Tiny declared it the best beer he had ever tasted. Billy explained who they were and that they were hoping to meet his friends Edward and Malcolm from the battalion.

'You're not a girl's father, are you?' said the landlord directly to Tiny. 'No trouble is there?'

Billy explained that they just wanted to see his friends and the landlord apologised saying, 'That Malcolm had the gift of the gab for sure, though I never heard any gossip about him,'

The landlord explained it had been quiet in the pub for six weeks now as all the soldiers were confined to barracks and could be heard drilling and practicing with their balloons at all hours 'poor buggers.' Billy ordered another round and said it was a shame as he had wanted to give Edward his address just in case he wanted to write after the war, 'Or maybe I'll make it to New York one day.' The landlord disappeared behind the bar and came back with a piece of paper and a pencil.

'If you put your address there the wife might accidentally drop it near a friendly soldier when she delivers some eggs tomorrow,' Billy thanked him and wrote wishing Edward and Malcolm and their comrades the very best and put his address on the bottom.

'Poor buggers,' the landlord repeated, this time adding, 'reckon in a few days they'll be over in France, God help 'em.'

Chapter 22
Neath (1945)

Grace remained unconvinced about the usefulness of standing against the Labour Party arguing long into a late April evening with Billy and Jock Haston at the RCP offices in the Harrow Road. She had remained active in promoting the anti-labour laws campaign which had continued after the case against Haston, Pearse and the others was thrown out last autumn.

'The mood of these big rallies and the committee meetings was for change, against Churchill and the old order and for a Labour government. The RCP will only gain tiny support, now is the time to work in the Labour Party perhaps get some comrades elected as MPs.'

Jock was in total disagreement arguing strongly that an independent party needed building to be in place to argue for a seizure of factories and the army to be placed under workers control, 'Our best chance for twenty years to show the power of the working-class, we need to recruit the best individuals now whilst the Communist Party is totally discredited.'

Billy agreed that the Communist Party was losing support as it continued to argue for a national government under Churchill but the working-class was loyal and this needed to be explained in debate.

'Well,' said Jock. 'That's why I'm standing in Neath in the by-election, I only expect to gain a few hundred votes at most but it will be a great opportunity too. Why don't you both come down, I'll see if Heaton, my election agent, has any places in the car on Monday when he goes back. Our car is full tomorrow, I'm afraid we're taking the London printing press to the office in Neath.'

Grace responded immediately that she would come and campaign for the RCP, 'It would be a good education for me also; I've never been to Wales or to a coalfield.'

Next day, Heaton Lee and Billy were sat up front discussing the prospects for the Party. Grace could hear them talking of the Socialist Appeal sales figures in Wales since the big miners' strike last year with Heaton saying, 'Eight hundred copies still being sold in Merthyr and Swansea and a couple of miners from Pentremawr are coming to campaign, good comrades from the anti-labour law campaign. Course the Stalinists will try and ignore us so it's up to us to force them into the open.'

'You ready to pound the streets, Grace,' he called back and Grace said she could not wait to start.

Heaton had decided against the ferry over the Severn, 'Queues are massive at the moment' and so they stopped at Abergavenny for a late lunch. They ate the sandwiches Billy had brought and then sat at a café drinking tea whilst Heaton told them about Owain Glendower and how Abergavenny was declared independent in 1404. Billy asked whether Heaton had researched all this for the trip but Heaton simply replied that back in South Africa they had studied all opponents of colonialism. He added that he had decided to take a long route home from Neath so he could visit Newport, 'The home of the last armed working-class rising,' and, if they wished, he would take them.

Grace said she would love to for John Frost was one of her father's heroes and one November he had organised a Chartist commemoration meeting for the 90th anniversary of the rising. Billy asked what she would tell Willans about this holiday and Grace said she had decided not to go back to the factory.

'I'm thirty-two now and I've spent too much of my life in a noisy factory. Like Brigid and Amy, I need to be back in the fresh air.'

It was getting dark by the time they reached Neath and pulled up alongside Victoria Gardens. Heaton had to find the election office to check all the leaflets were being printed but Grace had been allocated lodgings with a family in Henry Street and Jock had sent maps of the location. The door of the terraced house was opened by a small wiry man who greeted Grace and asked if she was from the ILP. Grace said she hoped there had not been a mistake but she was here to support the Revolutionary Communist Party.

Just then a large woman in a pinny looked appeared behind him and said, 'Dai, what are you doing? Come in Grace, Jock Haston said you'd be here. Welcome to Wales.'

Grace went inside with her bag and was offered a seat next to the fire and Sara explained that she was still baking cakes for the party tomorrow.

'Is it someone's birthday?' asked Grace, causing Dai to laugh.

'Not Hitler's at any rate.' Sara explained there was to be a street party the next afternoon to celebrate the German surrender in Europe.

'It'll be a good chance to talk to all the neighbours in the street, whilst they've got time.'

Grace said she would be honoured to come and asked Sara if she could help with the baking and Sara replied that she had been given 'half the streets rations,' but still needed two Victoria sponges.

'My speciality,' said Grace.

The party was a big success, every child had been scrubbed up as if they were going to church but as the day wore on, they were chasing each other in endless games of tag. Grace discovered that Sara was hugely respected in the street and once Sara introduced her as someone from London who had only arrived at ten o'clock last night and had immediately started baking cakes, she had the ears of all the mothers stood around the trestle tables. It seemed none of the women had ever been to London and so she was asked if she had seen the King and what was Big Ben like. In turn she asked about their lives and it soon became clear they expected big changes after the war. Many were married to miners and said their husbands were treated like slaves, in dangerous conditions, 'Every shift you're never sure your husband is coming home.'

Grace said it was important that the mines be nationalised so that wages and safety could be improved.

'We have no need for a national government with the bosses, we need a workers government and to ensure that we need to vote Jock Haston to make sure Labour gets a strong message.'

There were murmurs of agreement and talk of how more housing was needed for younger people and jobs so they did not need to leave the valleys. By the time Billy arrived late in the evening with some Haston leaflets some of the older children raced round giving them out and posting through the doors of these who had gone home.

The week passed quickly with leafletting and canvassing and selling the election special of Socialist Appeal and Grace found herself enjoying the open air and the discussions. A message came from Heaton that they were not to visit the Alfred Street office as an outbreak of scabies there had affected him, Jock Haston and others.

Billy passed on the news and could not help pretending to scratch himself as he did so, 'The Fourth International infiltrated by the mite of the Communist Party,' he said prompting those around him to endless comments until Grace held up her hand calling for silence.

'Comrades, we must get back to work, though it has clearly been a rash decision to come to Wales.'

More laughter as the large team dispersed to their allocated streets although Grace had to explain to an exasperated Sara that it was a joke and she knew how spotlessly clean Welsh workers kept their houses.

The South Wales Communist Party was very strong and at first it had tried to ignore the RCP campaign. As the street meetings increased and Haston's previous imprisonment for supporting the miner's strikes became widely known, the attacks of the Communist Party increased accusing the Trotskyists of supporting the enemy. Eventually the demand by the RCP that these slanders be the subject of a public debate was conceded and an eve of poll debate set was arranged for the Gwyn Hall. Grace was building support for the meeting in Creswell Road and had several RCP supporters with her.

Explaining the nature of the war for Empire to three men at the end of the street one suggested bringing his stepladder so Grace could make a speech to more people. A crowd of fifteen or so gathered in the sunshine and someone pointed out that Alun from Arthur Street, the next along, would want to be there so a small delegation was sent. Grace rehearsed the main points to make with Billy and wondered how the Party could afford so many supporters to come to Neath.

'Most of them have hitched and are living hand to mouth on what they make from sales of the newspaper.'

A Glaswegian comrade called Duncan had listened to this and simply said he had hitched down last week and pulled his trouser pockets out to show they were empty. A cheer and jeer went up as a crowd of twenty or so accompanied by children came round the corner.

'It's the Red Army from Arthur Street,' shouted Dai who had come with Sara to help.

Grace was forced to stand on the top step of the ladder which was being tightly held by Dai and Duncan. Her demand for the nationalisation of the mines under workers control drew the biggest cheer but the crowd listened patiently as she attacked the coalition government and explained that a continuation of a war for the greedy capitalists was wrong and Welsh workers had the same interests as English, Scottish, Irish and yes German workers.

'Except the fascists,' shouted a young man and Grace agreed saying that the capitalists had used the fascists to divide the working-class and now international solidarity was needed more than ever. Grace ended with an explanation of how, whilst the Soviet Union, should be defended against the capitalists it was a state in which workers democracy had been defeated by Stalin and his clique.

Afterwards Billy, Grace and Duncan sat leaning against a house wall with Grace confessing that she was exhausted. Duncan told her that he had seen many speeches on the campaign and Jock Haston had been well received across the constituency, 'But that was the most attentive crowd I've ever seen, you really have a gift, Grace.'

Grace knew the crowd had listened carefully but after Duncan had gone to sell papers with a cheerful 'otherwise I'll not eat tonight.' She told Billy that she still believed that work in the Labour Party would be the best strategy.

'The best people here just want change, it's a once in a lifetime chance to get a better deal for their children and they know voting Labour is the best chance of that.'

Billy did not reply he did not want to end the day in a political argument for he was amazed too at how Grace had held the crowd. Grace suddenly remembered she had a letter to show Billy and produced it from her bag. It was from Brigid describing the walk on the beach, the dogs they took there and how happy they were to be away from the factory. A poem by Amy was enclosed too, urging London friends 'to come and sample. Breathe in the Kerry sea spray, let your lungs be full of love.'

Billy said that was wonderful and he would love to visit them when the war was finally over. Billy too had received a message but had left the telegram at home. He had memorised it. 'Malcolm OK stop. I am getting married stop. Hope to see you in NYC stop. Edward.'

The debate in Gwyn Hall next day was packed, Grace thought the Communist Party members and Haston supporters were at least half the audience. It was gratifying to hear Ted Grant and Jock Haston repeat many of her arguments but she regretted not using their phrase 'His Majesty's Communist Party' to describe her opponents. As the meeting progressed the language became more heated though the crowd insisted on listening in silence.

Then Alan Thomas, speaking for the Communist Party, declared, 'In Russia, they defeated fascism because they shot all the Trotskyists and the Fifth Column scum, and if we had our way, these people on the platform would be shot.'

Uproar followed and a call of "withdraw" from the crowd.

Grace and Billy walked afterwards to the bandstand at Victoria Gardens. They sat at a bench and Grace said, 'So, we are to be shot if the Communist Party comes to power. I wondered if I may hold your hand before that happens,' she said, slipping her fingers between his.

He gripped her hand but said nothing as she leant over and said, 'And perhaps a parting kiss.'